MAR - - 2007

Chains of Folly

Other Five Star Titles
by Roberta Gellis:

Overstars Mail: Imperial Challenge

Chains of Folly

A Magdalene la Bâtarde Mystery

Roberta Gellis

Five Star • Waterville, Maine

A Magdalene la Bâtarde Mystery

This novel is a work of fiction. Names, characters, places and incidents are either the product of the author's imagination, or, if real, used fictitiously.

First Edition
First Printing: April 2006

Published in 2006 in conjunction with Tekno Books and Ed Gorman.

Set in 11 pt. Plantin by Ramona Watson.

Printed in the United States on permanent paper.

Library of Congress Cataloging-in-Publication Data

Gellis, Roberta.
Chains of folly / by Roberta Gellis.—1st ed.
p. cm.
ISBN 1-59414-472-9 (hc : alk. paper)
1. Bishops—Fiction. 2. Nobility—Fiction. 3. Knights and knighthood—Fiction. 4. Prostitutes—Fiction. 5. England—Fiction. I. Title.
PS3557.E42C47 2006
813′.54—dc22 2005030208

Chains of Folly

PROLOGUE

The man hauling on the rope paused, panting heavily. The body he was pulling up through the window was, literally, a dead weight and somehow heavier than any live body. It was stiffer than it should be, he thought, almost as if it were alive and afraid. But that was ridiculous. The woman had been dead for some time, and his companion, who was steadying the body from below so it did not bump against the wall of the house, would have had hysterics at any sign of life.

He snorted softly and began to haul on the rope again. Steadying the body was about all his companion was good for. Well, the idea of bringing it here to be rid of it had been his, but the fool had meant it for a joke. And for a while, when he had pointed out the advantages of doing it, he had thought the lily-livered churl might run away and leave him with the woman's corpse. How he had ever been knighted was a puzzle; as for knightly skills or courage . . . pfui!

The next drag brought a sharp check. The man pulled again but could not gain an inch. Cursing under his breath, he walked forward, gathering in the rope as he came toward the window. When he leaned out, however, he was relieved to see that the woman's head had caught on the windowsill, preventing her from rising further. He cursed again briefly, but without real anger, thought for a moment, then wrapped the rope around his waist so the body would not slide down.

With both hands free, he could lean out, free the body's

head from the sill, and drag the corpse in. In spite of the woman being small and light, he had to lift and rest, lift and rest, several times. At last he had her laid out on the floor and he stood above her sighing with relief. It had never been likely that anyone would notice what he and his companion had been doing, but now, with the corpse inside, an accidental exposure was impossible.

After a few minutes rest, he unwound the rope from his waist and crouched beside the woman to untie it from around her. That took longer, the pressure on the knots had drawn them tight, but he undid them at last and was able to unwrap the blankets with which they had concealed and padded the corpse.

It was not nearly as dark in the room as it had been when he had first climbed up the rough stones of the house and slid his knife between the shutters to raise the bar and open them. The moon had finally risen. That would make getting out a little more dangerous; climbing up had been slow, but he did not need to climb down—only a moment to get out the window, hang by his hands, and drop the few extra feet to the ground. His companion should help break the fall, too.

He looked down at the body on the floor. He could not leave it there, so near the window. That would give too strong a hint as to how the dead woman arrived. He glanced around the room. Too bad the bed was gone, but that was too expensive a piece of furniture to duplicate. Ah. Beyond the hearth was a table and behind it . . . oh, joy! . . . a chair.

With a slight grunt he lifted the corpse, frowning as he felt its resistance to bending. He hurried, but with care to be silent, to the table, laid the body down on it so he could move the chair away without scraping its legs on the floor. It was cursedly heavy and he had to stop to breathe when he had set it gently down again. He was not certain where the two servants and the old clerk slept and did not wish to chance waking them.

Then he lifted the body again and tried to seat it, but it did not simply fold into the chair. He had to exert a fair amount of force to bend it to fit. He stood frowning in puzzlement, and then smiled. Why did not matter. The woman *was* dead and he realized he could fix her corpse upright and it would not sag. He giggled softly. Yes, she would not be slumped over the side or fallen to the ground. She would be sitting upright to greet the great man when he came in.

The man's good humor survived until he was hanging by his hands from the windowsill and his companion did not reach up to support his legs. He blasphemed luridly as he let go, cursing the fool and coward to the deepest hell for not waiting to help him; however, he did not waste any time on it, rising quickly from the crouch into which he had fallen and running toward the gate, which he had carefully barred to keep from alarming the watch.

It was open, held by no more than the latch! If the watch had raised an alarm . . . Panic tightened the man's throat a moment, but a soft snort and the sound of a horse's hoof scraping the ground steadied him. At least that weak bowelled fool had not stolen his horse, and he could see that his saddlebags were fastened as he had left them.

He shrugged. Good enough. He had been abandoned and he need not consider that fool any longer. He could find a haven in Baynard's castle; those there would be very glad to hear of what he had placed in the bishop's house.

CHAPTER 1

No matter how carefully one prepared, Magdalene thought, events would take one by surprise. When she had left London to stay in Oxford three weeks ago, she had bought everything she could think of that the women of her whorehouse might need. She had been right about the linens and most of the staples, but of all things they were nearly out of honey. William's clerk had a passion for sweets. He even added honey to his wine, and other spices too.

Magdalene paused for a moment with a pot of honey in her hand, thinking about William of Ypres, who had protected—and used—her for so many years. He was with the king now, preparing to take the massive stronghold of Devizes. Inside, Magdalene shivered, her hand tightening on the honey pot. She prayed for his safety. A tight bond had grown between William and herself over the years, and it was no longer only because William stood between her—a whore with no rights and no other protection—and the law that she worried about him.

"It is the best honey, mistress," the grocer said. "I do not think you will find better anywhere in this market."

"I do not doubt its quality," Magdalene replied, smiling. "I was trying to think whether the guest who is so fond of it will be staying long enough for me to buy two pots."

The grocer looked gratified. "It will not spoil, mistress. You know how well honey keeps, but it is not cheap."

He named a price and Magdalene raised her brows. "If I buy two pots," she said, "surely you can make it cheaper."

They chaffered for a while and came to an agreement. Magdalene really had not minded the price. William had been *very* generous when he compensated her for her trip to Oxford. Perhaps he had felt a little guilty because she had remained to serve his political purposes against her lover's will, and that had infuriated Sir Bellamy of Itchen so much that he had left her.

Tears rose in her eyes and she set her teeth and blinked them away. A whore does not cry over a man, she reminded herself, keeping her gaze on the coins she had emptied into her hand from her pocket. She chose out what to pay the grocer and found a smile as she handed him his money.

When the honey and spices and some specially coarse ground wheat that Dulcie wanted had been added to what was already in her basket, Magdalene pulled her veil across her face and left. Not that a woman's veiling her face was common in London this year of Our Lord 1139, but Magdalene, who was cursed with startling beauty, had found it safer to go veiled when she was in the streets alone.

She hesitated on the step a moment, letting her ears grow accustomed to the bedlam of the market, to the apprentices calling their wares to passersby, to street vendors appealing for custom, to sellers and customers shouting contrary offers at each other to come to a bargain.

Magdalene smiled. It was a cheerful din. She made her way around the outdoor counter where the grocer's journeyman sold less pricey goods, turned right, and began to walk briskly—or at least as briskly as was possible in the East Chepe. She did stop several times to examine goods, but bought nothing.

When she came to Lime, she turned her head briefly to look north, wondering whether her friend, the saddler Mainard, had yet sold the expensive house he owned there.

His first wife had insisted he buy it for her, but after her murder he had married the blind whore Sabina, whom he had met in Magdalene's house. Sabina insisted on living in the rooms above Mainard's shop. She said it was because she needed to be near him, which made the horribly birthmarked Mainard weep with pleasure, but Magdalene suspected it was because Sabina wanted him to be sure that no man but he was ever admitted to her rooms.

That thought made Magdalene's throat tighten. Bell had never been able to accept the fact that she was a whore, that although she was retired, except if William wanted her, she could not change her past. A sudden stench of fish, fresh and foul, assaulted her nose and she hurried past Fish Street on the far side of the market, started to cross to the south side, and then changed her mind and continued ahead toward Gracechurch Street. She was really in no mood to visit Mainard and Sabina. Their cloying affection would turn her sick today.

Despite good intentions, Magdalene's basket was a good deal heavier by the time she had fought her way across the bridge. She had bought three pounds of apricots, some early apples, a large round of candied violets wrapped in cool water lily leaves, and a whole side of a smoked salmon. Fortunately the Old Priory Guesthouse was only a short distance from the foot of the bridge down the road that ran along the wall of St. Mary Overy Priory.

Thinking of her goal, Magdalene smiled. She hoped the souls of the very strict order of nuns who had had the Guesthouse built were not tormented by its current use. Their order had excluded all males, except the priest who said mass and confessed them, and even females who had not taken religious vows, so a fine guesthouse had been built outside the wall of the convent to accommodate visitors.

The monks who now lived in the priory were not so strict. Finding the guesthouse outside the walls inconvenient, even though it was connected to the priory by a gate in the wall, a new guesthouse had been built as a wing of the priory itself.

The monks had been far too practical to destroy the old guesthouse, which was a very good building. It was stone built with a tile roof and protected by a high stone wall with a strong gate. Thus it had been rented for various purposes until, after falling into very low hands indeed, on the urging of William of Ypres it had been rented by the bishop of Winchester to Magdalene.

There was nothing shocking to the bishop of Winchester about Magdalene intending to use the premises as a bawdy house. Something on the order of two-thirds of the stews in Southwark were owned by the Church . . . most of the remainder belonged to the Crown. However, Magdalene knew the bishop was particularly happy with her as a tenant. She paid her exorbitant rent promptly and there had never been a single complaint about her well-run premises. Moreover, when a Church messenger had been murdered on the north porch of St. Mary Overy Church, Magdalene had solved the crime and saved the bishop's life.

As she approached her home, however, Magdalene forgot history and began to think about how she was going to manage to juggle her burdens so she could lift the latch of the gate and open it. At the gate, she realized it would be easier to pull the bell rope because the latch was heavy and firmly set. A few moments later the latch lifted and the gate opened to the extent of a sturdy chain that allowed Diot, one of the three whores Magdalene employed, to peer out.

"Oh my goodness," she cried, laughing, as soon as she

saw Magdalene's veiled face and overflowing arms, "you really have been shopping."

The chain was immediately unhooked, the gate swung open, and Diot relieved Magdalene of a few of the packages in the basket. This created almost more of a problem than it solved by unbalancing the rest of the bundles. Magdalene and Diot hurried to the house and through the open door, without another word, rushing to set everything down on the table before they dropped the easily bruised fruit or tore the fragile wrapping of the candied violets and smoked salmon.

Everyone in the house rushed toward the table to prevent anything from sliding down on the floor, all laughing heartily, but Magdalene froze momentarily with shock. Overriding the high, childish laughter of the exquisite but simple-minded blonde Ella was a strong baritone voice Magdalene knew all too well. She looked up. It *was* Bell. She had not, out of longing, mistaken another's voice for his.

Bell was his usual elegant self, except that his face was flushed. He was wearing, over a shirt a great deal whiter and cleaner than most men's—Magdalene knew he paid his laundress extra to produce the effect—a sleeveless tunic of bright blue that came only to midthigh. The neck and hem of the tunic were bordered with dark blue ribbon, fancifully embroidered. Magdalene did not need to look at that; it was her own work. The dark blue matched the footed chausses that covered his legs, held to their shapely form with cross garters of the bright blue of the tunic.

He had removed the broad leather belt that supported his sword, but it was draped over one of the short benches near the table with the sword propped so he could seize it easily. Not that Bell expected to be attacked in Magdalene's house but, like always wearing a tunic short enough not to tangle his legs and interfere if he had to fight, the sword was always ready.

"I see that you expected Bell," Ella said, as she peeped under the wrappings of the violets and the salmon. "Why did you not tell us he was coming?"

"No," Magdalene said, "I did not expect to see Bell here today. I just thought a little celebration was in order. I am so very glad to be at home." She had swallowed down the shock of joy she felt on seeing him, damping it with the memory of the misery of the last three weeks.

"I did not expect to be here either," Bell said, voice harsh. The flush had receded, leaving him very pale. "I am here on the bishop's business. Let your women put your shopping away while I tell you."

She stared for a moment, then said, "Come into my chamber where we can be private."

Ella giggled, but Diot and Letice exchanged troubled glances. They had been aware, as Ella was not, that Magdalene's spirits were not what they should have been. Until now, they had put her oppression down to the dangerous political situation and the danger into which Lord William, her protector, was going. Now each suspected the trouble was more personal.

"This had better be urgent business for the bishop," Magdalene said as soon as she had closed the door of her bedchamber behind her. "You are not welcome here. You cannot tear a great hole in my heart and expect to hop back into the space whenever it pleases you. The hurt is sealed over already. A whore learns not to trust men."

"Is a dead woman sitting in the chair behind the table in Winchester's bedchamber urgent enough?" Bell snapped.

"What?" Magdalene gasped. "I never heard a hint that women were Winchester's vice."

"No, nor are they," Bell snarled. "Winchester was leagues away from London in my company and that of at least twenty other clerks and armsmen when that woman was placed in his chair."

"You mean she did not go up to his chamber and sit in the chair and die . . . or . . . or take her own life?"

"Not with a broken neck and fingermarks on her throat. I never yet heard of anyone who could break her neck and then walk up a flight of stairs and seat herself in a chair."

There was a silence and then Magdalene asked angrily, "But what have I to do with this?" She wondered suddenly if Bell's love had turned to hate as it sometimes did and he was attempting somehow to involve her in the death. "My women are all here safe and sound, and I certainly would not wish to embarrass or annoy the bishop of Winchester who has been kind to me."

Bell grimaced. "You have nothing to do with the woman or her death, but she was dressed as a whore and the bishop bade me ask if you would discover who she was and why she was brought to his bedchamber."

"The bishop sent you here?"

Flushed again, Bell said, "He thought it very funny. He said he had a mission for me that he was sure I would enjoy."

Magdalene said nothing, and after a moment Bell went on. "There is something else, something that could be very bad in these times. The woman was carrying a letter addressed to Winchester from Robert of Gloucester."

"What?" Magdalene said again. This time as if she could not believe her ears. "It cannot be real. Where would a whore get a letter from Robert of Gloucester addressed to the bishop of Winchester?"

"It is real enough. Winchester recognized the seal. He saw it often enough before Gloucester cried defiance. As to how she got it, there are a number of answers to that, but the simplest is that it was given to her to deliver to Winchester."

Magdalene stared at him for a long moment, slowly shaking her head and then said, "I cannot believe it. If the letter was meant to be given secretly to the bishop, all the messenger had to do was go to his house and ask for audience. Winchester is well known for listening to petitions."

"Unless the messenger who had the letter from Gloucester was already known as Winchester's enemy."

"Even so, to entrust such a thing to a common whore—"

"I think she was better than that," Bell said. His lips tightened as he added, "Not so grand and rich as you, but not out of the common stews."

Magdalene almost smiled at the painful admission, but managed to control her lips and only nodded acceptance. She knew he had said it to hurt her, but it did not. Indeed it gave her the only glimmer of hope she had felt since he had rolled his armor in his gambeson in Oxford and walked away.

If only she could bring Bell to accept what she was—to acknowledge that nothing could change the fact that she had been a whore for many years and, for a favored few, still plied the trade—perhaps they could come to a *modus vivendi*. No, she would not allow herself even to think about it.

"How was she dressed?" she asked, sternly quelling a hope she should not feel. "What did she look like?" And then before he could answer, she added, "No. Stay for dinner with us and tell everyone. It is possible that Diot will recognize her, or Letice, although Letice does not mingle much with the other whores. Among her people, whoring is a respectable trade, so she is welcome to them and she finds those who practice the trade here disgusting because of their filth and crudity."

"Stay for dinner? But . . . but . . ."

Bell's heart seemed to squeeze hard in his breast and then began to pound. His constant longing for Magdalene in the three weeks since he had broken with her was like the ache of a wound that had never healed. Before parting with her, he had managed to blind himself to the fact that she still serviced William of Ypres. He had told himself she performed an unwelcome duty, bowing to William's power. But then she had confessed it was not only duty. That she should share her body he had been able to ignore; he did not see it happen. But that he must share her heart—that he could not bear. He started at Magdalene's voice.

"Why not? You are on the bishop's business and if we say so, no one will expect you to stay or even come back tonight."

He rubbed his hands nervously along the sides of his tunic. "Well . . ."

"It would be much better for the women to hear all the details exactly from you . . . only I do not think you should mention the letter to them. They are close-mouthed, but . . ." Bell nodded quick agreement and Magdalene went on, "And do not use the word murder when Ella can hear—"

"You may be sure I will not do that!" Bell exclaimed, his taut face relaxing into a smile. "I and my long sword, which can protect her, would never be allowed to leave without wails and reproaches." He laughed aloud as Magdalene opened the door and stepped out. "And actually the sword is almost useless in a house. It is the poniard—" he tapped the well-worn, leather-wrapped hilt of his long knife, which he had hooked next to his eating knife "—that is useful."

Magdalene sighed. "Yes, I have seen you use it in close quarters. I do hope this problem will not come to that."

"I, too," Bell agreed, and stopped abruptly as he entered the common room.

While Bell and Magdalene had been absent, the women had set the table for dinner. Bell's eyes misted a little when he saw that they had laid a place for him on the end of the long bench to the right of the short bench at the head of the table where Magdalene sat. He looked around the room, suddenly seeing the place with new eyes because he had thought he would never see it again.

Nobody entering that chamber would believe he was in a house of prostitution. The large room, the refectory when the house had been a monastic guesthouse, had the comfortable appearance of a well-to-do merchant's home. To his left, near a wall that had two open but solidly barred windows, was a large table. Two short benches were set at the head and foot of the table, two long benches along each side.

Across from the table was a generous hearth, now empty in the heat of summer. But around it were set four stools, three with work baskets beside them and the fourth facing a large embroidery frame that held an almost-completed altar cloth. Taking a deep breath, Bell walked toward the place set for him.

"Magdalene says she is very glad to be home," Ella said in her high little-girl voice. "I am glad. I was afraid that she would find some place she liked better and would not come back. Diot was very good, but it was not the same." She smiled at him with blinding happiness. "You are glad to be home, too. That is very good. I have missed you. I know you cannot be my friend, but it is comfortable to have you here."

Ella, small, plump, utterly adorable, with the mind of a child of five and an insatiable craving for sexual congress. Her golden hair hung in soft waves and curls down to her hips. Her skin was white, just enough touched with rose on the high cheekbones and lips to prove that she was in glowing health. Her nose was short and snub and her eyes were as blue—and as completely empty—as a cloudless summer sky.

Bell smiled back at Ella, although her words made him feel more like crying. "Yes, I am glad to be back too," he said, "but I am not likely to be here much. This is a very bad and sad time for my master and I will be very busy."

"Bad and sad?" Ella's eyes grew round, her expression apprehensive.

"Nothing to do with you, love," Bell said hastily. "And nothing to do with Magdalene or this house. It is all owing to a quarrel about what the Church owns and what the king owns. You may listen if you like, sweet, but I don't think you will find it very interesting."

"I am sure I will not," Ella said, giggling. "And there is no sense my listening when I will not remember anyway."

The faintly anxious expressions on the faces of the other women told him that they feared it was more than the bishop's problems that would keep Bell from the Old Priory Guesthouse. He looked from one to the other.

Letice was a perfect contrast to Ella, dark of skin and eyes, with hair that hung to her knees as straight and smooth as a black curtain. Also small, her smooth curves hid a wiry strength that, Bell had been told, permitted some remarkable sexual convolutions, which captivated a number of devoted clients. And perhaps some of them were captivated by the fact that Letice was mute and, they thought, could tell no secrets. About that, they were wrong.

Diot's bright emerald eyes met his, their expression hard and calculating. He had brought Diot to Magdalene's house out of one of the worst stews in Southwark. Diot, who had once been a lady . . . as Magdalene had once been a lady. Bell's mind winced away from that fact. He did not really want to know how or why Magdalene had become a whore, but she seemed much too calm in the face of violent death.

As for Diot, she was very beautiful, tall and lush with a skin smooth and lustrous despite being very white. Her hair was a rich brown with enough red in it to be called auburn, thick and waving and hip-length. His lips twisted wryly; he could guess what brought Diot from the manor where she had possibly reigned as mistress to the stews of Southwark. She was promiscuous by nature.

Nonetheless, Bell liked her. Diot made no secret of the fact that she craved—not one man, which was common to most women, but all men. Her bold green eyes assessed every man in a way that could not be mistaken. And although she was smooth as silk, a polite lady with her clients, with him she was blunt and honest.

Bell had to swallow hard as he picked up his belt and sword and moved toward his seat. It was not only Magdalene's beautiful, fragrant body that he missed. The truth was that the loss of her exquisite beauty and the joys of bedding her had become the least part of his torment. One of the greatest pleasures of being Magdalene's accepted lover had been the warm friendship of the other women of the Old Priory Guesthouse.

Lonely. Bell suddenly realized he had been lonely for years because he was trained and educated above the level of most of his equals. He could not find true companionship among men who thought of nothing but wenching, drinking, and gambling. Not that he did not enjoy those pursuits in those men's company, but there was something missing.

Diot patted the seat beside her, and Bell swung his leg over the bench and sat, propping his sword between the leg of the table and the edge of the bench. His mother, he thought, would have a fit if she ever learned that he had found his family pleasures again among the women of a whorehouse. He bit his lip to hide a grin. Bread and cheese was on the table and he drew his eating knife and speared a piece.

"So," Diot said, "Magdalene told us that the king dismissed the bishop of Salisbury from all his offices and demanded that Salisbury and his relatives yield their secular castles, but between Ella interrupting every moment and Magdalene herself trying to make ready to receive our clients and answer their questions, I am afraid I did not take in the whole tale nor the reasons behind it."

"The reason is simple enough," Bell said after swallowing the cheese. He broke off a piece of bread and stared at it thoughtfully. "Stephen was convinced, largely by Waleran de Meulan, that Salisbury and his relatives were planning treachery, that they had stuffed and garnished their keeps, and intended to use them in support of Robert of Gloucester, who would try to wrest the throne from Stephen and place his half-sister Matilda on it. The old king had forced the barons to swear to make Matilda queen."

"And I always thought Henry was a realist." Diot snickered. "Imagine Henry believing men would support a queen once he himself was gone."

Bell shrugged, swallowed a piece of bread he had broken off with more cheese. "They would assume, of course, that Robert would rule, and Robert is loved and respected by many. If Robert of Gloucester leads Matilda's forces, Stephen does have some cause for worry."

"Some, but I know that William—" Magdalene's voice faltered as Bell's face darkened and then she went on "—was not best pleased with the king's dealing with Salisbury."

"Now that is where I get lost," Diot said. "For what did the king blame Salisbury?"

"A riot." Bell sounded grim and Magdalene shivered, remembering how Sir Ferrau had helped foment that riot and then tried to kill her. "Oxford was overcrowded. Salisbury came very late to the meeting and his men had no lodging and it rained, and it rained. Salisbury's men went to ask Alain of Brittany to share his lodging. Alain's men said Salisbury's people had been threatening and offensive. Who struck the first blow depends on which side you question, but soon all the men were involved and Alain's nephew was sore wounded. The king wished to blame Salisbury, and he did."

"Ah, I see." Diot nodded. "Then Stephen was able to say that Salisbury had broken the king's peace and no longer deserved to be the chief minister of the kingdom."

"That was not all," Bell said between gritted teeth. "The king also demanded that Salisbury yield all of the castles he had built and what was therein. Salisbury refused and the king had him arrested together with the bishop of Lincoln and Salisbury's son, Roger le Poer."

"But surely Stephen is not so mad as to treat his own brother and the pope's legate in the same way," Diot said.

"God knows," Bell sighed. "The problem is that my master cannot ignore the affront to the Church."

"But is it an affront to the Church?" Magdalene asked. "The king has not seized any of Salisbury's benefices nor threatened his position as bishop. The only things Stephen wrested from Salisbury are his castles, owned by the man not the Church, his secular offices, his place as justiciar and other appointments. That is surely the king's right."

"But it is not his right to seize Salisbury, Lincoln, and Roger le Poer physically. The person of a man of the Church is sacrosanct, and specially the person of a bishop."

Magdalene shrugged. "What did you want Stephen to do? Look the other way while Salisbury and his kin fled into their stuffed and garnished keeps? Come Bell, you are a soldier and know that the king, having exposed to them his suspicion of their treachery, could not let them slip out of his grasp."

"It is very strange indeed to hear you singing Waleran de Meulan's song," Bell snarled.

"Why are you angry?" Ella cried, looking from one to the other, tears rising into her eyes.

"Oh love," Magdalene sighed, leaning over to pat Ella's hand, "we are not angry with each other. We both desire the same thing but are convinced that different ways of obtaining it are best. So we talk quick and loud, but . . . but we are still . . . friends . . ." She took a quick deep breath, glanced sidelong at Bell, and began to laugh, realizing that the word "friend" meant something different to Ella.

Bell, understanding quite well that to Ella "friend" meant a man you serviced, flushed, and then also laughed. "But in a way you are quite right, Ella," he said. "There is no sense at all in Magdalene and me quarreling about this because we have no power to change what will happen. My master has decided what he will do, and I am bound to carry out his orders. Besides, what I came for was something quite different."

"I thought you came to see us," Ella remarked, pouting.

"That was an added pleasure, but not what brought me.

I told you that I was here on business."

At that moment, Dulcie came from the kitchen carrying a large platter of beef slices swimming in their own gravy and a smaller one on which slices of the smoked salmon were laid out. She went out again, but Bell, stomach growling, drew his eating knife, speared two slices of the beef, and dropped them on the broad trencher of stale bread that marked his place at the table.

By then Dulcie was back with a deep bowl of greens and another of turnips and carrots. A third trip brought a tureen from which rose the odor of a savory fish stew. With a broad smile, Letice filled her bowl with that and put some smoked salmon and some vegetables on her trencher. Then she fixed her eyes on Bell and as soon as she caught his, she made a sign for him to continue.

Bell chewed and swallowed, glanced at Ella, and sighed. "You know my lord has been at Winchester for some weeks past. Yesterday afternoon, late, we rode into London where he stopped at St. Paul's to talk to Father Holdyn, the episcopal vicar, and then went on to his house. He had, of course, sent the servants and the carts ahead, but when we arrived instead of finding all ready, the house was in turmoil."

"Oh I hope no ill has befallen Father Wilfrid," Magdalene said. The old clerk who remained in London to attend to any minor problems with Winchester's property had always been fair and reasonable when considering her requests—which was not always true when churchmen dealt with whores.

"No, no. He is well, except for feeling that he had somehow failed the bishop. When the servants went up to set up the bishop's bed, you see, they had found a woman . . . ah, in the bishop's chair, seated at his table, and . . . ah

. . . it was impossible to . . . er . . . ask her to rise and leave."

Letice and Diot stared at him; both then glanced at Ella, who was busy picking pieces off the slice of smoked salmon she had taken, pushing aside the pieces of beef that Letice had cut up for her.

"I suppose she had a reason," Diot said.

"Yes. The poor woman seems to have been badly beaten and a day or two later she somehow . . . ah . . . damaged her neck . . . ah . . . permanently."

Letice's eyes opened wide. She signed one finger going down several others, then sliding, then lying bent on the table, then getting up and climbing the stair again. At which point she shook her head vehemently.

"Yes, just so. The bishop and I went up at once to look at her and it was clear that she could not have climbed up to Winchester's bedchamber on her own. Moreover I found marks on the windowsill that showed she was pulled up by a rope."

Diot shuddered, made sure Ella was concentrating on her food, and put her hands around her own throat. Bell shook his head.

"I will explain that later," he said, glancing at Ella. "But what brings me here in particular, is that she is dressed as one of your sisterhood. Obviously, since the servants who found her cried out in alarm so that everyone in the house rushed up to see what was wrong, there is no way of keeping this secret. Plainly it was intended to embarrass the bishop, but he has *no* idea who would do such a thing—"

"Nonsense," Magdalene said. "Anyone who wished to make the conclave the bishop has called into a travesty might try to show Winchester as sorely stained with secular vice." She frowned. "That is not fair. Winchester has his faults, but he has kept his vows of abstemiousness and chastity."

"No, it is not fair, but his opponents do not play fair. So, will you help us, Magdalene? The bishop hopes you will be able to find out who the woman was and to whom she was connected."

"Yes, of course. I will try, at least. I do not know every whore in Southwark, but what does she look like?"

"Alas, very ordinary. Brown hair, brown eyes, a pleasant face—well, it would have been pleasant if it were not slack and fallen in. Oh, yes, she had a mole right here."

Bell touched the edge of his right brow. Magdalene shook her head but, oddly, both Diot and Letice frowned.

"It might be that I know her," Diot said uncertainly, and Letice nodded agreement. After a glance at her sister whore, Diot added, "I would have to see her." And again Letice nodded agreement, but she did not look at all happy.

"It is too late now," Magdalene said. "Our guests will be arriving very soon. Tomorrow morning?"

CHAPTER 2

Bell had not returned to share the evening meal with the women of the Old Priory Guesthouse despite Ella's warm assurances that she had no friend coming to visit her that night and would be glad to play any game he liked. The few glances he cast at Magdalene showed her to be perfectly expressionless. Bell had sighed and shaken his head. It would have served no purpose to return.

With Ella free he would not have been able to discuss the woman's murder with Magdalene and it would have been difficult to explain to Ella why he was not simply walking into Magdalene's bedchamber to spend the night as he had been doing for months. It would have been hard to explain to his body also. And probably he could have her. All he needed was five silver pennies, which was her price. She said she was a whore. Then he could buy her like any other whore.

Only Bell knew that was not true. Magdalene was not for sale to *any* man. Oddly that thought gave him more comfort than pain, but he pushed it out of his mind and stretched his long legs, cursing himself mildly for walking out the front door of the Guesthouse instead of out the back. Now he would have to walk all around St. Mary Overy priory instead of just going through the gate at the back of Magdalene's garden, crossing behind the church, the graveyard, out the front gate of the priory, and across the road to Winchester's house.

When he arrived at the bishop's house, however, he saw that arriving earlier would not have been any advantage.

Phillipe, the scholarly and learned young clerk in minor orders seated at the table partially blocking the door to the bishop's private chamber, shook his head at Bell.

"I can tell him you are here, but he is deep in the affairs of London diocese with Father Holdyn."

Bell nodded and sat down on the stool near Phillipe's table. "Tell him. He was so overset by finding that woman in his bedchamber that he did not tell me what more he wanted me to do today."

The young clerk shuddered and turned pale as he rose. "Terrible. That was so terrible. Why? Who would do such a thing?"

"I need to discover who she was before I can hope to discover who placed her in my lord's chamber. I have set that first matter in hand, I hope, but—" he was about to say that the women who might give him information would be occupied until the following morning, but he decided to spare young Phillipe's blushes and went on "—my informants cannot tell me more until tomorrow morning."

Poor Phillipe blushed violently anyway as he hurried to enter the bishop's chamber. Bell chuckled softly. Apparently the young man already knew to whom Bell had gone for information. But he liked Phillipe, who had his opinions but never allowed them to interfere with his duty.

To Bell's surprise Phillipe was back in a moment, holding the door open and gesturing for Bell to enter. He did so at once, and saw Father Holdyn gathering up and putting in order the documents that were strewn over Winchester's table.

Bell swallowed a grin. It always seemed so inappropriate to see documents in Father Holdyn's huge hands. He towered over the bishop, topping Bell's own considerable height, and he was as hard and fit as Bell too. There wasn't a church in London that needed repairs that did not find Father Holdyn carrying stones and mortar for the walls or raising heavy beams. His lank black hair and deep-set dark eyes only added to the impression of strength and determination.

As he straightened the documents into order, the episcopal vicar said, "What is this terrible thing I hear about your servants finding a woman in your bedchamber?"

Winchester's brows rose and Bell bit his lips to hold back laughter. Father Holdyn was a true ornament of the Church. He was very nearly as clever and as efficient as Winchester himself and he was much more truly pious.

"She was in no condition to be a temptation to me, I assure you," the bishop said dryly, and then, his eyes being drawn to Bell by the knight's approach added, "And when I think of the appearance of some of my tenants, not much of a temptation even had she been alive. Very ordinary. Brown hair, brown eyes, a mole near the end of her right eyebrow, and a full bosom . . . Oh, sorry, Holdyn, did I offend you by noticing that?"

"No, no, of course not," Father Holdyn said stiffly, but he scrambled the remainder of the documents together and pushed them hurriedly into a large leather satchel. "I will attend to the matter of St. Columba's church as you decided, and I will speak to the dean of St. Paul's about better controlling the churchyard vendors."

"Good," Winchester said. "Thank you." And as soon as the door closed behind Father Holdyn, sighed to Bell, "He is *such* a good man. Not only is he a wonderful administrator but he is a good priest, truly compassionate to the worst sinners. But why does he believe that taking holy orders caused me to go blind? I vowed to be chaste, not an idiot."

Bell chuckled. "No, my lord, and even if you took a vow to be an idiot, I doubt you could keep that one. Besides, I suspect it was not the temptation of the woman's bosom that made you think of it but what I found beneath it."

The bishop sighed. "You may be right, Bell." He stiffened for a moment—Bell guessed he was repressing a shiver—and added, "Thank God you decided to examine her to see if she had any other wounds. If we had just sent her over to St. Mary Overy . . . That accursed letter would have been common knowledge."

"Well, the infirmarian would have had to tell the prior, of course, but Prior Benin is no fool. He might well have sent the letter directly to you or asked you to come for it. Still, I agree that it is much better that only you and I know of it. It leaves you free to do as you like."

"Unfortunately it does not. What I would like to do would be to put that parchment in a fire, but I dare not."

Bell looked offended. "My lord, if you think that I—"

"Do not be ridiculous. If betrayal was ever your intention, you could have put that letter in your pouch and I would never have known about it. You called me and showed me that she had something wrapped in her breastband. It is nothing to do with you, Bell. It has to do with how many others know of the letter. Gloucester knows, of course. How many in his court know he wrote it? If it were destroyed, what might be said of its contents—that we were in agreement that I would support him?"

"I see." Bell gnawed gently on his lower lip. "At least if you have the letter, you can prove that it was in fact, harmless. Only sympathy over the way the king cheated you by not naming you archbishop and a wish if it is possible to be your friend."

Winchester's lips twisted. "Not so harmless with those two thoughts together." Then he shook his head. "I cannot believe it. I cannot believe that a common whore would be carrying a letter from Robert of Gloucester wound up in her breastband. And dead. Seated at my table in my bedchamber. Is it possible, Bell, that the woman was killed here just to make sure that there would be a scandal?"

"She was not killed here, my lord. I showed you the marks of the rope on your windowsill. The body was drawn up by a rope and whoever put her in the chair then went out the same window to escape. They came over the outside wall, too. This morning before I went to Magdalene's I examined the wall around this house. Two horses were tied down at the far corner in the alley; they were grazing and there were hoof prints where the earth was soft. I also found signs on the wall where the men climbed over."

"But why would a *whore* have a letter from Gloucester? And why should Robert write me such a letter?"

"Because you are the pope's legate and Gloucester hopes you will hold neutral if he should invade? Because he knows of your influence with your fellow bishops? My lord, surely you know the possible answers to that question better than I. And there is another possibility. Someone could have gone to Gloucester and urged him to write the letter."

"To take advantage of my anger over Stephen's latest outrage. Yes. I thought of that. But to give the letter to a whore? A *dead* whore?"

"For that I cannot suggest a reason, my lord. Frankly, I think it ridiculous. If the intention was to smirch you with friendship to Gloucester, who is a traitor to the king, surely the enemy who obtained the letter could have pretended to have discovered it by accident and carried it to the king or bawled aloud of what he had found."

The bishop's lips folded into a thin line. "So I thought myself."

"There is one other possibility, my lord. The woman was

not a *common* whore in the sense that she lay in ditches or worked in the stews. She was likely a woman who had a keeper or several clients and she entertained those clients in some chamber of her own. It is possible that she stole the letter from one of those clients."

"Stole a letter? How would a whore know anything about the importance of a letter?"

Bell shrugged. "Magdalene says that men tell whores the strangest things. Could he have been attempting to make himself important in her eyes? Could he have boasted that he had come from the great Robert of Gloucester's court?"

"Boasted to a whore?"

Bell shrugged again, a tinge of color in his face. "Men do. Especially to the better kind of whore. And this one—she did not look very attractive dead, but her face was pleasant and if it were full of expression, lit with laughter and playfulness, she might have been quite enchanting. At least attractive enough to make a man wish to please her."

Winchester sighed. "Perhaps I have been a priest too long. I cannot see it." Then a brief smile touched his lips. "No. No. I cannot say that. The delicious Magdalene is still far too tempting and requires stern discipline and a prayer or two to dismiss from my mind. Well, what did she say?"

"That she would do whatever she could to discover who the woman was and to whom she was connected. And when I described the woman, Diot and Letice both said they *might* know who it was. I will take them to the mortuary chapel tomorrow morning."

"Why did you not take them then?"

"It was too late. Clients were on their way. Magdalene will serve you to the best of her ability, but—" Bell smiled bitterly "—she will not allow anything to disrupt the smooth functioning of her business."

"And what is the point of taking the mute with you? She cannot tell you anything."

Bell laughed. "Do not you believe it, my lord. Oh, Letice cannot make a sound. She cannot scream if she is hurt nor laugh aloud when she is happy, but look . . ." Bell's fingers played out the pattern that Letice's had shown him.

The bishop frowned. "She implied that the woman we found had fallen down the stairs and broken her neck. How did she know that?"

"I don't think she did know anything, my lord. That was just the easiest way to point out that a woman with a broken neck does not get up, walk up a flight of stairs, and sit down in a chair."

With a discontented moue, Winchester said, "All those women are far too clever for anyone's good but their own."

Bell swallowed, a cold finger running down his back. He felt like the worst kind of traitor. If what he had told the bishop caused Winchester to turn against Magdalene, Bell would never forgive himself, but he did not dare say anything in defense of the women of the Old Priory Guesthouse. The best he could do for them was to look patient and indifferent. And to his relief, the bishop turned to a low pile of parchments at his elbow.

He picked them up and handed them to Bell. "Here are complaints, some from Father Holdyn, a few from local people about churches ill maintained in one way or another. I want you to visit them and see with your own eyes whether the complaints are justified. If the complainant was not Father Holdyn, speak to the person, and try to speak to others in the parish. If the complaint is justified, then speak to the priest and . . . ah . . . see that the problem is amended. With this other trouble we have, I do not want to use Church discipline if I can avoid it."

"Yes, my lord." Bell glanced out the window, saw that the sun was still well up. "If you have nothing else for me to do, I will start on this at once."

Magdalene watched Bell go out the door and then returned her attention to the smoked salmon on her trencher. There was a warmth in her, a sense of familiar comfort that slowly cooled into misery. He had been much as always, but she knew the breach between them was not mended.

More the fool he. He was happy here. His patience with Ella was remarkable. He was as quick to understand Letice's signing as any of them, and he knew Diot for what she was. Why, why could he not just accept the Old Priory Guesthouse as his home, the women as his family, take his joy with her when he desired, sleep in her bed like a long time husband when he was weary? He did not despise the other women for being whores. He understood their necessity and, despite Church training, did not judge. Why did the fact that she loved William too drive him mad?

What a fool she had been to tell him that! It was one of those things he had no need to know. She should have found another excuse for staying in Oxford . . . that she dared not refuse any request William made. Bell would have believed that. He had learned to accept the fact that she lay with William when he asked . . . her lips curved wryly. Well, if no one mentioned it, Bell would not think about it, but acceptance was too positive a word for his reaction.

Suddenly Magdalene stopped chewing and swallowed the mouthful of fish. She took another with more appetite. It had occurred to her that just thinking about Bell made her feel better. Why should she be miserable? It was ridiculous. Because she feared to be hurt again she would suffer for who knew how long now?

Utter foolishness, specially when Bell missed being with her—with them all—as much as she missed having him. She had seen tears in his eyes twice. She had seen how he looked at her women, as if they were dear ones he had believed dead and had found restored to him.

Moreover, Ella was not all wrong about Bell and his long sword making the house safer. Magdalene pursed her lips. Now there was a ploy she had never thought of using. What if she paid him for his protection of their premises with her body, as most whores paid for services provided for them? If she suggested it, Bell would have a fit! But really it was not such a bad idea to remind him that she *was* a whore, not a wife who happened to be running a peculiar business. A stifled giggle escaped her.

Diot's head lifted. "Has that dark cloud begun to lift?"

"Perhaps," Magdalene said. "Perhaps it has. It is something I need to think about. We will see."

"He is a very peculiar man—half very fine, half a natural killer. Do you know how he got that way?"

Magdalene smiled. "Yes, I do. Pillow talk, but not secret. He would tell you if you asked. He came from a large and happy family. His father was a knight of very comfortable circumstances but little ambition and he had two older brothers and three older sisters."

"Ah. And he was the pet of the sisters, no?" Diot asked with a smile.

"He did not put it that way, but yes, I think so. He is very comfortable with women and does not immediately see them as bedmates."

Diot nodded. "But how did he come by reading and writing and not only French but Latin?"

"What was his father to do with a third son? The estate would bear a small living for a second, but to divide it farther would make all three too poor, so Bell was educated for the Church."

Letice laughed soundlessly and shook her head.

Magdalene laughed too. "You are right. Bell was not cut out for the Church. He told me that at first he was quite content. He has a keen mind and he enjoyed what he was taught at the abbey and readily learned to read and write and cipher. But unfortunately—or fortunately, depending on the way you look at it—included with the saints' lives were tales of the Knights Templar and the Hospitaliers. And there was a knight who held abbey lands and came with his troop."

Diot shook her head. "Once. I would wager he would not need to see armed men more than once. I said he was half killer."

"He is *very* good. I have seen him fight." Magdalene nodded. "And he enjoys it. He craves excitement the way a drunkard craves drink. Apparently when he first said he wished to be a knight, he was lessoned in how hard a path it was by—" Magdalene's voice faltered as she remembered Sir Ferrau, who had murdered three people and had nearly killed her before Bell came to her rescue "—a man now dead."

"I warrant Bell did not need a second lesson."

"No, he bribed the men-at-arms who stayed at the abbey to teach him, and at fifteen he ran away. He took service as a mercenary aboard a trader."

"Ah, clever. That way his father could not reach him and drag him back."

Magdalene chuckled. "He told me his father was furious and it was years before his mother could soften him. But she, poor woman, all that time had been having nightmares of her baby dead and drowned and she wept and pleaded until Bell's father relented and appealed to Winchester for a place for his son. That Bell could read and write Latin as well as French was enough of an advantage to win him a trial. That he was Bell made him a favorite."

Diot nodded again. "From what you have told us, Winchester is the kind to appreciate Bell's cleverness."

"Oh, yes, and the fact that he is not coarse and crude but can be vicious when necessary. But did I not see you frown when Bell described the dead woman? Do you think you know her?"

"I hope not," Diot replied. "When I first came to London, before I found a place for myself, I stayed with a brown-haired, brown-eyed woman who had a mole just where Bell pointed. Her charge was reasonable and she was pleasant enough, but she would not let me bring men to her place and when she heard her patron was about to return, she told me to go. She did not want me to meet her patron, I suppose."

"And you, Letice?"

The mute nodded, then made a sign for her compatriots and then, looking frustrated, signed that it was too complex to explain, even to write. Nonetheless she went and fetched her slate.

"Se," she wrote and then, *"Cum wit to . . ."* and she drew a head wearing a turban.

Magdalene nodded and pushed away the remains of her meal. "If it is the woman you think it might be, I will have to come to the Saracen's Head for an explanation."

Letice smiled and nodded also. Then she stepped back over the bench and began to gather up bowls and spoons. Diot collected what remained of the fish stew and the vegetables and carried them into the kitchen. Dulcie also went to the kitchen to return with a damp cloth and vigorously clean the table. In just a few moments more, all the women were seated around the hearth with their work in their hands.

None too soon. They had hardly set five stitches, when the bell at the gate pealed. Magdalene smiled and went to answer. She tempered her smile as she opened the gate. Master Gerome was terminally shy. If she smiled too broadly, he might flee.

Master Gerome, a cordwainer, had been brought by Mainard who had explained Gerome's needs to Magdalene. She had first thought of Letice, who could not speak and thus might seem not to require him to do so; however, perhaps her knowing black eyes frightened him. He shrank back toward Mainard when Letice approached him, but when Ella bounced into the room and held out her hand with a giggle, he followed her.

He had been a *very* good client ever since, coming three, sometimes four times a week. There was something in Ella's childishness that made him comfortable, and he very nearly matched her sexual insatiability. Many men tired of her near mindless babble and some were embarrassed by her urging them to couple repeatedly because they could not perform. Not Gerome. Ella said he seemed too shy to initiate sex, but was more than willing each time she did.

"Ella has been looking forward to seeing you," Magdalene said softly.

Master Gerome twitched and Magdalene was sorry she had spoken, but after a moment he whispered, "Is that true?"

"Indeed it is," Magdalene assured him.

Suddenly he stopped dead in the path. Magdalene went on a step and then also stopped and turned back toward him. She was afraid to ask him a question, so she just tilted her head a trifle and waited.

"Longer," he said.

For a moment Magdalene was blank, then she thought of Letice to whom every word needed to carry more meaning. "You mean you would like to stay with Ella longer." She did not make it a question so he would not need to answer. "That can easily be arranged. Perhaps you would like to spend the whole night with her?"

His eyes widened and he nodded.

"That is more expensive," Magdalene said. "It costs five pence, but if you like the evening meal will be included and a little supper during the night and you are also welcome to break your fast with us."

He wrung his hands.

"You need not if you would not like that. Nothing is mandatory. I just wished to explain why the cost is so high. Ella has something she must do after you leave her this afternoon, but she is free this evening. If you come after vespers, she will be ready to welcome you."

He did not reply, only took five pennies out of his purse and handed them to her, and before she could thank him and assure him again that Ella would be his for the night, he scurried quickly through the door. Magdalene stood staring after him and shaking her head, wondering whatever could have happened to the poor man to reduce him to such a state.

The bell pealed again and she pushed her hand through the slit in her skirt, loosened the ties of her pocket, and dropped in the coins. Her smile was much broader when she saw who had rung.

"Master Buchuinte," she said, holding out her hand. "Do come in out of the sun. We have missed you. I hope that Diot did not offend you in any way?"

"Oh no." He laughed. "I was away on business for near two weeks. Diot? That one is too clever to offend. But sometimes I do miss my little girl."

No, Merciful Mother, don't let him ask for Ella today, Magdalene thought, as she shepherded him in through the door. Ella and her swain were already gone. Magdalene breathed a sigh of relief, although she had expected it. Master Gerome never lingered in the common room talking to the other women, as did a number of men who did not mind having their patronage of the Old Priory Guesthouse known.

Buchuinte did not linger either, but went off with Diot. Magdalene followed them with her eyes and then shook her head very slightly. Letice cocked her head interrogatively.

"No way could Diot manage to look like a little girl." Letice laughed soundlessly and Magdalene laughed too. "I think Master Buchuinte needs a session with Ella again. He has this thing for little girls—not that he would ever violate a child in reality, but I remember that Ella would braid her hair for him and sometimes wear a little shift, half falling off a shoulder. He is an intelligent man, however, and after a while Ella . . ."

Letice made a gesture implying one time this and one time that. Magdalene nodded but frowned. "If Diot is willing. Ella will be delighted, of course." She hesitated and then added, "Oh, very interesting. Master Gerome will be back to spend the night with Ella."

Letice widened her eyes and made a very crude gesture and then a sign for long continuation. Magdalene giggled. "Well, I suppose he will have to sleep some time and we will discover whether Ella has a limit." Then she sobered. "If she has and he overreaches it, I will not accept another full night's time with her."

Letice raised her hand, but the bell pealed before she

could gesture and she rose to answer it herself. Magdalene picked up her needle and set a stitch. When Letice had led her client in and closed the door behind him, Magdalene went and listened at Ella's door. She heard Ella say something, although she could not make out the words, and for a miracle heard Master Gerome laugh. She did not bother to pass farther down the hall to listen at Diot's door. Master Buchuinte had been a client for many years and she knew he would not harm his partner.

She returned to her seat and began to embroider with rapt attention, but it was only her eyes that were busy with the beautiful altar cloth. Her mind touched briefly on the problem of the dead woman and then by natural progression moved to Bell. How fortunate that someone should drop a dead body on the bishop, she thought, and then bit her lip.

It was not good fortune for the poor woman, whoever she was, and Magdalene knew it was only by the Merciful Mother's care . . . and William's favor . . . that she had not ended up the same way. Magdalene's lips folded together into a hard line. She regretted her careless thought and she grew angry when she remembered the indignities that had been heaped on the dead woman, hauled about like a lump of trash. Whore or not, once dead the corpse should have respect and dignity.

Magdalene sighed. That was not the fate of most whores, who were often buried like offal, but this one, dispatched untimely, would have her revenge, Magdalene vowed. Whoever killed her—a man from what Bell said about the bruises—would pay for his crime . . . and for embarrassing the bishop too. Which brought Magdalene's mind back to Bell and back to the question of how to seize him again and hold him.

CHAPTER 3

Magdalene had found no decisive answer to the question of how to induce Bell back into the fold either in the hours she patiently embroidered while her women worked or after she had settled them for the night with their new clients and herself went to bed. Her first concern when she woke was for Ella, but she heard her laughing as she led her client, staggering a little, out the front door.

Ella herself was rather heavy-eyed but had a most smug and satisfied expression. "I am hungry," she said, "but I think I will go back to bed after I have eaten."

"By all means, love," Magdalene replied gratefully. If Ella was asleep, she would not need to explain why she, Diot, and Letice went out with Bell and Ella was not invited. "I am sure you worked very hard last night."

"Not really," Ella said, liberally smearing honey on a thick slice of bread. She took a bite, chewed, and added thoughtfully, "Often when a friend spends the whole night, I do have to work hard to make his man stand more than twice, but not with Baby Face. If I just turn toward him or put my hand on him, up jumps his standing man, red-headed and ready."

"You do not mind, love?"

"Oh, no. Not at all. It is delightful to be really, really satisfied. I hope I pleased him. I hope he will come again for the night."

Ella finished her bread and honey and drank down the cup of watered wine she had poured for herself. Magdalene, recalling Gerome's bemused expression and unsteady departure, assured her that her friend would come again, and Ella smiled sleepily and went off to bed. Magdalene shook her head. She could only hope that the exhausted cordwainer would not cut off a finger with those knives he used to trim leather or put a needle through his hand instead of through a sole.

She jumped as the gate bell rang, and hurried out to answer it. It could not be a client at this hour of the morning. Occasionally they did have an early patron, a ship captain due to leave on an early tide or some similar case, but she would not accept any man this morning, Magdalene decided. Ella was hors de combat and the other women had done their duty and deserved their rest . . . not to mention needing to identify the dead woman.

The several glib excuses on her lips were unnecessary, however. It was Bell she faced when she opened the gate to the length of the security chain. She was very surprised to see that he was dressed only in his stained and mended gambeson, and not wearing the armor that usually covered it. She remembered the last time she had seen that gambeson, but did not allow the pang that pierced her heart to reflect in her face. Only, as she unhooked the restraint and swung the gate wide, she swore to herself that Bell would hear no more of her affection for William.

Some day perhaps, he would grow up and realize that a heart could hold more than one person. If Bell was unable to face the truth, then let him hold to a pretense that her bond to William was only duty and fear. What was important was that she and Bell would be happy and William would neither know nor care so long as she did his bidding.

In the blandest voice she said, "Oh, Bell, good morning.

Come in. You are early. You do not seem to have finished dressing. Have you eaten?"

He had been looking very grim, but her bland impersonal manner seemed to help. He smiled slightly. "I could not see any sense in putting on clothing I would only have to take off in a little while. Not to mention wearing anything that did not already stink to examine a corpse. And I certainly was not going to wear armor to walk about in if it was not necessary. I am bound to accompany the bishop to Lambeth, where he will dine with the archbishop. And no, I have not eaten. I hoped you would feed me."

"Then I shall with a good will. You also look very pleased with yourself. Have you discovered who the dead woman was?"

"No." The smile was replaced by a frown. "To speak the truth, I did not give her a thought all day yesterday, poor thing. You know the bishop has been away from London somewhat longer than usual and Father Holdyn had a big pile of complaints that he could not—or did not wish to—settle. Winchester does not want to use his power as bishop or legate right now, so I got the chore of seeing to the complaints."

"Successfully, from your looks," Magdalene said with just a bare touch of admiration in her voice.

She saw with satisfaction the infinitesimal body language that marked his pleasure in her admiration but only gestured him toward his usual seat. As he started to remove his sword belt, she went to the kitchen for more substantial fare than bread and honey, taking half of a cold pasty and some slices of beef. Setting what she held on the table, she went and got him a flagon of ale; she knew he preferred that to wine, especially for breakfast.

"And so, can you tell me what pleased you so well in yesterday's work?"

Bell laughed. "That it all went so smoothly. At least three of the complaints were without basis. I think Father Holdyn knew it, but he wanted another more powerful opinion to back his. He is a little too sanctimonious for my taste, and though he tries to hide it, a little contemptuous of Winchester's worldliness. Nonetheless, he is a good priest, surprisingly compassionate."

"So did you dismiss the complaints?"

"I have not the power to do that." Bell laughed again. "But the arrival of a knight in full armor, solemnly demanding to see *cause* for the reduction of tithes—"

"Sometimes even a wealthy family falls upon hard times," Magdalene said.

Bell hesitated, wondering if poverty had caused Magdalene to sell herself, and then shook his head. "Yes, but not this family. I came within and saw the pewter and silver—even glass—on the shelves and the gold chain around Mistress Brewer's neck and the rings on Master Brewer's hand. No, I do not think the paying of the tithe was threatening their daily bread. But I asked about losses . . . vats do break or go bad. A whole brewing can be lost."

"But not in this case?"

There was a little silence while Bell chewed the bite of pasty he had taken and washed it down with ale. "Not in this case," he agreed. "They said perhaps they had been mistaken in the weight of the tithe and that they would reconsider." He folded a slice of meat onto the point of his knife and bit off a piece. "The other cases were much the same. One man was marrying off a daughter. He said his business would be diminished by her loss, but I suspect he hoped to make up in lessened tithes what he was paying in dowry."

Magdalene made "listening" noises while breaking off a

small piece of the pasty and putting it in her mouth. Bell continued to talk, telling her about the one serious problem. There had been a complaint that a church was dirty, and it certainly was. However the neglect was not deliberate. The priest was very old. Not only was his eyesight failing but he had fallen ill, barely able to drag himself to the altar to say Mass.

"He should be retired," Bell said, "perhaps brought to the infirmary here in St. Mary Overy, where he could live out his years in comfort. But he does not wish it. He begged me, weeping, not to betray him. He said he would soon be well." Bell sighed. "But no one recovers from old age."

"But why? If he is old and ill . . ."

"It is a very poor parish. He is afraid no one will be willing to serve. The church is tiny and without the smallest comfort. He says the people need him, and I agree. They need someone—" his lips twisted "—and not some holier-than-thou young zealot who would condemn even those who came to church and frighten them away."

Magdalene frowned. "Something is not right. He sounds to be the kind of priest his flock should love. I know they are poor and likely criminal, but some I am sure attend Mass. Why did none of them try to help him?"

Bell shook his head. "That I do not know. Possibly Father Holdyn saw the place before the parish could act—and felt he had to report it. He should have removed the priest, but I think the old man pleaded with him also and he hopes that Winchester will find another solution."

"Will he?"

Bell smiled at her. "Oh yes, he has the power. He will find a young clerk or lay brother to watch over the priest and send his servants into the parish to warn the people that if they do not help the priest they will lose him—"

He broke off suddenly to greet Letice who had just entered the common room, and he bellowed for Dulcie, who always seemed to hear his voice and came trotting. Diot must have heard also, because she came from her chamber only a few moments later. Magdalene continued to nibble a bit of this and that while Letice asked (by touching it and looking curious) about his gambeson and Diot went to fetch him more ale. When he had explained about needing to escort the bishop, who would be dining with the archbishop, Diot asked whether Winchester and Theobold of Canterbury had been reconciled.

"Not to say reconciled. I doubt they will ever love one another, but this outrage against Salisbury has certainly given them a common cause. And both are good men. I hope as Winchester's hurt and disappointment over being deprived of the archbishopric fade that they will learn to work together."

"I hope so too," Magdalene said. "Unfortunately the legateship dies with the pope and then Winchester will come under the authority of Canterbury."

"Who might hold a spite?" Diot asked.

Bell nodded, his mouth grim for a moment, but then he shrugged. "I do not believe Theobold of Canterbury to be a fool. If he has the brains of a pea, he will see how useful Winchester could be to him. Legate or not, Winchester has the respect of all his fellow bishops."

Letice tapped her knife on the table and everyone looked at her. She made a cross for the Church, then the sign she used for the bishop and repeated that sign but above where she had signed at first.

"The archbishop," Magdalene translated.

Letice thought for a moment, then shook her head and ran off to her room from which she emerged carrying her slate. *"Ded in bed,"* she wrote, and pointed to the place where she had made the sign for archbishop.

"Oh, no!" Bell said. "No. I cannot believe that the archbishop had anything to do with placing the dead woman in the bishop's bedchamber."

After shrugging and grinning, Letice returned her attention to her breakfast, but Diot was now frowning. "Why are you so sure?" she asked Bell. "If the bishop were truly disgraced, would not that diminish his authority? Surely the archbishop must be frustrated by his relegation to second place when he should have first."

"I am sure he is frustrated and angry too, but scandal would not remove the legatine power Winchester holds, and, frankly, I do not believe the other bishops would believe that Winchester had anything to do with the dead woman. Women have never been his weakness and he was on the road the day or night she was killed with some dozen clerks and twenty men-at-arms and God alone knows how many servants. During the pope's lifetime, the only way Theobald can be rid of Winchester is if Winchester dies."

Diot laughed and applied herself to finishing what she had chosen for breakfast. When Letice, too, had swallowed the last of her watered wine and Bell finished his ale, they all carried the remains of the meal to the kitchen and from there went out the back door.

The gate to the church was, as usual, invitingly open. Magdalene smiled and touched the gate lightly as she passed. Prior Benin, a gentle and very pious man, found any sin, small or large, a heavy burden. He was sure that a man who had fornicated with a paid woman would be crushed beneath the weight of his remorse. It seemed cruel to the gentle prior to make the sinner, carrying that huge weight, walk the long way around the outer wall of the priory to reach the church. Thus he was willing to leave the gate between the church and the Old Priory Guesthouse open so the repentant sinner could sooner reach the church and a confessor.

Of course the Priory did not lose by the gesture. Although very few of those who visited the Old Priory Guesthouse had Prior Benin's delicate conscience, enough felt better for leaving an offering for the church. Thus the priory benefited, in a few cases, substantially. Magdalene uttered a little giggle.

Bell glanced at her sidelong. Diot and Letice were walking close together, holding hands, their faces downcast, both obviously uneasy about seeing the corpse. Magdalene . . . Magdalene was entirely too much at ease with violent death. Bell did not want to think about that and was irritated by her laughter.

"You find the bishop's situation funny?" he asked sharply. "Or the woman's death?"

"No," she replied, lips thinning. "I find the latter so unfunny that I will discover who did it and see that she is avenged, one way or another."

That was not the answer he had been expecting, and Bell said warningly, "Magdalene—"

But before he could finish they had reached the north porch of the church. All three women pulled their veils over their heads and Bell opened the door.

Near the altar, two young brothers knelt in prayer. As Bell and the three women genuflected to the altar, one rose and came toward them. His tentative smile of greeting and indifferent expression made clear that he did not recognize them. The other did not lift his head and Magdalene assumed he was fulfilling some punishment. She heard Bell's voice, lowered to a murmur, explaining for what they had come. The young brother shivered, then led the way across the church. The chapel in which dead bodies were placed was on the south side, closer to the infirmary.

The young brother shuddered again as he opened the door, and he stepped aside, gesturing for them to enter. Bell went in first, Letice, Diot, and finally Magdalene following him. A blob of incense slowly smouldered in a small dish near the covered head and fortunately that odor was still stronger than the odor of putrefaction. The woman had only been dead for a little over a day, and she had not been exposed to the summer temperature for long. The chapel itself was cool.

Light came in through four high windows just under where the roof met the walls. Letice and Diot hung back near the door. Bell gestured and Magdalene came forward followed by her women. He then went to the head of the table and pulled down the stained and tattered blanket with which the body was covered. The clothing she had worn was folded by her feet. Diot and Letice clung together, shivering. After a minute hesitation, Magdalene took a step forward and looked down.

"No," Magdalene said. "I have never seen her before." Regret and relief warred in her voice.

"Yes," Diot said, almost simultaneously. "I know her." She shook her head. "I cursed her when she put me out, but I never meant this to befall her."

Letice nodded too and shrank closer to Diot, but she made no attempt to explain how she knew the dead woman. Diot meanwhile pointed to the bruises and shook her head.

"She did not permit that," she said. "I never saw her bruised when I lived with her. Her name was Nelda, often called Roundheels."

"But the bruising is some days earlier than her death,"

Magdalene said. "See on her cheekbone and arm, the color must have been yellow before . . . But the fingermarks on her neck—" She turned to Bell. "Do you think the man broke her neck with his hands?"

"I don't know," Bell answered. "You can't see it because of her hair, but there is a soft place on the side of her head."

"She was hit with a club?"

"I don't know," Bell repeated. "I don't think she could have done so much damage just by falling down. Also there are some fresh bruises." He pointed to a livid mark on her shoulder and upper arm. "But most of them are on her back."

"Someone whipped her? Hit her with a cane?" Diot asked. "I know I said she would not permit herself to be beaten, but she was a greedy piece and if enough money were offered . . ."

"I don't think so," Bell said, but doubtfully.

He reached over and turned the woman. Although his fingers dented the softening flesh somewhat, she turned all of a piece, like a log of wood. Diot cried out and Letice buried her face in her hands. Magdalene gasped, but a moment later had leaned forward to examine the marks that now showed on the woman's back.

It was hard to see them clearly because of the discoloration, but after a moment she said, "Look, Bell, I do not think there is any of the old bruising on her back."

"Yes. It was clearer when I first looked at her because she had been put in a sitting position and the upper part of her back was not all stained. The old marks were from a beating. Someone held her by the arm and hit her with a fist or an open hand. The bruises on her back are from something with a broad, blunt edge but a definite edge."

"Stairs?" Magdalene asked. "Could she have fallen down the stairs?"

Bell laid the woman down again and drew the blanket over her. "Stairs?" he mused. "Yes. I think they would make such marks."

"She lived up a flight of stairs," Diot offered, pausing on her way to the door to speak over her shoulder.

Bell nodded acknowledgment, but said no more until they had closed the door behind them. The young brother was gone, already on his knees beside his fellow monk and neither turned to look at them. They crossed the church again, genuflecting in the main aisle, and went out onto the north porch.

"You know where she lived?" Bell asked Diot. "Of course you do. You said you lived with her for some time. And you say she generally lived alone?"

"I think her patron either paid the rent for her or owned the building, but as far as I know he did not live there. I never saw . . . well, any of the sort of thing a man leaves in a place he lives . . . changes of clothing, oddments one picks up and then does not want to carry, that sort of thing."

Bell glanced up at the sun and then grimaced. "I wish we could go there, but I must arm now if I am to ride escort to the bishop to Lambeth. I told the men to be ready, but there are always one or two that need prodding."

"I doubt it will make any difference whether we go now or tomorrow morning," Magdalene said, patting Bell's arm comfortingly. "Whoever killed her had time enough that night to take anything he wanted from her room, and all the next day also. And my women will soon be running short of time also, as both Letice and Diot have clients coming directly after dinner."

He did not need that reminder, Bell thought and grunted, starting to turn away. Before any of the women could step off the porch, he swung back. "See if you can find out what Letice knows," he said to Magdalene.

"Yes, of course," she replied, patting his arm again.

It took all his will power not to jerk away from her, to step down off the porch and turn left along the path that would take him to the front gate of the priory. Not to look back. From the priory gate he had only to cross the road to be at the bishop of Winchester's house. Slowly as he walked along, he rubbed the arm she had touched with his other hand.

Although he knew it was impossible because the sleeve of the gambeson was padded, he felt each of her fingers like a red-hot wire against his flesh. Mad. There was nothing in Magdalene's comforting touch to arouse lust. Lust? Bell swallowed hard. The burning, the longing he felt, had nothing to do with lust. That, he could assuage anywhere.

He nodded to Brother Porter, who opened the gate for him, frowning, Bell guessed, because the brother knew Bell had not entered the priory that way. There was no other way into the priory than the whores' house. As Bell passed through the gate he heard Brother Elwin sniff and imagined him thinking, "So early in the morning, too."

And he could have been coming from Magdalene's soft bed if only he had not . . . But for her to love . . . As he crossed the road, it was Bell who sniffed, thinking he could bed her anytime for five silver pennies. She would give him, as she had told him many times, what she gave all her clients—all of her attention, every joy her body could offer . . . for the hours the five silver pennies bought. But not what that hand laid gently on his arm offered—sharing, comradeship. That was why the fingers burned him so.

The gate in the wall that surrounded the bishop's house was closed, signaling that the bishop was either not at home or not receiving petitioners. Bell simply opened it and walked through. One of the men-at-arms lounging on the other side nodded and Bell told him to see that Monseigneur and the bishop's palfrey were saddled and walked on and into the house. In the past he had not lodged with the bishop, which meant sleeping on a cot or a pallet in the common room with the other men, his possessions bundled into a single chest.

He was well enough paid to afford a private lodging and after he came into the bishop's service he had rented a room in a widow's house only a street away . . . until he had moved to the Old Priory Guesthouse. He knew he should see if the widow had room for him again, but somehow he had not done it.

Lodging had not been necessary before the bishop decided to come to London. After Bell's parting from Magdalene, Winchester had merely sent him alone to London to do whatever business was necessary so the house had been virtually empty. Now with twenty armsmen sharing the room, it was crowded. He would have to find another place . . . but not today.

Bell threw open his chest and removed his mail shirt. A shout brought a servant who held the armor for him while he removed his sword belt, wriggled arms, head, and shoulders into the armor, and stood up so the mail would slide down his body. He held the ventail for a moment, loathe to fasten it when the chance of any attack in the few miles between here and Lambeth was very small . . . or was it? Recalling the dead woman carrying a message from Robert of Gloucester, he pulled the ventail across his chin and fastened the ties.

Helmet and shield were with his destrier, Monseigneur. Buckling the swordbelt around his waist, Bell made for the back of the hall that had been partitioned off into a private area. Phillipe waved him past.

The bishop looked up from the sheets of parchment spread on the table before him when Bell opened the door; his eyes widened and he raised his brows. "Are you planning to fight a war? Between here and Lambeth?"

Bell shrugged. "Foolish, perhaps," he said, "but it costs no more than the mild discomfort of wearing armor on a summer day and I keep thinking about that woman. Someone brought her here to do you hurt, my lord."

Winchester sighed. "Of course, Bell. You are quite right." He smiled wryly. "After all, I pay you to worry about such things so I do not need to." He got to his feet. "And the woman? Have you any information about her?"

"Yes, my lord, I do. I know her name and tomorrow will know where she lived and likely who was her keeper."

"Ah. The inestimable Magdalene."

Bell laughed. "No, Magdalene did not know her but one of her women did. Unfortunately I had no time to pursue the matter further, but as Magdalene pointed out there is no particular hurry since the man who killed her had all that night and all the following day to remove anything incriminating from her lodging."

The bishop had looked back down at the table while Bell was speaking. Now he gathered up some half dozen of the parchment sheets, and made his way to the door. He dropped all but one of the parchments on the table where Phillipe sat and bade him have three copies made of each. The last sheet he folded and pushed into his purse. By then, Bell had sent a servant scurrying to the stable to have the bishop's palfrey and Monseigneur brought to the door.

The ten guardsmen Bell had chosen were already ahorse and waiting near the gate when Bell offered his hands to help the bishop mount. "You will make a religious of me yet, my lord," he said when Winchester was firmly seated in the saddle. "I thank God most sincerely whenever you mount that you are not of the girth some of the lords of the Church have achieved."

Winchester smiled but abstractedly and when Bell was mounted and they had moved out of the gate and were riding south along the road, side by side, he asked, "You learned nothing but the woman's name?"

"I had no time to ask questions, but I think my informant, the woman called Diot, knew more about this Nelda, called Roundheels—"

"How appropriate."

"Unfortunately yes, my lord."

"Unfortunately?"

"Yes, because it implies that she was not faithful to the man who kept her."

"But surely the keeper would not kill her over jealousy? A whore?"

Bell was suddenly grateful that so much of his face was concealed by the mail hood. He could feel the warmth that meant his color had risen. *Yes,* he thought, *oh yes, my lord, a man can be jealous enough over a whore to kill.* And then, over the sudden clutch in his heart, *but not her; not Magdalene. If I had a hope in Hell of killing Ypres . . . I might . . .* He checked the thought. That was truly treason. Whatever he felt about William of Ypres, he knew Lord William was faithful to the king, more faithful than those Stephen held in higher favor.

"Likely not," Bell replied to the bishop's question about whether Nelda's keeper might have killed her out of jealousy. "Although it must be considered. But if she entertained other men, it unfortunately widens the field both of those who could have beaten her and those from whom she could have received . . . or stolen . . . the letter."

"Ah, yes, I see—" Winchester began and then straightened higher in his saddle in an attempt to see ahead.

There was a lot of unusual noise—oxen lowing and men shouting. Bell touched Monseigneur with his heel and the stallion plunged forward past the six men at arms who had been riding ahead. At first all he could see was confusion. A large wagon that had been loaded with barrels was athwart the road, one wheel broken so that it had tipped to the side and spilled barrels all over. Another cart, possibly the cause of the broken wheel, shafts splintered and draft animal gone, was half under the larger wagon. Around both vehicles were perhaps a dozen men shouting and wielding cudgels and fists.

Bell shouted for his men-at-arms, drew his own sword, and began to lay about him with the flat of the blade, shouting for order. For a moment he was not surprised when both parties turned on him in concert. He had memories of brawls in which both he and his opponent together furiously attacked the peacekeeper who was trying to separate them. In the next moment he realized that none of the fighters was an innocent civilian caught up in the altercation.

"To Winchester," he bellowed. "To Winchester. It is a trap!"

The order was barely in time. As his men turned their horses back toward the bishop, men began to run from the alleyways between the shops and houses. Suddenly, Bell was tipped forward in the saddle so violently the pommel caught him a nasty blow in the belly. Monseigneur, feeling movement behind him, had lashed out with his heels. Bell heard a scream and, as the horse kicked again, another.

Now he turned his sword in his hand and the next stroke he made drew a scream instead of a shout. A burst of red blossomed between the head and the shoulder of one of the men advancing on him as his blade struck. He twisted his body, striking again to the right as his left hand fumbled reins around the pommel and bent inward, trying to pull the shield strap from his shoulder so he could slide his arm through the hold.

Fortunately the man still screaming and writhing on the ground provided enough grim warning to the others to give Bell a moment's respite. He had just seized his shield and thrust violently out and away with it, catching two men advancing on his left, when some of the new opponents reached him. They were carrying swords, not cudgels, but, one seeing Bell's shield extended to the left, thrust unwisely at what he thought was Bell's exposed belly. Bell's sword took him on the extended arm. The clang of metal as the sword fell and the shriek of the wounded man again provided a respite; others drew away and Bell used knee and heel to turn Monseigneur.

The men Bell had thrust away with his shield were coming forward again, but Bell could do nothing. His shield was tipped forward to hold off one attacker's sword while he dealt with the other. However the smell of blood and the movement of weapons—although Monseigneur would have reacted the same way to waving empty hands—threw the battle-trained stallion into a frenzy. While Bell attended violently to the man attacking on his right, Monseigneur bit one of Bell's attackers in the face, tearing off his nose, and shouldered the other so hard he fell. That was the end of them both.

Monseigneur lifted just enough to permit him to kick the wounded man, who was trying to turn to run, in the side, and when he came down made sure his hooves landed square on the man he had earlier felled. Whether or not his keener than human hearing heard the ribs snap would have meant nothing anyway. Under his hooves in a battle with no orders by knees or reins meant that Monseigneur then pounded both fallen men into red jelly.

Both men had had swords and could have hurt, if not killed, the horse, but the armed men had experience of war destriers and their fear had made them hesitate . . . which brought the fear to fruition.

The lightly armed men who had set the trap now fled away from the varied and instant death Bell presented. Of the four better-armed fighters who had attacked him, three were dead and one dying. Bell took the opportunity to turn Monseigneur. He could see that there was no need for his help; his well-trained armsmen had beaten back those who had tried to attack the bishop. But Bell was furious. He fell upon those who were trying to flee and three more lay dead before he realized that the few left were crying for quarter and Winchester was shouting at him to stay his hand.

Bell swallowed hard, wiped his sword on his surcoat, sheathed it, and curbed his restive stallion before Monseigneur could attack anyone else. "Softly, softly," he murmured, stroking the beast's neck. "It's all over now, all done." To the men he said, in a steady, even voice, "Is anyone too hurt to ride?"

A chorus of "No, sir" followed. Bell nodded and continued, "Bind the living. Four of you drive them back to the bishop's house. They are not to escape. I have a few questions I wish to ask them."

His men moved quickly to obey, exchanging glances. There was something in the voice that was terrifying, not anything they were accustomed to in their firm but generally good-natured commander. Monseigneur snorted and nodded, pulling at the bit. Bell tightened his rein and patted the stallion soothingly. Monseigneur pranced, shook his head, chewed the bit.

"My lord," Bell said. "Do you wish to go forward to the archbishop's house or back to your own? It would be best if I remove Monseigneur from all this blood."

"Back home," Winchester said. "I am sure Theobald had no part in this attack but I am not in a mood now to discuss the formalities of a convocation."

"Yes, my lord." Bell turned his head to the men. "Levin and Kemp. Collect the dead and guard them. I wish to know what they carried. I will send a cart. The rest of you. Two ahead of the bishop and two behind."

"How did you know this would happen, Bell?" the bishop said as they passed the men-at-arms roughly binding the prisoners and looping them together neck to neck. "You are armed for war. You took ten men. All to ride just a few streets in broad daylight in a populous area. I thought you had taken leave of your senses."

As they drew away from the shambles left by the attack, Monseigneur grew calmer and Bell could give more of his attention to the bishop. He said, "I didn't *know*. Just . . . something stinks. That dead woman in your chamber . . . Someone wanted to shame you publicly, and when it did not happen . . . to remove you."

CHAPTER 4

When Magdalene let Bell in through the gate of the Old Priory Guesthouse the next morning, she drew a sharp breath and said, "What happened? You are hurt."

Bell was stiff and sore but not wounded, so he shook his head. "Only bruised. We were attacked on our way to the archbishop's house."

"The bishop?"

Magdalene's eyes were wide with concern. Henry of Winchester was as rapacious a landlord as any other who owned a whorehouse, but he had not raised her rent until she could no longer pay just because he knew her business was good. Moreover, Winchester valued her as a tenant and knew her as an individual. She could fare far worse under another.

"Unharmed, but as you can imagine, greatly distressed."

"Yes, I . . . oh, why are we standing here? Come in."

She closed the gate behind him and watched as he made his way into the house. He was not favoring any limb nor was his walk crooked; just, he lacked his usual grace of movement. Diot looked up from the cheese and bread with which she was breaking her fast. She too, looked concerned.

"You've been fighting," she said.

"The bishop was attacked on his way to the archbishop's house," Magdalene explained, and then to Bell, "Do you want more than bread and cheese? Sit, and I'll get you some ale."

Instead of simply stepping over the bench, Bell pulled it

out, walked around, and eased himself down, resting his sword beside him. "Bread and cheese is enough," he said, and as he took a cup from Magdalene's hand, "Thank you."

"Attacked the bishop?" Diot muttered. "Who would attack a bishop on the streets of Southwark? It isn't as if he were traveling with valuables—or was he? Bringing tithes to the archbishop?"

"No." Bell drank, set the cup down, and looked rather blankly at a piece of cheese he had speared on his eating knife. "He was going to dine with Theobald to discuss the convocation he called to examine the king's conduct with regard to the treatment of Salisbury and Lincoln."

"Calling a convocation will not endear him to Stephen," Magdalene said and then suddenly covered her lips with her hand as she realized what the king's displeasure could have implied about the attack. "Oh, no. I know they have quarreled but Stephen would not! Winchester is his *brother*."

"No," Bell agreed. "Stephen would not agree to harm coming to Winchester, but unfortunately those we captured and questioned . . . straitly . . . all said that the bishop was not to be hurt. So Stephen could have been involved or could have known nothing about it. Sometimes his 'advisors' do not bother to mention to him what they plan, particularly if they believe they will not be found out."

Diot looked brightly from Bell to Magdalene, but it was Magdalene who said, "That is a mark of Waleran's finger in the pie. There was no hint at all of who planned this?"

Bell shrugged. "Perhaps. They were supposed to take the bishop prisoner and carry him off to some den opposite Paul's Wharf, light two lanterns and set them side by side, then leave." He grimaced. "I lit the lanterns—as if anyone could see them during the day—and spent all of yesterday afternoon and most of the night down there watching, but no one came."

Diot shook her head. "I must suppose that bringing the bishop opposite Paul's Wharf and lighting signal lanterns means that a boat would come to move him across the river. And Paul's Wharf is not far from Baynard's Castle. And Baynard's Castle is held by Waleran's youngest brother, Hugh Beaufort." Once more she shook her head. "Could the Beauforts be so stupid and obvious?"

"I don't know," Bell said, voice rising and face twisted with frustration. "They might have thought it was better to be quick. If Winchester had ridden with only myself unarmed, and he had been seized quickly, me dead or too hurt to follow, he might have been hidden away and none even sure he had been taken. But what you say is also true. If anything went wrong, which it did, the hiding place would cry aloud that Waleran and his family were involved."

"Yes," Diot said. "Why not find a hole to hide the bishop in on this side of the river? There are enough holes in Southwark and Lambeth."

Bell opened his mouth, but before he could speak Magdalene said thoughtfully, "Could this be the work of someone who wanted to blacken the Beauforts *and* frighten the bishop? Someone like Geoffrey de Mandeville, who would wish to support the king's seizure of Salisbury's castles but would also like to slip into Waleran's place close to the king?"

"I don't know," Bell's voice, although still kept low, carried the feeling of a howl. "I don't know whether whoever planned the attack had someone down there watching and saw me and my men and thus did not send the boat. I don't know whether it was because we were later getting there than the attackers would have been. And the whole thing may have been only a ploy, an attempt to frighten Winchester. In that case no one would ever have come and the bishop would have been allowed to escape. It is possible someone those men knew nothing about—" Bell's mouth grew very hard "—and believe me they told *everything* they knew, would have come later, not necessarily from Paul's Wharf, and killed him."

Magdalene raised her brows. "They told everything . . . but not who sent them?"

"We had some bad luck there. I assure you that every man I questioned would have been only too glad to tell me. But the leader of the group, who had likely made the bargain, was killed." Bell finished the ale in his cup and slammed it down on the table. "It seems that I killed him myself."

"You couldn't have known," Diot said, patting his shoulder and refilling the cup with ale.

For a moment Bell was very still, then he said, "No. I couldn't have known." He sighed. "But I learned the men were not from Southwark, which is why they knew no holes here for hiding. They were from east of London. Two saw their leader with a very big man, well wrapped in a cloak. One saw him twice, once about a week ago and again yesterday morning."

Magdalene's brow furrowed and she bit her lip. "To give orders for the attack?" She shrugged. "I don't suppose the bishop's plan for dining with the archbishop was a secret." But before Bell could reply, she said, "I cannot see how these things can be connected."

"What things?" Bell mumbled around another mouthful of bread and cheese.

"Leaving Nelda's body in the bishop's bedchamber and setting a troop to capture him. It seems to me that although both were intended to damage Winchester, they are the product of entirely different ways of thinking."

"Hmmm. I had not connected them at all." Bell broke off a small piece of bread and chewed it slowly. "But they are both attempts on Winchester and likely both because of this convocation he has called. Still you are right. They . . . ah . . . *feel* different."

"But Nelda is dead," Diot said sadly.

"Yes, so perhaps the two attacks are not so different after all." Magdalene looked around the table. "If you are finished, perhaps we had better go and see whether we can discover anything from where and how Nelda lived."

Both Bell and Magdalene were slightly surprised when they realized how close Nelda's rooms were to the Old Priory Guesthouse. However, neither was particularly surprised when the hard-faced woman guarding the heaps of ragged remnants of garments that were piled outside of the old clothes shop turned her back on them. They were too well-dressed to try to steal her wares and it was to her advantage not to know anything about what went on above her shop.

The flight of stairs was sound enough. Bell paused to examine the stair treads carefully. A few had broken off, leaving sharp edges. Bell thought it likely that falling down the stairs had bruised Nelda's back. The older bruises—he squinted in thought as he climbed the rest of the stairs—one broad one on her upper arm where whoever had beaten her held her tight and the others on her face and upper body were not directly connected with her death.

He found Diot and Magdalene searching through their pockets, and both turned to him as he came onto the landing.

"The door is locked," Magdalene said. "Do you have a

piece of wire in your purse or a long, thin nail?"

He did not have a nail, but he did have a very thin file that he used for removing and smoothing nicks in his sword. Wordlessly, he proffered the file to Magdalene, who just handed it to Diot. Bell sighed as she bent and probed into the lock with the file. He was not really surprised that Diot could pick a lock, and had a quick caustic thought about whether she had learned the skill to open the chastity belt her husband had no doubt tried to make her wear.

"Crude thing," Diot muttered after a few moments, then turned the handle and opened the door.

They all paused just inside and looked around. "Whatever happened didn't happen in here," Magdalene said.

The chamber was not disordered and yet not neat enough to have been rearranged to hide disorder. Bell nodded agreement and Diot remarked that it looked much as it did when she had shared it with Nelda.

"She had a small strongbox, which she hid in a different place every day or two," Diot said. "It never had much in it. The most it held was five pence, but she never seemed to be short of money. I always thought she brought her money to a goldsmith to hold for her."

Bell grunted and began to examine the walls, but they were all solid. Diot pulled away the front board of what looked like a box bed—only it was not—built out from one wall. There was nothing in the space exposed. They went back to searching, and Magdalene eventually found the strong box at the back of the small hearth behind a false wall of thin bricks. It was locked, but Bell's file and Diot's skill soon had it open.

Hardly worth the effort, Diot thought. It held only two pence and two farthings . . . and then she swallowed bitter laughter. Now two pence and two farthings were nothing to her, but before she came to the Old Priory Guesthouse, she would have killed for it. Two pence and two farthings would have saved her—she swallowed sickly at the memory of the things she had been forced to do.

Nelda's strong box told them nothing about why she was killed, why she was carrying a letter to Winchester from Robert of Gloucester. They continued to search carefully, upending the stools and the small table, and the bench near the wall opposite the bed, testing for hollow legs, stripping the blanket from the thin pallet that served as a mattress and examining it very carefully for hidden parchment or the shape of coins or jewelry. They found nothing, not a slip of parchment and certainly no indication that Nelda could read or write.

Then they moved into the bedchamber. This bed, which seemed to be fixed to the wall, took longer to examine. It had several pillows and the mattress was thicker, stuffed with wool and horsehair. The examination, however, produced nothing except a few six-legged pests. Again the walls kept no secrets, nor did the chest that held Nelda's clothing.

While Bell pried at the base of the chest to see if it had a false bottom, Magdalene sat down on the stool near the empty brazier and stared around.

"Finished?" Bell asked, adding, "There's nothing hidden in the chest."

"No, we can't be finished," Magdalene replied absently, her eyes roaming restlessly around the room. "It has to be somewhere and more likely in here than in the other chamber."

"What has to be somewhere?" Diot asked.

"Nelda's real cache. That strong box was to convince a thief that he had found her treasure and could stop looking.

But the rooms are too good, the clothing too good. I think it likely that she was a thief too, and needed someplace safe for her takings. She must have money somewhere."

"A goldsmith, as Diot suggested?" Bell said.

"No. Diot thinks of goldsmiths, I think of goldsmiths, you think of goldsmiths, but Nelda would not put her money in a goldsmith's care. She would not trust anyone with her life savings, with what was all she had to keep her in her later years. She would think he would steal from her and what recourse would she have—a whore's word against that of a rich and honored goldsmith."

"It isn't in the walls," Bell said.

"Or in the bed," Diot added.

"In the bed, no. But it must be near the bed. She would want it close, where if there was fire or some other disaster in the night she could get it quickly."

"The bed is fastened to the walls," Bell remarked dryly.

"No, no it isn't. Not the way you think," Diot said, voice high with excitement. "Once I was in here talking to her . . . she had just got out of bed and I leaned against the footboard, and it moved. The whole bed moved. She was dressing. She didn't notice—or maybe she did and that was why she got rid of me. It . . . it must slide forward . . ."

But pulling and pushing had no effect, until Magdalene got on the bed and kneeling up slid her hand along the headboard. Her fingers caught on a metal bulge—a latch. When that was unhooked, the bed did slide forward, exposing a small ring. Pulled, this drew out a square of plaster on a thin board and behind that was a hollow in the wall in which lay a flat, well-smithed metal box.

That lock was much harder to open, but patience was eventually rewarded, exposing several pounds worth of silver pennies. Diot watched Magdalene, but the whoremistress was clearly not interested in the coins. She lifted them out, handing them to Bell who stood beside her, until what was hidden beneath the coins was exposed.

"Ah," she said with satisfaction, then turned to look at Bell, who had gasped.

He was staring at the most remarkable item, a large crucifix. Magdalene also stared at it, not ever having seen Christ on the cross depicted in jewelry. Bell put the pennies aside and picked up the crucifix, frowning at it.

"I cannot imagine how this came here," he said.

"You know to whom it belongs?"

"Yes, but I . . . I do not believe the man who owned this would violate his vow of chastity with . . . with . . ."

"A whore?" Magdalene asked, smiling bitterly.

"A whore like that." Bell's voice was harsh.

"Look at this," Diot interrupted. "Magdalene, did you not say something about Mandeville being involved in the attack on Winchester?" She fished about in the box and came up with an enameled house badge on a ribbon.

"That is certainly Mandeville's badge," Bell said, taking it from her hand and examining it closely. Then he looked around the chamber, grimaced, and added, "But can you see Geoffrey de Mandeville in these rooms?"

"Not Geoffrey himself," Magdalene replied, "but one of his captains? Could it be possible that Nelda had an arrangement, as I have with William, that for a set payment each moon he can send his men to my women? And these rooms are none so bad. We are used to the Old Priory Guesthouse, but I had been in business for some time in Oxford before I came to London so I came with money to spend on the Guesthouse. And since I came by a patron's order, I had help. Does it not seem to you that these rooms are more than what an ordinary whore could afford?"

"Well, Nelda had a patron . . . that I know. He was away when I first came to stay with her, and when she bade me go she said it was because her patron was returning to London."

"Yes, you said she did not want him to meet you."

As Magdalene spoke she had been turning over the trinkets in the box. She had put aside several valuable rings, which may have had lettering or simply a decorative border on them, and now she lifted out a handsome seal and uttered a low whistle.

"Is this what I think it is, Bell?" she asked, holding out the seal to show the device carved into it.

He took it and hissed gently between his teeth. "Beaufort . . . Waleran's house . . . marked with a bend sinister. A bastard of the house? One that Waleran's father old Robert did not want to acknowledge openly but did not want to ignore and abandon? Interesting. I have no idea to whom this belonged and however did he lose so precious a thing? It and a few words would identify him to the Beauforts—"

"Unless he is already known to them and thus less careful of his trinket. What odds will you wager that if Nelda serviced Mandeville or his men, Waleran would want to know what she could find out? And they are all lodged in those houses around the Tower from time to time. The men would talk to each other. Doubtless Nelda would be mentioned and knowledge of her drift back to the masters."

"No odds," Bell said. He shook his head and handed the seal back to Magdalene. "Pack it all up," he ordered. "We have been here long enough. I will go back to the Guesthouse with you and take the money to the bishop. He will set his clerks to searching out whether Nelda had heirs. If she did, he will see that the money goes to them; if she did not, he will use it for charity. Keep the other things safe for me. The badge or the seal or some other trinket may be the answer to why she was killed."

"But not to why she was placed in the bishop's bedchamber or where she got that letter." Diot sighed. "I did not like her, but I cannot feel she deserved to be murdered."

Bell shrugged, his mouth a thin line. "People are murdered every day just for being in the wrong place at the wrong time." He shook his head. "I want to look at the stairs and at the landing more carefully. Put the box back in the wall. I doubt any but Nelda knew of it, but perhaps her patron was involved in the thefts and did know."

Outside the apartment, Bell looked carefully at the wall near the edge of the landing. It was rough plaster over lathe and not far from the door, about the level of his waist, there were several threads caught in the plaster. They looked the same color as Nelda's gown. Perhaps her elbow had slammed into the wall while she was being choked. He pulled the threads free and put them in his purse.

Also he noticed there were scuff marks right at the edge of the landing, roughly below where the threads had been. Bell got down on his knees to look more closely. No one ordinarily walked that close to the edge.

"What the hell are you doing?"

Bell jerked upright in response to the angry male voice. His hand touched the hilt of his poniard. "Who are you to ask?" he retorted.

"I own this house. Who are *you?*"

Bell grinned. He was willing to concede that the man who owned the place had a right to ask why a stranger was examining the floor and walls. "My name is Bellamy of Itchen and I am the bishop of Winchester's knight. The woman who lived in this house was murdered and—"

"What? Murdered? That is impossible!"

Shock wiped the anger from the man's expression. His eyes bulged and his face whitened so much that Bell thought he would fall. Indeed, he put a hand against the wall to support himself.

"Impossible or not," Bell said, "she was discovered on Friday, sitting in a chair in the bishop of Winchester's bedchamber. Needless to say, the bishop wishes to know how she came there and has bidden me to discover the answer. And since you were her landlord—we know she lived in this house—I need to know who you are."

For one moment Bell thought the man would take to his heels, but then he no doubt realized that his ownership of the house would be a public record. He pushed himself away from the wall and shook his head.

"I can hardly believe you. Nelda dead? My name is Sir Linley of Godalming, and I am in service with William of Warenne, earl of Surrey. It is true that Nelda lived in the two front rooms, but how she came to the bishop's house . . . I have no idea. I suppose she was invited—"

Bell made an unpleasant sound in his throat and Linley stopped speaking.

"If she was sitting in a chair in the bishop's house—" Linley continued stubbornly, but his voice was not entirely steady "—I do not know any other way for her to be there."

"I can tell you how she came to sit in a chair in the bishop's house." Bell's voice was cold and his face so hard that Linley backed down a step. "Her body was pulled up through the window and someone carried her to the chair and forced her body into it."

"Who would do such a thing?" Linley whispered. "I cannot believe it. She was no one." He shrugged. "Who would bother to kill her . . . Are you *sure* she was murdered?"

"Her neck was broken."

"Oh . . . oh, but that could have happened many ways. She could have fallen down the steps, or . . ."

"There were fingermarks around her neck. If she went down the stair, which I think she did, she was choked first and then dropped."

"No!" Linley was holding onto the wall again. He closed his eyes and drew a deep breath. "Oh, poor Nelda. Sometimes she could be irritating, but—"

He stopped speaking abruptly when the door to Nelda's rooms opened and first Diot and then Magdalene stepped out. Linley's eyes bulged again.

"What are you doing in Nelda's rooms? How did you know she was dead? How did you get in?"

Magdalene looked at Bell, who nodded and said, "This is Sir Linley of Godalming. He was Nelda's landlord."

"Ah."

Magdalene's arms were crossed under her breast and her veil was draped loosely over her shoulders, pulled forward and tucked around her arms. She smiled at Linley and his face regained some of its color. His eyes drifted from her face down her body. Diot passed Magdalene and then turned sideways to pass Linley where he stood halfway up the stair. Her veil was drawn over her head and gathered by her arms around her waist and she bent forward a trifle, as if she were not sure of her footing.

As Diot passed Linley, Magdalene continued, "I suppose as landlord and patron you have a right to ask. My friend and I were trying to see whether there was a hint in Nelda's possessions of a reason for anyone to kill the poor woman. As to how we knew she was dead, I was asked by Sir

Bellamy to see if I knew her because she was dressed as a whore. I am whoremistress of the Old Priory Guesthouse."

Linley seemed to have recovered from the pleasant bemusement of seeing Magdalene smile at him. "How the devil did you get into her rooms?" he asked sharply.

Magdalene looked at him blankly. "Through the door."

"You couldn't have. The door was locked."

"Was it?" Bell asked. "How did you know? When were you here last?"

Linley turned toward him, looking affronted. "Nelda *always* locked the door."

"I suppose she would if she were going out," Magdalene put in, "but I doubt she would lock the door if she just stepped out to see a client off or to welcome someone in."

"But she—" Linley stopped speaking and shook his head, then said angrily, "I do not need to explain myself to you. You are intruders here. I will complain to the sheriff."

"I doubt he would object to my investigation," Bell said. "I have the bishop's authorization."

"Which right now will have little influence with my master, the earl of Surrey, who is utterly appalled at the bishop's being so disloyal as to try to call the king to account. He will be most interested to hear of a dead whore in Winchester's bedchamber."

"He is a worse fool than I believe if he finds that information interesting," Bell said coldly.

"Women are not Winchester's vice," Magdalene remarked. "The whole world knows that."

Bell swallowed a laugh, thanking God and all the saints that Surrey could not know what the whore had been carrying; *that* would have been interesting. Bell could just see Surrey rushing to Stephen to tell him that Winchester was in communication with Gloucester.

He snorted. "But to clear your mind and save Surrey trouble, I will tell you that Winchester has not been in London for weeks, and on the day Nelda died, he was on the road, in the company of myself, at least half a dozen clerks, and twenty men-at-arms. And when his servants discovered the poor woman, Winchester was in London, in conference with the episcopal vicar, Father Holdyn."

"Then why do you say she was murdered?" Linley frowned.

Bell stared at him for a moment and then said, "Because there were fingermarks on her neck and her neck was broken."

"Oh, yes," Linley said, shaking his head again. "You told me that. I just cannot bring myself to believe it. That she fell down the stair, that is possible . . . She did drink sometimes, but that any of the men she futtered would . . ." He let his voice drift off, shook his head once more, and started up the stair.

"Where are you going?" Bell asked.

"You said Nelda was dead. I am going to remove her things so I can rent the rooms again."

"Oh no you are not," Bell said, stepping in front of the door. "When I find out who slept with her most frequently and most recently, I will bring them here and hear what they say they remember about the rooms and about the likelihood of Nelda falling down the stair. I think I am safe to say that the bishop would forbid removing anything at all from Nelda's chambers."

"My God, she was only a whore." Now Linley sounded angry and exasperated. "So she quarreled with one of her marks and he lost his temper. I doubt the man meant to kill her. Why cannot you just forget about it?"

"Because someone went to a lot of pain and trouble to

get her into the bishop's bedchamber. The bishop likes to know all his enemies."

Linley paled and was silent and after a moment muttered, "I had forgotten that."

Bell put out his hand. "And since you expected the door to be locked, you must have brought the key. I will take it so that you will not be tempted to ignore the bishop's preference and just remove anything you think meaningful."

"You have no right!" Then Linley flushed. "Why did you say I had the key? At this time of day, Nelda would have been home. I would not need a key."

"Or she might not be. I doubt you would have come here without a way into her apartment." Bell wriggled his hand impatiently.

"Surrey will not like your attitude!"

"I am sorry for it, but I still want the key. Do not, I beg you, make me take it by force."

Bell reached out. Linley backed down a step, but not quickly enough. Bell caught him by the shoulder with his right hand. With his left, he seized the purse that hung from Linley's belt.

Linley howled with pain as Bell's powerful fingers dug into his flesh. "All right! All right!" he shouted. "I'll give you the damned key."

Bell removed his hand from the man's purse, but not from his shoulder, although he did soften his grip somewhat. Linley plunged his hand into his purse and withdrew a brass key.

"Magdalene," Bell said.

She came forward and took the key from his hand, still holding her veil over her other arm and breast. The key moved easily, locking the door and then unlocking it. Bell released Linley's shoulder and the man turned and bolted down the stair. Magdalene handed Bell the key, and returned her arm to support the jewelry she had wrapped in one end of her veil and was carrying pressed under her breasts.

"He must have another key," she said to Bell.

"I supposed so," he replied, smiling. "I would like to know whether he knows of the box behind the bed and what he would like to remove from the rooms. I will send a man. He can hide in the old clothes dealer's shop and watch."

"He is the one with the best opportunity to have killed her," Magdalene said, "but I cannot imagine why he would do so. It is clear that he expected her to service other men, so he could not have been jealous."

"Perhaps they quarreled over her ill-gotten gains."

Magdalene laughed bitterly. "If he knew of them, can you believe he would have allowed her to keep pounds of silver and valuable jewelry?"

Bell did not reply to that, but plainly he agreed with her. He shrugged. "I will see what I can discover about him and about where he was on Thursday night."

CHAPTER 5

Bell and Magdalene sat together at the table in the Old Priory Guesthouse counting the pile of silver pennies amassed by Nelda. Later, closed into Magdalene's bedchamber while the first set of clients arrived, Bell had made two lists of all the jewelry. He did not think about how comfortable and content he felt, until Magdalene came in to put the jewelry and one list away in her strong box—all except the silver crucifix, which Bell noted on the list that he had taken. When that was in his purse, Magdalene invited him out into the common room so they could count the money together.

He had to get up rather suddenly and look away to hide the fact that his eyes had filled with tears. A momentary and most unworthy hope that they would never find the killer so he would have a reason to go on working with Magdalene flickered through his mind. He dismissed it; such a hope would make the bishop vulnerable. But he began to count the coins from the open bag, which Magdalene had set on the table, with desperate attention. Magdalene looked a little surprised, but she carefully counted the coins he pushed aside. When they agreed on the amount, Bell sighed irritably.

"I need a witness," he said.

Magdalene did not look surprised. Although she had counted with him, she could not serve as witness. She was a whore and excommunicate; therefore she could not swear an oath. There were three solid citizens in three bedchambers disporting themselves with Magdalene's women, but neither she nor Bell thought of asking them to witness the count of silver. For one thing, Magdalene did not dare allow any of them to see that pile of coin; no matter what she said they might think it was hers. For another, she did not think that any of the gentlemen would be willing to give a time and place for having witnessed the count of coin.

Then she said, "Tom Watchman. He should still be in the stable."

Bell hesitated, but finally nodded agreement. The men of the Watch were venial and their sworn statements often challenged, but if Tom swore here and Bell had the coin recounted in Winchester's house and the sum was the same, that should validate his claim. He went out to fetch Tom while Magdalene wrote out where the money had been found and to whom it had belonged.

When Tom came in, he obediently made his mark where Magdalene pointed and she wrote in his name and the date and place. Under Tom's reproachful eyes, all the coins were then packed into a strongly stitched bag, which was twisted around them and firmly strapped so it could not fall open.

"I will see you when I see you," Bell said. "I have no idea how long it will take me to ascertain where Linley was on Thursday. And the bishop may need escort somewhere. He still needs to talk to the archbishop."

"When you can, then," Magdalene said and smiled goodbye as he walked out the door.

She did not overtly watch him walk to the gate, but she nonetheless noted that he was moving more easily and sighed with relief. If the bishop were attacked again, Bell would have to fight and she wanted him at the top of his ability. The smile lingered on her lips as she thought about how he had volunteered information about what he would be doing—as if it were her right to know. She would win in the end, she thought, but she was still not certain how to circumvent his stubborn pride.

Tom was just about to follow him when Magdalene turned to him and spoke in English instead of French to say, "Wait, Tom. Your Watch covers Dead Pond Road, doesn't it?"

"Not all the way to the pond, but the part near the bridge and near Abbey Road, ye-arh."

"There's a street off Dead Pond that has a shop that sells old clothes and rags. Do you know it?"

"Rags Street. More 'en one shop on it."

"The first one, the one nearest Dead Pond."

"Ye-arh, I know it." Tom laughed. "Woman runs that shop's blind and deaf. Never hears or sees nothing."

"That's too bad. The woman who lived up above the shop was murdered and—"

"Nelda or Tayte?"

"Tayte? Is there someone else who lives above the rag shop?"

"Ye-arh. Second door on the landing."

"I thought that door was to Nelda's back room."

"No. Tayte's got one room up there. They're both whores. Who got killed?"

"Nelda."

Tom nodded. "Figures. Tayte's real quiet. Nelda . . . couple times she yelled for us 'cause there was a man up there bangin' on her door. Men said she stole from 'em."

"Do you know who the men are? Could you recognize them?"

The Watchman shrugged and shook his head. "Don't give their names to the Watch, do they? Lie when they do.

Naw, I might recognize one or two if I was brought to 'em, but mostly it was dark and I really didn't see."

"All right, Tom. Do you think a couple of pennies might cure the rag-woman's blindness?"

"Waste of money. She'll just lie. Maybe if Sir Bell beat her up . . . Suthin' there though. Suthin' she's real feared of."

Magdalene nodded acceptance and told Tom he could go. The house he had lodged in had burnt down and she had offered him the loft in the stable temporarily. He was useful if there were drunken assaults on the gate and for carrying messages, but the stable loft would be too cold in the winter. And he was no help at all if there were trouble in the house. If Bell would only . . .

Wrenching her mind from that hope, Magdalene thought about what Tom had told her. Whatever the rag woman was hiding was something in her past and unlikely to have bearing on Nelda's murder. Too much effort to crack that nut. Tayte might have seen or heard something. But there was no sense questioning her yet. Likely Linley would have lost his temper over something with Nelda and killed her . . . but what about Gloucester's letter and why would Linley drag Nelda into Winchester's bedchamber instead of dropping her into the river where she would disappear for good?

Bell crossed the church grounds rapidly, nodded to Brother Patric at the gate, and crossed the road to enter the gate of the bishop's house. Winchester was engaged, which Bell had expected, but Philippe said he would tell him that Bell was back as soon as he was free. Meanwhile, Bell found Father Wilfrid and explained his need to recount the coins he had found in the whore's house.

By the time that was done and the second statement written and signed, the bishop was free. He pushed aside the parchments in front of him and looked up at Bell expectantly.

Bell told him about the money they had found in the hidden box, laid the bag of coins and the account on the table, mentioned the jewelry that he had left with Magdalene, and showed the bishop the crucifix. Winchester sighed.

"I would not have expected that, but . . . we are all human." He snorted gently. "And most human are those who try hardest to rise above that condition." He took the crucifix. "You do not think Father Holdyn could have killed the woman for this? No. How would he have got her into my chamber? And what about the letter from Gloucester?"

"I have a much better suspect," Bell said, and described the confrontation with Linley. "He did seem truly shocked when I told him that the woman was dead, but it is still most likely that he did away with her. More possible because it may well have been an accident. I found signs of a scuffle on the landing, so he might have been choking her and she went down the stairs. There were bruises on her back that looked as if they could have been made by tumbling down the stair. And I found some threads caught in the plaster that I want to compare with what she was wearing."

"And that still leaves the question of why this Linley should bring the woman to my bedchamber and why she should be carrying that letter from Gloucester."

"As to bringing her here . . . Linley is in service to the earl of Surrey."

"William of Warenne! Waleran's step-brother." Winchester's lips thinned, but after a moment he shook his head. "I cannot believe that Surrey would order a woman murdered only to prop her in a chair in my bedchamber."

"No, my lord, I don't believe that either. What I do believe is that if the woman died by accident Linley might have thought his master would be pleased if he rid himself of the body in a way that would embarrass you."

"And the letter?"

"I cannot believe Linley knew of that. Surely the letter would be most deadly in Warenne's own hands. I suspect Nelda stole that. She was a thief." He gestured toward the silver crucifix lying on the table. "And it is barely possible that she knew Gloucester's seal. She might have seen it while Lord Robert was here in London . . . or she might have been told to watch for a document so sealed. But there is no way now to find an answer to those questions."

Winchester nodded. "As usual, Magdalene has been most efficient. I was sure she could discover who the woman was. What will you do now, Bell?"

"That depends on you, my lord. If you need escort, that comes first. If you do not, I will go to Warenne's lodging on the Tower grounds and discover what I can about Linley and most particularly where he was on Thursday afternoon and into Thursday night."

"I will remain quietly within today," the bishop said, smiling. "So you can pursue your investigation into Sir Linley's doings. Tomorrow I will meet the archbishop at St. Paul's."

"We will take all twenty men," Bell said grimly.

Winchester smiled. "I will do as you advise. I pay you to be wary, but I do not believe there will be any other attack on me. And I am certain that the archbishop knew nothing about it. I sent Father Wilfrid to explain why I never arrived for dinner. You know Father Wilfrid is no fool. He said

Archbishop Theobald did not know and was truly appalled. More, Theobald related the attack on me to the king's treatment of Salisbury, saying that it had opened the door to all sorts of abomination against the Church. He is heartily in favor of the convocation."

"I never thought Theobald was involved," Bell said. "That we were on our way to his house is meaningless. When and where you were going was no secret and had not been for several days. No one would have thought it wrong to speak of it. There can be no doubt that many keep a watch on what you say and do, so anyone could have known you were to visit the archbishop. Beyond that, Theobald is a virtual stranger in England himself and I do not believe he yet has anyone on his staff who knows London's underbelly."

"Yes, I agree." Winchester hesitated, then reached out and touched the silver crucifix. "And I will arrange to speak to Father Holdyn either before or after talking to the archbishop."

"Before if possible, my lord? If you do not like Father Holdyn's answers about the crucifix you might want to speak to the archbishop about it?"

The bishop's brows rose over Bell's tentative half questions. "Trying to teach your grandfather to suck eggs, Bell?"

Bell flushed. "Forgive me, my lord. I am . . . eager to see you and Archbishop Theobald in harmony."

Winchester laughed, shook his head, and waved Bell away. "Take the money to Philippe and ask him to mark it to be held until we can determine if the woman had any heirs."

When Bell dropped the heavy package on Philippe's table and repeated the bishop's message, the young clerk looked from the account tucked into the fold of the bag to Bell.

"All this from a whore's house?" Philippe asked with considerable surprise. "What was she selling besides herself?"

"Hmmm," Bell said, looking down at the bag of coins. "That is a very good question and not one we thought to ask. I know she was a thief as well as a whore, but she could not have stolen *large* sums or a more determined effort to catch and punish her would have been made. Thank you, Philippe. I will certainly think about it."

It occurred to Bell, as he walked across to the priory, that the silver crucifix and the rings and seals that he had seen among the jewelry Magdalene had could be used to extort money. But that was self-defeating surely. Any man from whom she demanded money would cease to be a client . . . and would have a good reason to be rid of her.

Brother Patric was still serving as the porter at the gate. He frowned when he saw Bell. "We do not like to be used as a short way to Hell," he remarked.

Bell laughed. "You need not fear for my soul on that account. I am not on my way to the Old Priory Guesthouse but to the chapel where the dead woman lies."

"Did you not look at her yesterday?" Patric asked.

"It is not her body but her gown I wish to look at this time," Bell replied.

The porter, of course, had a right to enquire into the purpose of any who came to the priory, but Bell was well known to them as the bishop's knight and he was growing annoyed. Brother Patric sniffed.

"You are too late both for the body and the gown," he said. "She was buried early this morning and Father Holdyn took the gown and belt and shoes—"

"Buried?" Bell repeated. "But—but we found what money she had saved. The bishop intended to see her decently interred. Who arranged her burial?"

"I just told you," Brother Patric said irritably. "Father Holdyn arranged it and paid for it." The brother looked a little uneasy. "She is . . . ah . . . not buried in consecrated ground, not precisely, but . . ."

Bell was not at all interested in whether Nelda had been buried in consecrated ground or not. He doubted her soul could be saved no matter where she was buried. But he was so surprised by what the monk had told him, he doubted his ears.

"Father Holdyn arranged her burial and ordered she be placed as near consecrated ground as was possible? And he took away her clothing?"

"Yes. Is there something wrong with that? Why should St. Mary Overy be responsible for keeping the body? It was beginning to stink. And the bishop had not said—"

"No. Peace, Brother Patric. You have done no wrong and I am sure the bishop will be glad to know that she was buried without cost to the priory. I was simply surprised since Southwark is not within Father Holdyn's responsibility as episcopal vicar of London."

Bell saw again the silver crucifix lying on the bishop's table, thought of Father Holdyn's righteousness. Holdyn could not have known that they had found the crucifix. Why in the world had he exposed his connection to Nelda by arranging for her burial?

"He is a good and holy man," Brother Patric said, "and very charitable."

The monk did not sound absolutely certain, Bell thought, rather amused, but his purpose was not to blacken Father Holdyn, who might have an innocent reason for what he had done. He merely shook his head and said, "Then my purpose here is gone. Thank you Brother Patric." And he turned away and walked back toward the bishop's house to get his palfrey from the stable.

"Could he have truly loved her?" Bell asked Marbrer, the palfrey he rode when he did not expect to fight.

The gelding turned his head to look inquiringly at his master, who took the opportunity to jab him strongly in the ribs so that his breath whooshed out. Bell quickly tightened the saddle girth. The large dark eyes took on a decidedly reproachful expression but Marbrer only turned his head away. Bell laughed. He had, he thought, as he led Marbrer out of the stable, been fortunate in both his mounts.

Monseigneur was the perfect warhorse; he was awesome to look at and had a good disposition, for a stallion, so long as he was not involved in fighting. Marbrer the palfrey was as sweet and placid as blancmange but was intelligent (possibly more so than Monseigneur) and lively. And his gaits! Bell could doze in the saddle and never be jolted even when Marbrer moved from walk to trot. Bell knew he could never have afforded Marbrer—except for his size and appearance.

The horse trader had told Bell, rather bitterly, that the horse was a delicate pale strawberry roan when he obtained him as a yearling and was then small and slender. A pink horse! The trader was delighted, imagining the price he could ask for a pink horse from a doting father or husband, and he trained the gelding most carefully to be gentle and have smooth gaits.

Because he saw the animal every day and was so pleased with Marbrer's (then named La Douce) sweet and affectionate nature, the trader hardly noticed that the gelding had put on two hands in height and considerable girth. Sweet tempered La Douce was, but he was now far too large to be a lady's mount. Nor, the trader groaned, did he recognize the cause of the strange dark marks that appeared on the gelding's coat. He had severely beaten several stable boys for not keeping the horse clean until he discovered that the markings could not be washed away.

Bell laughed again as he mounted. There could be no doubt that the renamed Marbrer was of a most peculiar color, streaks and splotches of dark gray spread indiscriminately over the pale strawberry roan. Bell had been doubtful that he wanted a pink horse splotched all over with dirt, even for a bargain price; however, once he had ridden the gelding and considered the condition of his purse, he had closed the deal. The one drawback was that once seen, Marbrer was not forgotten; occasionally Bell had to deal harshly with those who thought he was silly because Marbrer looked funny.

Once he reached the bridge, Bell had no attention to give to idle thoughts. Even Marbrer might take exception to having trays of goods thrust into his face while the peddler shouted in his ear. But Marbrer was calm and clever. Instead of dancing and bucking, he took his own revenge, turning his head swiftly to snatch a bun from the tray being proffered. Bell laughed uproariously but found a farthing when the astonished peddler began to weep while Marbrer chewed and snuffled with satisfaction.

The byplay bought some space around the horse, at least from those who had seen what had happened, so that they reached the north bank a little more quickly. Then a right turn on Thames Street, the thieves and drunks no danger to a man on a horse. As he rode toward the Tower, Bell considered how to get information about Linley. He could go directly to Surrey's lodging and ask . . . but he might find Linley himself there and he did not yet want to accuse the man.

Thames Street ended on the road that circled the hill on which the Tower had been built. Bell looked left and then right. To the left was a low building with what looked like the fence of a paddock to one side and the back. Likely a stable. He could leave Marbrer there and walk down toward the river, where he suspected he would find alehouses.

The ostler's eyes widened a little when he saw the dirty pink horse, but Bell's size and the heavy war belt with sword and poniard kept him respectfully silent.

"I won't be long," Bell said. "Just loosen the girth. No need to feed or water . . . well, maybe water. It's a warm day. And he's safe with other horses."

The ostler nodded. Bell proffered a farthing and the man smiled. Bell understood. Since the ostler did not have to feed the horse or even put him in a clean stall, the farthing was his. And Marbrer would make no trouble; the bun he had on the bridge would satisfy him for a while. Bell wrinkled his nose as he realized he could have asked the ostler to clean Marbrer's bit, which was no doubt fouled with pieces of bun, but likely the horse would chew and suck it nearly clean.

Bell crossed Thames Street and began to walk south, looking idly at both sides of the road that circled the Tower, which cast a long shadow as the sun dropped lower in the west. As he half remembered, shops, cookshops, and alehouses lined the road. He passed an armorer and, unable to resist, stopped to look at the weapons displayed. The journeyman watching the counter stepped forward eagerly but Bell shook his head and touched his own weapons.

"These are molded to my hand. I just like to look," he said, and the journeyman nodded and smiled.

Beyond the armorer was a cookshop. Bell sniffed and passed without pausing. He had dined at Magdalene's table and the strong smell of pepper hinted to him that the spices were hiding something. Next was a mercer on whose counter were shirts and braies, even several tunics showing some signs of wear but not near rags. Another armorer. Bell stopped to look more closely at a fancifully chased, silver-hilted eating knife. It would look well hung from a long chain around her neck against the blue gowns Magdalene often wore.

When his free hand started to move toward his purse to buy the trinket for her, Bell dropped the little knife as if it were hot. Startled, the merchant exclaimed in distress and asked whether Bell had detected something wrong. Bell apologized.

"No. It is a fine knife. Just . . . I had forgot that the person I thought it would suit . . . is gone."

He backed away from the merchant's expression of sympathy, so eager to get away from the mistaken sentiment that he crossed the street to the west side of the road. He found himself fronting another mercer's shop, and turned somewhat blindly back in the direction of the stable.

I will never be free of her, never! She is always there in the back of my mind, a warm comfort—and a sharp stab of pain. How can I want her when I know she offers me only the leavings of her love for another man?

Instinctively, he turned toward the smell of wine, into a wine shop a few steps farther along the road. Once inside, his attention was immediately called as he stumbled over someone's feet and was told in no uncertain terms to watch where he was going.

There was no drunkenness in the voice so Bell realized it was no simple man-at-arms that had been emboldened by drink to speak with so little respect. He muttered a "Sorry," as he blinked and looked around. The place was more than half full, the men settled into three separated groups and those then broken further into men sitting singly or with a few friends. And all the men were dressed as well as he—if not necessarily as cleanly—and with similar weapons. These must be the captains and sub-captains, perhaps also the masters-at-arms, of those nobles quartered in the Tower.

Accident—and running from the thought of Magdalene—had brought him to just the right place. Then he angrily dismissed Magdalene from his mind . . . again. Walking into the right place was not really much of an accident. The wine shop was near the gate into the Tower, specialized in wine rather than ale and beer, and was a logical place for those who wanted a convivial gathering not too close to their master's eye and not too far to be summoned at need.

Now Bell looked around more alertly. The room was dim, as all such were, lit only by several small windows on each long wall; however, there was light enough for him to see Mandeville's badge and Surrey's—those groups hardly separated—and then farthest from him so that he could not make out the badge clearly, a third group. The center of the room had two long scarred tables; the rest of the space was filled with smaller tables, a few round and several square, all hard used. Bell passed down the room, nodding as he skirted a square table where three of Surrey's men sat.

He picked up a cup of wine from the hard-faced woman who sat at the back of the room, presiding over a tray of cups and mugs and blocking the way to a number of broached barrels. Actually Bell would have preferred ale, but the men wearing Surrey's badge were drinking wine and he did not want to seem countrified or crude. Cup in hand, he stopped where Surrey's men sat.

"By your leave, a word or two?"

"Yes?" A dark-skinned, dark-eyed man with just a touch of silver in his black hair raised his head.

"Would any of you gentlemen know Sir Linley of Godalming by chance? I know he serves the earl of Surrey and your badges say you do also."

"What do you want Linley for?" the man to the right of the dark man asked. He was younger, brown-haired and blue eyed, scowling now, but otherwise pleasant looking.

"His whore was killed on Thursday and, for my sins, I am bidden ask him if he knew any reason for anyone to kill her."

A chorus of voices. "Nelda? Nelda is dead? Where? When? How?" Shock was written on every face. Bell would swear that none of the men had known of the whore's death before he announced it. So Linley either did not know before this morning or had kept the secret very well. Bell confirmed the death without details and asked again for Linley.

"You mean Linley is suspect?" The third man at the table frowned, knitting pale blond brows.

Bell shrugged. "She was his woman. He knew her best. And nine times out of ten it is the closest to the dead who make them that way."

The dark man shook his head. "Not Linley. He had no reason to harm Nelda." He then waved toward an empty chair and added, "Sit, if you will. I am Sir Filbert. I've known Linley for years and he is not violent toward women."

The blond snickered. "He's not violent toward anyone."

Sir Filbert scowled at the blond. "Besides, Linley and Nelda got along very well."

"He certainly wasn't jealous of her," the blond said, his lips pursed as if he tasted something unpleasant. "He owed me a small sum and offered her favors as payment. I told him I would rather wait for the money."

"Well, what you both say is interesting," Bell said, "because someone beat Nelda severely several days before she died. Oh, my name is Bellamy of Itchen."

"Not Linley," Filbert repeated. "In all the years she has lived in his house, he never laid a hand on her. I used her once or twice when Linley was away. He had suggested that I visit her to see if all was well. I think he genuinely liked her . . . but there was no heat between them. Anyway, I do not understand why you have been ordered to examine the death of a whore—they die all the time in the stews."

Bell raised his hands and shoulders in a gesture of helplessness—implying that he was a man following orders he did not understand.

Filbert also shrugged. "If your master really desires an answer, I would look for whoever it was who beat her."

Bell nodded. "Well, that is one of the reasons I would like to speak to Sir Linley. It may be that he can tell me who would be likely to mistreat Nelda."

The brown-haired, fresh-faced man laughed. "You can find him readily enough by stopping at the mercery of Rhyton of Guildford. His place is in the East Chepe—"

"Bereton, why can you not keep your mouth closed?" Sir Filbert snapped. "Linley will not be best pleased to have a sheriff's officer inquiring about his dead whore at Master Rhyton's house when Rhyton has just agreed to permit Linley to be betrothed to his daughter."

"And heiress," the blond said, and lifted his pale brows at the man called Bereton. "Looking to slip into Linley's place? Rhyton won't have you. Linley will be lord of Godalming when his father dies and Rhyton wants a baron, not a penniless knight."

"Hmmm." Bell did not correct Filbert's mistake in

thinking him the sheriff's officer. He preferred to keep the bishop out of any discussion of Nelda's death. "About to be betrothed, is he? Perhaps being rid of Nelda was one of the conditions?"

All three men looked at him as if he had grown a second head, and the blond, despite the fact that he obviously did not like Sir Linley, was the one who asked a surprised, "Why should Master Rhyton care about Nelda?"

"That could not be a reason," Filbert said. "Linley did not pay her, beyond letting her live in the rooms above the rag shop. Surely you do not think the rich mercer would care so long as Nelda cost nothing or that his daughter would be jealous? And even if she were, all Linley would need to do was tell Nelda to go."

"Sometimes it is not that easy," Bell remarked. "Nelda might not have been willing to be put aside."

"Wait, wait," Bereton said. "When did you say that Nelda died?"

"On Thursday," Bell replied.

"Then Linley had nothing to do with it," Filbert said with satisfaction, nodding and smiling at Bereton. "He was at Rhyton's house on Thursday. He went mid-morning, stayed for dinner and most of the afternoon and evening. He and the mercer were working out the details of the betrothal agreement. Then Linley came here to the Cask of Wine to finish celebrating. Plenty of men saw him and so did Mistress Pechet." He nodded toward the woman who served the wine.

Bell frowned, seeing the easy solution to Nelda's death disappearing. "Are you sure? Were you here? And how do you know that he did not go to his house in Southwark after he celebrated here?"

Filbert laughed. "Because he was dead drunk, and I

mean *dead* drunk. I was not here while he was drinking. Thursday was a duty night for me, but Bereton and Radley had to carry him to Surrey's lodging because neither of them knew where he lived and he was too drunk to tell them. He lay there until morning, when I was able to rouse him and get him home."

"I would have left him," Bereton said. "I told him that he had had enough, but he said he was toasting his lady's fortune. Then he fell across the table and started to snore. Mistress Pechet wanted him out of the house before he began to spew."

Radley laughed aloud. "She even lent us a barrow to carry him to Surrey's lodging. That will make a tale to be spread among Mandeville's men. The gate guards saw us bringing him in."

Bell grimaced. "All I wanted was to know where Linley was, and I find my best suspect declared innocent. I hope you will all forgive me if I confirm your tale with Mistress Pechet, who might have less interest in protecting Linley."

The chorus of "Go ahead" and "Please do" and "Be my guest" only confirmed to Bell that the men were speaking the truth. Nonetheless he carried his half-full wine cup to the back of the room. When Mistress Pechet reached for it, Bell put his hand over the mouth of the cup but drew a penny from his purse. He held it in his hand without proffering it.

"I have some questions to ask you about Thursday. You were here, were you not?"

"I am always here. But I sell wine, not information."

"This will harm no one and I could ask it of any of the men here. Do you know Linley of Godalming?"

The woman snorted a laugh. "Didn't know him except as one of the men who drink here until Thursday. You want to know if he was here that night? Damn near emptied a half-barrel by hisself. And he wasn't walking altogether steady when he came in, either. Already drunk. Wouldn't have served him, but there was sign on him that he'd spewed already, so I didn't send my man to push him out."

"Did he say anything to you?"

"No more than that he wanted a whole flagon. I thought a bit about giving it to him, but he had the silver in his hand and I figured the worst he could do was bring back the wine. He'd clearly emptied his belly before he came in."

"Do you know when he came in?"

She shrugged. "It was dark. Can't say better nor that."

"Nothing else?" Bell lifted the penny suggestively.

The woman shook her head. "Unless you count when he joined a couple of his friends, he raised his cup and said, too loud—you know how drunks are—that he drank to Claresta and her dear papa, Rhyton."

Bell sighed and handed over the penny. Nothing was ever easy. Unless Mistress Pechet had truly remarkable hearing, she could not have overheard what Linley's companions had told him, yet she had given almost identical evidence. Her testimony as confirmation of that from Linley's fellow officers must clear him.

Leaving the half-filled cup—the wine was nothing to rave about—Bell started for the door. He would have to go and tell Magdalene that their principal suspect could not have committed the crime. For some reason that did not make Bell feel at all discouraged. At the door he paused to look at the sun. It was near setting. If he took his time riding back, he should reach Magdalene's house after the second set of clients was gone . . . He hesitated and then shook his head. It was Sunday; there would be no clients. Involuntarily, Bell smiled. He would arrive just about the time they ate their evening meal.

"You." A finger poked his back so hard that Bell staggered a step forward; he whirled around, his hand on his knife. "Did you say that Linley's woman Nelda was dead?"

Bell looked up and up farther—a most unusual situation because he was very tall compared with most men. This one was almost double his width too. His clothing was not as fine as that of the knights and bore a few more stains and smudges. Bell saw the man glance with little concern at his hand on his knife. He would be a master-at-arms, Bell guessed, and the badge on his shoulder was Mandeville's.

"Yes," Bell said neutrally, "Nelda is dead."

"Deserved it, the thieving bitch," the giant said, and pushed past Bell into the street.

CHAPTER 6

"What with Linley cleared of Nelda's death, I suppose I should have tried to stop the man," Bell said to the women at the table, who were listening intently, when he reached that point in describing his afternoon's activity.

"That would not be nice if he wanted to leave or was, perhaps, in a hurry." Ella's round eyes were worried.

"No, Ella is quite correct," Magdalene said, controlling twitching lips with an effort. "It is much better that you did not. Likely he would have struck out at you, you would have responded in kind, and either you would have been responsible for causing a riot or having a dead witness."

Bell laughed. "I thought much the same and that since he is Mandeville's man, he will be easy enough to identify. And if I speak to his captain first and the captain bids him answer my questions we will not come to blows over it."

"I do not remember seeing such a person while I lived with Nelda," Diot put in, pulling a platter of sweet and savory tidbits toward her.

"A new client, I suppose, and sharper or more suspicious than others," Magdalene nodded.

"New clients need special care," Ella said with great seriousness, also nodding agreement. "But why should this man want to hit you for just asking a question?"

Bell looked appealingly at Magdalene. It was Sunday night and none of the women had clients coming to keep them busy. They were all sitting around the table, completely at ease, picking at the remains of a very satisfying evening meal. Bell was full and content, but he had more to discuss with Magdalene and since he would not share her bed, he had to talk to her here.

He was fond of Ella, but her presence made it very difficult to explain what he had learned about Nelda's death. He knew he would slip and mention killing or murder and Ella would be terrified and require extensive soothing.

"Some men are like that," Magdalene said quickly in response to Bell's look of appeal. "You do not need to worry about it, Ella. We do not allow such men to come here. Tom Watchman does not let them in."

Ella's fair brows knitted. "It would be better if Bell stayed. I do not think Tom Watchman is strong enough or brave enough, although he is a nice man."

Letice touched Ella's arm, pointed to Bell, and then showed her fingers rushing here and there around the table. Then she touched Ella again and gestured for her to come.

"Letice says that Bell is very, very busy right now," Magdalene interpreted. "That is true, and he must stay near the bishop, who is in danger and may need him. You know Bell's first duty is to the bishop. And Letice would like you to go with her, my love. I think she has some mending that is too difficult for her. You will do it, will you not?"

"Oh, of course," Ella said, smiling at Letice and getting up at once. "I love to mend Letice's things. The cloth is so smooth and so beautiful. It calls for my smallest stitches."

A silence followed until Letice's door had closed, then Diot said, "Letice will keep her busy. She came back with a new gown but—" Diot laughed "—it would have fit two of *me*. You can imagine what it looked like against Letice. Hmmm. Ella is very clever about stitching. Perhaps she can fit it to Letice so that another gown can be salvaged from the extra. I think I will join Ella and Letice."

After she stood up, she added, "If there is anything you think I can add about Nelda's death, you can tell me later."

When she had disappeared into Letice's chamber, Bell shrugged. "Now that the shock is over, she doesn't care even though she knew Nelda well." He hesitated, looking into Magdalene's misty-sky eyes. "You care," he said.

Magdalene's lips thinned. "Because she was a whore. Because if she had not been carrying Gloucester's letter, if she had not been used to embarrass the bishop, no one else would have cared. Because when you no longer need her body, it will be cast into some pit somewhere—"

"No, Nelda has escaped that. She is decently buried . . . not in the church, of course, but right beside it. I almost forgot to tell you that, and it may be important. The man whose crucifix she had among her stolen trinkets paid for her burial . . . and took away the clothes she had been wearing."

"Who?"

Bell hesitated and then said, "Father Holdyn, the episcopal vicar of London."

For a moment, Magdalene did not react, then she said, "That is for you and the bishop to sort out. He has never been in this house. I can swear to that. If you wish, I can ask about him . . ."

"No. At least not until Winchester has spoken to him tomorrow. Interestingly, Holdyn is also a very big man, and strong, too. He does not spare himself in the building and repair of churches in London." Bell slowly shook his head. "That a man like Holdyn should slip with a woman like Nelda . . . yes, it could happen and she could steal his crucifix and he not notice until later. But that he should kill her to save confessing a sin and then put the body in the bishop's bedchamber . . . I cannot believe it. He does not admire Winchester, but—"

Magdalene put a hand on his arm. "Do not condemn the man before you hear him. I guess from your being so troubled about him that he is a good man. There are other ways Nelda could have got his crucifix and other reasons for his burying her than that he murdered her. Come back to the more likely suspect. About this other man?"

Bell's eyes narrowed. "From the way he poked me in the back, I would say he does not know his own strength or, more likely, he enjoys causing pain. That would make him a likely suspect for the man who beat Nelda, but if so we will lose another lead. If he had killed her, he would not need to ask if she were dead."

Magdalene looked at him with lifted brows. "Not all big men are stupid," she remarked, and smiled as she touched his cheek. "This one, however, is so distinctive from your description that if he had ever dealt with Nelda at all, he would be recognized. Thus, he had to pretend ignorance and the best way was to ask directly."

Bell had frozen for a moment when Magdalene touched his cheek, offering comfort and affection. But she was a whore! Her body and her affection were for sale to any man. As the thought came into his mind, he knew it was false, but he had to cling to it. If he did not . . . if he did not he would slip back into being her man and have to accept the fact that he shared not only her body but also her heart. Whore! With an effort, he recalled to mind what she had said.

"That is reasonable, but then why did he not say he was sorry, or some such? Why say she deserved it and that she was a thieving bitch?"

"I will lay odds because he fears or knows someone

heard him accusing Nelda of stealing something."

Bell nodded slowly and then sighed. "I suppose so, but when I will have time to question him I do *not* know. The bishop needs my escort tomorrow. He is going to St. Paul's where he will meet the archbishop and he will also question Father Holdyn about how Nelda came to have his crucifix. And I need to speak to Master Rhyton also. Linley seems cleared, but I wish to confirm with Rhyton that Linley was there."

"Do not bother with Master Rhyton," Magdalene said. "I will visit him to ask permission to show Claresta my embroidery. Perhaps she will wish to order trimmings for her wedding gown or embroidered linens for her dowry."

"And how will you have heard of this proposed marriage?"

Magdalene laughed. "Why from one of Linley's fellow knights, who was babbling of it to the woman he used . . . ah, no . . . that will not do. I do not wish to be known as a whoremistress but as an embroiderer. Oh, that is still easy. I will have heard from FitzRevery's daughter, whose husband knows one of Linley's fellow knights. FitzRevery still owes me for helping him win back Mainard's regard."

"You are jesting!" Bell exclaimed, laughing softly. "I cannot believe that Mainard could hold a grudge for five minutes together and more especially against FitzRevery, who is one of the few people who can look into his face with that horrible birthmark without wincing or turning away."

Magdalene laughed too. "When the men of the Bridge Guild searched Mainard's shop for the accounts Mainard's wife was using to extort money from them, some of them searched Sabina's rooms above the shop and disarranged the furniture. Mainard would forgive a man in five minutes for cutting off his arm, but to cause Sabina to bump into a chair, to throw Sabina's gowns on the floor—that was unforgivable." The smile disappeared from Magdalene's lips. "Oh, yes, if it touches Sabina, Mainard can hold a grudge."

"I believe you. She was a whore and yet he married her and seems more than content."

"She gives him no reason to doubt her, but to Mainard it does not matter. He would keep her and love her if she were as promiscuous as Diot. Jealousy would only tear *him* apart. It would not make him blame Sabina, nor quarrel with her, nor strike her, nor threaten her, nor leave her."

Magdalene's eyes flicked to Bell's face and then away. He had left her out of jealousy. He did not speak, however, and after a moment his jaw, which had clenched, relaxed, and he shook his head.

"How did we get to speaking of Mainard?"

"From Master Rhyton, whom I will approach tomorrow morning to show my embroideries. I think I can get the time Linley left from Rhyton, but far more important is that I can discover from Claresta whether they would lie for Linley."

"From Claresta?"

"If the marriage is of her making, if she has fallen in love with Linley or desperately craves the status of being a lady, a baron's wife, she will herself lie for him and, since she had influence enough to induce her father to make the marriage, induce him to lie also."

"Even if she learns that he killed a woman?"

Magdalene snorted softly. "The kind that desires the title 'lady' above all else will not care for the death of a whore. She might even take as a compliment that Linley would kill to have her to wife. Even if she guesses it is her father's money he wants, she will not care if she does not deeply desire the man himself. And likely Master Rhyton would not consider the death of a whore important enough to smirch a son-by-marriage who will some day be a baron."

Bell sighed. "I hate to agree with you, but likely you are right. Certainly it is better that you speak to Claresta. I would never be able to judge whether she was telling the truth about her feeling for Linley. If you can get information from Rhyton, that will be fine but it is more important that you be introduced to the daughter. If needed, I can speak to Rhyton later. He might not mind a son-by-marriage who killed his whore to soothe his betrothed's jealousy, but one who deals with letters from Gloucester might give him pause."

As he said the last few words, Bell started to rise. "It will be better if I go before your women return. They will want to start a game of nine-man-morris and—"

There was a rap on the door. Bell's right hand flashed to his sword hilt, his left to his knife, and the bench hit the ground with a clatter as he pushed it aside to get to his feet. "Who comes in without ringing the bell?" he snarled, rage and suspicion lighting his eyes in his quick glance at Magdalene.

"Just off, mistress," Tom Watchman's coarse voice came through the crack he had opened the door. "You'll want to lock up behind me."

"I will, Tom," Magdalene replied. "Don't worry. Sir Bell's here."

"Ah. That be good then."

The door closed and Bell stepped over the bench. "Why did you tell him that? I'm leaving too."

"No, not yet. Hearing Tom reminded me that he knew Nelda and he told me things you should know."

"Tom could afford Nelda?"

Magdalene laughed. "No, of course not. He knew her

because she was forced to call for the Watch several times when men tried to break into her chamber."

"She was not *that* desirable."

Magdalene laughed again. "Will you get your mind out from between Nelda's legs! Tom believes those were the men who were not much bemused and realized that she had stolen from them. He knows that there were complaints to the sheriff but nothing ever came of them. Nelda never sold any item she was accused of stealing and nothing was ever found. I suppose Linley also exerted some influence."

"As Lord William does for you." Bell's voice was cold.

Magdalene met his eyes and said, "Yes, and has for many years—ten at least. And I am very grateful. I shudder to think what troubles would fall upon me if he withdrew his protection."

Bell's jaw clamped tight again. What he wanted to do was cry out that he would protect her, but he knew that was ridiculous. William of Ypres might not be the king's favorite any longer, but Stephen still needed him and would surely accommodate him in so small a thing as squashing Bell like a bug. And to offer Magdalene the bishop's protection would be a dangerous lie. Doubtless there were things Winchester would be willing to do at his request, but to involve himself openly with a whore . . .

There was a short, tight silence before Bell said, "So what more did Tom tell you that I needed to hear. We both knew that Nelda was a thief."

"That she did not sell her gleanings was interesting when coupled with the coins in her secret box. To me that spells extortion."

Bell sighed. "To me also. We will need to identify the owners of the rings and the seal."

"Moreover, Tom told me that Nelda is not the only

tenant of the top floor. There is another whore, called Tayte, who lives in one room. He says Tayte is very quiet and the Watch has never been summoned by her or because of her. I will undertake to talk to Tayte. If she does not respond to a few coins, you can take over."

"What about the shop below?"

Magdalene shook her head. "Tom says the woman who keeps it is blind and deaf *always* to everything, not to be moved by coin or by threats. He thinks she is very much afraid of something or someone, but has no idea who or what inspires the fear. He thought real torture might—"

"I do not think the matter of what she saw or heard is important enough for that." Bell's mouth was tight with distaste and he shook himself as a dog does to free itself from water in an attempt to rid himself of the memory of questioning the men who had attacked the bishop. "However," he added quickly, "her fear is also interesting. Perhaps I will set a man or two to watching the shop. And now—" he bent and lifted the bench he had overturned into position "—it is time for me—"

The bell at the gate rang clamorously. Magdalene jerked and bit her lip. "Good God," she whispered, coming to her feet, "I forgot to lock it."

Bell already had his sword belted on and he followed a step or two behind Magdalene. The bell rang again, pulled so hard that it nearly sprang from the arm that held it.

"Be gone!" Magdalene called, hurrying to the gate. "It is Sunday night. We do no business on Sunday."

As she spoke, she reached for the bar that could fix the gate closed against anything less forceful than a battering ram. It was just out of her grasp, and she stepped sideways to seize it, which was lucky, because the gate sprang open under a forceful push, blocking Bell momentarily. A man stinking of sour wine and vomit staggered in.

"Who do you think you are to set times?" he bellowed, gazing around muzzily, until his gaze finally found Magdalene. "Filthy whore!" He turned toward her, knife out. "You and your kind will spread your legs when *we*—Aieee!"

Magdalene had swung the gate bar and caught him on the shoulder. The knife dropped from his hand and he staggered back. She swung again, this time catching him on the side of the head. He went down, just as two more men staggered through the open gate. Magdalene lifted the bar again, but Bell had already come around and tapped both with the flat of his sword. One had flown back out of the gate; the other was lying on the ground spitting out blood and broken teeth.

Bell stepped out of the gate and looked at the three men who had drawn swords and were about to rush in. "Pick up your offal and get out," he said. One stepped forward, and Bell knocked the sword out of his hand. "Next man who waves a sword at me loses his sword hand," he said. "Put your weapons away and remove the two pieces of garbage from the gate. I give you a quarter candlemark to be—"

"No, Letice! Don't cut his throat!" Magdalene's voice was high and urgent.

Bell stepped sideways away from the gate. His principal attention was still on the three men, who paused in sheathing their weapons to stare through the opening at Letice. Magdalene had a grip on her arm and was preventing her from stooping over the man Magdalene had felled. A long, wickedly curved knife—almost a scimitar—was reaching toward the man, who was starting to move.

Unable to resist, Bell grinned. He was not certain whether that was a bit of play-acting to convince the drunken group that the Old Priory Guesthouse was not a safe place to invade by force or whether Letice *had* intended to cut the man's throat. Now he stepped sideways and gestured with his sword.

Somewhat sobered by what had happened and watching Bell nervously the three entered the gate. They did not escape unscathed. Dulcie swung her fry-pan at the one who bent to help up the man Letice had threatened. She hit him on the behind with such force that he screeched as he flew over his comrade's head and fell face first in the dirt. But when he jumped up, yelling, Diot prodded him, just beyond his kidney, ungently, with the knife in her hand.

"Pick up that filth and get it out of here," she snarled, "or I will hold you down while Letice gelds you."

At which remark, Letice smiled and rotated the hooked tip of her blade suggestively. Bell stepped a little farther from the gate to give the men room, watched them as they picked up their damaged companions, and staggered north toward the river. He thought briefly of following them and pushing them in but then shrugged and came inside.

"I am so sorry we were slow in coming," Diot was saying as Magdalene put the bar into its sockets and hooked up the chain for good measure. "Letice and I were both undressed so that Ella could fit the gown to Letice and see if there would be enough silk for me to use. When we heard the noise, Letice went to get Dulcie and I had to get Ella into her room."

"It is my own fault," Magdalene said, sighing. Her hands were trembling and she knotted them together. "Tom told me when he left to lock up after him, but instead of hooking up the chain—"

"Yes," Bell said, "and so you should have done, but you never had a chain on the gate before. Why is Tom staying here? What happened in the weeks Magdalene was gone?"

"It was Father Etienne's idea," Diot said, as they all walked toward the house.

"Who is Father Etienne?" Bell asked.

"He is the clerk Lord William sent to help us if there was any trouble while Magdalene was gone. At first I was a little hesitant, thinking the chain might give clients the wrong impression atop having Tom sleep in the stable because his lodging burnt down, but Father Etienne said that with all the great men out of the city there might be some disorder. And he was right. We had several drunken groups who tried to force their way in."

"This place is not marked as a house of ease. How did they know?" Bell asked.

Diot's eyes widened. "I never thought. Someone had to tell them. Apurpose? But why?"

"Not necessarily apurpose for ill," Magdalene pointed out, her lips twisting wryly. "I am sure some mention disporting themselves at the Old Priory Guesthouse as a boast or innocently to praise the entertainment here."

"Not so innocently," Bell said, but he looked relieved.

Diot shrugged. "The chain prevented them from all rushing in together, and Tom was able to reach through the opening and prod them away with his sword." Then she nodded, also looking relieved. "They could not have come deliberately to do harm or they would have made a stronger effort. I do believe they were armsmen looking for a good time and annoyed not to be welcomed."

Bell nodded unhappily. "I would not be surprised if some were Salisbury's men, put out of the castles the king is taking. Winchester is hiring those he can, but—"

"He had better be careful," Magdalene interrupted sharply. "To hire Salisbury's men atop this call for a convocation will not endear the bishop to his brother."

"No." Bell sighed. "But he is so very angry. He does not show it much, but he is really furious. I spoke privately to the knights he set to the task of hiring the displaced men-at-arms and urged them not to spread abroad that it was Henry of Winchester who was hiring. They are doing their best, I believe."

They entered the house and shut the door behind them. Bell looked around at the neat room, at Magdalene's large embroidery frame, at the workbaskets set beside the stools near the hearth. He imagined everything overturned and trodden underfoot, wine spilled, perhaps lamps and candles overturned and setting the rushes ablaze.

He closed his eyes, reopened them. It was not his business. Let her beloved William protect her. He started to turn toward the door. Magdalene put a hand on his arm. He could feel it shaking.

"Don't go, Bell," she said. "Stay this night at least."

Letice also put a hand on his arm. Her knife had disappeared and her black eyes looked huge in her dark face.

"We would be much easier if you would stay," Diot said. "There is a small chance that those men will seek support and come back for revenge."

Ella opened the door of her room and peered out, her cheeks tear streaked. When she saw Bell in the middle of the group of women, she ran to join them. "You will not leave me to be beaten," she wept. "I have done nothing wrong."

"No, love," Bell said, unable to resist response to the fearful child. "You did just right by going to your room."

"But I cannot go back now," Ella whimpered. "I could hear the men shouting. I could not sleep. I would have fearful dreams. And I cannot even sew. Look at how my hands shake." She held out her small, plump hands, and they were trembling. "Dear Bell, will you not play a game with me so that I can forget the banging and shouting?"

"I do not think that we are in the right mood for playing games," Magdalene said, "but I have had sent to me from France a tale of love and adventure. You have a fine rich voice, Bell. Will you read to us of 'Aucassin and Nicolette'?"

"You will read us a story!" Ella exclaimed breathlessly and ran into her chamber to bring out a prized possession—in fact a gift that had been sent by Master Gerome—a stool with a soft leather pillow fixed atop.

Then she plumped herself down on her own stool and folded her hands into her lap, bright, empty eyes fixed on Bell in happy expectation. Magdalene slipped away to her chamber to get the scroll. From the corner of his eye as he looked at the stool, Bell saw Dulcie coming from the kitchen and going into the empty room beyond Diot's. She was carrying linens for the bed, a pillow, and a blanket.

Bell thought of the clean, quiet chamber, the sturdy, comfortable cot with its stuffed mattress, the warmth of the soft blanket; then he thought of his bed in the bishop's house—the pallet on the floor, the snoring or quarreling men, the sound of dice rolling, shouts and cursing. Bell sighed and unbuckled his sword belt.

CHAPTER 7

Magdalene broke her fast on Monday morning in the very best of spirits. She knew that Bell was long gone, which was just as it should be. He would be in good time for all to be ready when the bishop wished to leave. He would not feel rushed or guilty or that there was any inconvenience in lodging at the Old Priory Guesthouse.

Dulcie told her, speaking English instead of the French she seldom used, that Bell had wakened her at dawn to lock the gate behind him and she had brought him ale and bread and cheese and a piece of pasty for breaking his fast. While he ate Dulcie had asked, as if it was the most ordinary question in the world, whether he would be with them for dinner and the evening meal.

"Not for dinner," he had said, without the smallest hesitation, Dulcie reported. He would be busy with the bishop all day. And if he were dismissed early, he would ride over to the Tower to discover who the big man who wore Mandeville's badge was. As for the evening meal . . . There he had hesitated, but only as if he were considering what he would be doing, not as if he was reconsidering staying with them.

"He'll be here till the bishop goes back to Winchester for the convocation," Dulcie said, somehow her flat, deaf-woman's voice conveying great satisfaction. "Should I go over to the bishop's house and fetch his clothes?"

Magdalene giggled. "I think that would be going too far without his permission," she said in English. "But you can ask him, all innocent like, *which* clothes he wants you to bring in case he comes in armor and would want to change." She spoke slowly, not too loud, but saying each word separate from the others, which she had discovered Dulcie heard best.

"Load off'n m'mind him bein' here. That Tom means well, but he's nothin'." She looked at the table. "Had what y'wanted? You goin' out?"

"Yes. To the East Chepe to see if I can sell some embroidery. Is there something you want me to buy?"

"Dill. And rice. And saffron. Nothin' that'll mess your clothes. I'll get a haunch'v mutton myself. Need a bit extra. The man's got an appetite."

Magdalene laughed at Dulcie's pleasure. The maid was a good cook and liked nothing better than to see the meals she prepared devoured. She left the table and went to a shelf to the left of the doorway, where she took down a smooth-woven basket. Into it she put a clean muslin cloth and then several ribbons embroidered by Ella, who was developing into quite a seamstress, a square picture done by Diot, and a sleeve cuff which she had been doing for Bell but had left unfinished.

After a moment of consideration, she took one of the bands Letice had done, all intricate curving lines without any bird or beast or human form. Having tucked it down at the bottom, she covered the basket with a plain cloth and went to her room for her veil.

The bridge was its usual self, full of merchants and customers. There were fewer peddlers selling foodstuffs to eat because it was too late for fast breaking and too early for nooning. In any case, Magdalene did not hesitate over any ware, no matter how attractive apprentice or journeyman tried to make it sound. One did not carry odd items one had bought when trying to engage a client.

She walked as usual up Gracechurch Street rather than Fish Street to save her clothing and shoes from taint, then turned right into the East Chepe until she came to Mainard's saddlery. Henry had already backed away from the counter to make room for Magdalene to pass, but she smiled at him and shook her head.

"No, I don't want to come in, Henry. If I have time, I will stop on my way back. I presume all is well with Sabina and Mainard?"

"Yes, indeed, Mistress Magdalene." Henry laughed. "Sabina was singing yesterday afternoon and came home not only with a substantial gift over and above her fee but with the son of the household trailing along behind. Haesel said he had sneaked out and followed them. He did not believe a singer could be virtuous."

"Oh, dear, I hope Sabina did not thwack him with her staff."

"No, she would not attack the son of a client, and Haesel was with her. But it all worked to her benefit. He was a *very* pretty young man and she had told him several times that she was married. He did not believe her until she flung herself into Master Mainard's arms. Then, taking in the size of Master Mainard—although Mainard of course made no threatening gesture—the fool went away. And Master Mainard was so thrilled that she preferred him."

"Most wisely. I can see Mainard's face, which Sabina cannot, and I, too, would prefer Mainard to a pretty-faced boy. But what I came for, Henry, was to ask if you know where I could find a mercer called Master Rhyton of Guildford. I understand he is recently come to London."

"That is a really easy question to answer. It is Master Rhyton who has purchased the Lime Street house and taken

Josne's shop on the corner of Botolph."

"Ah, thank you Henry. How convenient that I do not need to pass the shop before I come to the house. I really wish to speak to Mistress Claresta and see if I can sell her some of my embroidery."

"You should have no trouble. Best of everything is what Master Rhyton wants and from what I've heard he can well afford it. It was said he nearly owned Guildford by the time he left. Came to London to look for a lord for Mistress Claresta so his grandsons will be noble."

"And she? Is she looking for a lord also?"

Henry shrugged, but a customer approached the counter and Magdalene waved Mainard's salesman away and walked to the next shop. She was welcomed there also, and passed at once beyond the counter into the shop where Perekin FitzRevery rose to greet her.

"I need a favor, Master FitzRevery," Magdalene said.

"You have it," the mercer replied without hesitation.

Magdalene laughed. "How trusting you are to agree without knowing to what. But this will do you no harm. I only want to be able to say that I heard of Master Rhyton of Guildford's daughter Claresta's forthcoming betrothal from you or your daughter."

"That is hardly a favor," FitzRevery said, smiling. "You could have heard it anywhere in the Chepe. Rhyton has been telling the 'secret' of his negotiations with Sir Linley of Godalming in a loud whisper to anyone who would listen. I think Mainard must have been the first to have heard, and since I was next door, I heard next."

Laughing again, Magdalene said, "And I was just talking to Henry. He could have told me and I would not have needed to trouble you."

"It is no trouble. Always a pleasure to see you, Magdalene, since I have no womenfolk at all to disapprove." Then suddenly his grin changed to a frown. "But when I told the news to my daughter, thinking she would be all atwitter, she was not happy over it. She said that Rhyton is making a mistake. Claresta is not the kind who wishes to be mistress of a landed estate."

"Ah, then it was not the daughter who urged the marriage?"

"No, not at all."

"Does she dislike Sir Linley?"

FitzRevery shrugged. "I have no idea. My daughter said nothing of that, only that Claresta was very much a mercer's daughter. Interested in the business. She is all her father has, and he often took her with him when he went to buy and talked to her about the goods as if she were a son."

"Ah well, if she has a lively mind, no doubt she can become interested in the working of her husband's manors. But I had no idea the news was all over the Chepe. I had hoped to sell her some of my embroideries for her marriage chest, but I may no longer be alone in my offer. Still, I had better go along and see her."

There was almost no purpose now to going to the Lime Street house, Magdalene thought. Obviously Linley had been telling the truth about his engagement with Master Rhyton and Linley's fellow knights in Surrey's household accounted for his whereabouts for the rest of the night. Nonetheless, Magdalene thought as she crossed the road and turned right again, it would be interesting to see how Claresta felt about the betrothal, and if she could sell some of Ella's embroidery the girl would be thrilled.

Magdalene still did not want to arrive loaded down with parcels, but she did stop to look at a selection of colored thread. That could go into her basket. She caught herself picking too many blues and greens, colors that flattered Bell's fair hair and blue eyes, and then chose more deliberately some of the brilliant shades that Letice loved and the pinks and yellows that were most attractive to Ella. For Diot . . . Magdalene did not know her taste so well but she found a rich amber that would show off her hair, and a glowing green that was much the shade of Diot's eyes.

Naturally, having stopped to buy, Magdalene was almost besieged by other apprentices and journeymen along the street, who called out and reached out to her to show their wares. Some very thin cloth caught her eye. The worst heat of the summer was yet to come. She looked, felt, said she had an appointment to which she could not carry anything beyond her basket but that if the cloth was still there when she returned, she would consider it.

Finally, having stopped only once again, this time to buy and pop into her mouth a small round of rose leaves in crystallized honey, Magdalene turned left once more onto Lime Street. About a third of the way north on the street, before one came to the crossing with Fenchurch, was what had been Mainard's house. It was a rather elegant two story structure, set well back from the street with no provision for a shop out front, which marked it ostentatiously as being a rich man's dwelling.

The servant who came to the door in response to the sound of the bell, opened his eyes wide when he saw Magdalene's veiled face. She was almost equally surprised by him. Jean had been Mainard's first wife's slave, starved to emaciation, dressed in rags. Now he was almost plump, his clothing was dark and plain but decent. His manner alone had not changed. Subdued and respectful, hinting that a harsh word would make him cringe.

"Mistress Magdalene," he nearly whispered, "Master

Mainard does not live here any more."

"I know, Jean. He sold the house to Master Rhyton. But what in the world are you doing here?"

"When the house was sold, Master Mainard offered us our freedom and asked if we would like to remain with the house. It seems that the purchaser was coming from Guildford and not bringing his servants with him. We were all afraid, but it seemed safest to us to stay where we knew we could go to Master Mainard for help . . . if, if the new master was not kind. But he is. Not like Master Mainard, but Master Rhyton pays us fairly and is in no way unreasonable."

"Well." Magdalene smiled. "I am happy to know that you are so well settled."

The man swallowed nervously. "But Master Rhyton is not here. He is in his shop at the corner of Botolph, but . . . but . . . I am afraid . . ."

Magdalene grinned under her veil. "It's all right, Jean. I am not come to solicit custom from Master Rhyton. I am come to see Mistress Claresta. I have heard that she is soon to be betrothed and I wish to show her my embroidery. Perhaps she will order items for her wedding chest."

"Embroidery?"

"Yes, Jean." She took the cloth off the top of her basket and displayed the wares. "We are listed as a house of embroiderers and we do embroider and sell our work. I am sure that Mistress Claresta would not be interested in our other activities."

"Your other activities?" Jean looked aside uneasily. "Oh, no. No. Mistress Claresta would not be interested in that but these—" he gestured to the embroidered ribbons and the sample square "—those are beautiful. Mistress Claresta might be interested in those."

"Then may I come in? And will you tell her that an embroideress has come to show her some samples?" Magdalene hesitated and then said pointedly, "And I hope that is *all* you will say of me."

Down the corridor, Jean scratched and then opened the door into the main room. Magdalene heard the soft murmur of Jean's voice and then a lighter, clearer voice saying, "An embroideress . . ." And then another male voice, young but a rich baritone: "Then I will leave the samples of cloth with you, Mistress Claresta, and you can tell your father—" But the woman's voice interrupted, "No, don't go Spencer. You might as well look at the embroidery also. And if it is such that we wish to buy, you can escort her to the shop."

Whereupon Magdalene loosened her veil and Jean came out to lead her into the room, after which he went out, closing the door behind him. The most interesting thing to Magdalene was that the young man Claresta had called Spencer was staring down at the girl and she up at him. Her hand lay on a small pile of cloth swatches, rich fabrics, but they were carelessly piled together as if she was not particularly interested in them.

Magdalene stood for a moment, realizing that she would need no adroit questioning to discover whether Claresta liked Sir Linley. It was all too plain that it was Spencer that held her interest. Magdalene assessed him and repressed a smile. She was accustomed to big men. William was tall and powerful, Bell even more so, but Spencer was a young giant—and a beautiful giant to boot. His hair was dark brown, thick and curly, his brows ran straight across his forehead but without being ragged and unkempt. No hair grew from his strong nose or from his ears and his rounded but determined chin was clean-shaven with no ugly stubble marring it or his cheeks.

Now all Magdalene had to learn was whether the girl yearned even more deeply to be called "lady." "I beg your pardon," Magdalene said.

Claresta started and turned to look at her. Spencer also looked at her . . . and looked back at Claresta. Magdalene's eyes opened a fraction wider. My, she thought, if my face will not distract him, he is truly devoted. Poor man. And stupid girl if she will give that up to be called "lady" in a marriage of convenience.

"Oh, yes, the embroideress," Claresta said. "My father does not usually deal in decorative pieces—"

Magdalene shook her head. "I am sorry. I am afraid there was a misunderstanding. I do not manage a large shop that sells to mercers and such outlets. We are only four women, and we do very special work. I had heard from friends in the East Chepe that you are on the way to being betrothed to a gentleman. I thought it possible you would be looking for some special ornamentation for the clothing and the linens for your wedding chest, something suitable for the lady of a fine manor."

"I must go," Spencer said, his voice harsh. "Your father will be wondering what could have taken me so long."

"Then you can take these back to him," Claresta said, snatching together the fabric samples and pushing them toward the young man's hand. "And you can tell him I said I would rather wear homespun all my life than need to go clothed each day in such finery."

Spencer's mouth opened, but nothing came out.

Well, that was the answer Magdalene had wanted and again she did not even need to put a question. Claresta had not been the one to initiate the idea of marriage into the nobility. Now all she needed to do was get Claresta to put a time to how long Linley had stayed on Thursday. It was clear enough that Claresta would not lie to protect Linley.

"If you do not mind, Mistress," Magdalene put in in a soothing, low voice, "please to leave the fabric. I am sure it can be returned at any time and I seldom see cloth of such quality. I would like to look at it."

As she spoke, Spencer backed away and without making a sound slipped out of the door. Claresta gasped—Magdalene could not tell whether with rage or loss—and jumped to her feet as if to follow. Magdalene caught at her sleeve.

"Let him go," she said. "If you send back the cloth with him and with such a message, it is all too likely that your father will guess or know more certainly what is between you. Likely he would dismiss him without his Master's badge and without recommendation. That would ruin him. Is that what you desire?"

Claresta stood still, staring at the door with tears in her eyes, but she made no further move to follow the young man. "I think my father has run mad," she breathed with a sob. "When we were in Guildford and my mother was alive, he was a good merchant and took pleasure in his work but he always had time to make merry. But after my mother died, he gave all his attention to business and laughed no more."

"Business was his anodyne for sorrow."

"I hoped he would marry again, but he never even looked at another woman. Instead he made me part of the business as if to turn me into the son my mother could not give him. Oh, I did not mind that! I liked it. And after some years he took Spencer as a senior journeyman from a small house that was going to close. I . . . I thought . . ."

"And Spencer also thought he had been chosen for you?"

"Oh." Claresta blushed. "Oh, no. He thought he had been hired because of his special knowledge of wool. He never . . . never looked at me."

Magdalene laughed softly. "He looked at you."

Claresta blushed again. "But we spoke only about the mercery. Spencer is quick and learned so much about the business. He took over . . . well, with my oversight . . . much of the everyday buying and selling. My father . . . he dealt with the other mercers and . . . and he grew richer and richer. And then he began to talk about founding a noble line, and no matter what I said he dragged us from Guildford to London."

"Founding a noble line? But I do not believe that King Stephen is so hard pressed, specially after taking what was stored in Salisbury's castles, that he is ready to ennoble a commoner. And surely the word is all over the Chepe that your father intends to marry you into a noble line."

"That was after he discovered that money alone will not buy a place among the lords. Dress and manner and speech and the ability to wield weapons are necessary. This desire to leave his class may be a little mad, but my father is not so mad he did not understand that he was far too old to learn. And then he realized that titles, unlike money, which can be passed by will to anyone, descend in the male line."

"Ah. Which brought him to look for a man willing to marry a commoner for a price."

Claresta stared at Magdalene and then put a hand to her lips. "What have I said?" she breathed. "Why am I telling you—a complete stranger—the secrets of my heart, speaking in such a way of my father who has always taken such care of me and treated me with such kindness."

Magdalene smiled. "Perhaps because I *am* a stranger and thus it seemed to you these secrets would go no further.

And that I can promise readily. I do not have a shop in the East Chepe. I do not have a shop at all. My three women and I do our embroidery in a private house and we have little inclination or time for gossip. Even my maid is safe. She is deaf. So what we say to each other does not get carried to the other servants in the neighborhood."

For a long moment there was a war in Claresta's face. A series of emotions flicked across—embarrassment, anger, shame, relief. The relief seemed to predominate at last, and Claresta waved toward the table on which the swatches of cloth lay and to the stools that stood near.

"You said you had embroidery to show me. Sit, and let me see what you have."

Magdalene first straightened the cloth that Claresta's angry gathering had crumpled. Then she uncovered her basket, took out the strips of ribbon, Diot's square picture, and after a very brief hesitation, the piece that Letice had done. Claresta leaned over the table, touching each piece of work gently, and then sat down. Magdalene also sat. Another moment passed. Claresta's fingers moved from Magdalene's work—a chase of silver hounds through green fronds on a darker blue background—to the non-pictorial swirls and interweaving of Letice's work.

"Where did you come by this?" Claresta asked. "By trade?"

"No, one of my women is from a far land. Unfortunately I cannot ask her which one or when she came because she is mute." Magdalene shrugged. "That makes no difference in the work she does."

"I could find a market for this work. And also for the embroiderer who did the dogs."

Magdalene laughed. "As I said before, there are not enough of us to provide you with goods for a market. I came because I thought you would want special embroidery for your wedding clothes and wedding chest. One piece at a time is what we sell. The price is not cheap, but the work is worth the cost."

"I have no doubt of that," Claresta said, touching with a gentle finger a jeweled blue eye on a silver dog. "But I have no heart to buy fine garments or rich linen. I do not want to marry Sir Linley of Godalming."

"Is there some fault you find in Sir Linley?"

Claresta sighed heavily. "No, not at all. He is well looking, well spoken, reasonably clever—although totally ignorant concerning trade. I can find no true fault in him. I wish I could." Suddenly her lips trembled. "If only he were crude or brutal, I could say I was afraid and appeal to my father not to put me in peril, but I cannot lie to my father, and he wants this so much. It is not Sir Linley I fear but just what my father most desires."

"The bearing of children?" Magdalene was puzzled.

Every woman feared childbirth and with some justice. Everyone knew of women who died in their attempt to bring forth new life. Nonetheless most women desired to marry and looked forward to having children.

"No." Claresta shook her head. "Well, no more than any woman fears it. I meant I fear to go to Godalming . . . I do not even know where Godalming is, nor do I care. I do not *want* to pretend to be a lady, to limpingly ape ways that are not natural to me, to hear whispers and titters behind my back as my mistakes make me ridiculous . . . to be forever a stranger in a strange place."

Magdalene really did not know what to say to that. Mostly those who were eager to climb up into a class to which they had not been born either did not understand the trials they would face or did not care. She had considerable sympathy for Claresta, however. She, coming down the ladder from baron's wife to common whore, had been sneered at and even beaten for her "false" high-class pretensions.

"It will not be so bad," she said, trying to offer some comfort. "You have already moved from Guildford to London, so you have some experience with adapting to new customs and manners of dress and speech. You will learn quickly."

"But I do not *want* to learn," Claresta wailed. "I want to marry Spencer and the two of us together assist my father and, when he is gone, continue the business. And now it seems all hope is gone. The bargain is made."

"When was it made?"

"Thursday. Sir Linley came before I had hardly choked down my breakfast and he and my father went apart. There must have been some sticking points because Sir Linley not only stayed to dinner but to the evening meal and beyond. Oh how I hoped they would not come to terms."

"How late did Sir Linley stay?"

"I do not really know, except that it was after dark. I had called the servants to light lamps and candles for me to see my sewing. I tried to speak to him when my father went to the jakes and said I did not want to intrude upon his life. But he only patted me kindly on the shoulder and said he had an aunt who would make all easy for me. You know what that means, do you not? The aunt will manage all, oversee the servants and what on the estate is women's work. I will be left to sit and sew and regret what I had lost. So then I went to bed to weep in peace."

CHAPTER 8

Bell arrived at the bishop's house in good time to choose the armsmen who would accompany them. After a moment's indecision he bade them arm as if for traveling and he went to get his own armor. He was nearly certain there would be no second attack, but he would need the men to clear the bridge so the bishop could cross with ease. Also, if he did have time to get to the Tower and look for the big man, a knight's armor would save argument and explanation.

He had given orders about saddling Monseigneur and the bishop's palfrey and just settled his mail as comfortably as possible when one of the bishop's clerks came to fetch him. On the table behind which the dead woman had been seated was the remains of a breakfast much like that Bell himself had eaten, but the bishop had left the table and was bending over a long chest to the right of his bed. To Bell's surprise, Winchester pulled from the chest a wicked looking mace.

"Good, my lord, but I hope you do not have premonitions of trouble," Bell said.

"No," Winchester replied, smiling grimly. "I leave that to you, my dear Bell. But I did not at all enjoy my feeling of helplessness the other day when men were fighting all around me and I had not even a poniard in my belt. This 'holy water sprinkler' is familiar to me, and I have not forgot how to use it. I will carry it henceforward."

The mace did not have the reach of a sword, but Bell assumed Winchester was not intending to attack. Certainly, the weapon would discourage anyone who wanted to seize the bishop physically or lead his horse away. One worry less he would have; Bell nodded.

"For today, my lord, hang it from the pommel. By tomorrow I will have a socket for it affixed to your saddle."

The bishop laughed aloud. "You do not, like my appalled looking clerks, think I should better rest my safety on praying for succor?"

Bell glanced at the clerks, who did look shocked, but he only said, "God succors most swiftly those who strongly defend themselves. And along that line of thought, if you will permit, I will carry the satchels of documents. Thus your clerks will be in less danger and you will be more certain that the documents will not be torn away."

This time, however, the preparations were not necessary. No one was lying in wait on the one street from the bishop's house to the bridge. The folk on the bridge cleared off when the men-at-arms ordered them away, grumbling but without real animosity, and the ride along Candlewick Street to Watling was without incident. Even in the bailey of St. Paul's they were not mobbed, as they had been the first time the bishop came through. Father Holdyn had apparently followed the bishop's orders about weeding out the dishonest and aggressive peddlers who used the open area as a market.

Holdyn himself was at the church door. The archbishop had arrived, he said, and was waiting in the chapel in which they would confer. Bell's lips thinned. That meant the bishop could not question Holdyn first. Apurpose? But Holdyn could not have arranged the time the archbishop arrived.

Bell watched as Winchester hurried into the church,

apologies already on his tongue. Bell did not think Winchester would ever accept this archbishop of Canterbury, who held the office he was convinced was meant for him, but he wanted the man's cooperation about this convocation.

The clerks took back the two satchels of documents and scurried after Winchester. Bell lingered a moment longer to tell the men-at-arms that they were free to wander about but not to go beyond the sound of his voice. That generated some laughter as many of the men claimed that persons in outlying shires could hear Bell's orders on a battlefield. Then, somewhat reluctantly, he went to the chapel where bishop and archbishop were opposite each other, flanked by their clerks, at a table that had been carried into the chapel.

Bell sighed softly and joined two of the archbishop's men on guard in the opening arch of the chapel. Father Holdyn had disappeared. The archbishop was indignantly clearing himself of any complicity in the attack on the bishop on Saturday. Winchester, at his most urbane, was assuring Theobald that he had never suspected him of any complicity, since he believed the only purpose of the attack was to interfere with the convocation—on which, he hoped, they were in complete agreement. The archbishop said that was true, but it troubled him that an attack should happen on the bishop's way to his palace at Lambeth. Anyone could have known of the appointment, the bishop said. Bell sighed again.

Eventually, although not nearly as soon as Bell hoped, the subject reverted to the convocation. In time a date was decided upon. That was not so simple because of the need to avoid holy days, meet soon enough to retain the outrage initially felt about the treatment of Salisbury, and yet long enough in advance for adequate traveling time. Many of the bishops were of advanced years and some of considerable girth. August 29th was eventually settled upon.

Bell sighed once more, unhappily. He understood why no nearer date could be chosen, but the end of August meant he would need to guard the bishop very strictly for more than a whole month. Had the date been later, he might have convinced the bishop to return to Winchester where he would be far safer—and where he, himself, would be safe from the temptation offered by Magdalene. He started to listen more closely as the place of the meeting began to be considered.

The archbishop suggested Oxford, the scene of the incident, because it might stir up the spirits of the bishops. It might also, Winchester pointed out, remind the bishops of the king's power and make them too cautious.

Bell looked across the church into which the sun, risen above the buildings of the city, was pouring a golden light. His jaw was set as polite argument waxed and waned. The two guards who had come with the archbishop were silent, perhaps also listening. Bell did not know the men and had no idea whether they had come from France with Theobald or had been provided to him by Waleran, who had arranged his election.

By the time the complaints of Bell's stomach were beginning to take precedence over his anxiety and remind him that his predawn breakfast was worn out, the conclusion that he had strongly hoped for—and he was sure Winchester desired—had been reached. The convocation would be held in Winchester . . . where the bishop held power.

Bell's last sigh was of relief. In his own cathedral city, Winchester's knights would arrange that the full strength of his armed forces could be collected without being obvious. The king would not seize him or even threaten to seize him or any of the other attending bishops no matter what the convocation concluded.

Very tentatively the substance of the convocation was approached. Winchester offered to defer to the archbishop in opening the convocation and stating the causes for its summoning. Acting as if stirred by impatience, Bell glanced over his shoulder. He saw at once that Theobald was looking somewhat alarmed and shaking his head. The archbishop said that surely the summoner and papal legate could best lay out the subject for the attending bishops.

Bell straightened his head and once again stared out into space. This, he was sure, was what Winchester desired. Naturally his summons to the bishops throughout England would carry the information that he had received a bull naming him the papal legate, but actually seeing the archbishop of Canterbury sitting before him in obedience would fix in the other bishops' minds that Winchester's authority was beyond that of Theobald's.

Then Bell stiffened a trifle, his hand falling to his sword hilt as he became aware of movement at the far door, but it was only a single shadow that crossed the church. In the next moment, he relaxed. From the size of the man and his genuflection to the altar, it must be Father Holdyn. The episcopal vicar did not approach the chapel; instead he knelt in prayer near the altar.

Bell could not help hoping that Holdyn was praying the bishop and archbishop would soon finish their discussion. Another few minutes passed and Bell's lips twitched. Father Holdyn must be a very holy man if the end of the conference had been his prayer because just then the bishop and archbishop rose and bowed gravely to each other. Bell turned to watch their clerks gather up the notes they had made.

Praying or not, Holdyn apparently had been keeping one eye on his illustrious guests. He now hurried toward the chapel to bow and invite Winchester and Canterbury to eat their dinner at his table, their clerks to eat with the cannons.

Winchester agreed almost before the words were out of Holdyn's mouth; Bell approved heartily since it would be an excellent opportunity to ask about Holdyn's crucifix. Almost as promptly as Winchester had agreed, the archbishop offered thanks but claimed he had a previous engagement. Bell was not certain whether Theobald actually had business or simply did not want to eat a meal with Winchester, but he was very grateful to the archbishop. Winchester, who Bell guessed was also thinking of the murdered woman in whose hoard they had found Holdyn's crucifix, was equally grateful. His farewells sounded warm and sincere.

Politely, Winchester and Father Holdyn, with Bell and Theobald's guards trailing behind, accompanied the archbishop to the door of the church. The archbishop's men and Bell sidled around and went down the steps. Winchester and Holdyn made deferential conversation while they waited for Theobald's men to get his horse and summon the rest of his escort. Meanwhile, Bell found one of his own men and bade him to tell the troop to find meals from the vendors of food in the churchyard.

When the archbishop was well away, Father Holdyn led Bell and the bishop to the refectory of the cannons. There a screen had been drawn across the north end of the room. Behind it was a table with one chair with arms, one chair without arms. A selection of stools and a small bench stood near the back wall.

Bell pulled out the chair with arms for Winchester, offering up a small prayer of thanks that the archbishop had decided not to stay. Which man, archbishop or legate, would have been offered the chair with arms? Then Bell wondered whether Holdyn had known the archbishop would leave. And where had he got a chair with arms anyway? Was that what he used in the privacy of his own quarters? Bell would not have expected it, but how had Nelda got Holdyn's crucifix?

Father Holdyn seated himself in the chair without arms and Bell drew up a stool for himself. Although Father Holdyn looked somewhat surprised and glanced toward the bishop, he did not protest. He rang a silvery bell and servants began to come around the end of the screen carrying bowls of pottage, bowls of vegetables, wedges of cheese, and cups and a pitcher. Bell thought briefly of dinner at Magdalene's house where there would have been roast meat and a hearty stew of mutton or pork accompanying the vegetables—as well as a sweet pudding and lively conversation.

Not that Father Holdyn and the bishop sat in silence. They were speaking animatedly enough, but about a theological question in which Bell took little interest. He ate in silence. At least the pottage was well seasoned, as were the roasted vegetables. He wasted no time in chewing and swallowing, interspersing the vegetables he speared on his knife and spoonfuls of pottage with mouthfuls of cheese. That was good too. The cannons of St. Paul's were certainly not starved, but the ale was terrible; watered, Bell thought.

Despite Bell's strict attention to his dinner, he could have eaten more when the bishop, who certainly kept his vows of abstemiousness, wiped his eating knife and returned it to its sheath. Father Holdyn immediately pulled his hand back from the piece of cheese he was about to pick up. Silent now, Winchester removed the crucifix from his purse and laid it on the table. Holdyn goggled at it, his eyes wide and his mouth half open.

"Why did you bury the whore who was killed and take away her clothing before Bell could examine it?" Winchester asked softly.

Holdyn managed one swift, startled glance at Winchester before his eyes returned to the crucifix. Still staring at it, Holdyn said, "I did not know Sir Bellamy was investigating her death. A whore . . . Why did I bury her? A good work. She would have been thrown into an unmarked pit. And why so quickly? In summer, a burial cannot wait. The clothing was good. There are many who need it urgently."

Aside from the comment that he did not know about the investigation, which was tinged with bitterness, Bell thought the man hardly knew what he was saying. He sounded as if he were repeating words he had committed to memory.

"You did not think I would order an investigation of a murdered woman found in my bedchamber?" Winchester asked.

Holdyn looked up at him, seemingly startled. "I had forgot where she was found."

Bell did not think that was possible. How could one forget the tale of a dead woman propped up in a chair in a bishop's bedchamber? From his expression, Winchester did not think so either.

"You did not know the woman?" the bishop asked.

For a long moment Holdyn was silent; his gaze dropped again to the crucifix. Then he lifted his eyes and shook his head. "No," he said. "I did not know her."

Bell thought Winchester did not believe that either and the bishop asked, more sharply, "Then how did it come about that your crucifix—I know it is yours; I have seen you wear it many times, and I do not think there is another such in England—was found in this whore's hoard?"

Holdyn swallowed. "How did you find it?" he whispered.

The bishop smiled slightly. "Through the help of another whore, who knows her kind well and showed my man—" he gestured at Bell with his head "—where to search."

"It was stolen," Father Holdyn said—Bell could see that his eyes were full of tears and suddenly looked away.

"I have no doubt of *that,*" Winchester snapped. "I did not imagine that you gave it to her . . ."

Bell heard Winchester's voice lose its brisk tone and falter to a stop. He guessed it had occurred to the bishop that Holdyn, who from his long record had never violated his vows of chastity, had slipped once and then, obsessed by the pleasure he had long denied himself, become enslaved. Bell knew of at least one client of Magdalene's who was treading that terrible path.

The idea was not one that would spring to the bishop's mind at first. Winchester was simply not the kind to be trapped in a pleasure of any sort. Seduced by power he could be, in Bell's opinion, but not by pleasure.

But I understand, Bell thought, raising his eyes again to look at Holdyn with some sympathy. Only what he saw in Holdyn's face was not what he would have felt if he had discovered Magdalene was dead—or if he had killed her. What was there was a . . . Bell could think of no words to describe it other than a distant sorrow, a grief for something far in the past.

Only the crucifix had not been stolen far in the past. Bell remembered it gleaming against Holdyn's dark gown the last time he had ridden to London some two, no three, weeks past. And why had he thought of Holdyn killing his love? Because he himself . . . What, take a life because he had fallen in love with a whore? No, he would not. Besides Magdalene had never lied to him, never deceived him.

Nelda, however, was a liar. If Holdyn had become so obsessed with her as to give her his dearest treasure and then discovered she was a whore—

"Or *did* you give it to her?" Winchester's voice, sharp and demanding, recalled Bell from his thoughts.

"No." Holdyn sounded more sure of himself; his mouth tightened into distaste. "No, I did not give the woman my crucifix." He took a deep breath and indignation colored his voice when he spoke again. "And if you suspect that I lay with her and that I paid with my crucifix, I did not do that either! Nor was the crucifix stolen while I slept after my illicit congress. And I will swear an oath at the very altar of this church, with my hand on the great cross, that what I have said is true."

Winchester stared at the priest for a handful of heartbeats. "Then perhaps you will explain to me how it came to be in Nelda's possession?"

Holdyn's shoulders slumped. "I cannot. All I can say is that I had taken off the crucifix because I changed to rough clothing. I intended to help with the cleansing of a church in which murder had been done. I laid the crucifix on my chest and it was gone when I returned."

"The church near Monkwell Street?" The bishop glanced at Bell, who nodded very slightly indicating that he would go and inquire whether Holdyn had been there and for how long. "I remember mention of the murder in the report I had just before we set out for London," the bishop continued. "The church will need reconsecration."

"Yes," Holdyn began rather eagerly, as if he hoped to divert Winchester to a new topic.

But the bishop was not easily diverted. What he said was, "So your crucifix was lost on Sunday night and you did nothing? You did not question your servants, your clerks?"

"My lord, you know I have been lodging in the bishop's palace to attend better to the needs of the diocese. However, there is no retinue and very few servants. I know my clerks and my servants. They would not steal . . . but a large number of people come and go in the palace on church business. My servants might easily not notice a stranger who seemed harmless. And such a stranger might have been able to find my chamber and steal my crucifix."

He knew who had taken it, Bell thought. But would his servants allow a woman dressed as Nelda had been dressed to wander about the bishop's palace or go into the episcopal vicar's bedchamber? Bell thought back on how long a silence there had been before Holdyn answered Winchester's question about whether he knew the woman. A mark of his struggle with the need to lie to his bishop?

"I think perhaps you should press your servants more closely about who might have been loose in the palace. Has anything else been found to be missing?"

Holdyn swallowed again. "Once, a gilt cup. I replaced it, my lord, and after that all valuables were locked away."

"You did not discover who committed that theft either?" Winchester asked.

"I—it came at a bad time. I fear I was so busy I did not pursue the matter. I replaced the cup with one of equal value. The punishment fell upon me for my carelessness, and that was just."

"Perhaps, but I would have my servants make sure that strangers did not wander about the palace."

"I did, my lord, but the palace is large, the servants are

few. The front doors are kept locked, of course, but there are necessary entrances for service . . ."

"I see." Winchester rose to his feet and Bell followed. Holdyn moved his hand tentatively toward the crucifix, but Winchester picked it up and returned it to his purse. "You will have it back when we discover who killed the poor woman and so indifferently used her dead body."

When Magdalene returned from the house on Lime Street where she had spoken to Claresta, she found Letice at the table eating cheese and cold meat with hunks torn off still-warm golden bread. To her surprise Letice smiled and signed toward the door. Her women worked hard when they had guests at night. Then she remembered that the man who had come for Letice came at night only so no one would see him and never stayed very long. He paid the full night's fee, too, so Magdalene had no complaint.

Then Magdalene also remembered that Letice had implied it was too complicated to explain how she knew the dead woman and wanted to take her to the Saracen's Head. She nodded and said, "Is there a time that is better than others to see your—uncle?"

Letice first shook her head, making a gesture for encompassing all, which Magdalene assumed meant that all times were the same, and then nodded, which Magdalene took to mean the man was her uncle. Magdalene almost forgot again in her eagerness finally to discover where Letice went and who were her people—questions despite her curiosity she had never felt she had the right to ask—that her purpose was to find out what connection Nelda had with Letice's compatriots.

While Letice finished her meal, Magdalene went to tell Dulcie that she and Letice were leaving and to instruct the maid to pull in the bell cord and lock the gate behind them until Diot was up and ready to answer the bell. Then she and Letice veiled their faces and went out. Letice turned right, away from the bridge to London, but they only went a short way before they turned left into the lane that led to the church of St. Thomas.

The lane was narrow and crooked, and the counters that protruded into it held mostly worn out gowns and tunics. One or two frankly sold rags—garments too torn and stained to be remade into something wearable. Still the cloth was of value. It could be used for patches or for stuffing a gambeson or for layering the inside of a gown or tunic to make it warm for the winter.

Beyond the church, which Magdalene had never entered—what need when St. Mary Overy, larger and more beautiful, was right beyond her back gate—the lane narrowed even further. Magdalene's glimpses of the filth-encrusted inhabitants who occasionally peered out the open doors made her grip the knife hidden in the folds of her gown, but Letice walked without either hurry or nervous glances. Indeed, she waved a hand occasionally to this or that seamed face and matted head. Most acknowledged the greeting; some even smiled.

They did not go much beyond St. Thomas'. Within little more than a hundred yards, they turned left again into what began as an equally narrow and dirty lane. This, however, soon widened, then widened again into a little square. It was no cozy village green—there was no sign of grass—but the stalls around it and the goods laid out on mats were recognizable. Fruits, vegetables, and to Magdalene's surprise rice and spices. Those were expensive items and did not seem to fit with the squalor they had passed. All of those vendors greeted Letice, only they called her Leilia, and she waved and made some signs with her hands at them.

On the northwest corner was the ale house called The Saracen's Head. It had, as well as the bundle of brush that marked a drinking place, a roughly painted head wearing a turban. Magdalene recognized their goal at once from the times Letice had drawn the sign on her slate.

The exterior of the building was, if not decrepit, old and worn. The interior was a surprise. It was well-lit from some windows, unshuttered in the summer heat, and brass lamps hanging from the ceiling. Even more surprising, the heavy wooden tables were clean and the rushes on the floor fresh. There was a decided smell of wine and almost none of ale.

Several voices called "Leilia, what are you doing here today?" And at the very back of the room a man stood up and came forward toward them. Letice put a hand on Magdalene's arm and gave it a hard squeeze. Then the man was before them and Magdalene understood the warning.

Bell had said that Letice's uncle had the most villainous face he had ever seen. It was no exaggeration. The skin was ravaged by pock marks until it looked leprous. On the right side, a terrible scar from forehead to lip drew both eye and mouth upward into an ugly leer; on the left, the lid of the eye was scarred by the pox so it could not open fully and a large black wart twisted the lips. Magdalene was grateful for her veil, which hid her no doubt blanched complexion.

"Leilia," the man said, giving Letice a quick hug. "Is something wrong? What are you doing here today?"

Magdalene did not expect Letice to shrink away; her face had always expressed real affection when she acted out visiting the man. But Magdalene did not expect her to kiss his horribly scarred cheek, then step back and begin waving her hands about and making quick gestures with the fingers.

"Ah," the man said when Letice's hands had come to

rest. He smiled at Magdalene, which made her swallow hard. "So you are Mistress Magdalene, Leilia's employer. I am very glad to meet you. Leilia is very happy at your house."

"Thank you," Magdalene replied, "but how did you know I was not just a friend?"

"Because Leilia just told me. She speaks with her hands in signs that permit the deaf and mute to be understood."

"Oh, for goodness sake," Magdalene exclaimed, almost forgetting the man's face in her interest in what he had said. "Why in the world didn't she teach me? I would have gladly learned. I have been teaching her to read and write, but writing is so slow."

The man laughed, which, although it did nothing good for his appearance, made Magdalene even better able to forget it. The laughter was warm and merry.

"She did not try to teach you because she can only sign in our own tongue, not in French. She would have had to teach you Persian first, and that would have been no easy task when she cannot speak and at that time could not write either." He bowed. "My name is Abd al Zahir. I am the brother of Leilia's father."

Magdalene looked away for a moment but then could not help saying, "Could you not have given her a home? I do what I can to make my women happy, but it is not a good life."

Zahir raised his eyebrows, which made Magdalene look away again for a moment. His cratered and furrowed skin seemed to crawl around the fixed lines of the scar and the black mole.

"You say it is not a good life," Zahir sounded rather condescending, "but that is because your faith considers the joys of the flesh evil. That makes you ashamed to use your body for pleasure. Our faith recognizes the joys of the flesh."

Now it was Magdalene who raised her brows with a touch of contempt. "Yet I understand that you keep your women locked up."

Zahir shrugged, smiling again. "Ah yes, because we do recognize the joys of the flesh and wish to know that our sons are our get. So we do prefer that our women lead safe and secluded lives." He sighed. "But for those women who cannot tolerate the confining conditions or who for some other reason cannot find a husband, there is this other life." He shook his head. "In any case I was too late to offer Leilia a home. Her father had already sold her into the house she left to come to you."

"Sold her?" Magdalene's voice was flat.

Abd al Zahir shrugged again. "Perhaps I would not have done the same, but she was his daughter and mute, which made it hard to find a husband or another way to live . . . and he was very sick. I do not think it was against her will—she says not, but that might be out of loyalty. The house was not a common stew. He did not know the keeper was cruel and dishonest. And he did not know that I was on my way here."

Letice touched his arm and signed briefly. He nodded, smiled, and gestured for them to follow him. In the corner of the room from which he had come he set two stools for Letice and Magdalene and sat down himself across a small table.

"Leilia tells me that you have come for information about a woman who was killed?"

"Yes," Magdalene said, very glad that Letice had kept her mind on business, for she had once more forgotten all about Nelda. "Letice recognized the woman, who was called Nelda Roundheels, and remembered she had seen her here."

He frowned and said defensively, with an angry glance at Letice, "I do not even know when and how this woman died. We had nothing to do with her death."

Letice shook her head violently and Magdalene made a dismissive gesture. She had forgotten that foreign and non-Christian as Zahir was, he would fear being blamed for any crime—a convenient scapegoat, as were whores.

"No," Magdalene said emphatically. "I'm sure you did not because you would have had no reason to place her body in the bedchamber of the bishop of Winchester."

Zahir's mismatched eyes widened. "No, certainly not. The bishop has been tolerant of our residence here. As long as we pay our tithes, like any Christian, we are free to do business and even, privately, worship in our own way. I assure you we were very disappointed when His Grace of Winchester was not elected as archbishop. God alone knows what this new man will order."

"I am in much the same position as you are, Master al Zahir," Magdalene sighed. "If he can, I am sure Winchester will continue to protect us, but it would be easier for him if we could clear up this woman's death so no scandal would attach to his name."

"I see that," al Zahir said, then turned to Letice. "When did you see her here, Leilia?"

Again Letice's hands flew.

"Hmmm," al Zahir said. "Leilia tells me that she saw this Nelda with two dealers in drugs. Was she an apothecary?"

"No, she was a whore."

Zahir cocked his head. "I wonder if she bought to sell or to use?"

But he did not wait for an answer. He got up and walked

around the room, stopping at several tables. First a man and then a woman rose and followed him back to where Magdalene and Letice sat.

"This is Umar," al Zahir said, gesturing to the man. "He deals in drugs of various kinds and has sold to the woman Leilia has described. But he says she bought only cakes of dried poppy juice."

"She did not take it," Umar said. "Did not eat the drug herself. I know the look. She did not have it. Those who do eat it can become very desperate. Perhaps that was why she came with a guard."

"Or because she did not trust us," Zahir said, his lips twisting.

"A guard?" Magdalene repeated thoughtfully. "Then she was afraid of something. That is interesting. What was the guard like?"

"Big," Umar replied, and the woman with him nodded.

"Ugly too," the woman said. "Not so much in the face, in the look. Mean. Cruel."

Magdalene immediately thought of the man who had accosted Bell, asked if Nelda was dead, and said she deserved killing.

"Can you say more closely what he looked like?" al Zahir asked.

Umar shook his head but the woman said, "Brown hair, brown eyes, and his nose was broken maybe more than once."

"All I saw, Fatima," Umar said, "was the way he looked at the cakes of poppy seed juice. Not bound to it hard yet, but he knew the delight it can bring."

The woman shrugged. "A foolish delight. False. With much sorrow to follow. I sold only peace—sleeping draughts. But you said she was a whore, not an apothecary.

Well, perhaps she feared sinning and slept ill."

"You said she was killed?" Umar asked. "It would have been an accident. A poppy-eater would not wish to kill the supplier."

"We do think her death was an accident," Magdalene agreed, "but what was done with her body afterward was not, which is why we wish to find the person who killed her."

Both Umar and Fatima nodded and murmured that the reason they had been willing to speak to her was that they did not desire trouble to fall upon the bishop of Winchester.

"Likely no one will ever need to know what you have told me," Magdalene said slowly, "but I fear Nelda might have put the sleeping draughts to less innocent use than her own need to sleep. We found evidence in her rooms that she was a thief. It is possible that she drugged her clients so she could steal from them when they were sleeping deeply."

"That does not seem very reasonable," Fatima said. "It could happen once, possibly with a very stupid man even twice but then the client would not return. Or are your men more stupid than ours?"

"No, but I think what she stole was more often something secret rather than valuable. Something that could mark the man in some way. I think she did not care that the client did not return because she then threatened to expose his secret and extorted money from him."

"A good reason for her to be dead," Umar said. "Cannot you find who killed her from the secrets she had uncovered?"

"If there were only one item," Magdalene said wryly, "we might, but there are several and we are not yet able to identify to whom each belongs." She sighed. "Well, I thank you all." She reached through the slit in her skirt to her pocket and took out two silver pennies, which she laid on the table. "For your time," she said.

Umar and Fatima each took a coin and nodded acknowledgment. To Abd al Zahir, Magdalene said, "Letice will tell me if there is some favor I can do for you in return."

"Teach Leilia to read and write well, and when she tires of work in your house, I will take her into business with me. That will repay any favor I do you many times, for once she knows the skill, I can find someone to teach her to write in Persian also."

CHAPTER 9

When Magdalene and Letice left The Saracen's Head, Magdalene's glance at the position of the sun showed that it was after Tierce but not yet close to Sext. There would be time, she said to Letice, to stop by the house in which Nelda had lived and see if she could manage to speak to the woman who lived next door—Tayte, Tom Watchman had called her. Letice nodded, but pointed onward, which Magdalene took to mean that Letice would go on to the Old Priory Guesthouse.

When they came to the turn onto Dead Pond Road, Letice nodded and continued along the main street while Magdalene turned first right into Dead Pond and then left onto Rag Street. The woman in the rag shop barely flicked her eyes at Magdalene when she opened the door and walked into the house.

It did not seem very safe to Magdalene, to leave the outer door open that way when the rag woman was known to be "blind and deaf." But then, as she looked around the bare space into which the stairs descended and the rickety stairs themselves, she acknowledged that there was nothing to steal. She remembered that Linley had told them that Nelda always kept her door locked. Tayte did too, no doubt.

Magdalene knocked, waited, knocked again. Even if Tayte had had a client the night before, she should be awake by now. Magdalene knocked a third time, somewhat longer and a bit louder.

"Tayte," she called, "it is Magdalene la Bâtarde. I wish to speak to you."

Still no answer. It was, of course, possible that the woman had gone out to shop or to visit a friend. Magdalene knocked once more and sighed. She was about to turn away when she heard the sound of bolts being withdrawn. She pulled her veil aside so that Tayte, even if she did not know her face, would see that it was, indeed, another woman.

A little mouse opened the door and peered out. She was diminutive in size though well rounded, with soft, fuzzy brown hair, small bright black eyes, a little pursed mouth, and a nose, just a little pink, that seemed to twitch a bit.

"What do you want?" The voice was mouselike too, high and squeaky.

Magdalene bit her lip to keep from giggling and spoke softly and slowly so as not to alarm the little creature. "You know, I assume, that your neighbor, Nelda, was killed—we think on Thursday night." The door started to close. Magdalene put out a hand to hold it open. "Believe me, we do not think you had anything to do with Nelda's death. We think it was an accident. We are fairly certain that she was quarreling with a man and that she fell or he pushed her down the stairs."

"Don't know. Had company Thursday. Busy, and then sleeping. Neither of us heard anything. And my man didn't leave till morning, so it wasn't him!"

The pressure on the door eased and Magdalene quickly pushed it more widely open and stepped inside before the little woman could prevent her. The room was small, holding no more than a wide bed, a chest under the one window, a stool, a chair, and a very small table. But it was not a typical whore's cocking place. There were a few touches of luxury: the chest was padded with a woven rug and the chair had a cushion on it. Moreover the room was clean and tidy.

"I mean you no harm, Tayte," Magdalene said hastily, "and I do not think—no one thinks—that you or the man who was with you had any part in Nelda's death. But Nelda's body was carried from here, where Sir Bellamy, the bishop of Winchester's knight, is sure she died, to the bishop's house and was set up in the bishop's very own bedchamber. Sir Bellamy is most eager to discover who moved Nelda's body. And, if we can, discover how the accident that killed her occurred. That, we hope, would remove any trace of blame from the bishop."

The little mouse's eyes flicked from side to side, seeming to look frantically around for a place to hide but saw that escape was impossible. She then gestured Magdalene toward the chair. Magdalene took the few steps necessary but before she sat reached through the slit in her skirt, took out her purse, and laid it on the table.

"Did you see anything at all that Thursday?" Magdalene asked when she had seated herself and Tayte had taken the stool.

Tayte eyed the purse with an expression of anxiety on her face that was puzzling to Magdalene. "It was hot," Tayte whispered. "I had opened my door so the breeze could blow through the room. I heard a knock on Nelda's door late in the afternoon and I . . . I did glance out. I saw a man standing there. It was not *her* man."

There was definite disapproval and contempt in Tayte's manner and expression. Magdalene first felt surprised that one whore should be contemptuous of another and then realized that Tayte must not be a whore in the common sense. Most likely she had only one lover, a man who for some reason would not or could not marry her—perhaps because she had no dowry or perhaps because he was married already—but who supported her. Well, Magdalene could not blame him. She was an adorable little thing.

Suddenly Magdalene also understood the expression of anxiety on Tayte's face when the appearance of Magdalene's purse provided a strong hint that she would be paid for her information. Likely, Magdalene thought, Tayte was from a decent family and maintained their standards; she would be troubled by the idea of being paid for information it was right to give. On the other hand, from the size of the room, Magdalene suspected that though Tayte did not go hungry or without shelter, there was little extra money.

"I am taking up your time," Magdalene said. "It is only fair that you be paid for that." And when Tayte finally nodded, after thinking over what had been said, continued, "Can you tell me anything about the man? Could it have been he who caused Nelda to fall down the stairs?"

Tayte bit her lip. "Well, I have seen him before, but not often; and once he came with her man." She shrugged. "He dressed like her man so I suppose they were in the same business, but he was very ordinary to look at. And I don't think that he did Nelda any harm. She was glad to see him. Oh!" She looked surprised and then said, "His name. He called out his name before she let him in! He said, 'It's Sir John.' Yes. I remember."

Sir John was too common a name to be much help in identifying the visitor, but that Tayte remembered might mean she would remember—and relate—other details.

"And then what happened?" Magdalene asked.

"She must have opened the door, because I heard him say, 'My God, Nelda, what happened to you?' If she answered, I didn't hear her, and then the door closed."

"What did this Sir John mean when he asked what happened to Nelda?"

"Oh!" Tayte's eyes got very round. "She was beaten. Monday, it was that it happened. It was awful! Awful! I heard her screaming, but I was so afraid. And whom could I call to help? It was that great big man."

Magdalene shook her head. "There was nothing you could have done." She was perfectly sincere. She could not imagine the man who supported the mouse or any other man in the area capable of interfering with the person that generated caution in Bell and likely no one would have been willing anyway. "You had seen him before also?" she added.

"Oh, yes. Nelda did not . . . solicit from the street. I . . . I would not have agreed to live next to a . . . a common whore. It was only men she knew," Tayte's small face pinched into disapproval. "But she was far too free with her favors."

"The big man. Did he come often?"

"Not often, and even then he did not always . . . ah . . . sleep with her. Usually Nelda was waiting for him and they went out together at once. Nelda usually carried a basket and she often came back alone. Once I heard them quarreling as they came up the stairs."

This must be the man that Umar and Fatima had spoken of. Nelda must have carried home her purchases in the basket. "Was that the time he beat her?"

"Oh, no, a week or two before that, and then he didn't do anything, only yelled at her. That Monday, I didn't hear him come at all. And—and I don't know when he left either. I—I closed my door. But—but Nelda was all right. I knocked on her door later. If he was still there or she hadn't answered, I would have called the Watch. But she did answer and I asked if she wanted me to fetch a leech or anything. She said no, and her voice was not weak."

Magdalene restrained a smile with some difficulty. For all her propriety, Tayte apparently kept a close watch on her neighbor out of curiosity or boredom.

"She was not seriously hurt by the beating," Magdalene agreed. "When her body was found, the bruises were all healing. But on that Thursday, the day she died, did you hear anything else? See anything? Anything at all?"

Now Magdalene took three silver pennies out of her purse and laid them on the table. Tayte looked at them, then looked away. Then she said slowly, "I told you that my man came that day and we were busy." Tayte looked down at the coins again. "Oh, wait. I do remember something strange, but it was nothing to do with the man who came. After . . . after a time for them to be together, Nelda went out with bowls and pots and then came back with food. But still later—it was almost dark—I heard footsteps on the stairs, and I opened my door and ran out because I thought it was my man."

"Yes?" Magdalene said encouragingly.

"But it wasn't my man, it was Nelda, coming up the stairs *again*—I hadn't heard her go out. She must have taken care to be very quiet because I was listening for my man and would have heard. And she was holding something folded in her hand. It must have been a piece of parchment." Tayte shook her head. "But what would Nelda be doing with a piece of parchment?"

"I have no idea," Magdalene said, and pushed the coins over toward Nelda. "And you heard and saw nothing else?"

"No." Tayte's eyes were on the coins, but she did not grab for them. "My man came in as soon as Nelda was back in her place. We went into my room and . . . and we were busy. Later it was so hot, we went out to walk on the bridge and to eat an evening meal at a cookshop. And when we came back we were busy again."

"Thank you," Magdalene said. "I hope you will not be offended if Sir Bellamy wishes to come and ask you some questions. I promise he will be gentle and do you no harm at all. If you do not want a man in your room—I understand that—we would meet you in some public place, like a cookshop or someplace in the East Chepe."

The mouse looked frightened, but then looked down at the three silver pennies again and nodded. Magdalene smiled at her and left. As she picked her way carefully down the stair her mind was very busy. Parchment? Nelda was carrying a folded piece of parchment? The letter?

Then she realized it could not have been Gloucester's letter. Nelda was coming *up* the stair, going into her apartment. A piece of parchment to *replace* the letter she was about to steal? That meant that the man in Nelda's room had been the man who was carrying the letter. And his name was Sir John.

Not so utterly useless a name after all. Between her and Bell, they should be able to decide who was eager enough to damage Winchester and also had enough influence to appeal to Gloucester. Then if there was a Sir John trusted enough in the service of those lords to be sent on such an errand, they might have the man who had his hands around Nelda's neck and killed her . . . apurpose or by accident.

Magdalene walked home briskly and found her women half through dinner. The women could not afford to delay the meal because their clients would be arriving soon. Although Magdalene did not really like to have anyone in the house when the clients came, today she was so eager to tell Bell what she had discovered that she was sorry he had not come.

She had to possess her soul in patience, however, for Bell did not come even after her women were all at work. A minor reward for patience made waiting easier when she recognized Diot's client as a successful apothecary. With satisfaction Magdalene told herself that he would know about the cakes from unripe poppy seed juice—what they did and what they cost. She had accepted what Umar and Fatima said without questions, not wanting to display her ignorance, but she really had no idea what they were talking about.

Thus, she waylaid Diot and her client on their way out of the back door, and drew them aside to a bench in the garden. He sat down heavily, with a sigh and a glance up at Diot, who stood just behind him and tickled his ear.

"I need a little of your knowledge, Master Apothecary," Magdalene said. "How common is eating poppy?"

He looked at her in patent surprise and shrugged. "It could not be common because of the cost. Wherever did you hear of such a thing?"

"It is not forbidden, is it?" Magdalene asked.

The apothecary laughed. "No more forbidden than swallowing diamonds. Who could afford to do so? Where agony is excruciating, the juice of the unripe poppy can be given to abate the pain and provide sleep, but it is a rare drug to find." Then the man's expression changed to sharp interest. "Do you know where cakes from poppy juice can be obtained? Only rarely do they come upon the market."

"Well, I do, and those who spoke to me of it did not make of it any secret. Only they spoke in a place private to them and perhaps spoke more freely for that, not realizing that I thought what they said common knowledge. Oh, I never would have mentioned it but for the ease with which they spoke. I can see you would be interested in hearing more, but I must ask first if I am permitted to say more."

Although the man looked faintly chagrined, he nodded, then glanced up at Diot with a smile. "I will be back on my regular date," he said. "May I hope that you will have more to tell me then?"

"Yes, I promise I will have at least a yea or nay for you and perhaps something even more."

On the words, Magdalene stood and the man did too. She waited while Diot accompanied her client around the house toward the gate, then went inside herself. She sat down before her embroidery frame and began to ply her needle while her women restored their rooms to an unused appearance. The men who came to her women all knew there were other men, of course, but part of what they paid a premium price for was that no hint of that usage should appear. The rooms were all clean and tidy, the beds made, the women washed and fresh.

If the dried juice of the poppy was so valuable, Magdalene thought, was that another reason for Nelda being beaten? Was the man who killed her trying to choke the source out of her? She embroidered carefully, considering whether the big man mentioned by Letice's compatriots could have been due a share of the profits out of which Nelda tried to cheat him, or just decided that it was worth while to take the whole of a shipment. Would Umar have sold to him directly if he said that he was acting as Nelda's agent or said she would come no more? Would that be temptation enough to dispose of Nelda?

She found no answers to her questions and wondered whether Bell had yet spoken to the man who had called Nelda a thieving bitch. When the bell rang, she jumped up eagerly to answer it, aware that it was earlier than any of the second group of clients should arrive. She hoped it was

Bell, and was considerably disappointed to see Raoul de Samur instead.

"Let me in. Don't want to be seen," he said.

Magdalene was half tempted to slam the gate in his face. Their acquaintance had not begun amicably. Raoul had first pretended to be a client but had threatened Sabina and Magdalene, too, when she came to her whore's rescue. Raoul wanted to force from them the whereabouts of a papal pouch gone missing from the body of the messenger, who had been murdered. Clever and brutal but contemptuous both of women and whores, he had underestimated Magdalene and the blind Sabina, who between them had rendered him unconscious and, with Bell's help, delivered him to William of Ypres' hands.

The capture had turned out none so ill for Raoul, although Magdalene knew he had not at first expected to survive his mistake. Instead of death, William had implanted firm hooks into Raoul that would ensure his destruction if he betrayed his new master. But Magdalene had reason to know Raoul did not fret against those hooks; he was now happily a double agent. William paid him well, not only in coin but also in news William wanted Waleran to hear; in return Raoul brought William information Waleran did not want William to know.

That knowledge made Magdalene open the gate and stand aside for him to enter, but she said, "I have no woman free for you."

"You never do, do you?" he snarled and then grinned. "And I can afford it on my own now. But I didn't come for a woman. I heard about the attack on the bishop of Winchester and I felt I'd better let Lord William know not to waste his time hinting to the king it was Lord Waleran or his brother Hugh. He'll lose even more of the king's favor if he does. Lord Waleran has no intention of interfering in any way with the bishop's convocation."

Magdalene's eyes opened wide. "Then it was *not* Beaufort who sent men to attack the bishop on Saturday!"

Raoul frowned and made a grimace. "That I cannot swear, but I don't think it was. And I think he was very angry about the signals that were set up as a lure opposite Paul's Wharf, as if, if the bishop were taken, he was to be carried across the river to Baynard's Castle."

"That is *very* interesting. I will pass the word to Sir Bellamy."

"Tell him he owes me," Raoul said, lifting his lip in an unpleasant gesture. "And about the convocation, too. Lord Waleran is very eager for it to take place."

"Eager? Why?"

"Why not?" Raoul said, sneering. "Lord Waleran bemoans Winchester's disloyalty to the king, but he has been laughing to himself about the convocation ever since he heard of it."

"Laughing?" Magdalene repeated furiously. She loathed Waleran de Meulan because of how he had hurt William and usurped William's place in the king's favor. "Winchester is now the pope's legate, not a man to laugh at."

"Oh, use your head. Can you think of anything that will make the king less fond of his brother than being called to order like a naughty child? Lord Waleran's purpose is to rule the king without Winchester's interference. So, of course, he's glad of the convocation. What, after all, can Winchester do, legate or not? If you think the bishops are going to dare threaten excommunication after what Stephen did to Salisbury, you're more a fool than I. And when the letter from Gloucester is made public—"

Magdalene caught her breath. "What do you know about the letter from Gloucester?"

Raoul was silent for a moment, his lips thinned to an angry line. "So you knew about it already? How do you know? God, don't tell me that loose-mouthed fool spilled it to his whore? I expected to be well paid by Lord William when you passed him the news."

Magdalene did not answer the remark about Sir John spilling his news to a whore. Let Raoul believe what he liked, but she asked in turn how he had learned of the letter.

Raoul shook his head. "That one really has a loose mouth. Two—no, three nights agone this idiot Sir John of Rouen came to Baynard's Castle begging lodging of Lord Hugh. He said he had arrived from Normandy, from visiting Robert of Gloucester's court, where he had told Gloucester of the renewed bitterness aroused in Henry of Winchester by King Stephen's assault on three bishops. He had spoken of Mandeville's, his own master's, uneasiness regarding the king's action."

"If Sir John was Mandeville's man, why not go to the Tower? What was he doing in Baynard's Castle giving such news to Hugh Beaufort?"

Raoul shrugged. "Why he did not go to the Tower for a bed, I have no idea. Why he told Lord Hugh about the letter is likely because he thinks Mandeville would not mind news damaging to Winchester be spread abroad, and—" his eyebrows took a cynical lift "—perhaps Lord Hugh found a trinket or two for him or contributed to his traveling expenses."

"I see. Perhaps for the same reason you should bring William the news about Gloucester's letter anyway," Magdalene urged. "You will be quicker to arrive wherever he is than any messenger I can send. And you will benefit by telling him yourself, even if going to him carries some danger. It will make him believe you are still honest."

"Bitch! I *am* honest with Lord William, and don't you go hinting to him I'm not. Why else would I warn him not to try to involve Lord Waleran in Winchester's troubles? But I'm not going back to where Lord William is. After Devizes yielded, Lord Waleran and the king went to Salisbury, taking the bishop of Salisbury with them. The king sent Lord William off to seize Malmesbury. I won't be near there, so you better find your own messenger."

Magdalene stared silently for a moment. Raoul was almost certainly playing a double game in the news he brought about Waleran, but even so it was likely good advice. She and Bell had guessed on their own that Hugh would not have ordered Winchester be held in a warehouse nearly opposite his stronghold. Then she nodded. Actually she did know of a way to find a messenger who would arrive as quickly or more quickly than Raoul himself. There were always a few of William's men in the house on the grounds of the White Tower. It was a convenient relay station if he needed to pass orders to his principal keep at Rochester. One of William's captains would arrange to send her news to William.

"And you tell Lord William that *I* brought the news about the letter from Gloucester!" Raoul's voice broke into her thoughts. "Damn that fool of a Sir John! No wonder he arrived when half the night was gone. He was busy spilling all his master's business to a whore. He said he had come off a ship that came in on the night tide."

Magdalene struggled to breathe evenly, as if what Raoul said had no special meaning to her. But if the Sir John Raoul named arrived at Baynard's Castle—that had to be where Raoul came from, carrying messages or news from Waleran de Meulan to his youngest brother, Hugh—if this Sir John arrived late at night, had he really come off a ship? Or had he come late at night after putting Nelda in Winchester's bedchamber? She would soon know. Tom Watchman could find out when the tide had come in Thursday night and whether a ship had berthed that night.

"Loose-mouthed he certainly was," she said, pretending irritation. "He apparently spilled his news all over Baynard's Castle readily enough."

Raoul only nodded sourly, assuring Magdalene that it was Baynard's Castle to which Sir John had gone. "Well," he said, lips twisted. "He was sure the news would please Lord Hugh, and that it would do Lord Mandeville good with Lord Waleran so it wasn't disloyal or stupid to tell Lord Hugh. But to spill the whole to a whore . . ." He shook his head.

So Sir John was in service to Lord Geoffrey Mandeville! Bell would surely be able to find him, and it was likely that they had their man, Magdalene thought. If he had discovered that Nelda had stolen the letter, he might well have killed her trying to get it back. And then, desperate to have something with which to please his master, he conceived the idea of placing Nelda in Winchester's bedchamber.

Magdalene was aware of a real gratitude to Raoul. Not only had he probably solved the question of who had killed Nelda and put her in Winchester's bedchamber, but the news that Devizes had fallen without need of an assault was precious to her. That meant that William was safe. She did not know what she thought about the king keeping Waleran with him and sending William off alone to take Malmesbury. She hoped it was not that Malmesbury Keep was expected to resist so that William would have to lead the fighting. He was getting too old to climb scaling ladders.

No, she thought, if there were going to be fighting at Salisbury, Stephen would not have divided his army. Doubtless Malmesbury was also expected to yield without a fight but it was not as rich a prize as Salisbury. Magdalene wrinkled her nose. She could only pray that Waleran would steal so much that the king would notice and withdraw his doting regard.

Possibly Raoul would say even more, but she did not want him to guess how much he had told her. She said ungraciously, "Come in, if you will. None of my women is free, but I can give you a cup of wine."

However, her effort to extract more from Raoul and even several cups of William's good wine were wasted. She heard more about how the Beauforts thought they could profit from Winchester's efforts to avenge the despite done the Church, but learned nothing new. When the bell rang again, this time to admit a client, Magdalene took Raoul out by the back door and made sure he took his horse and rode away.

Bell's afternoon was nearly as fruitful as Magdalene's, but at a much higher cost in effort and frustration. Having seen the bishop safely home, he had set off for Monkwell Street where he confirmed without difficulty that Father Holdyn had been in the desecrated church on Sunday night. Moreover, the priest of that church, impressed with Father Holdyn's dedication to solving a problem that was not his, had also told Bell that he had offered Holdyn a bed because he stayed until nearly Complin.

He then rode down to the bishop's palace, where a few questions to the servants told him what time Holdyn had returned to the palace on Sunday night. They remembered clearly, not because Holdyn had questioned them about the loss of his crucifix but because they had been concerned about his late return. It was just after Complin that he had come. Bell realized at once that there had not been enough time for Holdyn to do anything except walk from Monkwell Street to the palace. Holdyn could not have gone to Nelda's house and coupled with her and either paid with or had the crucifix stolen.

So that part of Holdyn's story was true. The crucifix must have been taken from the palace. However, it appeared that Holdyn had not complained to his servants about his loss at all. The servants knew about the lost cup; they were still upset about it. One said it had been "that woman" who had taken it. The other hushed him. When Bell asked further, he said, reluctantly, that he believed it was a particular charity case of Father Holdyn's, that over the years she had come sometimes openly, sometimes stealthily, into his house and later into the palace and often the father left a few coins out for her.

That was all the servants would say, clearly thinking what they said redounded to Father Holdyn's credit, showing his kindness and charity. Bell did not want to press them. He knew they were only answering his questions because they knew him to be the bishop's knight and he did not want them to feel Winchester was seeking to make trouble for their obviously beloved master. Bell felt that Winchester would have to ask Holdyn himself about whether the woman for whom he left money was the same as the woman he had buried.

That interview left Bell irritated and frustrated, but his afternoon went rapidly downhill from there. He had to ride all the way across London from St. Paul's to the White Tower, which was enough to try a saint. Then it took him a quarter candle to get to the captain on duty, who was up in the solar, further trying his patience so that Bell was seething. And then the man was surprisingly uncooperative, although at first, when Bell described the person to whom he wished to speak, the captain nodded recognition indifferently and said likely the man was Gehard fitzRobert.

In the next moment, the captain frowned and asked Bell what he wanted with Gehard and who he was. And when Bell said he was the bishop of Winchester's knight, which usually brought cooperation, the man's face closed—until Bell said his questions related to the death of a woman. Oddly, a flicker of what Bell thought was relief crossed the captain's face but then he shook his head and looked exasperated. It was quite apparent to Bell that news that Gehard had killed a woman would be no great surprise to the captain but he would not help bring the man to justice.

Then suddenly an expression of amusement drove out the worry. "Oh," the captain said, "you want to ask Gehard about the whore found in Winchester's bed? Don't think Gehard could have had anything to do with that. He couldn't afford to pay Winchester's price for a whore."

Bell's temper erupted. His hand shot out and took the captain by the throat so hard that any sound was cut off and his eyes bulged. For one moment, Bell's hand tightened; then sense conquered rage and he could have wept with fury over his lack of control. He could not kill a man for a stupid remark, yet one yell from the captain would bring too many men for him to fight. He slid his knife from its sheathe and let the point touch the man's neck, then relaxed his grip.

The captain understood. "Good God," he gasped, but softly, "are you mad? It was no more than a jest."

"I do not take kindly to jests about my master. He is a

good man and keeps his vows. He was midway between Winchester and London with about thirty attendants when that woman was placed in a chair in his bedchamber—and I am going to find out who did it and why. Gehard was known to use Nelda from time to time." That was an assumption for which Bell had no proof, but he did not care. "Now, where is he?"

"I don't know. Gehard isn't on duty now." The captain's eyes slanted sideways to the knife that rested just on the big vein under his ear. A hard prick, and he was dead. "I'm not his nursemaid. I have no idea what the man does or where he goes on his own time." The words were bold; the voice shook a little.

Bell swung the captain around and lowered the knife in one swift movement until it now pricked through the man's light summer tunic into his back. "Walk," Bell said softly, "down the stair and out the door to my horse. If one man of yours makes a move toward me, you will be dead."

"You will be dead too," the captain snarled.

Bell laughed bitterly. "If you think that satisfaction will make your corpse happy, you can call out to your men. But your master will curse your name for years. The bishop knows where I am and is likely to make trouble if I end up dead." Another lie, but a safe one.

There was a tense moment of silence and the captain said, "I will give my parole to see you safe out of the Tower nor send anyone after you. I do not wish to walk past my men with your knife in my back."

No man likes the men he commands to see him bested, Bell thought. "Accepted," he said, and withdrew the knife, although he did not yet sheathe it. Then he sighed. "I am very sorry. I have a nasty temper and I am attached to the bishop of Winchester."

The captain's lips tightened momentarily but he shrugged. "So I see. It was a stupid jest, and I didn't mean it the way it sounded. I certainly didn't mean to make you think Gehard had anything to do with that woman. He is a hard man but does his duty and I did not want to see him accused because of his manner and his attitude toward the whore."

"He told me she deserved what she got and was a thieving bitch."

Of course, Bell had no proof that the man who had said that to him was Gehard, but the captain's answer confirmed it. "He always said she was a thief, but he continued to use her so it is possible she did not steal from him."

Bell shook his head and gestured the captain to precede him down the stairs. "Until she did," he said, and neither of them spoke again as they went outside.

Mounted and out of the Tower grounds, Bell hesitated and glanced up at the sun. What he wanted to do was go back to the Old Priory Guesthouse and tell Magdalene what a fool he had been for losing his temper. Even if she agreed with him, the confession would ease his heart, and the other women would all find reasons for him not to call himself a fool. But the light said it was near or after Nones and the second set of clients would just be arriving. He would not be welcome.

Not having wished to sit still right outside of the gate in the Tower wall, just in case the captain decided not to keep his parole, Bell had directed his horse toward the river. A burst of noise—laughter and good-natured cursing—drew his attention and he realized he was passing an ale-house. His breath drew in. What was wrong with him today? The captain had said he did not know where Gehard was, but where was he more likely to be than in an ale-house? And it was important to find Gehard and speak to him before the captain warned him.

Farther down the street was a stable. Bell decided to leave his horse there and walk. After he dismounted and stalled Monseigneur himself—the stallion having tried to bite the stableboy who came to hold him—he thought for a moment about taking off his armor. To wear only his worn gambeson would not be noteworthy in the ale-houses used by the men quartered at the Tower, but then he decided to be safe instead of cool in case he made any more mistakes.

Bell walked back up the street, looked into one place but it was obviously used mostly by simple men-at-arms. The next, for some reason was nearly empty. The third, Bell recognized before he looked in. It was the ale-house in which he had found Linley's companions and where Gehard had spoken to him as he was leaving. And his luck, seemingly, had changed. As he entered, he saw Gehard alone at a small table with his back to the wall.

A kind of stiff silence fell as Bell entered, all eyes fixed on his mail-clad figure. To project peacefulness, he undid the ties of his ventail and threw back his hood. Talk started up again, although eyes followed to see where he was going. Soon as it was clear that he was going either to an empty table or heading for Gehard, conversations picked up again.

"Master Gehard," Bell said when he reached the man's table, "I am glad to find you."

There was the faintest glazing in the eyes that lifted from the liquid in the tankard to Bell's face. "Know you," he said. "You'wre in askin' 'bout Linley . . . 'bout Nelda."

"Yes." Bell tensed a trifle, hoped that Gehard couldn't see it under his armor, but he kept his voice easy and calm. "You called her a thieving bitch and said she deserved her death. I just began to wonder whether you arranged it."

"Me? Kill Nelda? Nuh! Why shed'I? Gave'er a beatin'. Careful though. Didn' break 'er nose er nothin', maybe give 'er a black eye. Told 'er if she didn' give back m'seal, I'd do 'er worse. Knock out 'er teef. Break 'er nose. Cut off 'er ears. But kill 'er? Nah!"

"Oh," Bell said, inadequately.

The utter casualness with which Gehard spoke, the ease of his voice, of his body, the faintly regretful expression, as if something not valuable but familiar had been lost, all implied he had spoken the truth. But Bell was uneasy. Just so would an expert liar look and Gehard was certainly strong enough to move Nelda, but why would he do it?

" 'Sides sh'paid when we went where those filthy pagans sold th'stuff." He paused and his mouth loosened as he apparently contemplated a pleasure. "Gave me some once." The mouth tightened again. "Would'n give me more."

"So you knew her well," Bell persisted, since Gehard seemed quite willing to talk. "You say you did not kill her. Do you have any idea who might want to kill her?"

The big man shrugged. "Nah! 'Cept maybe 'cause she's a thief. But tha's stupid. Kill 'er, lose what she stole. Or maybe some'un wanted the stuff so bad . . . Nah. Tha's dumb too. N'ver told no one where she got it."

"Ah, but you knew that."

Gehard snorted. "Whr'I'd get 't silver t' pay fer it?" He stared up at Bell, muttering, "Silver. Thought I'd have enough after . . ." slowly starting to frown. Then suddenly the man's face turned furious. "You're the one!" he snarled. "Yer 't one Snot tole me save't bishop." He started to lurch up, but the table caught him across the thighs and he dropped back onto the bench. "Stupid bastid! Wouldn' of hurt 'im."

"You arranged the attack on the bishop?"

The words came out hardly above a whisper and even as he spoke, Bell was appalled at his stupidity. He should have pretended not to understand or talked about Nelda again; then Gehard might have told him who had ordered the attack on Winchester and why. And then he remembered the captain's expression of relief when he said he wanted to question Gehard about Nelda. Relief because he had been afraid Bell was going to ask about the attack on the bishop? He opened his mouth, closed it, swallowed.

But he had not found silence soon enough. The damage had been done. Apparently Gehard was not so drunk he was going to admit the attack. He peered up at Bell and laughed.

"Me? Do such a thing against a holy man? Don't know the bishop. Never spoke to 'im. Why should I want to attack him?"

He relaxed on the bench so his back rested against the wall behind him, pretending to be at ease, but Bell noticed that the hand that held his tankard was pale with the tightness of his grip. Bell also noted that Gehard was no longer slurring his words. Alarm at his slip had sobered him.

Bell also laughed, as falsely as Gehard had. "I doubt *you* wanted to attack the bishop of Winchester," he said, keeping his voice very low. "You were only following your orders and are thus not to blame for what happened."

"Don't know what happened. Wasn't there. Had nothin' t'do with it!"

"That's certainly true," Bell agreed with another false smile. "I would not have missed a man like you. You were not there. And you said that no harm was to come to Winchester. Was it all a jest gone wrong? Should I warn Winchester that he has offended? But I must know who. Thus, if you tell me—"

The mug of beer went up, splashing liquid into Bell's face and the table slammed into his belly. He staggered back, his hand going to his sword hilt, but Gehard was out from behind the rocking table and already half-way to the door. Bell started after him, sword drawn, but half a dozen men were already on their feet blocking his way.

"There are more of you," Bell snarled, "but I am in armor. I can kill half a dozen before you can bear me down."

One of the men lifted empty hands. "No one wishes you any harm," he said. "We know Gehard's temper. But he was drunk and he is one of us. Let him go."

Bell sighed, realizing that it was possible the men had not heard what he and Gehard had been talking about. Perhaps they had just seen Gehard throw his beer into Bell's face and hit him with the table. If so, they would let him go, but he had better not take that chance.

"Then go and sit down again, all of you," Bell said. "The first man who rises is the first man who dies."

CHAPTER 10

"What is wrong?" Magdalene asked as soon as she made out the rigidity of Bell's body and the grim set of his mouth.

She swung the gate wide, then closed it behind him and after another moment pulled in the bell cord so no one could ring the bell. He did not answer, only strode forward to enter the house. Magdalene hurried after him and found him standing in the middle of the room, as if he did not recognize the place despite the light of candles and torchettes.

"Have you eaten?" she asked.

He swallowed. "No."

"Whom did you kill?"

He blinked and his lips twisted into a wry smile. "No one, but it is only by the grace of God that I am not dead myself, and all owing to my own bad temper and stupidity." He took a deep breath. "I do not like to feel stupid."

Magdalene uttered a half-strangled giggle. That was a miracle of understatement if she ever heard one. "Sit down," she said. "I'll bring you the remains of the evening meal."

He was in his accustomed place on the end of the long bench nearest the short bench on which she sat when she returned and set down a platter of thin-sliced cold mutton, a wedge of pork pasty, cheese, and half a loaf of dark bread.

As she went to fill a tankard of ale for him, she said, "You can thank Ella for the pasty. She insisted you would come today and made sure that no matter how late it was you would not go hungry."

"They are all working?" he asked, pulling his eating knife and stabbing a slice of meat.

Magdalene nodded without answering. She was struggling not to grin. Obviously Bell had hoped for the uncritical soothing admiration her women offered him. Ella would always say whatever happened was not his fault; Letice would make gestures that urged acceptance of bad luck and adverse circumstances, which she would imply were a result of fate and could never be utterly avoided; Diot would find a way to fix the blame on whoever opposed him.

Usually Magdalene played the impartial judge, speaking the truth as she saw it. But that had been when she and Bell were in a fixed and stable relationship. She was not sure telling him he was an idiot—if he had been one—was what he needed or what would best further her purpose right now. Still she felt a small glow of satisfaction. At least he had come to the Old Priory Guesthouse instead of working off his spleen on his men or getting drunk.

She stood beside him, watching him take a swallow of the ale and then break off a piece of the pasty. "I have some interesting news," she said tentatively. "Do you want to hear it or do you want to tell me what happened to disturb you so much?"

Mentioning the news brought Raoul de Samur to mind, and Magdalene nearly reached out to stroke Bell's hair, which was clean and shining. Raoul had not been particularly foul, but clearly he had not bothered to bathe after his ride from Devizes or Salisbury to London and he was ripe. His clothes had been stained and worn for too long, his hair was greasy and tangled, and the nails of the hand with which he held his cup had been black. The contrast with Bell, who had taken the time to change from his armor, made Bell seem even more desirable. True, Bell smelled of

horse and sweat, but today's horse and sweat, not a week's or several month's accumulation.

"Gehard fitzRobert is the man who beat Nelda," he said, startling Magdalene out of her thoughts, "and he may have been the man who killed her too."

Glad that he had diverted her, Magdalene still frowned. "Likely not. I think the man who killed her is Sir John of Rouen, although I have no better direction for him except that I think he is in the household of Geoffrey de Mandeville."

Bell choked on a bite of the pasty that he had tried to swallow too quickly. "Mandeville!" he got out. Magdalene pounded his back and he cleared his throat. "Mandeville is behind it all? But why? As far as I know, Mandeville was never of de Meulan's party."

"I do not think he is." Magdalene wrinkled her nose. "So far as I know he is always of his own party, but he is clever enough to let Waleran know when he does something that he thinks will work well with Waleran's plans. Raoul de Samur brought me the news that a Sir John was boasting that he had got from Gloucester a letter for Winchester. Not that Raoul knows the bit about Sir John was news to me. He thought I knew of the letter because this Sir John had been with one of my women and told her about it."

Bell opened his mouth for another slice of meat, but instead said, "Samur may be right. It is possible that Sir John did boast to Nelda about obtaining the letter from Gloucester. But I wonder how she could have got it from him?"

"Oh, I know that," Magdalene said. She moved around and sat down in her usual place at the head of the table and told him about her expedition to The Saracen's Head with Letice.

"So she drugged him and stole the letter. How come he

did not miss it when he finally wakened and dressed?"

"I know that too," Magdalene said, and described Tayte and how she had seen Nelda coming up the stairs and holding a piece of folded parchment. "I suppose she replaced the letter with the parchment she had obtained. Likely he would not take the letter out and look at it."

Bell shook his head. "That may well be true, but then it makes no sense," he said. "If this Sir John did not know Nelda stole the letter, why should he kill her apurpose or quarrel with her so violently that she was pushed down the stairs? And if he *did* know she stole the letter, why would he tell Lord Hugh that he had it?"

Magdalene frowned. "You are right." She snorted gently. "And I thought we had our killer. It seemed to me that if Sir John had killed Nelda by accident, trying unsuccessfully to get the letter back, he might have moved her to Winchester's house so he could say he had arranged for the bishop's embarrassment. Possibly he hoped it would save him some of Mandeville's fury when he learned the letter was lost. So Gehard may be our man after all."

Bell smiled at her. "Gehard may be, but you put that all together very cleverly, and it all fits—except his telling Lord Hugh he had the letter. Unless he and Nelda quarreled about something else. Could she have stolen something else from him, something he did notice so that he threatened her to make her return it? What was in that pile of 'keepsakes' you took from her rooms?"

Magdalene rose and went to her bedchamber where she drew a key from a chain hanging between her breasts and opened the steel-bound chest under the small, high window. She moved her clothing aside carefully and drew out a sturdy box that she opened with a smaller key from her pocket. From the box she removed a leather pouch,

which she carried with her into the common room after she had restored and relocked everything.

She emptied the pouch onto the table between Bell's seat and her own. "The Mandeville house badge? Could that have been Sir John's? And of all the rings she had, only these three and the seal have not been identified. I wonder how she got the rings? She could drug a man to sleep, but so deeply he would not feel a ring being pulled from his finger? And wouldn't even a half drugged man notice his ring was gone?"

Bell held what was left of the pasty in his left hand while he fingered the rings Magdalene had pushed toward him with his right. "I think she got these at least honestly," he said, then grinned. "At least honestly from your point of view in that they were likely given her for her service. They are not true gold, and I think this stone is only garnet."

"I knew they were not very valuable," Magdalene agreed. "But far too valuable to pay a whore for her service. She had to have a reason to keep them in her most secret place."

Having chewed and swallowed the last bit of pasty, Bell said, "Likely they were pledges of some kind. Or . . . wait. Gehard said he would not have killed her because then he could not retrieve his—ah! the seal is Gehard's. He said she had stolen his seal."

"Gehard fitzRobert," Magdalene murmured, taking the seal from Bell and pointing to the groove that broke the Beaufort arms. "See the mark from left to right?"

"To show that he had not full rights to the family?" Bell's voice rose as if to question, but he did not doubt what Magdalene had said. "Yet he was given the seal."

Magdalene shrugged. "You said his name was fitzRobert. A bastard of the old earl that he wanted to use but did not want to recognize? I heard he was a righteous old prig."

"But what is a Beaufort bastard doing in the employ of Mandeville?"

Magdalene did not answer at once. She pulled the branch of candles on the table closer and twisted the seal from side to side. After a moment she picked at it with the nail of her little finger.

"Wax," she said. "What odds will you lay against me that Gehard used the seal to identify messages about Mandeville's doings and plans which he sent to Waleran or to Hugh."

Having taken back the seal and examined it, Bell nodded. "No odds," he said. "I do not wager against sure things."

"Which makes it more clear why Hugh was so enraged by learning that Winchester was supposed to be held in that place across from Paul's Wharf."

"How do you know he was enraged? Oh, yes. Raoul. But why should Lord Hugh care? Nothing could be proven. Oh, I see. Gehard had made him look a fool, to put his victim in a place that pointed so directly to Baynard's Castle. Hmmm. I wonder just how much resentment Gehard has built up against his Beaufort half-brothers over the years?"

"I do not think you can suborn him," Magdalene said. "To serve Beaufort was likely set deep into his blood and bone from childhood."

Bell sighed. "He would be totally untrustworthy anyway. His conscience would nag at him and sooner or later he would turn on anyone who tried to make him betray the family. And one would never know when."

He tilted the tankard to get the last drops of ale, and Magdalene rose to refill it. When she returned to the table, she said, "What were you about to tell me when you suddenly remembered Gehard had said Nelda stole his seal? We were talking about the rings being pledges."

"Oh, yes. When Gehard said he was not so stupid as to kill a person who stole from him before he retrieved what he had lost, he said something about those who were desperate for more of the 'stuff' not killing her either because she never told anyone where she got it."

Magdalene's eyes opened wide. "That must be the poppy cake. The man who sold it to her, Umar, also said something about those who took it growing desperate."

"Likely that was what the valuable rings paid for," Bell said with a sudden sense of satisfaction. He reached out and cut a slice of cheese with the knife he had left on the table, slapped it on the bread and took a bite. In a voice somewhat impeded by his mouthful, he added, "And the less valuable ones, too. She might not have known the difference. And that was why she had ten pounds in her strongbox. I doubted any man would pay very high just to escape being accused of visiting a whore."

"I think you must be right." Magdalene sighed and shook her head. "And you know, Bell, that if her death was really an accident, if she fell down the stairs while struggling to escape a threat, the logic of not killing her because then one would not be able to retrieve what she had stolen or obtain more of the drug becomes meaningless. Which makes Gehard more likely to be the killer."

But Bell was looking past her, considering what he had said and thinking that Father Holdyn might pay high to keep his sin secret. And then the sense of Magdalene's remark hit him, and he groaned aloud and set his food on the table.

"I believe I've been even stupider than I thought."

Magdalene shook her head again. "You aren't stupid, Bell. You make mistakes, like any other mortal man. At least when you make mistakes you recognize them. What happened?"

"It was my cursed temper. It was rubbed raw and it mastered me. First I was annoyed because I needed to stand around for hours while Winchester and the archbishop fenced with each other about that cursed convocation. Then, we dined at the cannon's table—roast vegetables, turnips . . ."

Magdalene uttered a small giggle. Bell glared at her and then smiled sheepishly.

"Actually it was quite good," he admitted. "After dinner the bishop questioned Father Holdyn about that crucifix we found among Nelda's other trinkets. He admitted it was his—well, he could not well deny it, both Winchester and I have seen him wear it. He said it was stolen on Sunday night."

"Was it?"

"Oh yes, although to be sure I had to ride all the way up to Monkwell Street and then back to the bishop of London's palace, all the while broiling in my armor. But when I asked Holdyn's servants if he had complained about anything being stolen, all they knew of was a gilt cup lost a year or two ago. No one was ever accused; Father Holdyn simply purchased a new cup for the church. The servants said—thinking to praise their master's charity—that they believed the cup was stolen by a woman who periodically got into Holdyn's house and into the bishop's palace, too. They didn't even know the crucifix was missing. Holdyn never told them, never said the woman should be seized the next time she came."

Silent for a moment, Magdalene then nodded slowly. "Too bad Nelda was buried before the servants could be brought to look at her, but even without that I think the woman who took such liberties with Father Holdyn must have been Nelda. So he knew Nelda, knew her, seemingly

for years. Why should he kill her now?"

Bell sighed. "For the same reason as any other man. The gilt cup was nothing. He could replace that and it did not compromise him in any way. The crucifix was different. It was his and his alone, and many people knew that. So he tried to get the crucifix back, threatened to choke her, and she fell. It was an accident. Holdyn is bigger than me and hard as a rock. He spends all his spare time building or repairing churches."

"But?" Magdalene asked.

Bell looked down at the bread and cheese on the table. "But I cannot believe it. I simply cannot believe that Father Holdyn would not run weeping to his confessor if he had killed Nelda, even by accident. And then rushed to the bishop to confess his crime."

"Did you ask him straight out?"

"Winchester did ask him if he knew the woman he buried and he waited a long time before he answered. He had an odd look, too. As if he were rather surprised and sad when he said that he did not know her. I thought then that he was lying and was ashamed of it."

"But the bishop did not press him further?"

"No, because he cannot believe that Holdyn would put the woman in his room." Bell sighed. "I can't believe it either."

"I understand. You do not wish to suspect Father Holdyn but what he has said and done are suspicious. What then?"

So he told her about nearly killing Mandeville's captain for making a stupid jest and saying just the wrong thing to Gehard so that he could not learn who had ordered the man to have the bishop of Winchester attacked.

Magdalene's lips twitched, but she said soberly enough, "Likely you should not have throttled the captain, but you need not blame yourself for not wringing more from

Gehard. As soon as he said what he said, he must have shocked himself sober. No matter what you did, he would deny his words."

"Perhaps. Still it must be Mandeville who sent that order from Devizes or wherever they were. Unless Lord Hugh wanted to implicate Mandeville by using his man . . . No, then he would not have ordered Winchester brought to that place across the river from Paul's Wharf."

"Oh, yes, it must be Mandeville because the only purpose there could be for attacking Winchester is to frighten him enough to call off the convocation. And Raoul told me that Waleran has not the smallest intention of interfering with the convocation the bishop wishes to call."

"What?"

Magdalene nodded, knowing that Bell had heard her and was only expressing his disbelief of what she said. "I felt as you do at first, but Raoul pointed out that Waleran's purpose is to be the only influence on the king. Raoul reports that Waleran said nothing could widen the breach between the king and Winchester more than this convocation, during which, I suppose, the king is to be admonished and forced to return Salisbury's possessions."

Bell's mouth opened, but he did not speak and an expression of decided discomfort knitted his brows and turned his lips down.

"That is put in the most bald and unflattering terms," Magdalene said flatly, "but it is the meat of Winchester's intention. In the same bald terms, how likely do you think it is it will be successful?"

Bell looked down at the bread and cheese again; he did not want to meet Magdalene's eyes. "It is not often that Henry of Winchester lies to himself," he said softly, "but this time I think he has done so. Oh, only on the top of his

thoughts. Inside he knows. And inside I knew too. When the bishop and archbishop agreed that the convocation would be held in Winchester, I was relieved and thought at once that the bishop's whole armed might could be gathered there without being obvious about it. I remember thinking that Winchester and the other bishops could not be taken as Salisbury was taken."

There was a silence and finally Magdalene said, "What will you do?"

Bell shook his head. "I will tell him what we know—"

"Do not betray Raoul!" Magdalene interrupted sharply. "That will involve William."

Bell stiffened, and Magdalene cursed herself for mentioning William's name; however after a moment Bell said, "No. There will be no need. So many men come here. So many are cozened into talk. It is possible that Winchester will even believe that the woman who passed this news to you did not remember which particular man told her."

"Will you be able to convince the bishop—"

"No!" Bell's teeth snapped together and his jaw muscles bunched. After a moment he continued, "If you meant will he withdraw from the convocation? Nothing will convince him to do that. He has gone too far, even arranging time and place with the archbishop. But I will tell him what Waleran hopes."

Magdalene thought "men!" but she only nodded. "And it might help if from time to time before the convocation takes place, you can remind him circumspectly of the danger Waleran's single influence on the king holds for the realm and the Church. Winchester is a clever and subtle man. His mind will work on the facts until the 29th of August when the convocation convenes. He will realize that if he utterly alienates his brother the king no good can come

of it, not only to him but to the Church."

"The trouble is," Bell sighed, "that Winchester leans more to the Church Militant than to gentle pleading."

"I doubt he will get much support from the other bishops if he takes that tack. Salisbury's discomfiture is too near and too vivid."

Bell sighed again. "I think he knows it already from hearing what the archbishop had to say. Theobald is all for conciliation and compromise—perhaps an apology from the king but no punishment and no restitution."

"Ah!" Magdalene smiled. "He may get that and I hope that Winchester can be satisfied with that solution." She shrugged and her smile broadened. "*I* certainly do not mind in the least if the king's treasury has been refilled by Salisbury's hoard. Surely that will, for a little while, hold off more taxes. However, I do not wish to see Winchester stripped as Salisbury was because *someone* would have to replenish the bishop's exchequer." Her lips twisted. "And who do you think would bear the heaviest burden? No doubt the wicked."

"I will do my best," Bell said, stretching and yawning, "but do not expect too much. The bishop did not hire me for my sage advice in political matters."

"Go to bed," Magdalene said.

Bell stiffened but made no reply and after a little silence, Magdalene added, "None of the women knows you were here, and you will leave well before they rise in the morning, so no one will talk or wonder."

She got up as she spoke and went to get a sewing basket, which she set on the table and from which she extracted a ribbon she was embroidering. Bell watched her begin a new line. Then, still without answering, he picked up the neglected piece of bread and cheese and ate it. When he had

swallowed, he emptied what remained in the tankard on the table.

At last, he said, "Thank you," got up from his seat and moved down the hall.

Lowering her head over her embroidery, the second of a pair of borders to be sewn to the cuff of a sleeve, Magdalene smiled to herself. A few more days and he would slip back into the habit of living in her house. Now if only she could arrange to have someone threaten the peace of the Old Priory Guesthouse, she could offer him her bed as payment for his protection.

Her needle flew over the broad ribbon. The design, a simple one of leaves and flowers, would soon be finished. She had not yet decided whether it would be worthwhile to offer the cuffs to Claresta as an excuse to go to the Lime Street house again. Unfortunately the girl did not seem enough interested in Linley to urge him to talk to her and listen. Eventually Magdalene set the last stitch, bound off her thread, and packed all into the basket. She walked once down the corridor, listening. Behind one door were soft voices; the others were silent. She paused at Bell's door but heard nothing. She could only hope he was asleep.

In that Magdalene's hopes were fulfilled. When Magdalene had told him to go to bed, Bell had not hesitated because he did not want to take advantage but because he was afraid he would lie awake regretting he was not in *her* bed. The day, however, had been too long and trying. What came to his mind as he took off his clothes was not Magdalene but the fact that his master had two sets of enemies, each trying to destroy him in a different way.

Mandeville was not nearly so clever or subtle as Waleran. The letter he had arranged to obtain to make

Winchester seem a traitor was in the bishop's hands and could be presented to the king in such a way as to mark the bishop's loyalty. The other schemes had gone awry too, the woman in the bedchamber and the attack. He would be alert for any further tricks and between him and Magdalene they would discover who had killed Nelda and clear Winchester of any connection with the crime.

Bell drew a deep breath, lay down, and pulled a light blanket over his naked body. The danger from the Beauforts, just because there was no actual danger, was more acute. Waleran and his family had been implicated once or twice in false schemes to discredit Winchester so that the king had been made suspicious of them. This time, according to Raoul, Waleran was so sure Winchester would hang himself that he was taking care that no one in his family would even be seen handling rope.

Unfortunately, Waleran was likely right. If Winchester used the papal authority to try to cow Stephen, he would lose even if he forced Stephen to restore everything to Salisbury. The breach with the king would become so wide that nothing could bridge it, the other bishops would also feel the king's enmity and lose their trust in Winchester . . . Bell grunted and shifted. No. Winchester was no fool. Bell reasoned that all he had to do was present the information in such a way that it did not add to Winchester's carefully controlled rage. His eyes closed on that thought.

In the morning Bell did not stop to break his fast but made his way to the bishop's house and asked the clerk on duty—not Phillipe this morning—if Winchester could receive him now. The clerk climbed the stairs to the upper story and scratched on the door. A servant opened it. In less than a quarter candlemark the clerk came down and told Bell to go up.

"You are early this morning," Winchester said, turning away from a handsome crucifix where he had likely said mass.

"I have news, my lord, and I wished to be sure you had it before you became so busied that you had no time for it."

"News of note then?"

Bell hesitated. "Yes and no. I do not believe anything I learned calls for any action on your part, but you might know better than I whether that is true."

One servant was busied near the bishop's bed, folding the stole Winchester had worn to say his prayers. The other servant went out and down the stairs.

Winchester moved to the table and without hesitation sat down in the chair in which the corpse had been found. He gestured for Bell to take a stool and sit also.

"First," Bell said, "Father Holdyn told the truth about being at the church on Monkswell on Sunday night, and from what time his servants say he returned, he could have done no more that night than walk from the church on Monkswell to the bishop of London's palace."

"What do you mean?"

"I mean that he could not have visited Nelda—the whore who was killed—and had his crucifix stolen or given it to her that Sunday night."

"Ah, so Holdyn told all the truth. The crucifix was stolen from his chamber in the palace."

"Not *all* the truth, my lord. He did not tell his servants that the crucifix was missing or seek for it."

"Mayhap he did not notice it until he dressed on Monday morning. Then he would have thought it was too late to pursue the thief and did not wish to grieve his servants."

"Possibly," Bell said, but his tone was such that Winchester cocked his head in inquiry. Bell continued, "The

servants also told me—they are very fond of their master and wished to praise him—that for some years a woman has been somehow finding her way into Holdyn's house, and into the palace also. They think she stole a gilded cup some years ago which Holdyn replaced without inquiry, and he left out coins for her to take."

"Then he did know the woman he buried." Winchester sighed and bowed his head. "That it should not be the same woman as was found dead in my chair is too great a coincidence. I am disappointed. Not because Father Holdyn slipped in virtue. That can happen to any man. But I would not have believed he would lie about it." He hesitated and then added forcibly, "And I *will* not believe he set the corpse in my chamber."

"My lord, neither would I," Bell said. "But I find it curious that he took so long to deny he knew her. A prepared lie tumbles out quickly. When you question him about the woman—I assume you would wish to speak to him yourself?"

"Yes. So, when I question him about the woman . . ."

"Ask him *why* he said he did not know her. Mayhap you think the answer is obvious—that he did not wish to acknowledge acquaintance with a dead whore—but I just feel there is more to it than that."

The servant who had gone down the stairs returned bearing a large tray on which was a substantial breakfast. He set it on the table. Bell swallowed and his belly rumbled. The bishop laughed and bade the servant bring another cup for the wine.

"You did not break your fast?"

"No, my lord. I was afraid I would miss you or that you would have invited someone to break fast with you."

"Then I suppose the rest of your news is more important

than that Father Holdyn lied about the woman." He began to eat, swallowing a spoonful of frumenty before he nodded to Bell to continue.

"I am almost certain, my lord, that the attack made on you on Monday was ordered by Lord Geoffrey de Mandeville."

Winchester put down his spoon for a moment and asked, "How?" Then he looked down and began to eat again.

Bell told the tale of his interviews with the captain of Mandeville's troop and Gehard, not sparing himself over his mistakes. The bishop listened without comment. When he had finished his bowl of frumenty, he smiled very slightly.

"Likely you should not have choked the captain. My reputation is not *that* fragile." Then he sighed. "As to what the man Gehard let slip . . . I do not understand why Mandeville should wish me harm."

"Gehard said no physical harm to you was intended. But if you mean why Mandeville ordered an attack on you, I think he hoped to frighten you so you would not consult with the archbishop and let the idea of a convocation lapse. I suppose he believes that the king would be pleased and grateful."

"Frighten me?" Winchester's voice rose. "He thought I would run back to Winchester to hide because a few brigands . . . The man is not only unprincipled, he is stupid!"

Bell's lips twitched at Winchester's outrage over the slur on his courage. "He only sees you in the rich vestments of the Church," he said. Then could not help grinning. "And he did not see how lovingly you took your mace from its chest."

The bishop laughed and then said, "Eat."

Winchester addressed himself to a chunk of yellow cheese, which he sliced and laid on a piece of bread. Bell

reached for the white cheese, which he knew to be of milder flavor. He cut the wedge in half, broke a piece of bread, and took several healthy bites. Those he washed down quickly with the watered wine.

"There is more, my lord."

Winchester raised a brow. "You have been even more busy than usual. Can you be in more than one place at a time?"

Bell smiled. "The rest comes from Magdalene, my lord."

"Ah."

So he reported what Magdalene had learned from Tayte and what Magdalene's guess was as to how Nelda had stolen the letter from the man Tayte had heard name himself Sir John. Winchester immediately leapt to the same conclusion that Magdalene had—that Sir John had discovered his letter was missing and had killed Nelda in an attempt to retrieve it.

Now Bell hesitated. He was approaching the delicate ground of what Raoul had reported from Baynard's castle. Finally he shrugged and said, "That was what Mistress Magdalene thought until yesterday when one of her women reported that this Sir John had been in Baynard's Castle late Thursday night—near to Matins—and had told Lord Hugh that he carried a letter from Gloucester addressed to you."

"Peste!" Winchester exclaimed, slapping a hand hard on the table. "So the word is out to the Beauforts. I will have to go to Stephen with the accursed thing."

Bell's heart sank. He knew he should be glad that his master would take him away from temptation, but the warm comfort of talking over everything with Magdalene, of sleeping in ease and comfort in his private room, of looking forward as he had been doing to a bath when he was done

with this day's duty tightened his chest with loss.

"And chasing after Stephen from castle to castle," the bishop continued, "will keep me from receiving replies from the other bishops to my summons to the convocation. It could put the whole convocation at risk. Could someone at Baynard's Castle have stolen the letter and moved the poor woman's corpse for just that purpose?"

Bell barely stopped himself from raising his eyes to heaven and saying thanks for the opening Winchester had given him; however, he only allowed himself a troubled expression. "I do not know, my lord," he said, "but Magdalene's woman told her that Sir John had set off to find Mandeville—he thought he would be at Devizes—the next morning. Would he have done so if the letter had been taken from him? And, my lord, *would* Lord Waleran desire that the letter be delivered to your hand? Would he not hope that Mandeville would present the letter to the king at the worst possible moment . . . say, when the summons to the convocation was just known?"

"Then why was the woman brought here?" Winchester asked furiously.

"Oh, to do you a despite. There can be no doubt of that. The doubt is that those who brought her—there were two of them—knew she had the letter."

Winchester ground his teeth and got out, "Then I will have to go to Stephen. But to need to beg his pardon for something I have not done . . . To need to do so while he sits in Salisbury's castle, counting Salisbury's coin and weighing his plate . . . Surely this is de Meulan's work so that the convocation will fail."

Bell did not allow himself to sigh with relief; the bishop had given him exactly the right lead for what he had to say. "No, my lord. There is further information from Magda-

lene. She most earnestly desires your well doing and that your power not be diminished."

"She does?" There was a tinge of disbelief in the bishop's voice and a half-smile on his lips.

"Indeed she does, my lord." Bell smiled too. "She says compared with others, you are a good landlord and do not squeeze her so hard as to destroy her business."

"Ah." The smile lingered on Winchester's lips.

"It seems," Bell said, "that Lord Waleran sent messages to his brother Hugh that he not interfere in any way with your planning and summoning for the convocation."

Winchester had begun to lift his wine goblet to his lips and now sat with it arrested half way to his mouth. He stared at Bell. After a long moment he said, "Do you believe this? Do you believe that Waleran de Meulan wishes for the success of my convocation?" And he set the goblet down on the table.

Bell returned the bishop's steady gaze. He had come to the crux of his tale. "At first, when Magdalene told me I said it must be a lie set about by de Meulan to make me less wary to protect you or for some other hidden purpose. But she laughed and said no, the success of the convocation was the best thing in the world that could happen to Lord Waleran."

"It has nothing to do with de Meulan, except to make me look weak and a fool if it fails."

"No, my lord, now I, too, realize Lord Waleran's desire that the convocation succeed is most reasonable. What, Magdalene asked, could make the king more angry at you, more resentful of you, than forcing him to return Salisbury's hoard and his castles? Would the king not believe—if those who know of Gloucester's letter speak of it—that you, the king's own brother, want Salisbury in power so that he

can welcome Gloucester? What could make Lord Waleran's hold on the king stronger than that you be shown half a traitor, willing to hurt your brother in this way, to strip what he believes is his rightful prize from him?"

"That is mad," Winchester whispered. "I *set* Stephen on the throne. I convinced the old archbishop to anoint him as king. I convinced the Treasurer to open King Henry's vaults of treasure to him. I do not wish to hurt him, only to protect the Church. How could he believe . . . ?"

Bell had said what he had to say, and had no intention of allowing Winchester to argue the point he had made and perhaps convince himself it was not valid. Acting as if he had not heard the bishop's agonized murmur, he asked, "When would you have me make the men ready to travel, my lord?"

Winchester looked at him blankly then shook his head. "This needs thought, not riding hither and thither around England in pursuit of the king. I will send Father Wilfrid to Stephen. He was my brother's confessor when Stephen lived in King Henry's court and Stephen is soft to the old man."

Bell smiled broadly. "Very good, my lord. Father Wilfrid can convince me that the sun shines when it is raining. The king will believe the tale of the murdered whore."

"Better than if it came from me," Winchester agreed, his lips twisted wryly. Then he sighed and added, "I left a list with Phillipe of things my steward wanted ordered from London. Nothing, luckily, that could be considered the least warlike. I need hose for the singing boys in the cathedral, and gowns. They grow . . . I do not remember the rest but it is all on the list. You could take care of that. I will let you know or leave a message for you if I decide to travel."

"Yes, my lord."

Bell rose, silently replaced the stool near the wall, and left the bishop to his uneasy thoughts.

CHAPTER 11

After Bell had gone to bed, Magdalene had written to William detailing everything that had happened, starting with Nelda's discovery in Winchester's bedchamber and including what she and Bell had learned from each other that evening. Tom had taken the letter to William's house on the grounds of the White Tower with a request from her to the men stationed there that the news be sent on to William.

Then, restless and uneasy, she had sat up even later finishing the embroidered ribbons for cuffs, which she still had not decided to bring to Claresta. Still uneasy, she had wakened somewhat earlier than usual. She was a little worried when Dulcie told her that Bell had left without eating breakfast, but she deliberately put that out of her mind. Dulcie brought bread and cheese and ale, and Magdalene was nibbling at the food while she looked at the cuffs and thought about the pennies for which she could sell them if she did not give them to Claresta. Then the bell rang.

It was far too early for a client. Her women had seen their men off soon after sunrise and gone back to bed. However, there might be a message. Diot had no client for tonight because the apothecary had sickened of some disorder for which he was treating a patient. Magdalene was grateful that he had not come with the sickness on him, but she would be happy to find a substitute for him and went off to answer the bell quite cheerfully.

Thus, her expression was pleasantly welcoming when she

opened the gate—but only to the length of its chain. And she put her shoulder to it so she could slam it shut as soon as she saw a face that was familiar but to which she could not put a name. The man was wearing a sword belt and was too well dressed be a local messenger and now she saw a horse at rein's length to the side. The man riding to William who wanted more information? Someone from William? She did not know every man of his well, only those he favored by granting them recreation at the Old Priory Guesthouse.

So instead of slamming the gate, she said, "Yes?"

"You know me, Magdalene. I am Sir Linley of Godalming."

The man who kept Nelda and had found herself, Diot, and Bell examining the place Nelda lived. But Bell said Linley had not killed Nelda. He looked worried, but not angry.

"Yes?" Magdalene repeated.

"Let me in, Magdalene. I must speak to you."

For a moment longer, Magdalene hesitated. Then, recalling that Linley had no reputation for violence, she unhooked the chain and opened the gate. He came in, drawing the horse in after him, but he made no move to take the animal to the stable. Magdalene had not really thought he was looking for a substitute for Nelda, but not stabling the horse was an assurance he did not intend to stay.

"Well?" she asked, closing the gate but not chaining it.

"You took things from Nelda's rooms. You had no right to do that."

Magdalene stared at him and after a moment asked calmly, "How do you know that I took anything? How do you know what Nelda had . . . unless you were party to her thievery?"

He sighed heavily. "I . . . I suspected that she was not completely honest, but she did not steal from me and she was very good company. Not only in bed, but . . . she was clever, witty." He sighed again. "I suppose I should have checked her, but no one complained and I did not suspect the trade in poppy juice cakes. Magdalene, you must give back what she held. I wish to return the tokens to those who ask."

While he spoke, Magdalene had time to think. Although she actually would be glad of one irate poppy-craver banging on her gate when Bell was in the house, she had no guarantee that that was when such a person would arrive. She certainly did not want such a person arriving at the wrong moment and annoying her clients. Moreover, there might well be more than one. And she had no idea how strong the craving might be.

She shook her head. "I do not have what you want."

"I do not believe you!" Linley's voice rose and his hand tightened on the horse's rein. "You and your woman were alone in Nelda's rooms. The knight—Sir Bellamy—was outside with me. He had nothing of hers. He was examining the stair and the wall. So it must have been you and your woman who took Nelda's property."

Magdalene sidled away from him and walked quickly toward the house. He dropped the horse's rein and followed.

"Lying will not help you," he called after her. "When you and your woman came out, you both were concealing something in the folds of your veils. You have no right to those tokens . . . or to Nelda's money either. Nelda did harm enough to those poor men. Let me at least give them back their property without causing them more embarrassment and shame."

Having reached the doorstep, Magdalene stopped and

turned toward Linley again. "I tell you again that I do not have what you want. And even if I did, I would be doing those men no favor by giving you their keepsakes. Why should I believe that all you wish is to return the tokens?"

He gaped at her for a moment. "What else should I want to do with them but to rid myself of the importunity of those who knew that Nelda lived in my house and I often used her? They think I knew her secrets."

"Who was more likely to do so?"

"No." Linley reached to grasp her arm; Magdalene backed out of the way. He followed her but barely into the room and made no further move to seize her. "Look here, I am about to make a most advantageous marriage. I am on my way to show my father the proposed contract. I do not want argument and scandal to upset my future father-by-marriage."

That annoyed Magdalene, who felt that Linley should have mentioned Claresta as well as his future father-by-marriage. Of course he might know that Claresta did not wish to marry him, but that only made worse his indifference to Claresta's possible knowledge that he kept a mistress and his continued determination to make the marriage.

Magdalene fondly hoped that Rhyton *would* turn Linley away, although she was sure he would not. Rhyton had chosen Linley only because he was in line to inherit a barony and was willing to marry a rich commoner. Magdalene suspected that Nelda's connection with Linley and her death would be irrelevant to Rhyton. In fact, she thought that Linley was greatly exaggerating the effect complaints about Nelda would have on his future father-by-marriage.

"I cannot help you," Magdalene said coldly. "I tell you

that you are wasting your time here. It is useless to argue with me or threaten me."

Linley seemed to pale a little but his jaw jutted with determination. "You took the things from Nelda's rooms. You say you do not have them now. Only three days since I *saw* you carry them away. What did you do with them? To whom did you sell them? If you will tell me, perhaps I can buy them back."

It was now apparent to Magdalene that she would have to tell Linley *something*. He was not going to give up and he might well tell those who were plaguing him to plague her instead. That would be bad for business. To tell him that Bell had taken everything would likely make him rush to question Bell; Magdalene sighed. Bell did not really know how to lie. Thus he would refuse to answer, Linley would continue to question, and Bell would doubtless end up beating Linley, which in the long run would make trouble for Bell. Who would Linley *not* wish to annoy?

"I did not sell anything," Magdalene said. "As far as I know, the bishop of Winchester has what was found in Nelda's rooms. The woman was discovered in his house, and he is determined to learn who killed her and who brought her there."

"The bishop," Linley echoed softly. "How did Winchester know you had found anything in Nelda's rooms?"

"I was with his man, Sir Bellamy. And in a way it was Winchester who sent me to Nelda's place. He wanted to know everything that could be learned about her. When Nelda was found, the bishop recognized that she was a whore so he sent Sir Bellamy to ask if I knew her and what else I could find out." She paused and shrugged. "Winchester is my landlord. I try to find answers for any questions he asks."

Linley's shoulders drooped and he took a half step backward toward the doorway. Then he stopped. "Do you know whether Winchester intends to question the men whose tokens he recognizes about Nelda's death and how she came into his chamber?"

Magdalene laughed. "Do you think Winchester makes me his confidant? When he desires that I do something for him, he sends an order, often with Sir Bellamy who collects my rent—and I obey." She sighed. "I do not *know* anything, but I imagine Winchester is still trying to find out who carried Nelda into his house. It was plain she did not walk there with a broken neck."

"He was very angry about that, was he not?" Linley drew a hard breath.

Raising her brows, Magdalene laughed again. "How would you like to return from a long ride and find a dead woman propped at your table? *Specially* a dead whore, if you were a bishop? Yes, he is very angry and determined to discover who did him such a despite. He wasted no time at all in sending Sir Bellamy to ask whether I knew the woman and could guess who had killed her."

Linley stared at her for another moment and then finished his turn away from her, caught up his horse's reins, and led the beast out of the gate. Magdalene waited until she heard the hoof beats move away, then went and secured the gate again. She came back to the house and sat down at the table, but did not reach for the food she had abandoned.

After a while, Diot came from her room and then Letice. Magdalene told them about Linley's visit. "I am not sure what he will do," she finished, "but be very careful if you go out or go to the gate. It is not impossible that he will tell anyone who presses him about Nelda's ill-gotten gains that I took them away."

But there were no untoward incidents that day, and Linley's visit brought some good aftereffects too. Bell came to share their evening meal and to tell Magdalene about his meeting with the bishop. In exchange she described Linley's demand and how she had replied to it. "But I am sure he will not confront the bishop," she ended.

"Likely not," Bell agreed easily, "and with a demand like that—a return of tokens taken from a dead whore's room, not to mention that particular dead whore—Winchester's clerks and guards are not likely to let Linley anywhere near the bishop." He frowned then. "But did Linley believe you? Was he angry enough to be spiteful? To send those men here even if he did believe you?"

"What men?" Ella asked. "Will they want to be friends? I have Baby Face coming tonight and I do not think—"

"No, love," Magdalene said giggling and making a small gesture at Bell that he not ask. "Baby Face will keep you well occupied, and I do not think these men will want to be friends anyway. They just have some questions to ask."

Ella's lovely face clouded. "I do not like to be asked questions. Everyone gets so angry no matter how hard I try to answer."

"They won't ask questions of you, Ella," Bell assured her and she smiled again.

They were more careful of what they said until the meal was cleared away and Ella went off to make sure her room was fresh and clean. Free of the fear of frightening Ella, Bell said he would go and fetch some clothing from the bishop's house because he thought it best that he stay with them.

Although he said nothing about it to the women, Bell was troubled by the idea that Linley might tell those who craved the poppy cake Nelda sold that Magdalene had taken Nelda's possessions. While Bell had served as a man-

at-arms on various merchant vessels that traded with Spain and Italy and sailed the Mediterranean, he had several times come in contact with slaves of the poppy. They could be violent, very violent.

However he did not even need the excuse he had planned to use, that Linley might return, possibly with some of the men who had been robbed, to make sure that Magdalene had told the truth. His offer to stay was welcomed with such enthusiasm that no reasons were necessary. By the time he returned with his armor and servants carrying an assortment of garments, the three women were sitting at the table, bright-eyed, with the pieces for nine-man morris laid out.

As the hours passed, the giggles they had at first kept muffled to reduce any chance of disturbing Ella and her 'friend' became less and less muffled. And when Letice made a particularly clever play and swept the board, Magdalene and Bell both uttered not-at-all muffled guffaws. Diot shushed them with anxious hand wavings and they smothered their laughter. Then all sat quietly for a while to give Ella time to resettle her man if he had been disturbed.

After that they gave over playing games. The women fetched their embroidery, Bell got himself a tankard of ale, and they talked softly about whether the king would be content with what he had taken from Salisbury or seek out other sources of future trouble (and present profit) to subdue. Because near half a candlemark had passed since they had made rather too much noise, all were startled when Ella's bedchamber door opened and she came out, wrapped in her bedrobe.

"What is wrong, love?" Magdalene whispered, jumping to her feet and opening her arms to Ella.

To her surprise, Ella did not rush into that haven. She

stood, frowning and pressing her lips together. "Baby Face told me to tell you that the man you called Sir John did not come on a late ship on Thursday last. Baby Face saw Sir John here, at our gate, talking to Diot before Nones that day." Then she took a deep breath and opened her eyes wide. "Did I say that right? Did I remember?"

"Yes, love, you said it quite right and remembered every word. But what in the world made your friend send you out to us? Did we disturb him with our laughing?"

"Oh no." Ella looked delighted. "He loves to hear you laugh. He says it makes him feel as if he were still a boy abed in the loft and his family were all alive and enjoying themselves of an evening. He gets all warm and eager."

"Should you go back to him?" Magdalene asked anxiously.

"He's asleep now. That's why I came out. He told me to tell you tomorrow, but I knew I would not remember by tomorrow, so I came now. And I will go get him some wine and cakes. When I get back into bed, he will start all over again." Ella smiled with pure joy. "But after he will be ready for the wine and cakes."

"What of you, Ella, sweet? Are you ready also or are you too tired?"

Ella stretched languorously, her eyes half closing. "Not *too* tired. But after we have our little bed bite, I will sleep if he does. He is *such* a nice man, always concerned that he is wearing me out. But I am very strong."

"Yes, love. You are very strong, but if you *are* tired, do not hesitate to say so and rest until you feel better."

"Yes, Magdalene."

Ella trotted down the corridor to the kitchen. Magdalene resumed her seat, but she watched the corridor anxiously until Ella came back. She was walking carefully, but not as

if she were sore, only not to overset the flagon of wine and the cups on the tray. And she gave them her usual sweet smile and a little wave of one hand when she paused to open the door to her room.

All heard the latch snick and then Bell said very softly, "What was *that* all about?"

"We have a new client who is . . . truly I can only call him a satyr, except that he is the gentlest, sweetest person. And he is . . . ah . . . terminally shy."

"Really, it is the strangest thing," Diot said. "He was coming along the street toward the gate one day and I smiled at him, only smiled, did not speak. Oooh, you never saw such fear in a face; I thought he was going to turn tail and run away. Luckily Ella came to the gate and fetched him in."

Letice shook her head and sighed and snatched up her slate to write *"sad lif mizry."*

"It must be a misery to be so shy," Diot agreed, and Letice beamed her delight at being understood.

"But he is comfortable with Ella," Magdalene said, "and he has become a *very* good client. I believe he is a master leatherworker. You must remember the superb leather cushion on the stool Ella brought in when you read 'Aucassin and Nicolette.' I wonder if he has had little to spend money on before because he is so shy and so he has plenty to pay for his time with Ella."

"Yes, yes," Bell said impatiently. "But what he told Ella to say about Sir John . . . How did he know we were interested in Sir John? Did he mean the Sir John who brought the letter from Gloucester? *Did* you see this Sir John on Thursday, Diot?"

Diot blinked her gorgeous emerald eyes. "Good heaven, yes, I did! And . . . er . . . Baby Face must have seen him

too. That was the day I nearly frightened him away. Just as Ella said, Sir John had rung the bell and I came to the gate. He wished to be accommodated, but I did not let him in because we had a full house that Thursday—"

"You did not tell me?" Magdalene asked sharply.

"I forgot all about him by the time I saw you again. You had gone to the mercer in the East Chepe with our embroidery and by the time you returned my man was at the gate. We all had clients coming for the late afternoon and for the night. I remember I asked Sir John if he wished to make an appointment for another day, but he said he was leaving London and did not know when he would return."

"But if he was here on the day that Nelda was killed, surely when we began to talk about him—"

"I never heard Sir John's name mentioned until tonight," Diot said defensively. "You may have talked about him with Bell, but not with us. And anyway we knew nothing about Nelda's death until the Friday morning when Bell came."

"Hmmm, yes," Bell put in, not liking any friction in the place he felt to be home. "And actually Magdalene, *we* knew nothing about Sir John's possible connection with Nelda's death until you spoke to Tayte on Monday."

Magdalene sighed. "Sorry, Diot. All that is true. Nor do we know, even now, that it is the same Sir John."

"It must be," Bell said. "It is too much coincidence for two Sir Johns to be looking for a whore's services and riding out of London that same night. So he *could* have killed Nelda—that is, he was not on a ship that arrived late at night . . ." Bell's voice, which had started out firm and definite drifted away. "But why? If he did not know she had stolen his letter, why would he fight with her out on the landing of the stair? I mean, if he were going to quarrel

with her, why not in her rooms?"

Letice tugged on Magdalene's sleeve and made a sign for a man in bed and another knocking at the door.

Magdalene nodded. "Letice thinks maybe another man came and Nelda told Sir John to go." She shrugged. "If she had drugged him and had the letter, she would be glad of the excuse to be rid of him before he checked on his possessions. And if he were half asleep from the drug, possibly he would not have come fully awake and become angry until they were out of the rooms."

"So Sir John becomes a likely suspect again," Bell said, then cocked his head to the side. "And how did this . . . er . . . Baby Face—really, Magdalene, can you not find more . . . ah . . . dignified names for your clients?"

"Ella named this one."

Bell chuckled but then frowned. "Yes, but how did the man learn that we were interested in a Sir John?"

Magdalene shook her head. "Ella must have told him. He never comes anywhere near any of the rest of us and will hardly speak even a word to me to say what he desires. It took him weeks to say he wished to stay the full night with Ella. Mainard brought him originally . . . and do not ask me how he found the courage to tell Mainard he needed a woman, but perhaps Mainard guessed. Mainard often senses what others are feeling. And I have noticed that although most people are afraid of Mainard's ugliness, all dumb animals trust him."

"Sometimes the dumb animals are cleverer than we very clever people. When my horses jib . . . I pay attention."

Magdalene smiled at him and continued, "He stood behind Mainard—" she grinned "—which is not very hard to do, of course, big as Mainard is, and only came out with the two pennies in his hand as soon as Mainard and I agreed on

a time for him to return. We offered Letice, because she could not speak, but he shrank away. Only Ella came from the kitchen at the moment, took one look at him, held out her hand . . . and he went to her."

"That is all very interesting," Bell said, "but *how* did Ella know what to tell him? We have been very careful not to talk about Nelda's death in front of her. Have we ever mentioned Sir John to her?"

Magdalene shrugged. "I have no idea. Odd things stick in Ella's mind. If we were talking about something we did not think would frighten her we could have mentioned Sir John's name, or she heard Diot speak his name at the gate as she came to meet Baby Face."

"But why should she repeat that to . . . ah . . . her client?"

"If she heard Diot turn Sir John away, she might have mentioned that to Baby Face. She definitely favors him as he is nearly as insatiable as she. She might have warned him to be sure to make his appointments in time or urged him to arrange a permanent appointment." She glanced around at the other women. "We will have to be more careful. It seems to me Ella is remembering more than she used to."

They all nodded and suddenly Letice yawned and folded up the cloth on which she had been working. She rose, dropped a kiss on the top of Bell's head, took her sewing basket back to set it beside her stool near the hearth, and went off to her room.

"Me too," Diot said. "I will be glad of a full night's sleep. I have clients all the rest of the week." She did not kiss Bell but gave him a friendly pat as she, too, picked up her work and left.

When her door closed, Bell lifted his tankard for a last drink and sighed. "Oh, how I regret my temper. Now I

must find Sir John and the only way I know is to go to Mandeville's captain in the Tower and ask where Mandeville is. You can imagine how willing he will be to tell me anything. Perhaps Winchester will write the request and say he wishes to speak to Sir John."

"You need not bother to try to follow Sir John to Mandeville," Magdalene said, her eyes on a tricky stitch in a new piece of embroidery. "I will be much surprised if he is not here in London, very likely at this house, either to-morrow or the next day. Half the knights in England seem to be named Sir John. How was I to know the man Tayte spoke of was a client? We are very lucky he did not arrive sooner, before we had worked out his connection with Nelda. We would have welcomed him. He could have done us a mischief if we were unprepared."

Bell stared at her. "What the devil are you talking about?" And then angrily suspicious, "Are you trying to trick me into staying here to protect you?"

Magdalene dropped her work to the table and looked up, a startled and indignant "no" on her lips. She had not been thinking of Bell at all, but almost instantly she realized that Sir John could serve her purpose of providing a threat so that she could offer Bell her favors to pay for his protection.

"Yes," she said, and laughed. "But not for the reason you think, you vain man. Consider this. Say Sir John did push Nelda down the stair by mistake. He would have been badly shaken. Say he calmed himself to the best of his ability and went to Baynard's Castle. He gave the news of Gloucester's letter to make himself welcome, but I doubt he was in any mood for idle talk. In any case, even if he is one of those who babbles when distraught, he must soon have gone to bed, so he could leave for Oxford or Devizes early the next day."

"So?"

"So he did not check on the letter he carried because his mind was full of Nelda's death. When he arrived at Oxford he was told that Mandeville had gone on to Devizes, and when he arrived at Devizes that his master had gone on again to Salisbury. I do not know why he did not look at the letter when he arrived at Oxford, but either when he set out for Salisbury or perhaps when he arrived there, he *must* have checked it—and discovered it was gone."

"Oh!"

"Yes, oh. What do you think the kind of man who spilled his master's news in Hugh Beaufort's keep for a lodging would do when he found the letter had been replaced with a useless piece of parchment?"

Bell pursed his lips. "He would never go near Mandeville but head back to London at once. If he could retrieve the letter, he could escape any blame for losing it. No one could know when he would succeed in obtaining the letter from Gloucester. No one could know what ship he took or when it arrived so his coming to Mandeville a few days later would not matter."

"Of course. He would just say he came on a later ship, or whatever other excuse for delay he wished to give. Now I do not think he would dare accuse anyone in Baynard's Castle of stealing the letter—and why should they? It is another thing to discredit Winchester. What worries me is that Sir John might go to Linley to demand the letter, thinking that Linley would have collected all of Nelda's valuables and Linley will tell him at once that Diot and I had taken them. Then likely Sir John will come here."

"Would not Linley say the bishop had everything? That is what you told him."

"Perhaps." Magdalene shrugged. "Although I think Linley would guess that Sir John would be enraged and

want to give him a possible target for venting that rage. Linley would know Sir John could not attack the bishop, and Linley did not strike me as a particularly brave man." She bent her head and picked up the piece of embroidery again. "Most likely he will say he never found any letter among Nelda's things."

Bell had an instant memory of one of Linley's companions intimating that Linley was useless as a fighter. "And Sir John will press him, and Linley will say he saw you and Diot taking away Nelda's valuables . . ."

"It is unfortunate that Sir John has been a client here several times. He knows at what times we entertain clients. He might even know how to come through the back gate so he would not need to ring the outside bell. Dulcie would not hear him if he sneaked through the kitchen."

Bell looked at her, looked away from her lovely face. *I think this is a trap for my wary but too-eager feet. And yet, it might happen just as she says.*

"Ah . . . damnation visit all of them!" he burst out torn between suspicion and concern. "I cannot be here all day. The bishop plans to visit St. Bartholomew's and perhaps if he has time St. Catherine's also. I doubt there will be any further attempt made on him, specially since his visits to the hospitals can have nothing to do with the conclave, but I cannot send him with only the men-at-arms."

Magdalene smiled at him. "Tom Watchman will be here during the day. He is no match for two knights, but if he can distract them and raise an alarm, as you know the women and I can defend ourselves."

CHAPTER 12

Once again Magdalene's anxiety seemed to have been excessive. Bell did warn Dulcie to keep the back door locked, and she did, but no one tried to get into the house that way. Magdalene sent Letice to her uncle to ask if she should tell any poppy eater where to find Umar so that they could buy direct from him, and Letice returned with a nearly indistinguishable scrawl to the effect that Umar said he would sell to anyone with sufficient silver.

All the clients came on time and left on time. Nothing at all unusual happened all day long. Attacking before she could be accused of deliberately awakening fears, Magdalene apologized to Bell when he arrived for the evening meal for dreaming up dangers. He only shook his head and said that travel was chancy and Sir John might not yet have arrived in London.

If he had, he did not trouble them that night. All the women had bed partners and Bell and Magdalene spent the time before they, too, retired—alas to different beds—going over the rings and seals Magdalene had taken from Nelda's hidden hoard. They were able to identify all but two of the rings and Bell said he had a nearly free day on the morrow and he would try to find out where those men were and speak to them.

Bell left at his usual early hour to report to the bishop what he planned to do about the tokens Nelda had held. Having gone early to bed, Magdalene wakened early also. Diot and Ella were less than a quarter candlemark behind

her. Baby Face had given Ella a purse in addition to his payment to Magdalene, and Diot had offered to take Ella to the East Chepe so she could spend some of the money. The rest Magdalene would deposit with her goldsmith, building a fund for Ella to live on when her beauty faded.

Letice came from her chamber shortly after Ella and Diot left. She broke her fast and then devoted herself to copying on some scraps of old parchment a simple story that Magdalene had written out for her. Occasionally she touched Magdalene's hand and pointed to a word and Magdalene said it aloud. Letice worked with a passionate devotion, fueled by the need to be able to express herself and also by her uncle's promise that he would find a place for her in his business if she ever desired it.

When the bell at the gate rang, Magdalene made a face. All her women were occupied at every time interval for the remainder of the week. Nonetheless she got up to answer. Next week was not full. As she rose, she thrust her hand through the slit in her skirt that ordinarily gave access to her pocket. For the last few days, it had also given access to a well-honed knife strapped to her thigh. Magdalene touched the hilt gingerly; she hated to draw a knife. Every time she did so she could feel the rush of hot, sticky blood flowing over her hand, smell it, hear the thud when her husband hit the floor . . .

Pushing away the too-vivid memory—why would it not fade as most memories did?—Magdalene hurried out, unlatched the gate, and opened it to the length of the chain. At first she saw no one. Then she looked down, expecting a child who had been used as a messenger.

"Oh!" she said, surprised, undoing the chain, "Tayte. Come in. What brings you here?"

As she said the words, Magdalene wished them unsaid.

The very last thing she wanted was for Tayte to tell her she had been dismissed by the man who kept her and that she wanted a place in the Old Priory Guesthouse. Tayte was just not the type to satisfy Magdalene's clients.

"You gave me three pennies," Tayte said, coming in. "My man said that you would expect some service for that."

"Good God no!" Magdalene exclaimed. "I took up your time that day and I felt you should be paid for it, that is all. I . . . I do not . . . ah . . . use casual women . . ."

"Oh, no!" Tatye's little face turned bright red, and then she scowled angrily and said, "What kind of a man would send his woman out to pay a debt with her body? We are not rich, but Di—my man could find a way to pay you back—"

"Forgive me, Tayte," Magdalene said. "I have led a harder life than you, my dear." Her lips twisted. "The men who used me—even the best of them—" she thought of the many times William had sent men to her, men he wanted cozened out of information or fed lies, "thought of my body as coin. I should have remembered that you have a single man . . ." She cocked her head. "Why does he not marry you, Tayte?"

The red, which had been fading to pink while Magdalene explained, darkened again. "His father would not permit it. I was a servant, mostly a sempstress in the house, and when my man spoke of his preference for me, his father cast me out. But he is working and saving, as am I, and soon he will open a shop of his own. We will marry then."

"Ah," Magdalene said, trying not to allow sadness to change her expression. Once he had his shop, would Tayte's man not look for a wife with a decent dowry to increase his business? She pushed the thought away and smiled at the diminutive girl. "Will you not come in, my

dear, and tell me how you thought you should serve me for my pennies?"

"Oh, no, I . . ."

"There is nothing in the Old Priory Guesthouse to distress you, I promise. We have no clients at this time of day. It is already growing warm. Do come in and have a sip of ale or wine."

Curiosity warred with fear and then Tayte nodded and followed Magdalene into the house. She paused just over the doorsill, almost seeming poised to run, but then settled more firmly on her feet and . . . was that a shade of disappointment that flicked across her face? Magdalene restrained a grin. Had the child expected a huge tub in the middle of the floor with writhing couples in it? Or perhaps grunting pairs in the corners of the room?

Tayte took a half step back toward the door when she saw what Letice was doing and whispered, "Is she drawing spells?"

"No, indeed," Magdalene said reassuringly. "Letice is mute. She cannot speak, so she is learning to read and write in order to tell others what she thinks and needs. Now, do you want ale or wine?"

"Learning to read and write?" Tayte repeated with as much wonder as if Magdalene had said Letice was learning to fly. Then she frowned. "Is that not denying God's will? If He made her silent, perhaps it is to keep locked away what she might tell others."

"I do not know," Magdalene said, this time somewhat sharply. "I do not presume to know God's will. Since Letice is learning much faster than most others, I can only assume God is pleased with her progress. Now, have you decided what you would like to drink?"

"Wine, please, but with water." Tayte smiled shyly after

shaking her head at Letice's activity. "We do not have wine often."

Magdalene got a goblet from the shelf, poured a third of a cup of William's good wine into it, and filled the cup with water. She set that at Bell's usual place at the table, and seated herself. Having taken a swallow of her own drink, which was ale, she cocked her head again.

"So what service did you think you owed me for my penny?"

Tayte sipped from the cup Magdalene had given her and made an appreciative murmur. "When you asked me about doings in Nelda's rooms—that was what you paid me to tell you—you seemed interested in that big man who sometimes went out with Nelda, the one who once beat her."

"Yes?"

"I was working in the shop yesterday—I mend for the woman who keeps it—and I saw him come in and go up. I was surprised when he did not knock and come down again. I thought the door to Nelda's rooms was locked."

"It was. Sir Bellamy locked it when we left and he took away the key Nelda's man had."

"Well, I suppose this man had a key of his own because he was not waiting on the landing and he was certainly not in my room—where I can promise you the door *was* locked. He must have gone inside Nelda's apartment. I was a little surprised, but it was none of my affair. However, I had to leave the door of my room open. It was hot, you know, and I was preparing dinner over a brazier. So I was near the door for whatever cool air I could find."

Magdalene said nothing but she had much ado not to grin. It was a most curious little mouse and had the best reasons for everything it did, and always reasons that had nothing to do with its curiosity.

"Well, just about the time my stew had heated through, I heard a kind of hoarse shout as if . . . as if the man were surprised or in pain and there was a crash and then more crashes."

"Like a fight taking place?"

"Perhaps, but I would swear that no one else had gone up to Nelda's rooms. No, the sound was more as if the big man had lost his temper and was smashing the furniture. And then there was a heavy thud . . . and then nothing."

"What do you mean, nothing? I freely admit that if I had heard all that, I would have been standing with my ear pressed to the door for what happened next."

"Well . . ." Tatye's face grew a little pinker. She drank from her cup again. "I did not do *that,* but I could not help but pay attention. I even moved so I could see Nelda's door. But he never came out and I watched all afternoon, and when my man came I told him and he said he thought you would want to know and that I owed it to you . . . It was one of your pennies that bought the stew; we do not have meat very often. And when the man did not come out all night—" she blushed again "—although the door was closed then, of course, and we were busy so we might have missed hearing him go. Anyway, I decided to come and tell you."

You mean that you and your man want to know what happened, Magdalene thought, amused. But she chided herself for her criticism; after all, she wanted to know also.

"I am glad you did," Magdalene said, "but there is nothing I can do about it right now. Sir Bellamy is the one who has the key. When he comes, I will tell him what you have told me. Likely he will be willing to go to Nelda's apartment and look." She hesitated, saw the disappointment on the little mouse's face, and added, "I will come and tell you what we find, unless, of course, Sir Bellamy forbids me."

Tayte sighed. "I hope he does not, but men do seem to take a pleasure in telling women what to do."

They did, indeed, Magdalene thought, as she watched Tayte lift her cup and drain it, but she made no reply, and Tayte said a formal thanks, rose, and scuttled out of the door. Magdalene followed her to put the chain back on the gate. She stood a moment, looking rather blankly at the wood.

Magdalene itched to start for Nelda's place, but Diot, who could pick the lock, was heaven-alone knew where with Ella, and she had never thought to ask Bell for the key. When Diot returned—no, they had to eat dinner because all of the women had clients coming. Nor could Diot afford to be late because she had to be rid of that client in good time to take another. Magdalene sighed. She would have to wait for Bell.

She had hoped Bell would come in time to have dinner with them, but he did not. He did not, in fact, arrive until the evening meal was sitting on the table. He had not rung the bell, merely strode in through the open door and made for his usual spot. He looked hot and dusty and emptied the wine cup sitting by his place in a few long swallows. Then, he smiled at everyone and said, "Good day to you all."

A burst of laughter greeted his remark, and Bell laughed also and sat down. "A long, hot day," he said, "but nearly all my questions were answered and the answers will not make my life more difficult." A sidelong glance first in Ella's direction and then at Magdalene indicated that it would be too difficult to explain himself in Ella's presence.

Magdalene understood that he must have been able to track down most of the men who had given Nelda tokens and that they did not seem likely to be involved in her death. She could wait for further details without impatience.

"I have had a most interesting day myself," she said. "Do you remember the woman who lives in the other room in Linley's house? She was the one who told me about Sir John being with Nelda."

Bell nodded wordlessly, his mouth being full of a big bite of a goose and egg pie, and Magdalene recited to him the gist of Tayte's information.

"Gehard," Bell said when he had swallowed. "He must have gone there to look for his seal. How the devil did he get in? Not with Linley's key, I have that."

"He might have had his own key," Magdalene offered. "He went with Nelda to The Saracen's Head when she bought the poppy from Umar."

"Do you think Nelda would trust him so far as a key to her rooms?" Diot asked. "I find that hard to believe. She was not a trusting person."

"Keys should be hung on the wall. I would be afraid of losing a key if I carried it," Ella said.

"Hmmm." Magdalene, as she often did, followed Ella's innocent remark farther. "It is not impossible that Gehard somehow gained possession of Nelda's key long enough to have a copy made. And there was Nelda's own key. We had forgotten about that. I wonder what happened to it? But does that mean he never approached Linley about his lost seal? Possibly that Linley did not know he intended to search Nelda's apartment?"

Bell shrugged. "I do not know, but it does seem to me that if Gehard thought Linley had got Nelda's possessions and asked for them, Linley would have told Gehard that you, or the bishop, had them now. From what his fellow captains in Surrey's service said, Linley was no great hero. Yet Gehard did not come here."

"Thank God for that!" Magdalene exclaimed. "With a full house I do not need the kind of riot that one would make."

To that, Bell made no direct response, but he said, as if he hardly heard her, "So when he did not find the seal, he lost his temper and broke up the furniture." He nodded. "I can imagine him doing that, but why then did he not leave?"

"There was that heavy thud Tayte mentioned."

"Perhaps he tripped on something and fell," Diot said, and then shook her head. "But being the man you implied he was, Bell, tripping and falling should have made him more furious so that he broke up more furniture. Only Magdalene said it was quiet after that. And whatever happened, it still does not explain why he did not leave."

"Hit his head?" Bell suggested. "And we don't know that he didn't leave later. From what Magdalene says, Tayte and her man closed her door after the man arrived and—" Bell chuckled "—were busy."

The laugh died in his throat and his expression froze. Magdalene's hand tightened on the cup she held. Letice looked down at the piece of pasty in her hand. Diot looked away toward the window.

"I was very busy this morning," Ella said, smiling. "Diot was kind enough to take me to the East Chepe. Baby Face had left me a purse . . ." She turned to Magdalene and said earnestly, "I tried to give it back to him, but he would have none of it and said it was for me. I told him you gave me money enough—"

"It was something he wished you to have, likely so you could buy something that you could say came from him since he is too timid to buy you a gift himself."

Ella's eyes opened wide. "That is just what Diot said," she marveled. "And it sounded right, so I bought a really beautiful clasp to hold my hair, and when he comes I will show it to him and tell him what you said, Magdalene, and that I would always think of him when I put it in my hair."

Magdalene opened her mouth to commend this idea, but the bell of St. Mary Overy pealed the hour of Vespers. In a little while, the men who planned to spend the night in the Old Priory Guesthouse would be arriving. Bell hastily swallowed the remains of the pottage in his bowl and took more of the cold sliced meat, which he slapped on a piece of bread. He swung over the bench and pulled his sword belt over his shoulder. With both hands free, he added a wedge of cheese to the bread and meat, caught up the cup of ale, and walked down the corridor toward the room in which he slept.

"Where is Bell going?" Ella asked.

"To his room," Magdalene said patiently, but her voice trembled slightly. "You know some of our guests do not like it known that they come here. They would be uncomfortable and unhappy if they saw Bell or he saw them. That is why you must never speak to any of your friends when you meet them outside this house."

"Oh, yes." Ella smiled. "I never speak to any of my friends when I see them in the market. Today I saw Master Long Robe and I walked right by him, even though I will see him tonight. And now I remember about Bell."

"I am glad you remember."

"I saw that he took his sword with him. It is safe for us if he is in the house. I remember when that silly student came in the middle of the night and everyone screamed. Bell captured him with his sword. So if that man who fell and hit his head—was he running when he fell? My mother always told me not to run lest I fall."

"That is very wise," Magdalene said, smiling at Ella. The strain was gone from her voice. Sometimes Ella's babble was priceless.

But for once Ella did not respond with delight to the words of praise. She frowned, then nodded. "He will not come here and break our furniture because Bell will be here."

Magdalene could not help smiling. "Bell is very useful."

She lifted her cup and drained the ale, but she did not finish the food she had taken. Ella looked at the pasty and then shook her head. Diot and Letice put the last bites they had been eating into their mouths. Then all the women began to clear the table. Dulcie came and wiped it clean. They had hardly settled on their stools near the empty hearth, when the bell at the gate pealed.

When all the women were behind closed doors with their clients, Magdalene continued to embroider for perhaps half a candlemark. She looked up when she heard a door open and dropped her gaze hastily to her work again. Bell came softly down the corridor and sat on Diot's stool, across from Magdalene.

"Do you have the key to Nelda's rooms with you?" she asked.

Bell shook his head. "It is in my strongbox in the bishop's keeping. I thought of going to get it, but it is really too late to go to Nelda's rooms. By the time I got there, it would be too dark to see anything."

Magdalene laughed. "And I would have murdered you if you did not take me, but I cannot say I am sorry you do not have the key. You know I do not like to leave the house when my women are at work, even though the three men who are being entertained are hardly likely to cause any trouble." She sighed as she remembered her day-long frustration because she could not get into Nelda's rooms, and added, "You are a dreadful temptation."

"Am I?" A fist clenched on Bell's knee.

Magdalene laughed. "You know you are, you pretty peacock, but I am not talking about that. I have been burning up with curiosity ever since Tayte left. If you had had the key, I would have gone with you."

He was silent for a while, first looking down at his own hands and loosening the fists. Then he said, as if the previous remarks about temptation had not been made, "As you suspected, I spent the day chasing down the poppy takers. They were all merchants of one kind or another and their seals were easily traced. Fortunately, they had been supplied recently, but they were appalled when I told them that Nelda was dead."

"Did any seem to be hard pressed to pay for what they desired?"

"No. From what I saw they were all prosperous, but . . ." He frowned and then shook his head. "Perhaps it is old memories that make me distrust any man who loves the poppy. Still, as of today, I will take oath that none of those to whom I spoke threw her down the stairs."

Magdalene shrugged. "Whores hear about most dangerous vices, but I never heard of this one. In any case, I cannot believe—even if one of them did kill Nelda—that any merchant in the city would carry a whore's body to the bishop's house. And who did that, I think, is the important thing to discover. More and more I am convinced her death was an accident. The attack on the bishop was not. I think we need not worry about the poppy takers any more."

Bell nodded. "Most, I think will shake off their desire, but two . . ."

"They need not do without, any of them. I sent Letice to her uncle yesterday morning and he says that Umar will sell to anyone who comes with sufficient silver."

"Oh, good! Then I need not worry about them going to Linley and him sending them to you. I will return their rings tomorrow and tell them how to find The Saracen's Head."

For a moment Magdalene was surprised that he knew where the place was and then she remembered that he had taken Letice there one day when she had been threatened. He was a good man, kind, and truly fond of her women without the smallest desire for any of them. Most men, knowing them to be whores would think of trying them out, but Bell acted as if they were sisters. He had sisters, she recalled, and loved them and was loved in return. She had to strangle a laugh when she thought of those sisters' horror had they known where Bell's affection for them had led him.

But thinking of Bell's attitude toward her women reminded her of how her mention of temptation had stirred him. Now she grinned at him. "I am almost sorry that we will not suffer any threat of invasion by desperate poppy-takers."

He had been slumped forward a bit, elbows on his knees, idly watching her use her needle. He looked up, frowning. "That is not a matter for jest."

She had been about to suggest that if she had needed protection from desperate men, she could hire him to protect her and her house . . . and pay with her body. But suddenly her mouth went dry. She suspected if she made the proposal and he refused, he would leave the house and not return. She needed a real threat, needed to be truly afraid herself, before she made that offer.

So instead she said, “You know the oddest things, Bell. Like the fact that bodies get stiff after death, and what kind of wounds what kind of knives make, and now that eating poppy can make a man desperate to eat more.”

“I’ve had an odds and ends kind of life,” he said, now smiling more easily. “So my head is full of odds and ends things. You knew that when I fled the monastery where my parents had sent me to be educated to enter the Church I took a place on a merchant ship. I thought that would make it much harder for them to catch me and send me back. I could not thole the thought of a life of quiet prayer, not at fifteen when I had seen the flash of steel in a man’s hand and the joy of fighting in his eyes. Still the brothers, at least two of them, the prior and the infirmarian, were men with bright and lively minds. They taught me not only to read and to write but to look around me and truly see.”

As he spoke, his lips stayed curved in a faint smile, his body was relaxed, and his eyes were fixed into the distance of memory. He spoke about the sweet and the bitter of those days in the past, of the hardship of life aboard ship and the danger from pirates and from storm and also of his intense joy in being free and his passionate interest in the strange places where the ship made port.

He had been fortunate. The captain of that ship was a good man and he had favored Bell not only for his strong arm and skill with a sword, but for his education, his manners, and his ability to learn new things. He had taught Bell out of the experience of a lifetime of strange and harrowing situations, and when experience had honed Bell’s fighting skills to their peak he had made Bell the leader of the marines—where, as the youngest of them, he had to learn even more and faster about human nature to hold his place.

Magdalene listened eagerly. She knew some of what Bell was telling her from a comment here and there and brief snatches of pillow talk. But she had not heard a connected history, and she was very glad she had not tried to lure him back into her bed. It was too soon, she thought. He needed to remember those wild early years, remember the compromises he had made and that one could live with compromise.

One and then another of the women slipped out of her room, glanced back into the common room and waved gaily on her way to the kitchen to fetch a midnight bite to eat and drink. When the last had trotted back into her bedchamber, Bell suddenly yawned and stretched.

"Whatever started me on the story of my life?" he asked grinning at Magdalene and shaking his head.

Magdalene laughed. "I did. I wanted to know how you picked up all the things you know. You are quite a remarkable man, Bell."

He uttered an uneasy laugh. "No. I have many faults—" he hesitated and then added harshly, "And many weaknesses."

"I did not say you were a saint," Magdalene retorted. "I said you were remarkable. I would not like you much if you were a saint, but I am very fond of you just as you are."

Bell shifted uneasily on the stool. "You are fond of too many people," he said.

"No." Magdalene shook her head. "One cannot be fond of too many people. Did your mother love only one of her children? Was not her heart large enough to hold you all?"

He stood up abruptly. "But of men there is only my father."

Magdalene caught her needle in the fabric of her work

and looked up. "Your mother is a fortunate woman. Do not think I do not envy her—but the past cannot be undone. Life must be lived as a compromise between past and future. You have made compromises in the past."

Before he could speak or turn away, she put her embroidery frame aside, stood up, and said in an entirely different tone of voice, "Do not you dare go to Nelda's place without me in the morning. Send Dulcie in to wake me if I am not waiting for you when you come back with the key."

CHAPTER 13

Bell lay on his belly for some time thinking of what had passed between Magdalene and himself. To his surprise he was not particularly sexually aroused. Whenever he thought of Magdalene, he felt desire but now it was not an urgent need, just a longing for being with her, for talking as they had talked but lying cozily in bed, for the warmth of her soft body beside him.

Partly the lack of urgency was because he knew that he would only have had to hold out his hand to her and she would have taken him. It was very clear to him that she had thought again about the cold rejection of their first meeting. In a way that made him uneasy. He wondered if she would welcome him and then thrust him away as he had abandoned her.

Yet she was not abandoned, whether he left her or not. She had a haven and a protector. Bell could feel his teeth set. She had said she loved the man, yet William of Ypres drew her into danger for his own purposes without a second thought. And she knew it. And she did not care. What had she said? That when one was so deeply in debt to another, if you did not hate that other with every fiber of your being, then you loved him.

Thinking of sharing her was a burning in Bell's gut and a sour taste in his mouth. He shifted uneasily in the cot. But at least she had never lied to him, never pretended to be other than she was, never pretended there was no other man.

Would he have preferred the lie, he wondered? Honesty forced him to admit he would, but then when he learned the truth . . . Suddenly he snorted gently. If Magdalene had wanted to lie to him, he would never have learned the truth.

He flopped over on his back and stared up into the blackness of the ceiling. Perhaps she was not so far wrong in saying her heart was large enough to hold more than one. She certainly loved her women, and he did not begrudge them her affection. But another man . . . Could he tolerate that? Nonsense, he had tolerated it for months, just pushing it to the back of his mind. And she wanted him; he could feel that. And when she spoke of William . . . No, never desire. Affection, yes; desire, no.

Was that difference enough? His mind winced away from that question and away from why he had asked it of himself. Instead he deliberately turned his mind to Magdalene saying that discovering who ordered involving the bishop was more important than the death of the whore. At first she had wanted to avenge that death because no one else would think it important enough to avenge. Now that it seemed likely Nelda's death had been an accident, she saw the protection of the bishop as essential. Bell shifted. The cot creaked.

He must be careful not to read his own feelings into Magdalene. Her care for Winchester was because it benefited her, because he was a reasonable landlord, and perhaps because he was willing to talk to her; many churchmen were not. She had no loyalty to the bishop. Still she recognized his good qualities. It was most unlikely that he and Magdalene would find themselves at political cross purposes.

Bell drew a long, deep breath. He would take her back. But on his own terms. Suddenly Bell grinned into the dark. No, not his terms . . . hers. She insisted she was a whore and that he must recognize that fact. Well then, he would pay her like a whore. Smiling, Bell closed his eyes and slept.

He woke just at dawn feeling well rested. If he had dreamed, he did not remember. Dulcie was already awake; she readily put some cold meat and bread and cheese on the work table in the kitchen and went to the cellar to draw some ale for him from the barrel kept there.

At the bishop's house, he left orders for drill and guard duty with Levin and told his man if he were needed, he could be found at the house of the whore who had been killed. He left the same information with the clerk half asleep at the table near the stair to the bishop's rooms.

Bell was not surprised to find Magdalene waiting, just finishing breaking her own fast. She was no more likely to oversleep when she had decided to do something than he was. He smiled at her, thinking about how she would react when he offered to pay her. Her brows went up.

"You are very cheerful this morning," she said.

"I had a good night's sleep," Bell replied blandly and did not smile at her surprised and suspicious look. "I have the key," he added. "Shall we go?"

"Just let me get my veil."

Although she threw the fine scarf over her shoulders, Magdalene did not, in fact, veil her face. The distance to Nelda's rooms was short, and it was it was still warm enough to make covering her face uncomfortable. She did not think with Bell as escort that anyone would accost her. A single drunk, staggering down the main road, did make a grab, but Bell merely pushed him away. Magdalene's glance at his face told her nothing. His expression was still deliberately bland; she had to resist an impulse to kick him in the shin.

The shop on the street level of Nelda's house was closed

but the outer door was as usual unlocked and they went up without hindrance, Bell taking the key from his pouch as they climbed the stairs. What struck them both when Bell unlocked the door and swung it open was not the disorder, the table knocked loose from its trestles and the stools overturned and scattered around, but the terrible stench. Both started to back away from the door and then Bell stopped and pointed.

"Look."

"That is why he never left," Magdalene murmured. "He was dead." She peered through the gloom. "But how?"

"We need a light," Bell said, backing away farther and turning toward the other door.

"For God's sake, open the shutter and let in some fresh air," Magdalene urged, lifting her veil to cover her nose and mouth.

"Not yet," Bell said in a rather choked voice. "I want to look at it first." He took the few steps to Tayte's door on which he banged his fist. "There's been an accident," he called. "I need to borrow a light."

Meanwhile Magdalene had taken a deep breath out on the landing and, taking care not to breathe again, had stepped into the room. There was just enough light leaking through the shuttered window to see a candleholder on a shelf. She hurried to grab it and rushed out of the room again, proffering the candle to Bell just as Tayte's door opened and the mouse peered out. Bell held the candle forward as the door started to close again.

"Light the candle for Sir Bellamy, Tayte," Magdalene said around Bell's shoulder.

"What is that dreadful smell?" Tayte cried.

"A dead man after a day lying in this heat," Bell said.

"Dead?" Tayte whimpered. "Oh. Oh. Oh what will we

do? We shall be found. And we had nothing to do with the dead man. I swear."

A young man appeared suddenly behind Tayte's shoulder, carrying a burning spill. He put the girl gently aside and reached beyond her to light the candle Bell held. "How did he die?" he asked. "Tayte told me that she heard a lot of noise yesterday afternoon, like furniture breaking, but she only saw the one man enter Nelda's rooms."

"I don't know how he died," Bell answered. "I am not even sure who is dead. The room was too dark to see from the doorway and with the way it stinks I didn't step in. We need the sheriff or his deputy."

"No!" Tayte cried.

"Don't be silly," the young man said to her, putting an arm around her waist and giving her a hug. "I will go off to my work as I was just about to do, and you will help Sir Bellamy as best you can. There will be no reason for you or anyone else to speak of me, will there?"

"Not so long as Tayte can be found," Bell said promptly. "In the most unlikely circumstance that it seems you have information I need, I will be able to find you . . . if I must."

"Good enough," the young man said as he gave Tayte a last squeeze and stepped out past her. He paused for a moment at the top of the stair to add, "Truly I know nothing about any of this, beyond what Tayte has told me. And that she can tell you herself."

"I cannot go to the sheriff, I cannot," Tayte whimpered when her man had clattered down the stair and out the door.

"No," Magdalene said before Bell could speak. "There is no need. Run instead to my house—you know where that is—and tell the lady who answers the bell at the gate to rouse Tom Watchman and tell him I need him. He will accompany you back here. Can you do that, my dear?"

Tayte huddled her arms around herself, but nodded. She went back inside to put on her shoes.

"I was going to go to the sheriff," Bell said. "It would be foolish to send her. Who would listen to her?"

"I know you were," Magdalene said, "but I did not want to be left here alone with the body."

Bell blinked. "You were afraid?"

Magdalene shook her head impatiently, but she was afraid. The body on the floor sent chills through her, and brought back memories of past terror, such terror as froze the blood in her body. But there was no blood, she told herself staring at the corpse; there was no dark pool spreading from the twitching, dying hulk and dripping from the knife in her hand.

Again over the memory of freezing fear came a faint wash of satisfaction. Terrified as she was, she had not yielded. She had cleaned the knife on her gown and then torn it off and flung it on the floor not far from her husband's body. She had taken the key of the strongbox from around his neck, wiped her bloody hand on the already bloodied gown, taken the money, every broken farthing, and then begun to pack.

How fortunate his roaring rage had sent the servants running from the house. There had been time for her to escape. She knew the servants would not return until the next morning, usually to find her beaten bloody and unconscious. This time, staggering drunk, her husband had threatened worse than a beating. She was too beautiful, he said. Too many men praised her. He would cut off her nose and her lips. He had drawn his knife, laughing at her pleas . . .

"Magdalene?" Bell asked uncertainly into the silence.

"I am not afraid of the dead," she said, making sure her

voice was steady, "you know that. I am afraid of what the sheriff would say if he found me here alone. Would he not ask what I had stolen? What I had changed or rearranged so that my guilt would be hidden?"

"Why should you stay at all?" But as soon as the words were out of his mouth, Bell laughed. "That was a stupid remark."

"It certainly was. You think Tayte would not name me at the first question? Or her young man, if he were pressed? Oh no. Either we can send Tom for the sheriff and both remain here or Tom can stay with me outside the door and swear to that when the sheriff comes."

Bell was still grinning. "It is true that your presence here could not be hidden, but I was not thinking of that. I was thinking that your curiosity would kill you if you went away before we discovered who was dead and why and how."

In fact it was her curiosity that kept her there—and perhaps the need to bury her memories under the whys and wherefores of this body. Magdalene knew she had no need to fear the sheriff of Southwark. Perhaps if she had been found standing over a corpse with a knife or poison in her hand, he would have asked her some pointed questions . . . perhaps. His instructions from William of Ypres were clear and to the point. Magdalene was William's. She, her women, and the Old Priory Guesthouse were to be protected against anything.

Thus the sheriff on being told by Tom that Sir Bellamy and Mistress Magdalene had found a dead body, actually came himself with his two assistants to investigate. He was deeply relieved that Bell, whom he knew from other investigations, would stand witness that he and Magdalene had come to the house together and had not been apart since that time.

The stench of the corpse having been somewhat diminished by the exchange of air through the open door, the sheriff walked in, reaching to open the shutter too. Bell stopped him, breathing shallowly, but holding up the candle to examine the bar that held the ill-fitted boards in place. Then he lifted the bar, pulled the shutter from the window, and leaned out to look at the window sill and the outer wall of the house.

"What the devil are you doing?" the sheriff asked.

"Magdalene and I unlocked the door. I am making sure that no one left through the window. The young woman who told Magdalene about the noise in the empty rooms said she heard someone come in, but did not hear anyone leave."

"Why should she tell Magdalene about the noise?"

"The woman who lived here, Nelda Roundheels, she was called, was killed last Thursday. Her body, as you no doubt heard, was carried to the bishop of Winchester's house and left there for him to find. Since we did not know who the woman was and she was dressed as a whore, the bishop asked Magdalene to discover what she could."

The sheriff grimaced. "I knew about Nelda. Can't say I was sorry. I've had complaints about her."

Bell nodded acceptance. "We heard that she stole and used drugs to make sure her clients slept well. As part of her attempt to find out what Winchester wanted to know, Magdalene questioned the girl who lives in the room next door. And she told the girl that if she saw or heard anything strange in Nelda's rooms, she should bring that information."

"Ah," the sheriff said and then, still standing by the

window where the stench was not so fierce, gestured at the body on the floor. "So who is that?"

Bell turned from examining the window sill, the wall, and the unpromising packed earth below. In the light coming from the window, he saw the dead man's features clearly.

"Shit!" he muttered, and then added more loudly, "That is Gehard fitzRobert. He is, or rather was, Lord Geoffrey de Mandeville's man."

"FitzRobert?" The sheriff took a deep breath to hold, then went closer, looked down at the corpse, and snorted. He retreated to the window again. "So it is. He's not much loss either. Came roaring into my office a couple of times complaining about being thrown out by a brothel keeper for being too rough. Too rough? I can't think what he was doing if one of those stew-keepers thought it was too rough." He paused, looking at the body, which showed no sign of a wound, and asked, "Why do you care if he died?"

Now Bell had approached the corpse. He stared down at it, noting that the lips looked blistered and the chin and front of the tunic were marked with vomit. He then knelt, seized the body by an arm, and turned it over. It flopped limply—all the stiffness that came after death gone; Bell had to use both hands to turn it onto its belly. The limpness confirmed to his mind that Gehard had died a day and a half earlier, when Tayte had heard the noise.

There was no more sign of a wound on the back than on the front and not a speck of blood, but the man's braies and tunic were stained with once-liquid feces. Bell backed away, swallowing nausea, and stuck his head out of the window to breathe the less-tainted air. He straightened to find the sheriff staring at him.

"Well? So a man has a fit and dies. That happens to big

men like Gehard, doesn't it? Why do you care?"

"Because he didn't just die of a fit. Look at his mouth. It is burnt. He vomited and he voided. The man was poisoned."

The sheriff breathed an exasperated sigh. "Damn you, Bellamy, you always have to find the hardest way to do anything! He was all alone. If he was poisoned, he must have taken the poison himself. So he killed himself. That means an unhallowed grave and damnation."

So the sheriff had seen the signs of poison and decided to be deliberately blind to get Gehard the mercy of a grave in hallowed ground. Bell shook his head and uttered a mirthless crack of laughter. He had had too much of a Church background to think you could fool God and be saved from damnation by being buried in hallowed ground.

"Oh, I am sure Gehard will be buried in hallowed ground," he said, "but you will like the reason even less than my noticing the poison. This is no self-killing. No one who knew Gehard would believe that. He was murdered by poison. I am quite sure of it."

"He was alone."

"Yes." Bell frowned. "So either he was given the poison before he came to the house and it only took him when he was here, or someone gave him something to take with him and he ate or drank it here."

"Bellamy, you are a pain in the arse! Do you think I have nothing better to do than to search out every man who spoke to Gehard the day before yesterday?"

"Well, not every man—and woman too, of course. A woman could have poisoned him as easily as a man. No, there is no need to question very many. From what I have heard about Gehard and myself observed, his temper was not such as to provide him with many acquaintances. Beside that, the fact that he is here in these rooms implies to me that his death may be connected to that of the whore."

"Just because he is here? In these rooms? Nelda died a week ago. Why could he not be here to rent these rooms?"

Bell shook his head. "Gehard lodges in the Tower. He was leader of one of the troops Mandeville left as guards. He knew Nelda well and told me when I first met him that Nelda was a thieving bitch and deserved what befell her." He heaved an exasperated sigh. "Until I found him here, dead, I thought he was the one who had killed her. Now . . . I must begin all over again."

For a long moment the sheriff stared at Bell, then shook his head. "Who cares who pushed the whore down the stair? Likely that was not deliberate murder but an accident."

"Yes, but taking her body and setting it in the bishop's bedchamber was *not* an accident. I had strong suspicion, but no proof, that Gehard hired men to attack Winchester on his way to meet with the archbishop at Lambeth on Saturday last. Thus it seemed to me that it was possible that he had moved Nelda's body too."

"Why then do you care who killed him? Dead, he is no danger to Winchester."

"Because I cannot believe that Gehard would, all on his own, hire a troop to attack the bishop. I doubt he had sufficient coin. However, if he were bidden to do that and paid for it, might he not think that dropping Nelda's corpse in Winchester's house would be pleasing to the one who paid him to hire the troop? Might he not think he would be rewarded for that?"

"Hmmm. I suppose that is possible."

"I said I had strong suspicion that Gehard had hired those men, but that was not from the men—"

"No," the sheriff interrupted drily. "All of those are dead

in unpleasant ways. I am surprised you could not extract more information from them. They were not the kind to hold out against torture for loyalty."

Bell sighed. "I had killed the leader of the troop in the battle. He was the only one who knew who hired them."

The sheriff burst out laughing. "That will teach you to be so efficient."

Bell sighed again. "Well, I doubt it. In the heat of battle, one does not think too far in advance of the next blow. But the thing is that I came upon Gehard drunk and his tongue slipped. He said the men were instructed not to harm the bishop . . . which says to me that he gave, or knew who gave, that instruction. So, *why* is Gehard dead? Because the one who hired him to send that troop against the bishop heard of his drunken slip of the tongue and decided Gehard had become dangerous to him?"

"I see." The sheriff was no longer laughing. "But Gehard was Mandeville's man. Mandeville is with the king."

Bell shrugged. "No way do I think I can bring this to roost on Mandeville . . . but I want to *know* so that the bishop will know."

Now it was the sheriff who sighed. "I will go along with you so far as to send my men out to question the apothecaries in Southwark to discover if any sold . . . hmmm . . . do you know which poison it is?"

"No, but likely if you send the body to the hospital of St. Catherine, they will be able to make a guess at least."

The sheriff nodded and stepped out onto the stair landing to instruct his men. Bell mentioned that there was a bed in the next chamber with a blanket that they could use to wrap the corpse. When they had carried the body away, the sheriff glanced around the room, said to Bell that the disorder all seemed likely to have been caused by Gehard's death throes, and then took his leave.

Bell watched him go rather blankly and then, feeling quite sure he was forgetting something important, looked around also, jerking slightly as Magdalene seemed to appear from nowhere.

"Good God," he said. "I had forgot that you came with me. Where have you been all this time?"

Magdalene laughed. "Mostly standing by the bedroom door where the stink was less and listening to you." She sobered and frowned. "I don't think there was time enough after you spoke to Gehard for Mandeville to have ordered his death."

"No, neither do I, but the idea induced the sheriff to be of some help. He, too, would want to know if Mandeville was involved. Do you by any chance have a guess as to what the poison might have been?"

Magdalene shuddered. "I know nothing about poisons—" she hesitated, thinking that she knew too much about knives, and then went on hastily "—except . . ."

"Except?" Bell's brows went up.

"That man—oh, yes, Borc was his name—did you not tell me that when he was poisoned by lily of the valley he also voided and vomited?"

"Yes." Bell frowned. "But no. I do not think it was lily of the valley this time. Gehard's mouth was blistered, as if he had swallowed some corrosive. Nothing as strong, though, as lye. I hope the infirmarian at St. Catherine's will know."

"At least I know that it must be a quick acting poison."

"I thought you said you knew nothing about poisons."

"And so I do not, but I know how he took the poison."

Bell looked at her blankly. "How? How do you know that?"

Magdalene pointed. “Because that flagon was not here on the day we came to gather up Nelda’s possessions.”

Bell followed the line of her finger and, sure enough, lying on its side against the partition that separated the bedroom from the main room was a hard leather flagon. He looked from the flagon to the overturned table and saw that it was likely enough that the flagon had been thrown to the floor when Gehard’s death convulsions knocked the table over.

“Are you sure?” he asked.

“Of course I am sure. Diot and I looked in every vessel that could hold anything. Women often keep unimportant trinkets or something they are willing to give away in a cup or a pitcher not often used. That flagon was not here. In fact, there was a pitcher—yes, there it is on the shelf—but there was no flagon of any kind.”

Bell was staring at the pitcher standing on the shelf. Then he looked back at the flagon. “Then whoever bought the flagon of wine—it is wine, is it not?”

He went over to it. The curve of the lip had kept it from emptying itself completely and he took it carefully and set it upright, bending his head a little to look inside.

“Be careful,” Magdalene cried. “Do not smell it. There are smells that can kill.”

Bell smiled, pleased by her fear for him. “I remember. But there is enough in here I think to make it worth while to bring this to St. Catherine’s infirmarian. Then we will be sure if it was what was in this flagon that killed Gehard. But if it was, whoever bought the wine and poison did not come from these rooms. He would have taken the pitcher.”

“Oh. Yes.” Now Magdalene frowned and pointed again. “Look, there is a cup also.” She went and picked it up. “It is empty but there had been wine in it.”

Bell came and took the cup from her. "There may not be enough remaining, but I will take it to the infirmarian too. It is possible it will tell him something." He looked around. "Is there anything else we need to look at here?"

"Not in these rooms, but I must ask Tayte whether Gehard brought the flagon with him. I do not remember that she mentioned it, but she might not have thought that important."

Bell shook his head. "If he did not bring it, how did it get here? You said the girl swore he came alone and that no one else came."

"While she was watching," Magdalene said slowly. Her mind chasing another thought, she added somewhat absently, "You remember after her man came, they were . . . busy."

"I remember," Bell snapped angrily. "But that was after she heard the noise in Nelda's apartment."

Magdalene looked up, startled by Bell's tone. Then the word 'busy' connected in her mind with what Tatye was busy doing, and she barely suppressed a grin. Pretending she had not noticed his anger or understood it, she said, "Yes, of course, but there has been something tickling in my head and it just came clear. Whoever killed Gehard must be the one who knocked Nelda down the stair because only that person would have Nelda's keys. Either he took the key from her body or, if she had not locked the apartment, found it inside."

"Or Gehard himself killed her and took the key. But then, who brought the poisoned wine? Could it have been meant for Nelda by someone who did not know she was dead? Or meant for Linley, who owns the place?"

"No," Magdalene said, "because after you took Linley's key, we did lock the apartment when we left. No one who did not have the key could have got in without breaking the lock or the door."

Bell nodded. "True, thank God and all his saints. I did not need to suspect the whole of London and Southwark. Well, I will take myself to St. Catherine's and give the infirmarian this flagon and cup and then go on to the Tower to try to speak to Gehard's men."

Magdalene giggled. "I hope a new captain is on duty."

Bell sighed. "I hope so too."

"I'll speak to Tayte and then go back to the Old Priory Guesthouse. If the infirmarian can tell what poison was used, come and tell me. I know the Guildmaster of the Apothecary Guild. He might be able to tell us who regularly sells poisons."

CHAPTER 14

Bell wondered, as he made his way to the riverside and found a boatman to take him downriver and across the Thames to St. Catherine's Hospital, what tack he should take with the captain in the Tower. Perhaps he should try to find Gehard's men off duty and question them without the captain's order and permission? It was briefly a tempting notion, but second thoughts made it less appealing. Without an order, the men might not be willing to talk to him and finding them a few at a time in an ale house was too chancy. Besides, with any luck, there might be a new captain on duty.

That future problem was dismissed from his mind when he was directed to the hospital mortuary and found Gehard's body already unclothed and under scrutiny. The infirmarian looked up at him and shook his head.

"Sir Bellamy. Again. And again with a problem."

"Yes, brother. I need to know from what poison this man died. I have here a cup, but it is empty, and a flagon holding, I think, the remains of the wine he drank just before he died."

The monk's face sobered and he took the cup from Bell's hand first. He smelled it, rubbed his finger over the stain of wine near the bottom, sniffed the finger and then touched his tongue to it. After a moment he shook his head.

"Perhaps there was not enough dried on the cup, but it seems to be only wine." Putting the cup down on the table beside the corpse, he reached for the flagon. Very carefully he sniffed it, and quickly pulled his head away. He looked at the cup and shook his head. Then he tilted the flagon so that a single drop ran onto his middle finger. He then stared down at the finger, after a moment closed his eyes, and finally touched the liquid on his finger with the tip of his tongue.

Having placed the flagon carefully on the foot of the table that held Gehard's corpse next to the cup, he came to the head of the table and examined the face. After a moment he touched the slightly blistered lips.

"Monkshood also called wolfsbane and in the classical texts mother of poisons. But it was not in the cup, only in the flagon."

"Are you sure, brother?"

The monk shrugged. "I will ask our herbalist to look at the cup and what remains of the wine and let you know if my guess is wrong. Is he the kind of man who would not drink direct from the flagon?"

"No. If no cup were there he would have drunk from the flagon. But the cup *was* there." Bell shook his head. "And you are sure of the kind of poison?"

"Yes. The tingling on my skin is typical and the blistering around the dead man's mouth. Do you want to know how long the man has been dead?"

"We know that. There was someone in the next room who, we believe, heard him die. Tuesday afternoon that would have been."

"Yes. That sounds right. But why did we only get the body today? Did the person not go and try to help?"

Bell smiled. "Poor little mouse that she is, she would have been too afraid. She thought he was breaking up the furniture because he was angry. She did not know he was dying. But even if she had known, she could not have helped because the door was locked. She lives in a different room."

"She could not have helped anyway." The infirmarian shook his head. "I only thought that if she had seen him dying and called a priest, he could have had the last rites to help his soul. From the way that drop felt on my hand, the potion was very strong. Wolfsbane kills too fast for any help but the viaticum." Then the monk's eyes widened. "Did I not hear you say that the door was locked?" He lifted his hand from the table where it had rested near the corpse and stepped back. "He is a self-slayer?"

"No, no," Bell assured him. "This was murder, not self-slaughter. He was not the kind to die by his own hand, and he had enemies enough to help him along the way."

"Then God have mercy on him," the infirmarian sighed. "He died, as you said, by poison. There is some bruising, but I am reasonably sure that was from falling and striking some furniture in his death throes. There are no other wounds."

"Thank you, brother," Bell said. "If any man deserved dying, I think this man did. Yet to trick a man into taking poison is wrong."

"It is, indeed. Who knows, had he lived long enough even this sinner might have repented and mended his ways and found salvation. To send a soul, no matter how evil, untimely to Hell is wrong."

Bell thought briefly of the many souls he himself had sent untimely to Hell, but he only nodded and said, "If I can right that wrong, I will."

Monkshood, wolfsbane, mother of poisons Bell repeated to himself as he walked to the gate in the city wall that would let him into the grounds of the White Tower. Before entering the gate, he thought briefly of taking a boat upriver to the foot of the bridge to tell Magdalene which poison killed Gehard.

A glance at the sun told him he would probably be just in time for dinner with the women, but that meant that it would be too late to seek out the Master Apothecary. Magdalene's clients would be coming in soon after dinner and she never left her women when clients were in the house. Besides, he would get more reaction from Gehard's men when they first heard of his death. Seeking out the man who sold the poison could wait until the next morning when he and Magdalene could go together.

To the gate guard, he showed the bishop of Winchester's seal and said he wished to speak to Mandeville's captain. The man looked at Bell's clothing, at the richly adorned sword belt and the well-worn hilts of his sword and his poniard and passed him without difficulty. Nor did the door guard refuse entrance to the bishop of Winchester's knight. Bell recalled that he and the captain had walked down from his chamber without any display of animosity so likely none of the men knew what had happened. In any event Bell had no trouble in getting to the captain's quarters.

The man looked up at Bell as he opened the door and pulled his knife. Bell held out both empty hands, palms forward, in a placatory gesture. "I am come to bring news," Bell said, "not to make trouble, although the news itself may make trouble. Gehard fitzRobert is dead, murdered."

The captain looked surprised, then shrugged. "I suppose he committed one atrocity too many. I wonder how many men it took to bring him down and how many sword or knife thrusts to kill him."

"None."

"You said murdered?"

"Poisoned."

"Merciful Mary, a woman killed him?"

Bell shrugged. "I have no idea. No more has the sheriff of Southwark. The door to the rooms where we found Gehard was locked. The shutter of the window was secured on the inside, and there were no marks on the sill or wall or ground below the window to show that someone had left that way."

The captain stared at him, then breathed, "Witchcraft?"

Plainly, Bell thought, it did not occur to the captain for a moment that Gehard would kill himself. But witchcraft? Bell frowned. He had not thought of that. To die by witchcraft was possible, but he had never heard of a witch using poison. Men and women who died of witchcraft wasted away or suddenly strangled on their own breath or fell as if smitten when no blow had been struck.

"No. I think not," he said. "Gehard died of poison. He went to the room of Nelda Roundheels, she who died by falling down the stairs on, we think, Tuesday, and there found a flagon full of wine. We think he drank of it—"

The captain snorted. "If there was wine, Gehard would drink it." His lips thinned and he glanced sidelong at Bell. "He drank too much. Well, you can ask him no questions, so what do you here?"

"I need to speak to his men. The bishop does not tolerate murder, even of an enemy. I need to try to discover who would have wanted to kill him."

There was a long silence while, Bell thought, the captain sought for an excuse to refuse the request. Then his lips thinned again and he said, "Go speak to them, but if you cause any trouble in the troop I will complain to the bishop. Winchester cannot run roughshod over everyone because he was annoyed by a silly jest."

Bell opened his mouth and then firmly shut it. He did

not regard a dead whore carrying a letter from Gloucester propped in the bishop's bedchamber as a silly jest nor an attack by an armed troop, even if it was true that the troop had orders not to harm the bishop. However he noted that the captain was careful to avoid any salacious hints. It was more important to speak to Gehard's men than how this man thought of Winchester.

"Thank you," Bell said, and turned on his heel and went out and down the stairs again.

A question to the guard below got him direction to the men's barrack. He was considerably relieved when he heard the normal hubbub of a large group of men-at-arms at their ease. Now he thought what a fool he had been. He had never asked the captain whether the men were on duty, and therefore spread all over the Tower grounds, or on leave, and therefore anywhere at all. The bishop was evidently in favor with the heavenly host, so his man's path was smoothed by having Gehard's troop ready for duty but not yet engaged in it.

The door was open to encourage any breeze to come in, but the large open barrack was definitely cooler than the bare trampled earth outside in the full glare of the sun. Bell looked around. The place stank of many men who worked hard and did not bathe frequently enough. There was some disorder, clothing dropped on the floor and blankets crumpled on stained but not fetid pallets. However, the men's armor was laid neatly ready, pikes were stacked out of the central aisle but in place for easy seizure, and swords were propped or hung to be taken in hand. One or two men looked up as Bell's shadow fell ahead of him into the room.

"All right you men, listen up," Bell bellowed in English.

The battleground voice cut like an axe through the talk. Silence followed. Every head turned in Bell's direction.

"Gehard fitzRobert is dead," Bell continued in the same loud voice and then stopped speaking.

"Knew it," a man near Bell gasped.

"Nothin' else give us a rest an' keep 'im away," another fairly close muttered.

From the back of the room, a man called, "How? What happened?" and a bald, hard-faced man with small hooded eyes that had all the expression of dull marbles thrust through a group to whom he had been talking and came forward. "I'm Sedge Raffson, Gehard's second. Who the hell're you t'bring th' news?"

"I am Sir Bellamy of Itchen, the bishop of Winchester's knight. I have been seeking the answer to who killed the whore Nelda Roundheels and today went to Nelda's rooms because I was told of a disturbance there—which should not have happened because the rooms were locked up. And they were locked when I arrived. When I unlocked the door, I found Gehard dead on the floor."

"Witchcraft!" a voice Bell could not identify yelped.

"What else could kill 'im 'hind a locked door?" another voice intoned.

"Poison," Bell bellowed. Let these men believe Gehard died of witchcraft and not one would dare be of any help lest the witch be angered and curse him. "Gehard was killed with poison, left for him in a flagon of wine." He looked around, letting his mouth curl in open distaste. "I did not like Gehard fitzRobert, I will say that plain, but even less do I like this cowardly attack on him. If he had been challenged and killed in a fair or even a not-so-fair fight, I tell you true that I would have looked away and said nothing. But poison, poison not even given face to face but left as a trap . . . *pfui!*"

Murmurs of agreement, disagreement, question, comment,

even some nervous laughter made a rising sound throughout the room. Sedge Raffson stared without expression at Bell for a moment.

"You did'n come here t'give us news. You would've told th' captain first and he would've told me. What d'ye want?"

"I did tell the captain. He said I might question the men to discover whether they had any idea of who would want to kill Gehard."

Raffson laughed, but his eyes were wary. "Y' mean aside from th' men 'emselves? There're few who don't bear scars 'v 'is ordered whippin's or 've mem'ries 'v beatin's."

Bell shook his head. "Unless you know of a recent punishment that could arouse more than usual anger, it makes no sense. If he were killed by his men, it would have happened a long time ago."

The master-at-arms's second nodded and Bell saw the man relax somewhat as he began to hope that Bell was not simply seeking a scapegoat among the men-at-arms. Raffson uttered another nearly mirthless laugh.

"There's a army 'v 'em Gehard pissed off. He weren't easy tempered, an' 'e didn' care 'bout makin' enemies."

"Enemies who would have a way into Nelda Roundheels' locked apartment and were desperate enough to give Gehard poisoned wine?"

"As fer a way into Nelda's rooms," a man who had been listening intently said, "I wus gate guard by th' Thames Street gate 'nd I saw Gehard catch one 'o th' captains a'rter 'e come in. Did'n see 'oo it were; they us b'hind me. But Gehard wus angry. 'e said 'oo 'e was talkin' to better get Nelda t' giv' it t' 'im. But that wus afore Nelda died."

"How th' hell do y' know 'bout Nelda?" Raffson asked.

The man who had spoken was young with dirty tow-colored hair, but his eyes were a light, bright brown and

Bell thought full of intelligence—or at least shrewdness.

"I've eyes 'nd ears," the young man said. "Nelda come lookin' fer Gehard mor'en once. 'nd *he* wus flush 'ith coin arter he went 'ith her, 'stead 'v th' other way. Once wh'n he weren't 'ere, I asked 'v I could serve instead. I could do 'ith s'me extra coin." He looked squarely at Bell when he said that, but continued without pausing. "She looked me up 'nd down 'nd said, maybe some day but I weren't suited for her purpose yet."

"One of the captains," Bell muttered.

"Not ours," Raffson snapped. "Hmmm. There wus a captain askin' fer Gehard . . . ah yestiday. Lef' a message t' meet 'im arter duty in th' Cask 'f Wine. Yeah. Man called Linley." Raffson snickered. "Must'a waited quite a while 'cause Gehard must'a been dead a'ready."

So Linley had not known that Gehard was dead, Bell thought. *But could he have been the "captain" the gate guard heard Gehard threatening?*

"Did Gehard know Sir John?" Bell asked. Magdalene might say he was reaching for the moon, but Gehard *could* have known about the letter.

There was a glutinous chuckle. " 'nother one he didn' like." An older man, missing an ear and with a scar running from the stub across his cheek, pushed in beside the young tow-head. "Sir John, 'e wus one 'f Me Lord's pets. Gehard wus allus arter 'im 'bout where 'e'd bin 'n whut 'e did. Mostly Sir John wouldn' tell 'im."

That, too, was very interesting, Bell thought, and asked if Sir John had been at the Tower recently. No one had seen him since he had arrived from France Thursday past. Other men had tales of Gehard's unpleasant ways, but nothing so direct or any specific threat. It seemed unlikely to Bell that the men named would be angry or frightened enough to poison Gehard. Not enough was at stake to merit murder.

Bell found farthings for those who had volunteered information—but not until no one else came forward. If he had offered money in the beginning, the men would all have found tales to tell—true or not. To Raffson he gave a whole silver penny, saying that he might want to come back and ask further questions in the next few days. The man-at-arms second nodded brusquely, tossed the silver in the air, and said he'd be welcome but that he wouldn't trust the men not to make up things. In answer to which Bell laughed and said he would come with specific questions to which he knew the answers and only needed confirmation.

He had dinner in a cookshop in the East Chepe and then set out to find the men who had quarreled with Gehard. Not one of them was the least saddened by the news of Gehard's death; on the other hand Bell did not think any of them was sufficiently angry or bitter to commit murder. All seemed to be prosperous merchants from whom Gehard had made purchases at his captain's behest and from whom, with varying degrees of success, he had tried to extract a healthy commission. Bell made a mental note to get one of the clerks who handled Winchester's accounts to discover whether any of the merchants was in debt or otherwise in trouble so that the requested commission would be seriously damaging.

By the time he had spoken to the last man, the afternoon was well advanced. Bell set out for Winchester's house with a strong sense of satisfaction. Most of the bishop's business for the diocese of London was conducted in the morning. The late afternoon was often given over to his private affairs and messages from the diocese at Winchester. Having first made sure that all was well with his men and no problems had arisen, he asked for an audience with the bishop and was admitted immediately. He gave Winchester the news about Gehard's death and his investigation of it.

Winchester frowned even as he nodded. "Oddly, that kind of man, one anyone would believe would be the first to be murdered, often dies in his bed in miserable old age. So, you have no idea of who might have killed him?"

"I know that he threatened 'a captain' and that he was on bad terms with Sir John who obtained the letter you now have. But—" Bell shook his head slowly "—I cannot see how he would have access to Nelda's rooms to leave the poison, unless he is the one who killed Nelda and took her key."

"What of the landlord, Linley?"

"I took his key and he did not kill Nelda. He was either at Master Rhyton's house or dead drunk when Nelda died."

"Those who spoke for him are telling the truth?"

Bell shrugged. "According to Magdalene, the woman Claresta would be glad to be rid of him and would not lie to protect him. And by my judgement, his fellow officers in Surrey's household do not like him and also are not likely to lie for him. Of course, Diot picked the lock so it could not have been very hard to do. But it is not something one can do quickly—and I think the little girl next door would have noticed and told Magdalene."

"You are sure the woman Nelda did not give out keys?"

"Not sure, my lord, but from what we have heard of her, it is not likely. She was suspicious and, being a thief herself, I would think unlikely to trust others."

There was a little silence and the bishop sighed. "There was something between that whore and Father Holdyn whether or not he lay with her. She stole from him and he did not seek to punish her. Perhaps he is the one person whom she would trust enough to give a key."

"I had forgot Holdyn," Bell muttered. "Could Gehard have killed Nelda? We know he beat her two days before she died. And if Gehard killed her, could Father Holdyn have sought revenge for her death?"

"A priest commit murder with poison?" There was a bleakness, but no utter rejection in Winchester's voice.

"I think, my lord, you must confront Father Holdyn and discover what power the woman had over him. I cannot believe he is guilty . . . and yet . . ." Bell cleared his throat. "Meanwhile, I would like to borrow one of the clerks of your household to examine the businesses of those from whom Gehard tried to extort money to make sure his exactations would not have ruined anyone."

Winchester sighed again. "Very well. You know my chief clerk. Tell him which men must be examined and he will appoint someone with the skill appropriate for the task. If they find anything suspicious, they will let you know."

"Thank you, my lord."

The bishop looked down at his hands, clasped before him on the table at which he had been working. "You believe it was this man, this Gehard, who arranged the attack on me?"

"Yes, my lord. He did not confess in so many words, but he cursed me for interfering and said it was ordered that you not be hurt. That seemed sure enough evidence to me."

"Do you believe that no harm was intended to me?"

Bell paused, thought a moment with pursed lips, and then nodded. "Well, I certainly believe that if Mandeville gave the order, he would insist you be kept safe. He would know that if you were truly hurt or killed the king would pursue the guilty party until ten times vengeance had been taken—"

"You believe the king would wish to avenge my hurt?"

Winchester sounded a little uncertain and very pleased.

"Oh, yes, my lord. King Stephen can be told tales of you that make him act foolishly, but if you lay wounded or, God forbid, dead, all he would remember is that you were his brother, playing together as boys, and every service and kindness you have ever done him. The king is not a cruel or vengeful man, but even I, who I promise you would be the first pursuer on Mandeville's trail, would come to pity him."

The bishop laughed. "Even if I were not there to pay your wages, you would pursue?"

Bell did not laugh in return; his nostrils flared. "To the death. And with no knightly care for honor. Where there is too much power and no heart and conscience, one must use the means that come to hand." Then seeing Winchester's troubled expression, he did laugh. "You have given me work of such interest that every day is a new adventure for me. I will never find another lord as satisfactory. Have I not the right to punish the man who deprives me of such a master?"

That the bishop was pleased and flattered and that he knew Bell was speaking only the truth as he felt it was obvious, but he said only, "To each his own pleasure, but the man who arranged the attack is now dead. The scandal over the woman died without even a ripple. I have Gloucester's letter and the king has not mentioned it. I could wish this investigation was at an end before the conclave begins."

Bell wondered if Winchester was hinting that he accept Gehard's death as punishment for his sins, and forget about the murder, but he did not want to leave the puzzle unsolved. He nodded and said, "I hope it will be, my lord."

Winchester did not follow the hint, if it had been one, with an order. He said, "So what will you do now?"

Bell smiled. "That, of course, depends on you, my lord. If you travel or have any special task for me, I am yours to command. If not, I will go tell Magdalene what poison was used. She said she knew someone who might be able to tell us which apothecaries were likely to sell such substances. Once we know that, if we can find the man who sold the stuff, we may have a good lead to the poisoner."

The bishop snickered. "I should have remembered with whom you shared your ferreting. By all means go, but do not let your pleasure in the hunting delay your unweaving of the crime as soon as may be." Then he grimaced slightly. "That was unfair." He felt in his purse and withdrew two pennies. "Whore Magdalene may be, but she and her women have truly exerted themselves to solve this problem without thought of profit. When you speak to my clerks of account, tell them that the Old Priory Guesthouse is to be remitted a full week's rent. And," he handed Bell the pennies, "buy some sweetmeats that will give them all pleasure . . . and you, also . . . as my visible thanks."

Bell opened his mouth, but the bishop waved him away and he could do nothing but bow and go. He felt a flicker of irritation because he was being teased about a pleasure he had not tasted in far too long. Still, he was growing more and more sure that was a decision totally within his own power. He checked when he added the bishop's two pennies to his purse that he had five more to offer Magdalene.

A brief chuckle when he thought of her indignant reaction and his pointing out that being treated as a whore was at her own insistence, made the bishop's chief clerk comment dryly on his good humor.

"That is because I have found extra work for you," Bell said with spurious soberness, and laughed again when the clerk drew an indignant breath.

He then explained what the work was, asked for pen and parchment to write down the names and guilds to which the merchants belonged, and made his peace. The clerk assured him that over the next day or two he would have an answer for each man. Bell thanked him, apologized for his jest—which the clerk was now ready to laugh at too—and set off for Magdalene's house.

However, instead of crossing the road and going through the churchyard and Magdalene's back garden, Bell walked down until the street between the priory and the bishop's house ended at a small boat pier. To the right was a rough and narrow lane, rarely used, but far enough above and away from the river to allow him to cross to the High Street that came from the bridge. There he turned left. It was near dusk and many of the peddlers were heading home so he was able to buy at very good prices.

He found two large leaf-wrapped packets of candied violets somewhat broken apart but deliciously sweet, then a large bag of cherries—the bag had some red stains, marking a crushed fruit or two but Bell ran his hand in and found most of the cherries were sound—and last he took from a vendor the whole leavings of his stall, a woven grass basket full of mixed berries. Last, just as the bells of St. Mary Overy began to ring the Vespers, he found a milkmaid and bought a whole pitcher full of heavy yellow cream.

He was always greeted with warmth by Magdalene's women, but his purchases were fallen upon with squeals of joy and, in her enforced silence, claps of the hands and skips of delight from Letice. However, he was also rushed to the table, where the evening meal was already laid out. They needed to eat quickly, Ella said, if they wanted to enjoy his largesse. Diot brought the wine he said he would prefer to ale this night, and Magdalene squeezed his hand when he sat down at his corner of the table.

"You have a tale to tell, I expect," she said, smiling at the fruit, and then, glancing briefly at Ella, told him there would be a full house of "guests."

Although Bell wrinkled up his nose as if he were dissatisfied with that information, actually he was rather pleased. He would not have minded, of course, if Letice or Diot heard what he had to tell Magdalene—Ella was the only one from whom he had to hide the fact that murder had been done—but he was uneasily aware that he wanted to talk to Magdalene alone.

They lost no time in eating the fine meal Dulcie provided and topped it off with bowls of berries drowned in the cream and drizzled with honey for extra sweetness. The bell rang. Bell grabbed a handful of the broken bits of the violets and another of the cherries, then looping his sword belt over his arm, went off to his room. Ella chewing happily on cherries went to answer the gate—they were expecting Baby Face again; he was always a bit early. Nonetheless, aware that Sir John might by now have reached London, Magdalene watched warily from the doorway.

This time Ella remembered to look out the gate without undoing the chain, and Magdalene nodded praise and then hurried back to sit by her embroidery out of the way of her terminally shy client. Ella pranced in leading her prize and rushed to offer him the violets and cherries, which were still on the table.

"Did you remember to latch the gate again, Ella?" Magdalene asked.

"I did," Master Gerome said. He blushed furiously when he spoke, but then, as he came forward to pay his five pennies, he added, "The violets and cherries are very good. Thank you."

Magdalene was nonplussed. With any other client she would have taken that as an invitation to a conversation. With Master Gerome she did not know whether to speak or not, but he had not hurried away, so she said with a little emphasis, "Thank *you* for remembering the gate. Ella is always so glad when you come she sometimes gets a little forgetful."

"She is? She is not . . . ah . . . ordered to . . . to be . . . willing? I—" he blushed even darker "—I am aware I am . . . excessive."

Magdalene thought that if the kitchen fire had failed she could have lit her candles at his ears, but she only remarked with a touch—but not too much—of indignation, "No, indeed! None of my women needs to be with a client she does not like. I assure you we have business enough in this house. And I have sufficient protection not to fear to turn away any client. Ella truly enjoys being with you." Magdalene chuckled softly, beckoned and murmured to him, "Look at her. She knows she must not interrupt when I speak to a client, but if she could, she would drag you away to her room at once."

"Then I would like to make a permanent arrangement to be with Ella three nights a week—if possible Tuesday, Thursday, and Saturday. I have a guild meeting on Wednesday night. And if I could then pay four shillings for three months? I know that sometimes Ella is free for a night so over the time I am sure you would make up the discount you have given me. If Ella is still happy at the end of that time, I would extend the arrangement—in three month periods—permanently. I would also be willing to pay in advance . . ."

"I can see why you are a successful man of business, Master Gerome," Magdalene said. "If you will make that four shillings and six pence, I will agree. You will have nearly two free nights out of twelve." She waited for Gerome's nod, then gestured to Ella to come closer. "Love, here is Master Gerome who likes you so well that he wishes to come to you the same three nights every week. But only if you wish it. Would you like that, dearling? If you prefer—"

"Three nights a week?" Ella interrupted, smiling beatifically. She went and took Gerome's hand and kissed his cheek. "Oh, you are satisfied with me and happy. I will always do my best to please you, I promise, even if your coming again is a sure thing. Oh, yes, Magdalene. I would like that. I would like him to come even more often . . ."

"Ella!" Magdalene said in gentle warning.

Master Gerome's face was incandescent again, but he managed to say, "I am not sure I would survive that," as he turned away to follow Ella to her chamber.

CHAPTER 15

Magdalene sat quietly looking at her embroidery frame. With Ella out of use three days a week, she would have to shift one or two of Ella's steady clients to Diot. Probably that would cause no trouble, but Diot's time was getting more filled than Magdalene liked and of late Letice was also busy. It seemed that her countrymen had discovered and liked the amenities of the Old Priory Guesthouse. They paid in strange coin, once or twice even in gold, but silver was silver and weighed the same in the goldsmith's scale no matter what figures were stamped into the metal.

The other two clients arrived close on each other's heels. Magdalene added the ten pence to the five Gerome had given her and pulled the embroidery frame close. For a time, half a candlemark or so, she embroidered peacefully. When she heard the door of Bell's room click, she looked up with a frown. Bell hesitated, a brow raised in question.

"I am going to need another woman," she said to him. "Blind, if I can find one who is pretty and can be taught to manage herself."

Bell nearly choked on the last of the crystal honey that had crumbled off the violets that he had just licked off his hand. He was hearing his mother speaking to his father, new come from the stables. "Trude is some five months gone with child. I will soon need another maid . . ." He swallowed hard against the combined pain and pleasure that roiled in him. A bound woman speaking to the man from whom she had a right to help, that was what Magdalene sounded like.

Taking the time to seat himself on Ella's stool—why not choose the one with the comfortable cushion—let Bell control the odd mixture of emotions that racked him. "You want me to look at the girls that are left in the churchyards?"

Mingled with his surprise and pleasure at the intimation that he was again part of Magdalene's household, he was a little shocked at the idea of being asked to recruit an innocent girl—Bell considered that thought and dismissed it. No girl left to the charity of the Church and pretty enough to work at the Old Priory Guesthouse was likely to be innocent; more likely she would have been used by men all her life. The priests tried to prevent that once the girl was left with them . . . well, he hoped they tried to prevent it.

Magdalene looked up, smiling. "Mary help me for being witless. I never thought of that. I was just saying aloud what was in my head. But it is a very good notion, Bell."

"A very good notion for me to make a whore of a helpless girl?" His voice, although not raised—he was subconsciously aware of the business of the house progressing behind the closed doors of the corridor—was full of indignation.

"What are the odds that a girl abandoned or so unhappy that she has run to the protection of the Church has not already been broached?" Magdalene raised her brows. "You know I would never take a woman who did not understand and accept the life I offer. Would not the girl be better off here, well fed and cared for, safe from hurt?" She laughed gently. "It was you who brought me Diot, after all."

"She was already a whore. I brought her from a house where she was in danger of great hurt, not from a churchyard where she expected to be succored."

Magdalene shook her head and then bent it over her embroidery again. She realized that Bell was not really arguing, that he just wanted to hear said aloud what they both knew to be true. "You know where they go from the churchyard," she said. "If not to their graves most likely into one of the stews. The Old Priory Guesthouse is better."

That was true enough, and below the moral objections he had been taught, Bell was aware of a warm pleasure in the exchange with Magdalene. Man of the house was the way she spoke to him; the man who had the right to be consulted in any decision made about the household and who was obligated to contribute to it. A stronger sense of pleasure, near delight, flowed over Bell. That was something William of Ypres would never have. Not, Bell thought, choking back a laugh, that it was anything Lord William would ever want.

He sighed and shrugged. "I suppose so. And a blind girl could not even hope to be taken as a servant. I will look and ask about. But this is not something we must urgently do tomorrow. More important now is that I know what poison was used to kill Gehard and what Gehard's men—I do not think he had any friends—say about who had reason to kill him." And Bell went on to tell her what he had learned.

"So Linley left a message for Gehard to meet him after Gehard was dead." Magdalene picked up on that immediately.

"Which might mean he did not know. But Sir John knew Gehard also and Gehard would have wanted that letter for Waleran. Could he have told Nelda somehow?"

Magdalene shook her head. "How? It is a long way from the Tower over the bridge to Nelda's rooms."

"No, earlier. Gehard's man said he was always after Sir John to tell him where he went and why. Sir John told Lord

Hugh about the letter. Why not his own lord's man?"

"And it is true that they both used Nelda."

"The thought had crossed my mind. The man Gehard spoke to, the one he threatened and said he would get 'it' for Gehard . . . could that 'it' have been Gloucester's letter?"

"Why should Sir John give Gehard Gloucester's letter? No, that is too farfetched. How could Gehard even know about the letter?"

"Sir John must have gone to the Tower to give Mandeville the letter. He was telling everyone else about it. Perhaps he told the captain and Gehard heard."

Magdalene stopped embroidering to shake her head and laugh. "You are really reaching for the moon. Besides, Sir John wasn't in London to poison Gehard. He had ridden off to Oxford or Devizes to bring the letter to Mandeville."

"Did he? That was what we decided between us, but what if he *did* look at the letter when he spoke of it to Lord Hugh? What if he realized it was gone? What if he *then* went back and tried to get it from Nelda and killed her and failed to find the letter by searching her rooms and obviously did not think of searching her body."

"But why put her in the bishop's chamber?"

"A sop to Mandeville? That is the best reason, but he could also have done it because Linley knew he used Nelda and that she stole and he did not want Linley to find her there dead in case someone had heard him announce himself to her—which your little mouse did hear. We had better try to find out who sold the poison tomorrow."

"Yes, you said you knew what poison was used. What was it?" In her interest Magdalene anchored her needle into the cloth on which she was working.

"Wolfsbane, also called monkshood or mother of poisons."

"Oh! I have heard of monkshood. I remember my mother showing us the plant and warning us that when not in flower it might be mistaken for wild white radish." She frowned. "She told us that we must not ever touch it, that all parts were deadly poison and might even harm us through our skin."

Bell looked down at his hands, which were lightly clasped between his knees. Magdalene had never previously mentioned any life before she was a whore in Oxford. He hardly knew whether to pretend he had not heard . . . No, she would know at once that he *had* heard and that he marked her words as important. Better to act as if they were commonplace.

"You were born in the country?"

Inside, Magdalene froze. God help her, she had all but told Bell from where she came. If he enquired around the St. Foi estate, he would discover far too much. Many years had passed, but she had no doubt that in that quiet place the disappearance of the abnormally beautiful wife of St. Foi after his murder was still remembered. Next she would confess to him what she had done. She took her needle from the cloth and peered at it as if to judge the length of thread.

"Yes," she said as if it did not matter. "A small manor far west of Oxford—" The truth was that she came from the north, beyond Lincoln. "I would prefer if you did not try to discover more. There is really nothing much to learn. My life there was without interest . . . even to me."

"As you like," Bell said, "except—" he saw her stiffen and was pleased with the device he planned "—I would like to know whether you would still recognize the plant and whether it grows here in London."

She breathed out—too lightly to be called a sigh, but Bell knew it was a sound of relief and was satisfied. He had no desire to expose whatever shame she was hiding, except to show her he did not blame her for it. Had her parents sold her into prostitution?

"Not in my garden," Magdalene said. "But I cannot say I have ever looked for it elsewhere. I do not gather herbs, I buy them."

Magdalene was furious with herself. The comfort and ease she felt in Bell's company, the sense that he would gladly share her problems, was dangerous. She should do something that would drive him away. As the thought came, a gray pall seemed to dim the bright design she was stitching into the cloth on the embroidery frame. She wished she had never met him! Before they came together she had been content with her life. But now it was too late. She must either live in dull safety with an aching hollow inside her or accept the danger Bell brought with the pleasure.

Bell laughed. "I do not suspect you of murder."

Magdalene had a flashing image of St. Foi bleeding his life out on the floor at her feet.

"What I am asking," Bell continued without pause, "is whether you are willing to so far compromise one of your clients as to ask him whether he knows who sells wolfsbane?" He grimaced. "I do not want to ask these questions on the bishop's authority. Perhaps I am overcautious, but Gehard did die in the chamber of the whore who was found in Winchester's bedchamber."

"I cannot see how the bishop can be blamed for that, but it so happens that like everyone else I purchase herbs and simples. I have even bartered my embroidery for drugs, so that I am known in the apothecary's shop I frequent as an embroiderer. Also the apothecary desires some information from me. I asked him about use of the poppy and he questioned me straitly as to how I knew about the cakes made from poppy juice. He wishes to buy those cakes and, as I told you, Umar will sell to anyone with the coin to buy. If the apothecary answers our questions about the monkshood, will you guide him to The Saracen's Head?"

Bell frowned. "I am not sure I think it so good a thing to spread the use of that drug."

"Oh, no, this is an apothecary. I doubt he will sell it for common use. He spoke to me about using it for otherwise ungovernable pain."

"Good enough. We can go tomorrow morning, after I have made sure that my men have their duty set and that the bishop has not changed his mind about working at home. Likely I will be back before you are finished breaking your fast. Let us hope that the apothecary you use can tell us what we want to know." Bell grimaced again. "If not, I will need to go to Master Octadenarius, and request that he send out his men to ask about monkshood in every apothecary shop." Bell sighed. "He will not be pleased."

Bell was not forced to face the disfavor of Master Octadenarius. When he and Magdalene arrived at a large and obviously prosperous shop, Magdalene was greeted with a smile by the apprentice at the outside stall. Her request to speak to the apothecary brought an accepting nod without any sidelong glances and she was directed inside the shop. Nor did the apprentice make any objection to Bell following her.

Master Pasche, tall and thin with scanty dark hair and mud-colored eyes, was behind the counter inside. He bowed slightly in recognition. "Mistress Magdalene." He glanced uneasily up at Bell and changed his mind about what he intended to say. "How may I serve you?" he said at last.

"By telling me what you know about monkshood."

Master Pasche stiffened and sort of leaned back away from her a trifle, looking very alarmed. "What *I* know about monkshood?" he repeated, sounding horrified. "What would *you* want with monkshood, mistress?"

Magdalene realized at once that she had stepped on a sore toe, smiled gently, and shook her head. "I do not want anything to do with it. But Sir Bellamy here needs to know who sells it."

Pasche looked at Bell. "It is a very dangerous substance, very dangerous. You should not keep it in your house. It might cause harm by accident." His eyes glistened momentarily with tears. "There was a tragic case not long ago of a child who drank some of his mother's liniment—and died of it. No. I do not even sell the liniments or salves made with monkshood to ease joint pain. There are other things."

"But there *are* medications that use monkshood?" Magdalene asked. "And apothecaries do sell it?"

The apothecary was frowning now, lips thinned, clearly alarmed. "Some do. It is very effective in soothing bruises and for pain in the joints, but as I said I have much safer salves that work almost as well. In your business—" the muscles in his jaw bunched "—such a liniment should *never* be used near—"

"Oh, no, Master Pasche," Magdalene interrupted. She laughed and said, "Thank goodness none of my women is afflicted with joint ail." And then more seriously, "As I said, I do not want monkshood myself, but Sir Bellamy needs to know who sells it. Sir Bellamy collects my rent. He was telling me of a case being investigated by the sheriff of

Southwark of a man poisoned with monkshood."

"That is correct," Bell said. "I want to know who sold it and to whom."

"It is not the fault of the apothecary if someone misuses his drugs," Master Pasche said defensively.

"No, of course not," Bell assured him. "No blame will be affixed to the apothecary, but if he could remember to whom he sold enough monkshood to poison a man—a very big, strong man—that would be of considerable help to the sheriff, who might be grateful to you and to Mistress Magdalene."

"Hmmm." The apothecary now looked more thoughtful than worried. "There are only ten apothecaries in the East Chepe and two others, like me, do not stock or sell remedies that depend on monkshood. So, seven . . ."

He gave them the names and the locations of the shops but warned them that there were other apothecaries who did business outside of the market itself. And then there were the apothecaries who had shops in the West Chepe. He knew some of them, but not all. The Guildmaster might well have a list of all those who belonged to the guild. Bell sighed.

"Thank you, Master Pasche," Bell said, sighing again. "The sheriff of Southwark is questioning the apothecaries on the south of the river. If the killer did not buy from one of them or one of the masters in the East Chepe, I will go to Master Octadenarius, the justiciar, and he will send his men all through London."

Magdalene also thanked Master Pasche and then smiled happily at him. "Oh, I almost forgot. I have some good news for you. The seller of the poppy cakes is one Umar who can be reached at The Saracen's Head in Southwark. He will sell to you if you have the price."

"And the price?"

"I have no idea," Magdalene said. "I am not in any way involved in this. You must make your own bargain with Umar."

"But where is The Saracen's Head? Southwark is not as large as London, but one obscure ale-house . . ."

"I know where it is, Master Pasche," Bell said. "I collect rent there too. Since you have been so cooperative, I will gladly take you."

They made a time to meet the following afternoon, Bell only saying that he would send a message if he could not come to the shop at the arranged time. Then he and Magdalene set out for the apothecary shops. At the first two, they were offered salves but assured that no one other than regular customers for the salve had purchased any. In one shop no purchase had been made for a fortnight; in the other the apothecary named a woman called Old Mother Heulen and said she could barely totter to the market and home and he had been selling the salve to her for many years. Neither Bell nor Magdalene could think of a way to get enough of the salve into wine to cause a swift death, and they did not bother to discover where Old Mother Heulen lived.

The third shop had liniment as well as salve made with monkshood. Bell asked whether the liniment was dangerous, admitting he had been warned about it by Master Pasche. This apothecary agreed that the liniment if drunk could kill but said that after Pasche's client's child had died, he had added a substance so foul-tasting to his product that it would be spat out as soon as it touched the lips.

Then he frowned. "What is this interest in monkshood all of a sudden?"

"Then someone other than Sir Bellamy and myself has

been asking for monkshood?" Magdalene asked.

The apothecary did not answer at once, and Bell said, "Monkshood was used to kill a man in Southwark. The sheriff of Southwark is questioning the apothecaries there, and I was sent here to discover if I could who bought the stuff."

"No!" the apothecary exclaimed.

Bell held up a hand. "No blame to you if you sold it. People who buy liniment are not usually planning murder."

Revelation spread across the apothecary's face. "So that is why the man did not buy my liniment! Thank God! When I tried to make the sale, I explained to him how my liniment was safe because of the terrible taste. I thought he muttered it would not do, and he shook his head and left. He was the only one. I have not sold monkshood salve for some time."

"What did he look like?" Bell asked eagerly.

The apothecary frowned in thought but then shook his head regretfully. "He wore a sword and was well dressed, but nothing to note in special and . . . and the face was just a face. It made no impression on me. I am very sorry."

Magdalene smiled at him. "We are sorry too," she said, "but you have at least assured us that our effort is not all in vain. Now at least we know that this man intended to buy the monkshood, not simply go out into the country and gather some growing wild."

At the fourth shop, they struck gold. The moment Bell asked about liniment containing monkshood or wolfsbane, the apothecary looked highly suspicious. Thus Bell explained at once that they did not wish to buy but hoped to trace the substance used to kill a man.

"Heaven! Oh, heaven!" The apothecary covered his face with his hands. "I knew I should not have sold it to him. I knew it, but he seemed so distraught over his dog, a great mastiff, which had gone mad. They had the beast confined but even he did not dare go near it to kill it. It raged and howled so he said, near weeping, and he loved the beast and wanted it out of its misery. He wanted a poison that would be swift and sure, not something that would add to the poor beast's pain and let it linger. He had seen the effect of wolfsbane. He gave me his name . . ."

"Gave you his name?" Magdalene echoed. "What name did he give you?"

"Gehard fitzRobert, he said. It was not a name like John Smith, which is real enough but so common that people say it when they want to hide their true names. I believed him. God help me. I believed him."

"Gehard . . ." Bell breathed, and looked at Magdalene. "Could Gehard have bought the poison and somehow . . . He was not clever. Could he have mixed up the cups or decided to taste the stuff . . ."

Magdalene giggled. "He was not clever, but no one is stupid enough to drink poison he has himself prepared. No," she added more seriously, "from what you have said of Gehard he would never even think of using poison. He would kill with his knife or sword or his bare hands." She frowned. "And it was not Gehard who asked about monkshood in the other shop."

"No, it was not," Bell agreed, and turned back to the apothecary, who was still wringing his hands and biting his lips. "It is no fault of yours," he said soothingly. "It is a tale I might well have believed myself. There are several mastiffs in my father's house that are well loved. Do you remember what this Gehard looked like?"

"Yes, I do. We spoke for some time. First he asked for liniment and when I assured him it was safe to use because the honey in it was made horribly bitter, he asked if I had any pure tincture of the monkshood or some of the ground root. I looked at him hard then and asked what he wanted it for. That was when he told me the story of the mad dog."

"And what did he look like?"

"Ordinary," the apothecary said.

Magdalene and Bell exchanged glances. At first when the apothecary was so certain he remembered what his customer looked like, each had wondered if it had been Gehard. But no one would ever describe Gehard fitzRobert as ordinary.

"Can you say nothing more?" Bell asked.

"Well, he was wearing a sword belt and boots for riding, which made me believe he had come from the country . . . the dog, you see. For the rest, he was . . . ah . . . medium. Of medium height, his hair not fair nor dark, blue eyes, I think, or possibly gray. His voice . . . yes . . . he was soft spoken, even plaintive . . . about the dog."

"Not Gehard," Bell said. "Gehard was a giant of a man and anything but soft-spoken."

"I assure you," the apothecary said earnestly, "the man who bought the tincture of monkshood from me was no giant and seemed almost weeping when he begged for the drug."

"Oh, we believe you," Magdalene said. "Since murder was done with the monkshood, it is not at all surprising that the purchaser of the poison gave a false name. We were surprised because the name he gave was of his victim."

"Terrible. Terrible." The apothecary shuddered. "I will never sell the raw product again. Never."

"A good idea," Bell said. "And since it does not seem to be often requested in its raw form, you will lose little by it. Now, I will have to tell the sheriff of Southwark that you sold the drug, and he may come or send a man to hear the description you gave first hand—"

"Oh, please!" the apothecary moaned. "Can you not keep me out of this? I have been honest with you. Must I be punished for that?"

"I am sure no blame will attach to you," Bell said, but he knew it was not impossible that the sheriff or his man would take out his irritation on this relatively innocent bystander. He shrugged. "Well, I will tell the sheriff that we have found the source and give him a description of the purchaser. If he does not press me for where I found the information, I will not offer your name."

The apothecary confounded himself in thanks as Magdalene and Bell left his shop. Outside they walked back toward the bridge in silence for few moments.

Before they reached the noisy bedlam that crossed the Thames, Magdalene said, "You know who the description the apothecary gave sounds like, to me? It sounds like Linley."

"So it does," Bell agreed, "although I only saw Linley that once on the stair, and he was below me which disguised his height. I don't believe I've ever seen Sir John. Is he so different?"

Magdalene laughed ruefully. "Not really. He is of medium height. I would call his hair dark rather than neither blond nor black and I think his eyes are brown, but in the dimness of the shop they might look gray. Only, why are you so fixed on Sir John?"

"I do not mean to be. But the only other good candidate we have is Linley and he seems to have been . . . Perhaps you should try to pin down the time he left Ryton's house more firmly and I will ask again about when he arrived in the Cask of Wine."

"Very well. I have a pair of cuffs I have embroidered that I can bring to Claresta. Meanwhile, you should also ask in

Baynard's Castle when Sir John left there and in what direction he rode. We have only Raoul's word for that. I cannot see why he should lie about this, but I never trust him about anything."

"There is also Father Holdyn," Bell said slowly. "He is not the man who bought the monkshood. He is a very big man and dressed as a priest—"

Magdalene shook her head. "Is he such an idiot as to wear a priest's robes to buy poison?"

"No, but he is not at all medium, either."

Now aware of the reluctance with which Bell had named Holdyn, Magdalene hesitated. They walked in silence for a few moments. Then, because she felt even Bell might not see what he did not want to see, she spoke.

"A priest much addicted to good works would not need to buy poison from an apothecary," she pointed out. "He could go to the still room of any hospital and take what he liked, probably without any question. You know, Bell, the man who bought the monkshood might really have had a mad mastiff."

"And given the name Gehard fitzRobert?"

"No. You are right about that. The man who bought the monkshood must have been the murderer."

Bell sighed. "Nonetheless, I will remind Winchester that he must ask Holdyn why he lied about not knowing Nelda. But it still makes no sense. Even if he knew her and killed her, perhaps by accident, why should he kill Gehard? How could he even know Gehard? They had nothing at all in common."

"Yes they did. They had Nelda in common."

"Good God, so they did." Then Bell frowned. "And if Holdyn was obsessed with her—I cannot think of any other reason for him to give her his crucifix—and he discovered that Gehard killed her . . . No. I simply cannot believe that Holdyn would use poison. I cannot."

"Likely he did not. How would he get into Nelda's room?"

Bell snorted unhappily. "Unfortunately he may have had a key. Suspicious as she was, she might have given the priest a key so he would not need to knock on her door or call out to her."

They had reached the bridge by then, and Magdalene thought again about getting the cuffs and going to Lime Street to speak to Claresta. However, she saw that the shadow at her feet had shrunk to near nothing; it was almost noon. It was time for dinner and then the clients would be coming. She and Bell turned into the busy chaos of the bridge, weaving past stalls and shaking their heads at insistent peddlers who thrust trays and baskets at them.

When they had reached the relative quiet outside the Old Priory Guesthouse, she asked, "Will you come and have dinner with us?"

He glanced upward at the position of the sun. "I think I had better see if I can catch Winchester. I do not remember that he planned to have any guest to take dinner with him today. If no one is with him, I can tell him what we learned and urge him to summon Holdyn to explain himself."

Magdalene nodded and rang the bell. Diot came out of the house and opened the gate. They walked in together, but at the door of the house Bell turned left. Before he started around the house to go through the gate into St. Mary Overy churchyard, Magdalene patted his arm.

"I hope your doubts about Father Holdyn are resolved," she said softly. "You can tell me what transpired at the evening meal."

She turned away before Bell could find an answer. Both

her assumption that he would come that evening and that he would expose to her—a whore—possibly incriminating information about a relatively important Church official deserved a rebuke. Bell shrugged. Considering that the bishop had sent him to her for help, she had a right to assume. And despite what his head "knew" and propriety ordered, there was no comparison in pleasure and good conversation between taking his evening meal with the whores—yes, whores, not ladies although he often named them so in his own mind—of the Old Priory Guesthouse and the men of his troop.

Bell arrived at the bishop's house just as one of the servants was carrying up a well-laden tray. "Ask m'lord if he will speak to me while he eats," Bell said. And when the servant came down he told Bell to go up. To his pleasure, there were two places set at the table, and Winchester waved him toward the stool placed at right angles to his chair.

"So. You have more news for me, I suppose."

"Yes, my lord. We know who sold the monkshood and we have a description—such as it is; medium everything—of the man who bought it."

Winchester smiled as he speared some slices of pork on his eating knife. "Medium everything?" he repeated.

Bell smiled too and also set both pork and lamb (nearly mutton, he thought) on his trencher. "The apothecary who sold the poison, a flask of pure tincture of monkshood rather than a liniment, said the man was of medium height with hair neither light nor dark and blue or gray eyes."

The bishop sighed. "A description that will fit about two thirds of all the men in the city."

"Not quite," Bell replied around a bite. "The man wore fine clothes and a sword. Thieves and hired men may wear a sword, but seldom clothing fine enough to be noted by a successful merchant."

"A knight. But is the description really of any help? You cannot even say the tincture was purchased to do murder."

"That I can, my lord, because the purchaser gave the apothecary the name Gehard fitzRobert."

The bishop laid down the spoon he was about to dip into the pottage. "He gave the name of his victim? Why?"

"I cannot know, of course, but I think because it was on his mind. Thus that name was the first thing that came to his tongue when he did not want to sound as if he were hiding his true name by giving one too common, like John Smith."

Winchester raised an eyebrow, but then looked down to finish his aborted gesture and dip his spoon. "From your cheerfulness, you have someone in mind."

"Two someones," Bell said, looking less cheerful when he considered exactly what he was going to say, "but I have evidence that one of them was elsewhere when Nelda died and the other should not have even been in London—or just arriving now—when Gehard was poisoned."

The bishop looked exasperated and Bell explained more fully, mentioning that he believed Sir John was the man from whom Nelda had stolen the letter. That distracted Winchester from the murders to what was, basically, more important to him.

They discussed the mysterious silence about the letter. No one had mentioned it. Even Linley, who had tried to get back from Magdalene the tokens and money Nelda had hidden, had not asked about any letter. It was also curious that if the purpose of leaving Nelda's body in Winchester's bedchamber was scandal, that too had failed. Bell asked if it was safe for him to mention that Winchester already had the letter; the bishop thought and said yes, that he had informed the king.

The talk did not trouble either of their appetites, and they worked their way though more of the roasts, a pottage, stew, and a boiled carp. Then the subject shifted back to Nelda's and Gehard's deaths. Bell reported that he and Magdalene would try to make sure of the time that Linley left Master Rhyton's house and when he arrived at the Cask of Wine alehouse. Perhaps they had jumped to conclusions. Perhaps there had been time between those two events for him to have gone to Nelda's house and killed her, and taken her key.

Also, Bell said, he would ask more specific questions at Baynard's Castle about the elusive Sir John. Had he actually ridden to Oxford or Devizes, or had he discovered that the letter had been stolen and rushed back to Nelda's place where they quarreled and he killed her? If so, Sir John could have taken her key and searched her room. Perhaps he had been lying hidden in London in the hope of retrieving the letter. Winchester said he understood Bell might want to mention the letter to Lord Hugh and began to rise.

"My lord," Bell said reluctantly, without readying himself to rise also, "there is one other who could have had a key. Magdalene—no great respecter of persons—pointed out that the one person Nelda might have trusted enough to give a key, so that he would not need to knock or to call out to her and be noticed would be—"

Winchester's lips thinned. "Father Holdyn. But why should he kill Gehard? How could he even know him?"

Bell shrugged. "They both knew Nelda. As to why Father Holdyn should kill Gehard . . . you understand, I cannot believe this, but there are reasons presented by logic. Could Holdyn have been involved in Gehard's arranging an attack on you? He would have known where and when you would be going to see the archbishop."

"No." The word burst out and then Winchester said, "Why? What possible profit could Father Holdyn win by my hurt or death?"

"By your hurt or death he might have gained a less careful and honest overseer of the London diocese."

"That is ridiculous. I have been overseeing Holdyn's work as episcopal vicar since London's death and have not found so much as a whisper of corruption. As to wringing money from the Church, it is the other way. He gives much of his income back to the Church."

"It is even more ridiculous when you consider that your death or hurt were *not* intended. I do believe what Gehard told me. He was particularly angry that I had interfered in the attack because, he felt, it was unnecessary. You would have been safe and free within hours."

"So there is no reason to suspect Father Holdyn."

Bell shrugged. "There may be reasons that logic has not presented to me, but there is another that would spring to any man's mind. If Father Holdyn was obsessed by Nelda and learned that Gehard killed her, he could have desired revenge for her death." Bell sighed. "I do not believe it, but when I said that Father Holdyn could not have been the man who bought the poison, he being a very large and strong man and not likely to wear a sword, Magdalene also pointed out that he could walk into any hospital or infirmary and take what he wanted without question."

"Magdalene," Winchester said coldly, "is sometimes far too imaginative."

"I agree," Bell said dryly, "but every time I try to dismiss the idea as utterly out of the question, I remember that Nelda stole from Father Holdyn more than once and he never told his servants to hold her or punish her. And I remember, too, that he arranged for her swift burial in as near to consecrated ground as possible and got rid of her clothes. And when you asked if he knew her . . . it was a long, long moment before he answered that he did not."

"Why should he hesitate over a lie if he had already committed murder?" Winchester snapped.

"I do not believe that Father Holdyn committed murder." Bell was silent a moment and then grimaced. "I do not like Father Holdyn, my lord, but that is because he is so truly a good man that he shows me my black spots and blemishes. Only my head keeps telling my heart that I must know why he lied about Nelda. I will not raise the question again, my lord, if you forbid me, but it nags at me."

There was a long silence while Winchester stared at nothing. "If he is guilty, I will have lost my right hand in administering London," he snarled at Bell, and then, "It will nag at me, too, and poison every moment that he and I must work together. Go and get him, Bell, and bring him back here. I will ask and make sure that he answers."

CHAPTER 16

When Bell arrived at the bishop of London's palace, he had ample opportunity to understand why Winchester said he would lose his right hand if Father Holdyn was guilty of any crime. He waited patiently for the spate of clerks and petitioners to abate, standing aside and listening to the dispositions the priest made. Bell had to acknowledge that every decision was fair, perhaps a little harsher in penance than the bishop's judgement, Bell thought, but just.

Bell noted with some dismay, however, that Father Holdyn did not look well. His face was drawn and dark bruises showed under his eyes. At last, as those demanding his attention were satisfied, the priest looked around and noticed Bell. His face became more haggard, but he rose from his seat.

"I am summoned by the bishop?"

"Yes, father."

"Very well, I am ready." Holdyn turned to his chief clerk. "I am not sure when I will return. Either I or the bishop will send you word."

Bell's heart sank. Holdyn sounded as if he expected to be stripped of his rank and duties. Winchester would be fit to be tied and his own duties would be increased. He found, too, that his spirit was sorely oppressed. If a man like Father Holdyn could commit murder it seemed to Bell there was very little hope for anyone.

Not knowing whether Father Holdyn had a mount, Bell had walked. The return, south from the bishop of London's palace to Thames Street and then east to the bridge, was conducted in silence. Twice Bell saw Father Holdyn's hand rise to his chest as if he were seeking his crucifix for comfort and then drop away.

It was a relief to fight the crowd on the bridge; it made the silence between them less palpable. Once free of the bridge, Bell did not need to moderate his stride to suit his companion, who was as tall as he. They almost galloped past the Old Priory Guesthouse and along the wall of the priory until they came to the gate of Winchester's house.

Phillipe waved Bell and Father Holdyn past him as soon as they approached. Winchester was waiting in the area partitioned off from the main hall rather than in the more intimate chamber above. He had a number of documents open on the table in front of him, but the clerk farther down the table was sitting idle, his hands loosely clasped as if he had been idle for some time. He gathered up his quills and ink without surprise at Winchester's gesture and left, as he passed raising a brow at Bell, who had stopped near the door. When the clerk was gone, Bell closed the door and then moved along the wall until he could see Holdyn's face. There he stopped and leaned against the wall.

Winchester wasted no time. Pointing at a stool across from him he said, "Sit, Holdyn, and explain to me why you lied to your bishop about the woman Nelda."

"I did not lie."

Holdyn's voice, which could fill a church, was barely audible. Bell was quite certain of what he said, although he heard it as a faint murmur, not really distinguishable as words. He knew from the expression on the bishop's face as he leaned forward to hear better.

"And that is a lie," Winchester snapped, his own voice slightly raised. "You said you did not know her, yet she was the one who stole the gilt cup you replaced, she was the one who regularly took money that you, likely deliberately, left out for her. She was the one who stole your crucifix—if it was stolen. You said you did not lie with her, but . . ."

An expression of horror twisted Holdyn's face. "No. Oh, no! I never would. Never." Tears filled his eyes and spilled over. He hid his face in his hands. "And yet it is all my fault, my sin."

"*What* was your fault? Your sin?"

"I brought her here, you see." The priest had lifted his head, but his eyes were staring . . . blind.

"You brought her here?" Astonishment raised the bishop's voice. "Why? You say you did not lie with her. Then for what did you bring her?"

"Of course I did not lie with her!" Anger and disgust momentarily brought life to Father Holdyn's pale and tired face. "I brought her to keep my house. To lift my spirit when it was weighed down by labor and hopelessness. To be my light and laughter, as she had always been."

For a moment Winchester was silent, shocked. Then he said, distastefully, "You sound as if you loved her."

"Of course I loved her," Holdyn sighed. "She was my sister. She had always kept my house and made me happy." He put his face into his hands again and his shoulders shook with weeping. "That was my sin. I knew I should have found a husband for her. But she was such a precious comfort—a good housekeeper and always merry. Yet if I had found her a husband, she would have been alive today, surrounded by her children."

Or she would have been dead of childbearing, Bell thought; he had two living sisters, but there had been three. He did not move or speak and he kept his face expressionless.

Holdyn lifted his face again, looking pleadingly at Winchester. "But she said she did not wish to marry," he explained. "She said that she was happy keeping my household. And when London came and elevated me to overseeing the parishes in his diocese, she was thrilled. She greatly desired to come with me." He closed his eyes momentarily and swallowed hard. Then, as if he could not bring himself to say more about Nelda, he went on, "London said there was much looseness and corruption, the city being what it was and that he was getting too old to oversee matters as he should. But that kept me very busy. I was much away—"

"She was your sister," Winchester interrupted, voice tight and hard. "Yet when I asked if you knew her, you said you did not! Why did you lie?"

"I did not lie," Holdyn whispered. "You did not ask if I loved her. You asked if I knew her . . . and, alas, I had just discovered that I did not know Nelda at all."

"What do you mean you did not know her?"

"I knew she was light of heart and mind but I thought her clean . . . as clean as any woman can be . . . and loved her. When she left me a message that she had found a man she truly desired, I was saddened but not surprised that she had gone . . . outside of the bond of marriage. She came back to ask for money. I tried to reason with her, to plead with her, to offer a dowry and find a man who would marry her, even soiled as she was. She laughed at me. She said she would never marry a dull common clod. Her man was a knight, and she was as good as married being with him alone, although no priest would fasten the binding."

"You were jealous. Did you kill her for that?"

Bell frowned at Winchester's question. Nelda had been living in Linley's house for several years. If Holdyn was going to kill her out of jealousy, he would have done so much sooner, which Holdyn's indignant answer confirmed.

"Kill her? Of course not! I would never harm Nelda. And I was not jealous. I was troubled for her soul but I hoped her passion for the man would diminish and she would have time to repent. Meanwhile I saw that she was happy. She visited now and again and she looked well. She said her man was always kind to her, but that he did not have much money. I gave her a little, but the needs of the Church came first." He hesitated and looked up at Winchester, new tears running down his cheeks. "My fault. My sin. I should have seen sooner that she would find another way to get money."

"When you learned there was more than one man, you quarreled with her? She fell down the stairs by accident?" Now Winchester sounded sympathetic, inviting confidences.

"I never quarreled with her." Holdyn's voice was husky with weariness and grief. "I had not seen her since the Monday when she took my crucifix. I was annoyed, but I knew she would keep the crucifix safe until I was ready to redeem it. There was no great hurry for that. I was very busy. I knew you were coming on Friday and I was making all ready."

If Holdyn had not seen Nelda since Monday, Bell thought, Holdyn could not have known that Gehard beat her on Tuesday. Likely he did not know of Gehard's connection with Nelda at all and would not have suspected him of killing her. Thus, he would have no reason to murder Gehard. Holdyn now looked as if he were ready to collapse, as drained and white as any tortured man. And it had been torture for him, Bell thought. There was no point in pursuing him further, except for a direct question about where he was and what he was doing on Thursday night. Bell moved restlessly. The bishop turned his head and glanced at him. Then he sighed.

"Yes, all was ready for me. Holdyn, in the name of God, tell me, without all these delicate prevarications between knowing and loving, where were you and what were you doing on Thursday night?"

"Thursday night?" Holdyn sounded dazed and exhausted, but his voice had become firmer. "Oh, the night before you came? I was at home, working on the accounts and the reports of my oversight of the parishes. My chief clerk will tell you. He was with me working until after Matins, and he slept in my bedchamber on a pallet until we began work again soon after Prime." He uttered a tired sob. "I did not kill her or cause her to have an accident by which she died. I could not have hurt her, even had I known what she had become. Would I be such a monster as to kill her with all her sins upon her when if she lived I could hope still to redeem her?"

To both Bell and Winchester it was a convincing argument. They had known Holdyn for years and his piety and honesty, the strength of his faith, were long proven. That any man could sin and become entangled and struggle to free himself, was possible. That Holdyn would murder his sister—whose identity could be easily established—because she had become a whore and stolen his crucifix was not. The bishop breathed a huge sigh of relief. Bell nodded. Winchester would not lose his right hand.

Then turning his head, the bishop said, "Are you convinced, Bell? Do you have any further questions for Father Holdyn?"

"I will confirm that Nelda was Father Holdyn's sister," Bell said, "but the only other question I have is to ask if he knew the man Gehard fitzRobert."

"Gehard fitzRobert," Holdyn repeated. "I know the name, but I do not know why." He closed his eyes. "Perhaps my clerk will know. I—I find it hard to think."

"Can you ride, Father Holdyn?" Bell asked. "I will lend you my palfrey. You cannot walk back to the palace."

"Thank you," the priest said faintly.

Bell and Winchester looked at each other. Without words Bell conveyed the fact that he would accompany Holdyn. He would make sure the episcopal vicar's servants took him off to his bed before he spoke to anyone. Once Holdyn was out of the way, Bell would confirm with the clerk where Holdyn was Thursday night and where the late bishop of London had found Holdyn. A messenger could be sent to that parish to determine who had kept Holdyn's house and whether the woman was known to be Holdyn's sister. Bell would ask, too, about Gehard.

"There are none so blind as those who will not see," Bell said to Magdalene when he arrived long after Complin. He stretched tiredly and leaned forward to rest his arms along the table. "What she was must have been plain to everyone in the household except Holdyn." He shook his head. "She dismissed all the servants and hired new just before she left."

"And you spent the whole afternoon trying to find them."

Bell smiled. "It was not so difficult. Holdyn kept good records so I was able to find the servants' families and eventually speak to the servants themselves. I am sorry I never knew Nelda. She must have been a strange person, but Holdyn was not alone in finding her delightful. Even the servants she dismissed liked her . . . but she was whoring while she lived as his housekeeper. They told me."

"*Was* she his sister?"

"Are you asking whether he was lying with her, denials to the contrary? I do not think so. The servants certainly did not think so. They all agreed that sister and brother was how they acted. In any event, we will know tomorrow or the next day for certain. Winchester sent a messenger to the village where Holdyn was born. His father was the miller there, a prosperous merchant, and his brother still owns the mill. Holdyn writes to him and has letters in return. The bishop was so sure of the answer, that he sent back Holdyn's crucifix."

"Then he is almost certainly innocent. He would not have said she was his sister when he has a living brother who must know the truth."

"Oh, yes. Father Holdyn is cleared. According to his clerk he recognized Gehard's name because there had twice been complaints from women stallkeepers about rough handling. Father Holdyn did not meet the man. The local priest spoke to him . . . for all the good it would have done. But it doesn't matter now. Even if Holdyn had remonstrated with Gehard himself, there was no cause for murder. Holdyn did not know that Gehard had beaten Nelda. He had not seen her since before that happened."

Magdalene nodded. "So that leaves Linley and Sir John. Where *is* Sir John? Why is he not here, seeking his letter?"

"I cannot say except that it is possible he or his horse was injured on the road . . . or he never went on the road." He groaned softly. "*Peste!* I forgot to stop by Baynard's Castle to ask about whether Sir John said where he was going when he left them, and if they knew which road he took."

"Will they be willing to give you any information? Lord

Hugh is not a great admirer of Winchester nor likely to be too willing to be helpful."

Bell showed his teeth in what was not a smile. "But I have the word of the would-be abductors of the bishop that they were to bring him to that warehouse opposite Paul's Wharf—so convenient for Baynard's Castle. The testimony of my men about what they heard is good before the law, too. Those who gave the information were dying." His eyes were ice-cold and his lips set like two bands of steel. "They knew it. They even wished for it."

Magdalene shuddered slightly. She had seen Bell kill, but always quickly and cleanly. She did not *want* to know that he could torture also.

"I may drop a hint or two about that attack and about the strange death of the man who hired the attackers . . . They will wish to oblige me and if the answers are not important to them to be rid of me as soon as possible."

"Just be sure that they do not get rid of you . . . permanently."

Bell laughed. "Never fear. I am not an idiot. I will bring a full troop, half to come in with me and half to wait without to be sure we all come out." His eyes dropped to the bright cuffs on which Magdalene was binding off a short edge. "Those are pretty."

"Yes," Magdalene said, laughing. Bell did love fine clothing. "But they are not for you, my greedy friend. They are my excuse tomorrow for going to speak to Claresta. I will offer the cuffs and ask her to try to remember when Linley actually left Rhyton's house, but I really want to speak to the servants. They were Bertrild's slaves, who Mainard freed. They know me and trust me. Claresta may not know exactly when Linley left, but I hope that Jean will know."

Bell frowned. "It is possible that Linley will be there. From what I heard from his fellow officers, he is mostly to be found at Rhyton's house. I am not too happy about your meeting him. I would go with you, but I need to go to Baynard's Castle first."

"I cannot leave going to Lime Street too late or Claresta will be gone to the shop, and it is the Lime Street servants I must question. Possibly you will be back from Baynard's Castle before I leave, but if not . . . Yes, I would be happier if I knew you would follow me there. And you will not frighten Jean and the others; they know you as Mainard's friend."

Bell yawned and stretched again. "I am off to bed then. I think I have walked ten times around London today." He looked down as Magdalene set one cuff aside and began to finish the other. "Hmmm," he said, "if Claresta will not buy the cuffs—you said she did not want to buy for the unwelcome wedding—I will buy them."

Magdalene chuckled. "When did you ever buy any piece of my embroidery?"

And then the laugh froze in her throat as she saw the expression on Bell's face change. His hand dropped to the purse fastened to his belt, and he removed five silver pennies from it.

"I desire to buy something else also," he said, and put the coins on the table.

"I am not for sale," Magdalene hissed.

"You are a whore. You have told me so many times. You have insisted on it. A whore is for sale."

"Not a rich whore. A rich whore picks and chooses the men she wishes to take to her bed."

What a fool she was! She should have taken his five pennies. She could have returned them in the morning with a jest about the pleasure he had given her. Now she felt sick. She would lose him again. He would say that she then *chose* to lie with William. What could she answer? He had not forgotten she had told him in Oxford that she loved William too. If she used the excuse that William was too powerful to refuse, he would know she was lying.

But Bell did not mention William. He said, "When you claimed you were retired, you picked and chose me. I have not changed."

Hope stirred in Magdalene. It seemed that Bell, too, wished to pretend that William did not exist. She grinned up at him. "I chose you for pleasure, for laughter. I do not want your coin. I prefer to take my pay in other ways, Bellamy of Itchen."

"Oh." Now he grinned too. "Well, I am not for sale either. If you want your pay, you will need to take my terms for it."

And before she could reply, he walked down the corridor to the room in which he had been sleeping. He grinned again as he began to take off his clothing, remembering that Magdalene intended to take on another woman. There would be no convenient bed available for him once they found someone suitable, and he was quite confident that Magdalene did not intend to put him out. Then there would be only her bed . . .

He felt not at all frustrated and in very good spirits as he lay down, and he wondered how Magdalene would explain her invitation. He wondered, too, if he should simply yield at once or try to insist on paying her. He always enjoyed a tussle of wills with Magdalene. And before he had planned out what he would say to tease her, he fell asleep, still with the grin of satisfaction on his face.

Morning, though it was damp and foggy, did not blunt

his feeling of good cheer, and that sense of amused confidence must have communicated itself to Lord Hugh's men. The guard at the gate looked him up and down and sent at once for the master-at-arms. That man glanced sidelong at Bell when he identified himself and asked what the bishop wanted of his lord. Bell smiled.

"Nothing at all, except to ask about the Sir John to whom you gave lodging on last Thursday night."

The arrested expression on the master-at-arms' face told Bell plainly that the man knew of the letter Sir John thought he was carrying. He allowed himself to smile more broadly.

"Sir John is not Lord Hugh's man," the master-at-arms said uneasily.

"I never thought he was," Bell assured him. "I know he is Lord Mandeville's man. I merely wish to ascertain when he left Baynard's Castle on Friday—or on Thursday night if he had decided to travel at night—"

"No, it was Friday. He spoke to Lord Hugh before he left too, but—"

"Ah," Bell interrupted, "then I would be pleased if you would inform Lord Hugh of my arrival and ask if he could grant me just a few moments of his time. I wonder if from his window he could see a light from that warehouse that is across the river from Paul's Wharf."

"Lord Hugh's windows do not face the wharf."

Bell smiled again. "Then it would have to be from the battlements that a light would be visible. Was there a watch set?" Bell's voice was only mildly inquisitive, as if he could guess the answer without being told.

"A watch set when? For what? You are making no sense."

The tense anxiety of the questions told Bell that the man knew very well what he was talking about. "No?" The smile lingered on Bell's lips. "Possibly you were not told. But you will enquire as to whether Lord Hugh can grant me an audience? I promise I will keep him less than a quarter candlemark."

The master-at-arms hurried into the building. Bell nodded at Levin. "There is no reason to dismount. I do not expect to be within for more than a quarter candlemark. Eduin has the other men safe from arrow shot?"

"Right against the wall, Sir Bellamy, with shields ready."

"Good."

Bell smiled again, quite sure that the guards had heard the exchange, which assured that any harm coming to Sir Bellamy and his men would be swiftly reported to the bishop of Winchester. He began to walk slowly toward the door of the outbuilding that housed the stair going up into the keep. No one tried to stop him, and by the time he reached the door the master-at-arms was just stepping out. He led Bell up the stairs and through the great hall, which was actually not particularly great, to a low dais on which there was a table and behind it a tall cushioned chair with back and arms.

Bell came to the table and bowed, not smiling now, carefully keeping his face without any expression because he always felt a kind of contempt for Lord Hugh. It was not fair; there was nothing truly lacking in the man himself. It was just that he was a pale, rather unfinished version of Waleran de Meulan. That he resembled Waleran was natural; Waleran was his older brother. But Robert of Leicester, who was Waleran's twin, did not look like a washed out version of Waleran. The resemblance was strong, but Lord Robert looked like himself. Perhaps it was Lord Hugh's expression.

"Well, what do you want, Sir Bellamy?" Lord Hugh asked.

"Information about the Sir John who was your guest on Thursday night. Earlier that night a woman called Nelda Roundheels—"

Lord Hugh laughed. "The woman who was found in the bishop of Winchester's bed, eh?"

Bell said nothing while rage tightened his throat, but this was not a captain of a troop, and he still regretted the loss of control that had probably made him an enemy. Then he smiled, as sweetly as he knew how.

"She was dead before the bishop's bed arrived from Winchester with some twenty guardsmen and ten clerks, but the men who were told to bring Winchester to the warehouse across from Paul's Wharf were alive when I took them and had a most interesting tale to tell—"

"Lies. All lies."

"As is the tale of the whore in Winchester's bed. My lord the bishop was not in London when the whore was killed, but he was . . . ah . . . annoyed that someone had carried her corpse into his house. Which is why I am asking what time Sir John came to Baynard's Castle that Thursday night."

"How would I know? I was abed. Do you think my men wake me for every nobody who comes begging shelter?"

"No, but I thought since Sir John was a messenger to Lord Mandeville from Robert of Gloucester—" Bell kept his voice smooth, but he was interested to see a brief expression of surprise cross Lord Hugh's face; he was not supposed to know that Sir John had been to see Gloucester "—you might have asked him whether his message was secret or he was willing to speak of it to you and whether the message was urgent. I need to know whether Sir John actually rode north to find his master. You see, the man who hired the troop to attack Winchester was murdered only a few days later."

"Who hired them? Who?" Lord Hugh was furious. "I will . . . Oh, you said he was dead already."

The naked shock on Lord Hugh's face followed by fury and then frustration was all the proof Bell needed—not that he needed much after what Raoul had told Magdalene—that Hugh was in no way involved in the attempt on Winchester.

"Yes, murdered, as I said. In fact, poisoned. And the poison was purchased by someone who could fit Sir John's description."

"But Sir John had only just got off a ship from Normandy that arrived on the midnight tide. How could he—"

"He might or might not have got off a ship that day, but it did not arrive on the midnight tide. On that Thursday, Sir John tried for accommodation at the Old Priory Guesthouse before Nones. Thus, he was in London long before Vespers, not to mention Matins. And the murdered man, Gehard fitzRobert—"

Lord Hugh's lips had parted as if he were about to protest when Bell said that Sir John had been at the Old Priory Guesthouse before Nones, but by the time Bell registered the expression, he had continued to the mention of Gehard's death.

"Gehard?" Lord Hugh's voice came out in a surprised screech. "Gehard is dead?"

"Yes, m'lord," Bell said gravely, thinking, *so Magdalene and I were right about that seal. Lord Hugh knew Gehard and knew him well; the Beaufort seal marked with that left-slanting cut was Gehard's and he was serving the Beauforts despite being Mandeville's man.* "Did you know him? He was master-at-arms for a troop that Lord Mandeville left in London to guard the Tower."

"Yes, I knew him," Lord Hugh said reluctantly but

knowing he had exposed that fact too nakedly to lie about it. "I did not much like him, but I did not think he would be easy to kill."

"I do not think so either," Bell said, and then pretended a slight shudder. "Someone gave him poisoned wine."

"Oh, wine." Lord Hugh sighed, however his expression was contemptuous. "Gehard had a weakness for wine . . . and for ale . . . and for anything like that."

Bell had not liked Gehard either, but he felt a flicker of sympathy for the man, the unacknowledged bastard, used by the family but treated as unmentionable.

Then a frown darkened Lord Hugh's expression. "Poison," he repeated slowly. "That is ugly. Do you know who . . . Wait, did you not say the buyer of the poison could have fit the description of Sir John?"

"Yes, m'lord." Bell now wanted to be polite as it looked as if Lord Hugh felt some vague responsibility about Gehard's death and might wish to help find his murderer. He repeated the description given by the apothecary.

Lord Hugh snorted. "Yes. It might be Sir John, but it might be almost anyone else also." He frowned again, this time in thought. "But I am certain Sir John intended to ride to Oxford as fast as he could. He had with him a letter that he felt would make his fortune by increasing his importance to Lord Mandeville. He said as much."

"He did not show you the letter?"

"For what purpose? It was sealed and I knew to whom it was addressed."

Lord Hugh had no expression so purposefully that Bell was sure he was repressing glee at Winchester's stupid knight who, he believed, had no idea that the letter carried by Sir John bore a disaster for the bishop. Bell concentrated on concealing his own expression.

"And he left Baynard's Castle, when?"

Lord Hugh answered readily, obviously glad to be done with a subject on which he might betray something important. He said, "He slept late, having come in late. I had been long abed when he arrived. I suppose he broke his fast when he woke. He then came to thank me for his lodging and to bid me farewell . . . hmmm. Near Tierce it must have been, but I cannot remember whether I had just heard the bells or heard them after he left. He did seem anxious to be gone, but I have no idea which way he went."

That was the best he would do, Bell decided. Sir John had certainly implied that he wished to reach Mandeville as soon as possible. Lord Hugh did not seem to be concealing any guilty knowledge about Sir John's departure, and Bell could not think of any advantage to him in lying for Sir John.

"If I might have your permission to ask of your men just what time Sir John arrived and whether he said any more to them than he did to you, m'lord?"

Lord Hugh waved him away. "By all means, but what difference would it make what he told them or in which direction he started? Just out of sight, he could have turned any other way, and my men would have no way of knowing. But ask if you will."

"Thank you, m'lord," Bell said, backed a few steps and then went down the length of the hall and down the stairs.

What Lord Hugh had said was perfectly true. Nonetheless Bell did ask questions. He got confirmation that Sir John had arrived after Matins that Thursday night and that he probably had been ashore for some hours. One of the men remembered that the horse Sir John rode did not seem to have come directly off a ship. Horses did not take well to travel by sea, and Sir John's mount did not have that look of terror and exhaustion. The men who had seen him ride off agreed that he had set out toward the road to Oxford.

A wasted morning, Bell thought, as he remounted Monseigneur and led his troop along the Thames toward the bridge, but necessary. He had not learned anything he did not know, but sure as death would come to all men, had he *not* gone to Baynard's Castle and asked his questions, there would have been some essential fact he would have missed.

He stopped briefly at the Old Priory Guesthouse, but Magdalene had just left. In fact, Diot was surprised he had not met her on the bridge; however, the bridge was always so crowded that it was easy to miss people, and everyone had pressed back, away from the center, to give his mounted troop room to pass.

As he mounted, Bell considered sending his men back to the bishop's house and following Magdalene immediately. Then he imagined having to leave Monseigneur in the street where some fool would surely have approached the valuable horse and been maimed or killed. Monseigneur did not take kindly to unknown persons trying to touch him when he was saddled. Beside that, the effect of his entering Rhyton's house in full armor would doubtless have set everyone on edge. Moreover, he did not really believe that Linley would attack Magdalene in the house of his betrothed.

The servants were not likely to be of any help, but surely Linley would not want them as witness. As long as he arrived before Magdalene left the house so that Linley could not follow her, she would be safe. Bell touched Monseigneur with his heel. It would do no harm to take the time to change his clothing and walk back to the Lime Street house.

CHAPTER 17

By the time Magdalene had broken her fast and was ready to leave, the clouds had partially cleared and fitful sunshine was drying the damp from the streets. She paused at the gate, hearing Dulcie put the chain into place, and looked north toward the bridge but there was no sign of Bell. Shrugging mentally, she made sure her veil was firmly in place, and set out. She carried an empty basket for any small thing that caught her eye.

Her tale to Claresta would be that she had decided to do some shopping in the East Chepe and, since she was going to be so close to the Lime Street house, had brought the cuffs with the running hounds design that Claresta had admired. If Claresta purchased them, that would be fine. If Claresta did not want them, Magdalene would say she had lost nothing beyond a few extra steps and a little time.

The door of Rhyton's house opened so promptly that Magdalene had not completely lowered her hand from knocking. And the expression of disappointment on Jean's face was eloquent.

"Who were you expecting?" Magdalene asked, smiling.

At that moment a man's voice, loud and angry, came from the open door into the common room.

"Where is he? You said he would be here today."

Claresta's response was also louder than she usually spoke, but annoyed not frightened. "I said he *probably* would be here today. I told you yesterday that Sir Linley had ridden to Godalming for his father to approve some changes my father desired in the marriage contract. Usually he does his business with his father when he arrives, spends the night, and then he rides back to London the next day. I assumed he would come this morning to speak to my father—but that would be at his place of business. Why did you not seek him there?"

"Because what I have to say to him needs privacy, not the bustle of a busy shop."

Wide-eyed, while Claresta was replying, Magdalene had whispered "Who?" to Jean.

"He said his name was Sir John and that he was a friend of Sir Linley." Jean's very low voice trembled.

"Oh." Magdalene bit her lip with chagrin. She could not go in and confront Sir John. Unfortunately he knew her all too well as the whoremistress of the Old Priory Guesthouse. "I would rather not interrupt," she said to Jean. "Let me stand by the door to the kitchen." And as she followed Jean to the back of the house, she remembered the expression on the servant's face when he saw her at the front door, and asked softly, "But who did you expect when I knocked?"

"Master Spencer had some business with Mistress Claresta that he could not finish yesterday before he had to return to close the shop for Master Rhyton. He said he would come back this morning." He hesitated as Sir John's voice came to them saying he needed privacy and then whispered, "Mistress Magdalene what am I to do? He should not shout at Mistress Claresta, but . . . but she has not summoned me, and . . ."

Before Jean could finish his sentence or Magdalene reply to it, Claresta showed she needed no assistance. Clear and cold, her voice high with anger, she gave Sir John as good as he had tried to give her.

"If you do not moderate your tone to me, Sir John, you

can have your privacy out in the street. I am not yet the common wife of a baron whom you can treat with contempt. I am an honorable burgher's daughter, and I will not be shouted at in my own home."

A low mumble so choked with rage that at first Magdalene could make out no words came in response. However, soon, loud and aggressive again Magdalene heard Sir John say that Linley had caused him great harm.

"That is between you and Sir Linley," Claresta snapped, but she was no longer so angry and there was a decided note of interest in her voice, as she added, "If it is so very important, why do you not sit down and wait for him? I am sure he will be here sooner or later. Would you like some wine?"

Magdalene was sure that Claresta was about to ask in what way Linley had harmed Sir John, perhaps hoping that she would hear something so disreputable that she could still escape the unwanted marriage. But the door knocker sounded again. Jean hurried to answer it, and if Claresta spoke, the words were drowned in Jean's eager recounting to Spencer of the unexpected guest Claresta had. The big journeyman hesitated, half turning to leave, but Jean, desperate for support in case Sir John turned nasty again, described the knight's incivility.

"Shouted at Mistress Claresta!" Spencer growled. "We will see about that!" And he marched off into the common room.

"Oh, Spencer," Claresta said, sounding less than overjoyed to see him. "Did you see Sir Linley at my father's shop?"

"No, Mistress Claresta, but I did not come from the shop. I left soon after Prime to go, as you bade me, to Master Perekin FitzRevery about that heavy cloth you thought would do for the northern trade. I . . . ah . . . had to be careful what I said to him because—"

"You mean you don't even know if Linley will come here at all?" Sir John interrupted furiously.

There was a very brief silence, as if Spencer started to reply, equally furiously, remembered himself and was now seeking for something to say. Claresta came to his support.

"Sir John was just about to tell me in what way Sir Linley had injured him," she said.

And the knocker sounded again. Jean, who had remained near the door while Spencer marched into the common room, opened it. This time it was Linley.

"Oh, Sir Linley," Jean said, somewhat more loudly than he usually spoke and quickly closed the door as if he wanted to prevent Linley's escape. "Mistress Claresta is in the common room."

It was just as well that he had closed the door, because Sir John erupted from the room, shouting, "Whoremongering bastard, where is my letter?"

Magdalene, watching from the shadows, thought that Sir Linley would have backed out of the door had it been open. But that, she judged, was only because of the violence in Sir John's voice and gesture. Linley's expression was totally dumbfound. To Magdalene it seemed plain enough that Linley had no idea what Sir John was raving about.

"Letter? What letter? Have you gone mad?"

"Your whore stole my letter and you killed her to get it. What have you done with it?"

Linley opened and closed his mouth rather like a fish gasping out of water, and Magdalene thought his face had gone pasty white but she could not be certain in the dim light with the door closed. But what he said was, "For God's sake, Sir John. Watch what you say in the house of my betrothed. I have no idea what you are talking about. Go away now. I will meet you at the Cask of Wine—"

"Where all of Surrey's men who are bound to support you will be? I want that letter. I want it *now!*"

Sir John seized Linley by the front of his tunic and dragged him forward, which was fortunate as the knocker sounded yet again. Half stunned, Jean did what was strong habit for him and opened the door. Bell's massive form filled the doorway. He stepped in, and without a word unfastened Sir John's hand from Linley's tunic and began to herd both men toward the common room.

Magdalene slipped out of the kitchen and followed, half concealed by Bell's broad back. She lifted her veil to shield her face, but no one looked at her as she slid along the wall to stand in the shadow of some shelves holding handsome silver cups and plates.

Recovering somewhat from his shock, Linley turned on Sir John. "I do not know anything about any letter. I find it hard to believe that Nelda would have stolen a letter. She could not read. A letter would be of no value to her. How would she know it was important to anyone?"

"Because you would have told her!" Sir John bellowed. "Because you would have bidden her search each man you brought to her for Gloucester's seal or Salisbury's or his son's or nephews' and Winchester's too."

"You are mad!" Linley exclaimed, but faintly.

Magdalene thought he looked slightly frightened as if he might have mentioned—not a specific letter, but his interest in any information about Gloucester. From what he had said about Nelda in the past, Linley found her clever and an easy person to talk to.

In the shadow of the shelves, Magdalene nodded. It was not at all uncommon for a man to discuss what was uppermost in his thoughts in pillow talk. Linley might indeed have told Nelda how valuable it would be to him to lay hands on any proof of a connection between Gloucester and those the king wished to call enemies.

"Mad, am I?" Sir John snarled. "You tried to get the letter from her and she refused to give it to you. You tried to take it by force. She fought you and you threw her down the stair. You even tried to make me believe I killed her—"

"You drunken, drugged sot," Linley shrieked, pale and sweating. "I was not even there that night. You cannot prove I was there. I was here, and I drank too much of Rhyton's wine so that he bade me go, but I wanted more and went to the Cask of Wine. They will tell you there how I came in drunk and fell insensible—"

"You were not there?" Sir John gasped, outraged. "Who woke me? Who told me that Nelda was dead? Who, in God's name, convinced me to move her body to the bishop of Winchester's house?"

"I did not," Linley screamed. "No one saw me. You cannot prove I was there! It was you inside the bishop's house."

"Yes, you puling coward. You left all the labor to me, and you even deserted me, ran away and left me there."

"I was never there!"

While the two went again and again through "You were," "I wasn't," Magdalene went softly out and brought Jean to the entrance to the room. She had told him that he must speak the truth, that Mistress Claresta would be *very* pleased with him if he spoke the truth, and that Sir Bellamy would protect him from everyone else.

"Two witnesses are necessary," Magdalene said, breaking into another exchange of accusation and denial. Linley and Sir John gaped at her, shocked into silence.

"Jean was in the house that night. It is his responsibility to lock the doors after guests, if there are any, are gone and the family is abed. Some time ago Mistress Claresta told me that she went to bed after her father and Sir Linley began to drink their wine and did not know when Sir Linley departed. However, Jean must know—"

"Jean will be out in the street naked after I am the master of this household if he knows too much," Linley said threateningly.

"And he will be out in the street *immediately* if he does not tell the truth, whatever it is," Claresta said from where she stood beside the silent but glowering Spencer. "And I will stand witness of your threat to him. So will Spencer."

Magdalene patted Jean's arm. "Do not be afraid. Just speak the truth. We will all stand witness to what you say."

Not that Magdalene could stand witness to anything, since she was a whore and excommunicate and unable to swear an oath. However, Jean knew and trusted her and knew she would speak for him to Master Mainard, who was nearly his god, so it was the best thing to say to reassure him.

Jean swallowed hard. "When Mistress Claresta went up to bed, she bade me wait by the door for any order from Master Rhyton. Mistress Claresta is always careful that her servants understand what is needed so we will not be blamed for what is not our fault. I saw Master Rhyton start to rise, perhaps to call me to bring another flagon of wine, but he nearly fell. He said then that he had had enough. I saw Sir Linley to the door and locked it behind him and then helped Master Rhyton up the stairs to his bed."

"And the time?" Bell asked, blocking a movement by Linley with his body; his voice was softer than usual, calm. Bell had known Jean when he was so starved and constantly beaten that he was reduced nearly to idiocy by fear.

"A little after Complin," Jean whispered. "I heard the bells. I was tired and I wondered when Sir Linley would leave so I could go to bed."

"Thank you, Jean," Claresta said, smiling.

Bell looked down at Linley, who was cursing lying servants and fingering his knife suggestively. "And I have the word of Mistress Pechet of the Cask of Wine that it was near Matins when you came into the alehouse," Bell said loud enough to drown Linley's threats. "So where were you between Complin and Matins?"

"He was getting my letter from the whore!" Sir John burst out.

"I tell you I never knew of your letter, whatever it was and to whom," Linley shouted, but he was shaking and white. "If Nelda took it she did not tell *me.* I knew nothing of it."

"Then what were you quarreling about with Nelda that made you throw her down the stairs?" Bell asked.

"I didn't," Linley screamed. "I never wanted to hurt Nelda." He uttered a half sob and then said more quietly, "Anyone will tell you that I never beat her. She was clever and she was amusing. I knew she was not perfect, and she brought terrible trouble on me—"

"When she stole Gehard fitzRobert's family seal," Magdalene said.

Linley looked at her, but his thoughts were turned inward and he did not seem to recognize her. "Gehard beat her terribly but she . . . Perhaps she was afraid that if she admitted what she had done and returned the seal he would kill her, or perhaps she thought she could make some profit out of it." He sighed but looked at Bell, not at Magdalene. "She was terribly greedy."

"But Gehard threatened you." Magdalene's voice was soft, sympathetic; there was no accusation in it. "You could not fight him and you had to be rid of him. He was a terrible man. Even his own soldiers feared him."

"Yes, yes. There was only one way. No one grieved for *him*. But I never meant harm to Nelda. I pleaded with her but she would not give me the seal to return to him. I only meant to shake her. And she bit me, and I pushed her, and she fell . . . I doubt I will ever find a woman so companionable."

"How nice to know you find a whore more companionable than I."

Claresta's voice stabbed like an icicle pulled from a roof edge. Linley did not seem to notice. Spencer made a low, growling noise and his big hands clenched and unclenched. Bell spared a glance for the big journeyman and wondered just how long it would be before he took Linley apart.

"Companionable!" Sir John roared. "Companionable? Oh, yes. She made me laugh and fed me tidbits and sips of this and that between chuckles. She asked me where I had been, saying she smelled the sea on my clothing. She laughed and teased so I nearly forgot what she was and I told her I had been to Normandy, that the earl of Gloucester had received me. And then she drugged me and stole my letter."

"It is nothing to do with me," Linley said more briskly. It was plain to Magdalene that he was relieved by not needing to confess he had poisoned Gehard and expected Nelda's death to be accepted as accidental. "I knew nothing of it. I was busy here and had not seen Nelda for almost a week."

"But I am sure she knew you would be returning to her," Claresta snapped.

"That is none of your business," Linley said to her, with utter indifference. "Why should you care? You will be my wife by law, lady of Godalming, which is what your father wants. And the son I will get on you will be baron after me." He looked down his nose. "That is enough for such as you."

Claresta drew a sharp breath, but Spencer started toward Linley, his big hands out to grasp. Bell turned from where he stood, somewhat to the side but between Linley and Sir John and in easy reach of both. He took two quick steps to put himself in Spencer's path.

Seeing the threat from Spencer contained, Linley turned back to Sir John and shook his head. Now his voice had an easy confidence. He said, "If Nelda took your letter, it is gone for good. The whore—" he waved at Magdalene "—came with the bishop's man and cleaned out her rooms. She told me that everything Nelda had went to the bishop of Winchester. So Winchester must have the letter, too, if Nelda stole it."

"Winchester? Winchester has it? Then I am ruined!"

The husky whisper should have warned Bell, but the easy confidence of Linley's voice and his crude dismissal of Claresta had brought a snarl to Spencer's lips. For just one moment too long, Bell's eyes were fixed on the young giant and Sir John's knife was out and buried in Linley's throat. Then Bell was on him and the knife was pulled free and wrested from his hand.

But for Linley it was too late. The knife had severed the big vein in his neck. A fountain of blood followed the blade when Bell pulled it out, running over Bell's hand and spattering his tunic. Linley's hands flailed helplessly toward his throat but never even reached it before his body slid bonelessly to the floor.

Claresta screamed, high and shrill, and Spencer pulled her into his arms and buried her face in his broad chest.

Magdalene nearly fainted. The knife. The blood. The body falling all stained with red. Lashed by memory, she held out her hands, but they were clean. She had not shed this blood. She closed her eyes and swallowed her sickness, leaning on wall behind her for support.

"Why?" Bell asked, still stunned by what had happened, staring at Sir John's suffused face. "He was a nothing. Why kill him?"

"Nothing?" Sir John gasped, wrenching at his wrist in Bell's grip and pulling free when Bell relaxed his hold. "That nothing has destroyed me, utterly destroyed me."

"*He* destroyed you because *you* chose to sleep with his whore and she stole from you?" Bell said, disbelievingly. "That is ridiculous."

"I tell you he did it all! If he were not a puling coward, he would not have killed the whore. If he had not lied to me . . . He told me he found her dead. He shook me out of a drugged sleep and he accused me of killing her. And then when I could hardly think, he demanded that I help him get rid of the body. And he said, laughing, that we should put it in the bishop's house and let him explain it while he tried to call a convocation to reprimand the king."

Bell started to laugh. "You were truly hung by your own rope. Nelda had the letter you so urgently desire wrapped in her breastband. I found it when I looked her over to see if there was any cause, other than her broken neck for her death." He shook his head at Sir John and uttered another chuckle. "You are right. Had you left Nelda lying at the foot of the stair . . . Well, you would not have had the letter, but it would have made all the scandal your master desired."

"Laugh at me, will you?" Sir John's eyes narrowed. "You will laugh less when your bishop is reduced to the state of that other traitor, Salisbury."

Bell's lips thinned when he heard Winchester called a traitor, but he did understand the desperation of a man who had failed a master with little patience or compassion. He understood, too, that despite being addressed to Winchester the letter was never supposed to come to him. Likely Mandeville would have brought it to the king, with some tale of how his man had come by it that would blacken the bishop.

Mandeville, Bell guessed, hoped to raise himself in King Stephen's eyes by adding proof that Winchester was a traitor to the rage the king must feel over Winchester's call for a convocation. Having that ploy not only fail but backlash at him, when Winchester found the letter on the body of a whore, would infuriate Mandeville. His spite would turn on Sir John, who had not only failed him but actually helped the bishop. And Mandeville was the kind not only to dismiss Sir John from his service but to blacken his name so that no other noble would be willing to employ him.

"I will go back to Gloucester," Sir John said, staring up at Bell. "I will explain to him that I lost the letter and beg for another to be written. He will do it. It will cost him no more than the sheet of parchment . . ."

"That is useless," Bell said, almost with sympathy. "The bishop has already sent the letter to the king and explained how it came into his hands."

"Is that so? I am very glad you told me. Then I will not waste my time on a letter proffering friendship. I will bring back a reply from Gloucester . . . a reply . . . yes . . . that will prove Winchester is a traitor."

"Winchester is no traitor," Bell snapped. "Don't be stupid, man. The king is his brother."

"Stupid am I? We will see who is the cleverer."

Sir John started to turn away, but Bell's hand fell on his shoulder.

"Let me go," Sir John snarled, shaking free of Bell's light grasp, and stepping back almost onto Magdalene's toes.

"I cannot let you go," Bell said, frowning. "You say you had cause, but in my eyes you just murdered Sir Linley, who was not even holding a weapon. He is bleeding at your feet. I cannot allow you to take ship for Normandy . . . at least not until you have explained yourself to the sheriff and Master Octadenarius the justiciar. Come—"

"No!" Sir John bellowed, suddenly drawing his sword. "I *will* go to Normandy. You cannot stop me!"

Claresta screamed again, and Spencer pushed her behind him, himself backing as far away as he could get from the moving weapon. Bell danced aside from the stroke, his hand going to the hilt of his own sword. But as he twisted to avoid another slashing blow, his elbow struck Spencer's arm and he cast a single glance over his shoulder. There was no room for him to swing a sword; a backstroke might hit the two innocents behind him. Cursing luridly, Bell drew his long poniard. If he could catch Sir John's sword arm or hand, he could disarm him.

Magdalene neither moved nor cried out although the blood pounded in her throat so hard she thought she would choke on her fear for her lover. She knew that the very worst thing she could do was to distract him by any sound or movement. She saw him reach for his sword, felt a small flutter of relief. Sword in hand, there were few men who could match Bell.

The relief was short lived. Fear surged higher when Bell

backed to avoid Sir John's second blow and nearly collided with Spencer. Magdalene saw Bell glance over his shoulder at Claresta and Spencer, sobbed behind bitten lips as she saw his hand leave his sword hilt. No! she cried silently. Knife against sword. No!

Bell dodged again, but Magdalene saw he was closer to Sir John, saw the edge of Sir John's blade brush against Bell's sleeve, saw him lean precariously away from the slice, barely drawing his leg clear of the sword edge in time. He could not escape again.

Magdalene could not breathe. She heard Sir John cursing Bell with a stream of foul obscenities. She saw him raise his sword, gripping it now in both hands for a killing blow. She saw that if Sir John were closer to Bell, the sword would go beyond him, not strike him at all. Still silent, she leapt forward, arms rigid, both hands slamming into Sir John's back with her full weight and all the impetus she could get from her strong legs.

Sir John screamed. Bell shouted in surprise and belated warning as Sir John fell against him, fell against the knife he was holding at waist height, slightly tilted upward, ready to strike at the wrist of Sir John's sword arm as the arm came down. Instead when Sir John fell against him, both arms struck Bell's shoulder, but the sword he was holding was well beyond Bell's body.

Spencer also cried out as the sword seemed to come directly at him. He dragged Claresta sideways, still shielding her with his body, but that was scarcely necessary as the sword drooped downward and then dropped from Sir John's hand.

Sir John himself seemed to be clinging to Bell and then he screamed again as Bell pushed him away, pulling his knife free. Sir John staggered backward, crying out once more, his hands reaching for his hurt; then he began to fall. Bell caught at him, one-handed, holding his knife well away in the other hand. Sir John's body twisted in his grip and he wailed wordlessly, but Bell managed to ease him down to the floor, where he lay quite close to Sir Linley's body, moaning, hands pressed to his wound. Bell stood staring down at both bodies, eyes and mouth open with shock.

"What happened?" he gasped. "Why did he leap at me?" By long habit that operated without thought, Bell cleaned his knife on his already blood smeared tunic and sheathed it.

No one answered his question. Spencer had been watching only Sir John and the threat from his weapon. Claresta, terrified, had been hiding her face in the journeyman's broad back. Magdalene was backed against the wall again. If Bell had not seen what she had done, she decided, she would not admit it. He would be fit to murder her for interfering in his fight, even if her action had saved his life.

"Pu—pu—" Sir John struggled to lift his head, his voice a gurgling mumble.

Magdalene stiffened as Bell went down on one knee to listen, but the effort had done some final damage to the injured man. Blood ran out of Sir John's mouth, stifling anything more he might have said, and he fell back limply. Shaking his head, Bell pulled Sir John's hands aside so he could see the wound. Blood was pulsing out of it and air bubbles frothed the blood, but Sir John was still breathing. Bell hesitated for one long moment and then stood up.

Behind him Claresta was sobbing hysterically. Bell turned toward where the journeyman still stood, nearly paralyzed by shock. "Take her out of here," Bell said to Spencer. "Take her up to her solar and send the servant, Jean I think it is, in here to me."

Spencer nodded, looked at the two bodies, and lifted Claresta into his arms so she would not need to walk past them. He carried her out of the room with her face buried against his breast so she did not see the men, one dead, the other nearing that state.

"It is a kindness to let him die," Bell said to Magdalene in a troubled way when Spencer had left the room. "I have seen wounds like that. If I stopped the bleeding . . . if I could stop it, but I am not sure I could because I think the knife caught the edge of the heart or that big tube that comes out of the heart . . . But if I could he would die anyway, only in terrible pain and it would take days . . ."

He was babbling out of shock and guilt. Magdalene came forward, carefully lifting her skirt to keep it out of the blood on the floor.

"It was not your fault, Bell," she said soothingly.

Bell never seemed to feel any guilt over those he had decided to kill for what he considered a good cause, but for some reason Magdalene could not fathom he seemed to have sympathy for Sir John. Apparently, Magdalene thought with exasperation, Sir John's clear intention of killing Bell was not a good enough cause for Bell to kill him. She put a hand on his arm to give comfort.

As for her part in Sir John's death, her only interest in it was to keep Bell from discovering that she had been the cause. The blood no longer bothered her, nor did the two bodies on the floor. The shock of Linley's sudden death had brought back an evil memory, but she had buried it again.

Actually a definite sense of satisfaction covered any horror she might have felt regarding Sir John's death. He had tried to kill her dearling Bell; he had drawn his sword while Bell was unprepared, continued to wield it when he saw that Bell could not draw his own weapon without endangering Spencer and Claresta. No, she was not going to be worried about pushing Sir John into Bell's knife.

Unaware of Magdalene's thoughts and soothed by the comfort of her hand on his arm, Bell sighed. "No," he agreed, shaking his head, "it wasn't my fault. I saw no reason to kill him and didn't intend to do so. I intended to stab his sword arm, if I was lucky get my knife into his wrist so that he'd drop the sword. I can't imagine why he leapt at me."

Magdalene could feel Bell's arm trembling under her hand and she squeezed it gently. She did not like it that Bell was still so distressed. He would continue to worry about how Sir John died, might remember a half seen movement and suspect she had been involved.

"Perhaps he tripped on Linley's hand," Magdalene suggested blandly. "It is stretched out and I freely admit I was not watching Sir John's feet."

"I suppose," Bell said frowning as he looked down at the position of the bodies; then he laughed ruefully. "I was not watching his feet either."

Delighted that her suggestion was taking hold, Magdalene said, "Well, it would be justice if he tripped on Linley's hand, would it not? Perhaps Linley's lingering spirit moved the hand or even grasped at Sir John's foot."

That had a greater effect than Magdalene had intended. Bell shuddered and said, "We need a priest."

"We certainly do," Magdalene agreed.

She reconsidered an impulse of denial. It would be better to let the idea that Linley's ghost had tripped Sir John fix itself in Bell's mind. If that were true, Bell would be freed of all guilt for Sir John's death. If Linley's spirit had exacted vengeance through Bell's hand, Bell was not responsible. Also, Magdalene thought with satisfaction, it was not something he would wish to dwell upon.

Bell stepped away from Linley's body and asked irritably, "Where is that Jean?"

"Here," a choked and shaking voice replied from the doorway.

"For sweet Mary's sake, why did you not speak sooner?" Magdalene snapped, then shook her head when Jean cringed. "No, never mind that. Go at once to the nearest church for a priest so that he may give the last rites to these poor men. And as you go, send Hugo in here."

Jean rushed out and Bell looked puzzled. "Why Hugo?"

"Master Rhyton has a horse, I am sure. Hugo, I know from when Bertrild was killed, knows horses and can ride. If you tell him how to find Master Octadenarius's house, you can write a message to the justiciar and he can come himself or send someone to take the evidence about these deaths."

"You are right," Bell said. "It will be best if the tale is told when it is still clear in everyone's mind."

EPILOGUE

It was after dark before Bell finally reached the Old Priory Guesthouse. He came from the bishop of Winchester's house, across the grounds of the priory, and through the back gate. Thus he did not ring the bell at the front gate but knocked softly on the door of the house itself. For a moment his heart sank when no one answered. He was so tired he was near weeping.

He had raised his hand to knock again when Magdalene's voice came, tense and frightened, "Who is there?"

"Bell," he replied.

"Wait," she said, her voice light now, relieved. "I have to get the key."

When the door opened, he just stood in it, blinking stupidly, until Magdalene, smile of welcome fading from her lips in her concern, put her arm around his shoulders and drew him in. She pushed the door shut with her free hand, and Bell dropped his head to rest his cheek on her hair.

"What happened?" she asked. "Did Octadenarius make things difficult? After he sent you to the kitchen to get off as much of the blood as you could, he asked me what had happened. He knows my house and my reputation. I was sure he believed me. Then he went above to speak to Claresta and Spencer, and when he came down he said my tale fit perfectly with theirs, that he had two witnesses, and since I was excommunicate and could not bear witness, I could go home. I could swear he was satisfied."

Bell lifted his head and Magdalene pushed him gently

toward the table. She released his shoulders and he gathered enough energy to go to his usual place. Magdalene followed, unbuckled his sword belt, and propped the sword against the table for him. Bell muttered something, perhaps thanks, and sat down heavily on the bench.

Magdalene hurried to the shelves at the back of the room to bring a fine horn cup and a flagon of wine—William's wine, she thought, but she would not mention that to Bell and William would not grudge it. She sat down and poured a full cup for him.

He drank about a third of the cup in one swallow, then set it down. "No, Octadenarius gave me no trouble about the killings. Claresta and Spencer told him how Sir John had blamed Linley for all his troubles and then stabbed him in the throat when Spencer had distracted my attention. And Spencer insisted Sir John had gone mad, that he attacked me, and then not satisfied with trying to cut me in half with his sword, leaped on me despite my shouting a warning and skewered himself on my knife."

"Then you are clear of any blame," Magdalene said.

Bell shivered. "I know, but Octadenarius wanted to hear it all from me, from Nelda's death and the letter."

"Gentle Mother, why?"

"Because *he* would have to explain to both Mandeville and Surrey what had happened to their men. I had forgot that."

"Did you tell him that Sir John and Linley were the ones who carried Nelda's body into the bishop's house?"

"Yes. Once I mentioned that, Octadenarius realized why Sir John was angry enough to kill. And he understood why Sir John attacked me when I refused to allow him to leave for Normandy. But before I was finished, Master Rhyton arrived."

"He had heard about what happened?"

"No. He didn't even notice the bodies but went right up to the solar, thinking Linley was there with Claresta. It was something in the contract, apparently something that Linley had lied about." Bell smiled suddenly. "I do not think you need worry about Mistress Claresta being forced into another noble marriage. It seems Linley, or his father, had inserted into the contract a clause forbidding Rhyton to come as a visitor to Godalming or to have Claresta visit him here."

Magdalene shook her head. "It seems that Linley was truly his father's son, greedy to take but not to shoulder the results of the taking."

"Yes. Rhyton was livid. It shamed him, denied what he most desired, to be thought a landed lord. But it would not have mattered because Mistress Claresta told him in no uncertain terms—well, Octadenarius and I heard her all the way down the stairs and I think would have heard her through two closed doors—what came of trying to force his way out of his own class. She said she would have Spencer, no idiot nobleman who would no doubt ruin the business and think of her only as a brood mare."

"I would not wonder if she then told him about the two dead bodies in the common room and pointed out that respectable burghers would never behave that way."

"Ah . . . yes." Bell found a tired smile. "I was witness to that. Mistress Claresta brought her father down to show him the result of his unadvised attempt to bring noble blood into their family. She said that hope was dead . . ."

Hurriedly, because she saw Bell's expression change and wished to divert him from thoughts of Linley's dead hand, Magdalene said, "I wonder if she will buy those cuffs or the ones with leaves and flowers and some other embroidery?

But of course if she heard anyone calling me a whore . . . though why my being a whore should make my embroidery less beautiful, I have no idea."

But Bell was not listening. He finished the wine in his cup, and Magdalene took it from his hand and refilled it. "I asked if I could go report to the bishop while Octadenarius was explaining to Rhyton, but he said he was not through with me. Once rid of the merchant, he wanted to hear about how Linley had managed Gehard's death. I could only give him our guesses, and he sent for the sheriff of Southwark, and the two of them wanted proof. Fortunately I remembered the apothecary had said he would recognize the purchaser of the poison. They sent for him and he was able to identify Linley and told them of Linley giving his name as Gehard fitzRobert and the tale of the mad dog. So that was settled."

"Good. Can you eat?"

"No need. The bishop fed me while I was explaining the whole thing to *him*."

"Oh, poor Bell. Over and over."

He sighed heavily and drank again, but only a sip this time. "At least I was able to tell Winchester about Linley . . . Ask him, I mean, whether he thought it possible that Linley's spirit could move his dead hand." He took a slightly larger sip and shuddered.

"I have no idea what Winchester would say, except that whatever made Sir John fling himself on your knife, it was no fault of yours."

A faint smile bent Bell's lips again. "Yes, he said that, and also absolved me of any sin of omission, like looking away from Sir John at the wrong moment so that Linley was murdered." He sighed again. "I have no idea why it sticks in my mind so. I do not really feel guilty. I would have prevented Linley's death if I could, although he certainly brought it on himself by enraging Claresta and through her, Spencer . . . but I keep seeing that dead hand rise and grip Sir John's ankle . . ."

Now it was Magdalene who shuddered, very visibly. She was bitterly sorry she had used that suggestion to prevent Bell from thinking about how she could have pushed Sir John onto his knife. Many ghosts must haunt a long-time soldier. She had only one, and she could understand all too well that Bell did not need another.

"Sorry." Bell patted her hand, misunderstanding what had caused her distress. "I did not mean to raise horrors to trouble you."

And suddenly a new idea came to Magdalene. "Well, you did," she said, deliberately shuddering again. "And this is now a night when I do not wish to sleep alone. Come to bed—tomorrow you will know in your heart and head both that what the bishop said is true and the light of day will clear away my terrors."

Bell stared across the table at her. Slowly he emptied the cup of wine and replaced the cup on the table. "But nothing is changed."

Magdalene bent her head. "Nothing can change. Twelve years ago, to save my life, I committed a crime. No door but death was open to me, except that of a whore. I became a whore. I *am* a whore. Nothing can wipe out the past, no wish of mine, no prayer, not even a miracle."

"You think I will turn on you and call you whore and leave you?"

"Have you not done so once already?"

"And you said you would not have me back."

Magdalene sighed. "I did. And I tried, but I found that you were rooted deep in my heart. I could not tear you out.

Why should I suffer pain and misery now only because I fear that pain and misery in the future? It is better to have a present joy and endure the suffering when it actually comes."

Bell took the five silver pennies out of his purse and laid them on the table. "I have been carrying these since the day after the bishop sent me here. If you are a whore . . . I, too, do not wish to sleep alone. Take them."

"Well, I will," Magdalene said briskly, scooping the coins off the table; the shock on Bell's face made her giggle. "The condition you are in tonight, I do not think my usual payment of pleasure and laughter will be forthcoming."

"I am not so tired as *that,*" Bell protested.

But Magdalene only laughed and took his hand and pulled him to his feet and then, swordbelt trailing from his free hand, into her chamber. Within, he freed himself and put his sword conveniently to hand by the side of the bed on which he always slept. Then he pulled off his tunic and, seeking the chest on which he laid his clothing, turned to face her. He found that she had tied the five pennies in a wisp of fabric and hung them from the frame that held the oval of polished silver she used as a mirror.

She saw the relief on his face, relief because she had not put his coin with those that her women earned, thus setting it aside from pay for whoring. She grinned broadly. He did not know that the oval of silver had been William's gift, as were most of the costly things in her chamber. But she said not a word and went swiftly forward to untie the rolled ribbon that held his shirt closed.

"I could not root you out of my heart either," he murmured, dropping his head to meet the lips she raised to him, "nor this place. My mother and sisters would have a fit if they knew, but to me this is home."

ABOUT THE AUTHOR

Roberta Gellis has been a very successful writer of fiction for several decades, having published about 40 novels since 1964. She has been the recipient of many awards, including the Golden Porgy from West Coast Review of Books, the Golden Pen from Affaire de Coeur, the Romantic Times Reviewer's Choice award for Best Novel in the Medieval Period (several times), the Romantic Times Lifetime Achievement Award for Historical Fantasy, and the Romance Writers of America's Lifetime Achievement Award. Some biographical information, pictures, and a list of all Gellis's publications with details, covers, and excerpts from all her books in print can be found on her website: http://www.robertagellis.com/